THE GREEN MAN
Tales from the Mythic Forest

Other Anthologies by
ELLEN DATLOW and TERRI WINDLING

The Adult Fairy Tale Series

Snow White, Blood Red
Black Thorn, White Rose
Ruby Slippers, Golden Tears
Black Swan, White Raven
Silver Birch, Blood Moon
Black Heart, Ivory Bones

A Wolf at the Door

Sirens

The Year's Best Fantasy and Horror
Volumes 1 through 15

THE GREEN MAN

Tales from the Mythic Forest

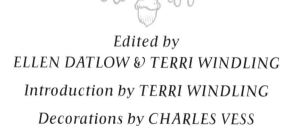

Edited by
ELLEN DATLOW & TERRI WINDLING

Introduction by TERRI WINDLING

Decorations by CHARLES VESS

VIKING

VIKING
Published by the Penguin Group
Penguin Putnam Books for Young Readers,
345 Hudson Street, New York, New York 10014, U.S.A.
Penguin Books Ltd, 80 Strand, London WC2R 0RL, England
Penguin Books Australia Ltd, Ringwood, Victoria, Australia
Penguin Books Canada Ltd, 10 Alcorn Avenue, Toronto, Ontario, Canada M4V 3B2
Penguin Books (N.Z.) Ltd, 182-190 Wairau Road, Auckland 10, New Zealand

Penguin Books Ltd, Registered Offices: Harmondsworth, Middlesex, England

1 3 5 7 9 10 8 6 4 2

LIBRARY OF CONGRESS CATALOGING-IN-PUBLICATION DATA
The Green Man : tales from the mythic forest
edited by Ellen Datlow and Terri Windling; decorations by Charles Vess.
p. cm.
Summary: A collection of stories and poems by a variety of authors
relating to the Green Man and other myths of the forest.
ISBN 0-670-03526-2
1. Green Man (Tale)—Literary collections. [1. Green Man (Tale)—Literary collections.] I. Datlow, Ellen. II. Windling, Terri. III. Vess, Charles, ill.
PZ5.G727 2002   808.8'0351—dc21   2001046976

Printed in the U.S.A.
Set in New Aster
Book design by Nancy Brennan

This book is dedicated to
CHARLES VESS and KAREN SCHAFFER,
who create magic daily
and share it with unstinting generosity.

CONTENTS

PREFACE

༄

ELLEN DATLOW AND TERRI WINDLING

WHEN WE JOURNEY deep "into the woods" in myths, fairy tales, or modern fantasy fiction, we travel to a place of magic, danger, and personal transformation. Forests have provided the setting for some of the most enchanted tales in world literature, from the perilous woods of medieval Romance and the faery-haunted glades of Shakespeare and Yeats to the talking trees of Tolkien's *Lord of the Rings* and the archetypal wilderness of Robert Holdstock's *Mythago Wood*.

In this book, we've asked the writers to journey deep into the Mythic Forest, to bring back tales of those wild lands, and of the creatures who dwell within them. Thus in these pages you'll find witches, wolves, dryads, deer men, a faery or two, and numerous magical spirits of nature (even a jolly green giant!) Charles Vess, our cover and interior artist, is a frequent traveler in the lands of myth, as well as the founder of Green Man Press. What better artist to send us off on the dark paths through the woods?

In the Scottish ballad *Thomas the Rhymer,* the Queen of Faery shows Thomas three mysterious paths leading into the trees:

See ye not yon narrow road,
so thick beset with thorns and briars?
That is the path to righteousness,
though after it but few enquire.

And see ye not yon broad, broad road
that lies across the lilie leven?
That is the path to wickedness,
though some call it the road to heaven.

And see ye not that bonny road
which winds about the fernie brae?
That is the road to fair Elfland,
where you and I must gae.

Like Thomas, we've chosen the bonny, winding road that leads into lands of magic—through forests, deserts, mountains, cities, suburbs, and mythical landscapes. Oak and ash whisper over our heads, and other green creatures watch from the shadows. We hope you'll enjoy this journey into the trees. But watch your step.

INTRODUCTION

༄

About the Green Man and Other Forest Lore

TERRI WINDLING

WHEN WE PEER into the shadows of the Mythic Forest, a startling face stares back at us: the Green Man, masked with leaves or disgorging foliage from his mouth. The Green Man is a pre-Christian symbol found carved into the wood and stone of pagan temples and graves, of medieval churches and cathedrals, and used as a Victorian architectural motif across an area stretching from Ireland in the west to Russia in the east.

Although the Green Man is commonly perceived as an ancient Celtic symbol, its origins and original meaning are actually shrouded in mystery. The name dates back only to 1939, when folklorist Lady Raglan drew a connection between the foliate faces in English churches and the Green Man (or "Jack of the Green") tales of folklore. The evocative name has been widely adopted, but the legitimacy of the connection still remains controversial, with little real evidence to settle the question one way or the other. Earliest known examples of the foliate head (as it was known prior to Lady

Raglan) date to classical Rome—yet it was not until this pagan symbol was adopted by the Christian church that the form fully developed and proliferated across Europe. No known writings exist that explain what the head represented in earlier religions, or why precisely it became incorporated into Christian architecture, but most folklorists conjecture that it symbolized mythic rebirth and regeneration, and thus became linked to Christian iconography of resurrection. (The Tree of Life, a virtually universal symbol of life, death, and regeneration, was adapted to Christian symbolism in a similar manner.)

The Jack in the Green is a figure associated with the new growth of spring and May Day celebrations. In Hastings, England, for instance, the Jack pageant is still re-enacted each spring. The Jack in the Green is played by a man in a towering eight-foot-tall costume of leaves, topped by a masked face and a crown made out of flowers. He travels through the town accompanied by men whose hair, skin, and clothes are all green, and a young girl bearing flowers, dressed and painted entirely in black. Morris and clog dancers entertain the crowds, while the Jack—a trickster figure—romps and chases pretty girls, playing the fool. At length he reaches a mound in the woods below the local castle. The Morris dancers wield their wooden swords, striking the leaf man dead. A poem is solemnly recited over the creature, then merriment breaks out as each member of the crowd takes a leaf from the Jack for luck. (According to mythologist Sir James Frazer, "the killing of a tree spirit is always associated with a revival or resurrection of him in a more youthful and vigorous form.")

In Bavaria, a similar tree-spirit called the *Pfingstl* roams through rural towns clad in alder and hazel leaves, wearing a high pointed cap covered by flowers. Two boys with swords accompany him as he knocks on the doors of random houses, asking for presents but often getting thoroughly drenched by water instead. This pageant also ends when the boys draw their wooden swords and kill the green man.

In a ritual from Picardy, France, a member of the *Compagnons du Loup Vert,* dressed in a green wolf skin and foliage, enters the village church carrying a candle and garlands of flowers. He waits until the "Gloria" is sung, then he walks to the altar and stands through the Mass. At its end, the entire congregation rushes up to strip the green wolf of his leaves, bearing them away for luck.

Such rituals are the debased remnants of pre-Christian rites and festivities. In early pagan religions, trees were held sacred; forest groves were perceived as the dwelling place of gods, goddesses, and a wide variety of nature spirits. A staunchly animist outlook (with a strong reverence for trees and the holiness of nature) was particularly entrenched among the peoples in the far north of Europe and in the British Isles—thus these were two of the areas where Christian priests of the Dark Ages (such as Devon's stern St. Boniface) waged war against older beliefs, cutting down sacred trees and putting whole groves of woodland to the torch. To the Norse, in the wild, wintry forests of Scandinavia, a giant ash tree called Yggdrasil was the center of the universe. Its three great roots linked Asgard (the realm of the gods), Rime-Thusar (the realm of the Frost Giants), and Niflheim (the realm of the dead) with the human world above.

The Celtic tribes of Britain and Ireland assigned each type of tree magical properties, and the twigs from the tops of trees were prized by magicians, warriors, and healers. Each letter in the Celtic *ogham* alphabet stood for a tree and its magical associations, and the symbology of trees is a richly poetic presence in Celtic myths. The English poet Robert Graves, in his extraordinary book *The White Goddess*, deals at great length with the order and meanings of the letters comprising this tree alphabet. He conjectures that the famous Welsh *Battle of the Trees* (a group of ancient poems preserved in the sixteenth century manuscript *The Romance of Taliesin*) refers to a druidic battle of words rather than a literal battle of vegetation.

Sacred trees and groves also played a central part in Greco-Roman myths. The oak was the tree sacred to Zeus, whose priests heard his voice in its rustling leaves. Adonis, the god of returning seasons and new crops, was born from the trunk of a myrrh tree. The nymph Daphne turned into a laurel tree in order to escape ravishment by Apollo. The laurel was sacred to goddess cults, and was the tree of poetic inspiration. Many scholars consider the god Dionysus to be a forerunner of the Green Man symbol, for Dionysus is often pictured masked, crowned in vines and ivy leaves. This compelling but dangerous deity was the lord of the wilderness; he was the god of wine (made from wild grapes), madness, and ecstasy. Dionysus is also a god of the underworld (in the guise of Okeanos), associated with death and rebirth—particularly as he was (according to some stories) thrice born himself: first as the son of Persephone and Zeus (devoured as a child by Titans), second as the son of Semele of Thebes (who died as a result of Hera's jealousy before the baby came to term), and third, as the fetus from Semele's body born out of the thigh of Zeus.

Various scholars have pointed out the parallels between Dionysus and the Celtic stag-man Cernunnos, consort of the Moon Goddess and lord of the forest in Britain and Gaul, who was also associated with the underworld and the great cycle of death and resurrection. Carved heads representing this forest god were once placed near doorways, springs, and woodland shrines, often carved with holes in which stag antlers or foliage was placed.

The Greek goddess Artemis was another creature of the forest, attended by beautiful tree nymphs (dryads) and bands of unmarried girls. Although she was a virgin in the later Greek and Roman traditions, in earlier accounts she was the Mother of All Creatures, and not virginal but free of the control of men, as were her priestesses. Artemis was revered as a great huntress, and feared for the wild side of her nature— many forest groves were sacred to her and thus could not be entered without peril. In the famous story of Actaeon, a beautiful young man out hunting with his friends stumbles into one of her groves and spies the goddess bathing in a pool. For this crime, Artemis transforms Actaeon into a stag (with full human consciousness). Unaware, his own dogs and friends hunt the young man down and tear him apart.

Despite her later incarnation as a virgin, Artemis was also the goddess of childbirth—under the name Eileithyia, she was the goddess of release to whom pregnant women prayed during the pain of delivery. In this guise, she is related to the Green Man's wild female counterpart, the Green Woman, depicted in stone carvings as a primitive female form giving birth to a spray of vegetation. This Green Woman symbol is far less common than the Green Man, being rather harder to adapt to Christian iconography or Victorian decoration— and yet quite a few Green Women appeared on Irish churches built before the sixteenth century, where they were known by the name Sheela-na-gig. Some of these figures are still intact, others were destroyed or buried during church renovations in the nineteenth century. As with the yoni figures of India, it is customary to lick one's finger and touch the Green Woman for luck.

The city of Rome was born of the forest, according to its mythic origin tales. Rhea Silvia (Rhea of the forest) was the daughter of the king of Alba Longa until her uncle stole the throne. She was packed off to the Roman equivalent of a nunnery, but gave birth to twins, Romulus and Remus, after being raped by Mars, the god of war. The false king ordered the twins to be drowned, but instead (in the best fairy tale fashion) they were left abandoned in the forest. A she-wolf suckled the infants; then the children were raised to manhood by a forest brigand. When Romulus emerged from the woods, he helped his grandfather recover the throne of Alba Longa and then returned to the forest, cleared a hill, and founded the city of Rome. By Roman law, the forest at its gates belonged to no one and lay beyond civil jurisdiction. This was the realm of Silvanus, the god of sacred boundaries and wilderness. As Rome grew, the power of Silvanus dwindled, not only locally, but in all the lands where the Roman empire extended. In those times, explains Robert Pogue Harrison in *Forests: the Shadow of Civilization*, "the forests were literally everywhere: Italy, Gaul, Spain, Britain, the ancient Mediterranean basin as a whole. The prohibitive density of the forests once preserved the relative autonomy and diversity of the family- and city-states of antiquity. The forests were obstacles—to conquest, hegemony, homogenization. By virtue of their buffers, they enabled communities to develop indigenously; hence they served to localize the spirit of place. In their woodlands lived spirits and deities, fauns and nymphs, local to this place and no other. In their drive to universalize their empire, the Romans found ways to denude or traverse this latent sylvan mass . . . building roads, imperial highways, institutions, a broad integrated network of 'telecommunications.'"

Mass clearings of land for building and agricultural use had profound ecological implications even in antiquity, as forest after forest was demolished and the soils of once fertile lands eroded. As early as the fourth century B.C., Plato wrote with grief in the *Critias* of the barren hills surrounding Athens as grove after grove fell before the plow or the shipbuilder's ax.

According to Greco-Roman tradition, dryads die when their personal tree is cut down. This is also true of other tree spirits who inhabit the forests of Europe, including the vegetation faeries of many different cultures. In some cautionary tales, the faery folk take their revenge upon humans who dare disturb their haunts. In others, the faery quietly pines away when her habitat is destroyed—and when she dies, the beauty and magical soul of the land dies with her.

Supernatural forest spirits take many forms, ranging from the exquisite dryads of the Greeks to the ugly tree trolls of

Finland and Norway. The *swor skogsfru* (wood wives) of Sweden are seductive and utterly beautiful . . . from the front. In back, these faery women are made of bark and are hollow as logs. In Italy, the *silvane* (wood women) mate with *silvani* (wood men) to produce the *folleti*, the enchanting faeries of the land. In England, many earthy brownies and hobgoblins make their homes in oak tree roots, and each kind of tree has its own faery to tend it and enable its growth. Men made of bark seduce young maids in the fairy tales of eastern Europe—some of them dangerous, others making tender, courteous lovers.

The wood spirits in the forest of Broceliande (now known as Paimpont) in Brittany also range from the benevolent to the malign. In one old tale, a lost traveler finds his way to a strange chateau in the woods. The beautiful lady of the house offers him food, drink, and her own arms to sleep in at night. He gallantly refuses the latter, which breaks the faery's hold on him. The morning light reveals the chateau in ruins, empty, reclaimed by the forest. Broceliande is the woodland where Merlin the magician lies entrapped in the bowels of a tree, tricked or seduced by the faery sorceress Vivian (also known as Nimue). Merlin is a figure intimately connected with forests in Arthurian lore, for it was during his years of madness roaming the forests of Wales, after the disastrous Battle of Arderydd, that he learned the speech of animals and honed his prophetic powers. A similar tale recounts the trials of Sweeney, an Irish hero cursed in battle, forced to flee to the woods in the shape of a bird. Like Merlin (and other shamanic figures who seek Mysteries in the wilderness), Sweeney goes mad during his long exile—but when he emerges from the trial, he has mastery over creatures of the forest.

In epic romances, heroes enter the woods to test their strength, courage, and faith; yet sometimes, like Merlin, they find madness there—as does the lovelorn Orlando in Ariosto's *Orlando Furioso*, one of the great poems of the Italian Renaissance. In the famous medieval tale *Sir Gawain and the Green Knight*, a mysterious knight rides out of the woods and into Camelot on New Year's Eve. His clothes are green, his horse is green, his face is green, as are all his bright jewels. He carries a holly bush in one hand and an ax of green steel in the other. The Green Man issues a challenge that any knight in the court may strike off his head but, should the challenger fail to kill him, in one year's time, he must come to the Green Chapel and submit to the same trial. Gawain agrees to this terrible challenge in order to save the honor of his king. He slices off the Green Knight's head; the creature merely picks it up and rides back to the forest, bearing the head in the crook of his arm. One year later, Gawain seeks out the Green Knight in the Green Chapel in the woods. He survives the trial, but is humbled by the Green Man, who catches Gawain in an act of dishonesty.

In the French romance *Valentine and Orson*, the Empress of Constantinople is accused of adultery, thrown out of her palace, and gives birth to twins in the wildwood. One son (along with the mother) is rescued by a nobleman and raised at court, while the other son, Orson, is stolen by a she-bear and raised in the wild. The pair eventually meet, fight, then become bosom companions—all before a magical oracle informs them of their kinship. The wild twin becomes civilized while retaining a primitive kind of strength, but when, at length, his brother dies, he retires back into the forest. This epic presents another great archetypal figure: the Wodehouse or wild man, a primitive yet powerful creature one finds in tales ranging from *Gilgamesh* (in the figure of Enkidu) to *Tarzan of the Apes*.

"The medieval imagination was fascinated by wild men," notes Robert Pogue Harrison, "but the latter were by no means merely imaginary in status during the Middle Ages. Such men (and women as well) would every now and then be discovered in the forest—usually insane people who had taken to the woods. If hunters happened upon a wild man, they would frequently try to capture him alive and bring him back for people to marvel and wonder at." Other famous wild men of literature can be found in Chrétien de Troyes's romance *Yvain*, Jacob Wasserman's *Casper Hauser* (based on the real life incident of a wild child found in the market square of Nuremberg in 1829), and in the heart-stealing figure of Mowgli in Rudyard Kipling's *The Jungle Book*.

Mythic tales of forest outlaws are a sub-category of wild man legends, although in such stories (*Robin Hood*, for example) the hero is generally a civilized man compelled, through an act of injustice, to seek the wild life. Magical tales of hermits and woodland mystics form another sub-category, and Christian legends are filled with tales of saints living in the wilderness on a diet of honey and acorns. This, again, is bolstered by the actual experience of people in earlier times, when it was not uncommon for folk marginalized by the community (mystics, herbalists or witches, widows, eccentrics, and simpletons) to live in the wilds beyond the village, either by choice or by necessity. An elderly neighbor of mine in Devon, England, remembers such a figure from her youth—a harmless old soul who lived in a cave and was believed to have prophetic powers.

To the German Romantics, forests held the soul of myth and thus of *volk* (folk) culture, believed to be more pure and true than the artifice of civilization. E.T.A. Hoffman, Ludwig Tieck, Baron Friedrich de la Motte Fouqué, Novalis, and other German writers entered the fairy tale forest to create mystical, darkly magical works making deft use of mythic archetypes. In the early nineteenth century, the Brothers Grimm published their famous German folklore collections, full of tales in which a journey to the dark woods was the catalyst for magic and transformation. The passion for folklore spread across Europe, touching every area of popular arts in addition to fostering a new academic climate for collection of oral tales and ballads. In Scotland, the Reverend George MacDonald, inspired by the works of the German Romantics, began to write folkloric stories—like "The Light Princess" and "The Golden Key"—which are now classics of magical literature. In the faery woods of MacDonald's imagination, talking trees (both wondrous and wicked) are drawn directly from mythic archetypes, forming part of a literary tradition that runs from the prophetic trees in the magical adventures of Alexander the Great, through the "Wood of Suicides" in Dante's *Inferno*, to the Ents in Tolkien's *Lord of the Rings*. The Victorian painter Edward Burne-Jones and his fellow Pre-Raphaelite artists returned again and again to the Archetypal Forest in their paintings, poetry, and prose—including novels such as *The Wood Beyond the World* by

Burne-Jones's great friend William Morris. As the century turned, Celtic Twilight writers like the Irish poet William Butler Yeats found magic in the twilight woods with which to fuel their art. In the early twentieth century, writers such as Hope Mirrlees (*Lud in the Mist*), James Stephens (*The Crock of Gold*), and Lord Dunsany (*The King of Elfland's Daughter*) created modern mythic tales to explore the woodlands that lie (to borrow Dunsany's phrase) "beyond the fields we know." Then three Oxford dons came along—J.R.R. Tolkien, C.S. Lewis, and Charles Williams—calling themselves the Inklings, whose work has profoundly influenced most magical fiction written since.

It is the challenging task of modern fantasists to assimilate the works produced by these three (Tolkien in particular), while avoiding the pitfall of merely producing pale imitations of it. Modern writers who have managed this most successfully (Alan Garner, Ursula K. Le Guin, Jane Yolen, Philip Pullman, etc.) are those familiar with the mythic source material which the past masters used to such great effect—as well as those for whom a strongly personal vision shines through Professor Tolkien's long shadow.

Neil Gaiman is a good example of a modern myth-maker who avoids being derivative, even when he gives a tip of the hat to Dunsany, Mirrlees, and Christina Rossetti, as in his charming faery novel *Stardust*. This story, set in an English woodland at the Wall separating our world from faeryland, reads like a classic nineteenth-century story yet is utterly fresh and original. *Stardust* began as a collaborative work first published in narrative graphic form with enchanting paintings by Charles Vess. The woodland created by this talented pair is not a generic Fantasy Forest—through Gaiman's clever yet gentle prose and Vess's Rackham-flavored pictures these woods are specifically English and yet archetypal as well, filled with true magic. The spirit of the woodland is also a captivating presence in the Japanese animated film *Princess Mononoke*, with its English screenplay adapted by Neil Gaiman, a deeply folkloric work in which all the power and terror of the Mythic Forest is brought vividly to life. Robert Holdstock is a writer who has traveled deeper into the woods than any other mythic writer, and the books of his Mythago Wood sequence are essential reading, as well as his Breton novel *Merlin's Wood*.

Charles de Lint writes interstitial works which bring the potent archetypes of the mythic woods into modern urban settings, particularly in his novels *Forests of the Heart* and *Greenmantle*.

In *The Wild Wood*, inspired by the art of Brian Froud, de Lint takes us deep into the woods of northern Canada—a prismatic landscape where magic and madness waits, as in shamanic tales of old. The woodlands of Patricia A. McKillip's tales are some of the finest in fantasy literature; I recommend her novels *Winter Rose* and *The Book of Atrix Wolfe*, as well as her unusual contemporary story *Stepping from the Shadows*. I also recommend Sean Russell's *World without End* and its sequel *Sea without a Shore; Rumours of Spring* by Richard Grant; *Engine Summer* by John Crowley; *The Word for World Is Forest* by Ursula K. Le Guin; *Cloven Hooves* by Megan Lindholm; *The Stone Silenus* by Jane Yolen; *Enchantments* by Orson Scott Card; and *Thomas the Rhymer* by Ellen Kushner. *The Bloody Chamber* by Angela Carter and *Red as*

Blood by Tanith Lee are good story collections filled with deliciously dark, Freudian flavored fairy tale woods. And for fine novels set in American wilderness, try: *Wild Life* by Molly Gloss, *Nadya* by Pat Murphy, *The Flight of Michael McBride* by Midori Snyder, and *Power* by Linda Hogan.

Visual artists have also been caught by the powerful spell of the Mythic Forest. In addition to the art of Charles Vess, which beautifully ornaments this volume, I recommend seeking out art books on the work of two English sculptors: Andy Goldsworthy (*Wood*) and Peter Randall-Page (*Granite Song*, available through the Internet Bookshop, www.bookshop.co.uk), as well as the Scottish photographer Thomas Joshua Cooper (*Between Dark and Dark*), British painter Brian Froud (*Good Faeries/Bad Faeries*, and *Faeries*, with Alan Lee), and the fairy tale art of "Golden Age" illustrators Arthur Rackham, Kay Nielsen, and Edmund Dulac.

For further reading on the subject of the Green Man, forest folklore, and nature mythology, try: *Green Man* by William Anderson and Clive Hicks, *The Wisdom of Trees: Mysteries, Magic and Medicine* by Jane Clifford, *Celtic Sacred Landscape* by Nigel Pennick, *A Dictionary of Nature Myths* by Tamra Andrews, *Forests: The Shadow of Civilization* by Robert Pogue Harrison, *Meetings with Remarkable Trees* by Robert Packenham, *Discovering the Folklore of Plants* by Margaret Baker, *The Practice of the Wild* by Gary Snyder, *The Spell of the Sensuous* by David Abram, *The Power of Myth* by Joseph Campbell, and *The White Goddess* by Robert Graves.

The Mythic Forest is every forest—we enter it whenever we enter the woods. The Green Man dwells there, called by different names all over the world. When we hear the rustling of the leaves, we're still hearing the Oracle, and the oaks are still the home of faeries . . . or at least of tales about them. In California, there are living trees, the bristlecone pines, that are thousands and thousands of years old. So are the stories of the trees. They are ancient, deeply rooted in the loam, yet still unfurling bright new leaves.

GOING WODWO

NEIL GAIMAN

SHEDDING MY SHIRT, my book, my coat, my life,
Leaving them, empty husks and fallen leaves,
Going in search of food and for a spring
Of sweet water.

I'll find a tree as wide as ten fat man,
Clear water rilling over its grey roots.
Berries I'll find, and crab apples and nuts,
And call it home.

I'll tell the wind my name, and no one else.
True madness takes or leaves us in the wood
halfway through all our lives. My skin will be
my face now.

I must be nuts. Sense left with shoes and house,
my guts are cramped. I'll stumble through the green
back to my roots, and leaves, and thorns, and buds,
and shiver.

I'll leave the way of words to walk the wood.
I'll be the forest's man, and greet the sun,
And feel the silence blossom on my tongue
like language.

NEIL GAIMAN is a transplanted Briton who now lives in the American Midwest. He is the author of the award-winning *Sandman* series of graphic novels, and of the novels *Neverwhere* and *American Gods*. He also collaborated with artist Dave McKean on *Mr. Punch* and the children's picture book *The Day I Swapped My Dad for 2 Goldfish*.

In addition, Gaiman is a poet and short story writer whose work has been published in a number of the Datlow/Windling adult fairy tale anthologies, in *A Wolf at the Door*, and in several editions of *The Year's Best Fantasy and Horror*. His short work has been collected in *Angels and Visitations* and *Smoke and Mirrors*.

His Web site address is www.neilgaiman.com.

Author's Note:

A wodwo (or wodwose, or woodwose) was a medieval wild man of the woods. Sometimes they are identified with the Green Men.

This came from wondering what it would mean to be a wodwo now; and from the carvings of Green Men as human-faced men with leaves growing from their mouths.

GRAND CENTRAL PARK

DELIA SHERMAN

WHEN I WAS little, I used to wonder why the sidewalk trees had iron fences around them. Even a city kid could see they were pretty weedy looking trees. I wondered what they'd done to be caged up like that, and whether it might be dangerous to get too close to them.

So I was pretty little, okay? Second grade, maybe. It was one of the things my best friend and I used to talk about, like why it's so hard to find a particular city on a map when you don't already know where it is, and why the fourth graders thought Mrs. Lustenburger's name was so hysterically funny. My best friend's name was (is) Galadriel, which isn't even remotely her fault, and only her mother calls her that anyway. Everyone else calls her Elf.

Anyway. Trees. New York. Have I said I live in New York? I do. In Manhattan, on the West Side, a couple blocks from Central Park.

I've always loved Central Park. I mean, it's the closest to nature I'm likely to get, growing up in Manhattan. It's the closest to nature I want to get, if you must know. There's wild things in it—squirrels and pigeons and like that, and trees and rocks and plants. But they're city wild things, used to living around people. I don't mean they're tame. I mean they're streetwise. Look. How many squished squirrels do you see on the park transverses? How many do you see on any suburban road? I rest my case.

Central Park is magic. This isn't a matter of opinion, it's the truth. When I was just old enough for Mom to let me out of her sight, I had this place I used to play, down by the boat pond, in a little inlet at the foot of a huge cliff. When I was in there, all I could see was the water all shiny and sparkly like a silk dress with sequins and the great grey hulk of the rock behind me and the willow tree bending down over me to trail its green-gold hair in the water. I could hear people splashing and laughing and talking, but I couldn't see them, and there was this fairy who used to come and play with me.

Mom said my fairy friend came from me being an only child and reading too many books, but all I can say is that if I'd made her up, she would have been less bratty. She had long Saran-Wrap wings like a dragonfly, she was teensy, and she couldn't keep still for a second. She'd play princesses or Peter Pan for about two minutes, and then she'd get bored and pull my hair or start teasing me about being a big, galumphy, deaf, blind human being or talking to the willow or the rocks. She couldn't even finish a conversation with a butterfly.

Anyway, I stopped believing in her when I was about eight, or stopped seeing her, anyway. By that time I didn't care because I'd gotten friendly with Elf, who didn't tease me quite as much. She wasn't into fairies, although she did like to read. As we got older, mostly I was grateful she was willing to be my friend. Like, I wasn't exactly Ms. Popularity at school. I sucked at gym and liked English and like that, so the cool kids decided I was a super-geek. Also, I wear glasses and I'm no Ally McBeal, if you know what I mean. I could stand to lose a few pounds—none of your business how many. It wasn't safe to be seen having lunch with me, so Elf didn't. As long as she hung with me after school, I didn't really care all that much.

The inlet was our safe place, where we could talk about whether the French teacher hated me personally or was just incredibly mean in general and whether Patty Gregg was really cool, or just thought she was. In the summer, we'd take our shoes off and swing our feet in the water that sighed around the roots of the golden willow.

So one day we were down there, gabbing as usual. This was last year, the fall of eleventh grade, and we were talking about boyfriends. Or at least Elf was talking about her boyfriend and I was nodding sympathetically. I guess my attention wandered, and for some reason I started wondering about my fairy friend. What was her name again? Bubble? Burble? Something like that.

Something tugged really hard on about two hairs at the top of my head, where it *really* hurts, and I yelped and scrubbed at the sore place. "Mosquito," I explained. "So what did he say?"

Oddly enough, Elf had lost interest in what her boyfriend had said. She had this look of intense concentration on her face, like she was listening for her little brother's breathing on the other side of the bedroom door. "Did you hear that?" she whispered.

"What? Hear what?"

"Ssh."

I sshed and listened. Water lapping; the distant creak of oarlocks and New Yorkers laughing and talking and splashing. The wind in the willow leaves whispering, *ssh, ssh.* "I don't hear anything," I said.

"Shut up," Elf snapped. "You missed it. A snapping sound. Over there." Her blue eyes were very big and round.

"You're trying to scare me," I accused her. "You read about that woman getting mugged in the park, and now you're trying to jerk my chain. Thanks, friend."

Elf looked indignant. "As if!" She froze like a dog sighting a pigeon. "There."

I strained my ears. It seemed awfully quiet all of a sudden. There wasn't even a breeze to stir the willow. Elf breathed, "Omigod. Don't look now, but I think there's a guy over there, watching us."

My face got all prickly and cold, like my body believed her even though my brain didn't. "I swear to God, Elf, if you're lying, I'll totally kill you." I turned around to follow her gaze. "Where? I don't see anything."

"I said, don't *look*," Elf hissed. "He'll *know*."

"He already knows, unless he's a moron. If he's even there. Omigod!"

Suddenly I saw, or thought I saw, a guy with a stocking cap on and a dirty, unshaven face peering around a big rock. It was strange. One second, it looked like a guy, the next, it was more like someone's windbreaker draped over a bush.

But my heart started to beat really fast anyway. There weren't that many ways to get out of that particular little cove if you didn't have a boat.

"See him?" she hissed triumphantly.

"I guess."

"What are we going to do?"

Thinking about it later, I couldn't quite decide whether Elf was really afraid, or whether she was pretending because it was exciting to be afraid, but she sure convinced me. If the guy was on the path, the only way out was up the cliff. I'm not in the best shape *and* I'm scared of heights, but I was even more scared of the man, so up we went.

I remember that climb, but I don't want to talk about it. I thought I was going to die, okay? And I was really, really mad at Elf for putting me though this, like if she hadn't noticed the guy, he wouldn't have been there. I was sweating, and my glasses kept slipping down my nose and. . . . No. I won't talk about it. All you need to know is that Elf got to the top first and squirmed around on her belly to reach down and help me up.

"Hurry up," she panted. "He's behind you. No, don't look"—as if I could even bear to look all that way down— "just hurry."

I was totally winded by the time I got to the top and scrambled to my feet, but Elf didn't give me time to catch my breath. She grabbed my wrist and pulled me to the path, both of us stumbling as much as we were running.

It was about this time I realized that something really weird was going on. Like, the path was empty, and it was two o'clock in the afternoon of a beautiful fall Saturday, when

Central Park is so full of people it's like Times Square with trees. And I couldn't run, just like you can't run in dreams. Suddenly, Elf tripped and let go of me. The path shook itself, and she was gone. Poof. Nowhere in sight.

By this time, I'm freaked totally out of my mind. I look around, and there's this *guy*, hauling himself over the edge of the cliff, stocking cap jammed down over his head, face gray-skinned with dirt, half his teeth missing. I don't know why I didn't scream—usually, it's pitiful how easy it is to make me scream—I just turned around and ran.

Now, remember that there's about fifty million people in the park that day. You'd think I would run into one or two, which would mean safety because muggers don't like witnesses. But no.

So I'm running and he's running, and I can hear him *breathing* but I can't hear his footsteps, and we've been running, like, *forever*, and I don't know where the hell I am, which means I must be in the Ramble, which isn't that near the Boat Pond, but hey, I'm running for my life. And I think he's getting closer and I really want to look, just stop and let him catch me and get it all over with, but I keep running anyway, and suddenly I remember what my fairy's name was (is) and I shriek out, "Bugle! Help me!"

I bet you thought something would happen.

So did I, and when it didn't, I started to cry. Gulping for breath, my glasses all runny with tears, I staggered up a little rise, and I'm in a clear spot with a bench in it and trees all around and a low stone wall in front of another granite cliff, this one going straight down, like, a mile or two.

The guy laughs, low and deep in his throat, and I don't

know why because I don't really *want* to, but I turn around and face him.

So this is when it gets *really* weird. Because he's got a snout and really sharp teeth hanging out, and his stocking cap's fallen off, and he has *ears*—gray, leathery ones—and his skin isn't dirty, it's gray, like concrete, and he's impossible, but he's real—a real, like, rat-guy. I give this little urk and he opens his jaws, and things get sparkly around the edges.

"Gnaw-bone!" someone says. "Chill!"

I jump and look around everywhere, and there's this amazing girl standing right beside the rat-guy, who has folded up like a Slinky and is making pitiful noises over her boots. The boots are green, and so is her velvet mini and her Lycra top and her fitted leather jacket—all different shades of green, mostly olive and evergreen and moss and like that: dark greens. Browny, earthy greens. So's her hair—browny-green, in long, wild dreads around her shoulders and down her back. And her skin, but that's more brown than green. She's beautiful, but not like a celebrity or a model or any-thing. She's way more gorgeous than that. Next to her, Brit-ney Spears is a complete dog.

"What's up?" she asks the rat-guy. Her voice is incredible, too. I mean, she talks like some wise-ass street kid, but there's leaves under it somehow. Sounds dumb, but that's what it was like.

"Games is up," he says, sounding just as ratty as he looks. "Fun-fun. She saw me. She's mine."

"I hear you," the green girl says thoughtfully. "The thing is, she knows Bugle's name."

I manage to make a noise. It's not like I haven't wanted to

contribute to the conversation. But I'm kind of out of breath from all that running, not to mention being totally hysterical. I'm not sure what old Gnaw-bone's idea of fun and games is, but I'm dead sure I don't want to play. If knowing Bugle's name can get me out of this, I better make the most of it. So, "Yeah," I croak. "Bugle and me go way back."

The green girl turns to look at me, and I kind of wish I'd kept quiet. She's way scary. It's not the green hair or the punk clothes or the fact that I've just noticed there's this humongous squirrel sitting on her shoulder and an English sparrow perched in her dreads. It's the way she looks at me, like I'm a St. Bernard that just recited the Pledge of Allegiance or something.

"I think we better hear Bugle's take on this beautiful friendship," she says. "Bugle says you're buds, fine. She doesn't, Gnaw-bone gets his fun and games. Fair?"

No, it's not fair, but I don't say so. There's a long silence, in which I can hear the noise of traffic, very faint and far away, and the panicked beating of my heart, right in my throat. Gnaw-bone licks his lips, what there is of them, and the squirrel slithers down the green girl's shoulder and gets comfortable in her arms. If it's even a squirrel. I've seen smaller dogs.

Have I mentioned I'm really scared? I've never been this scared before in my entire life. And it's not even that I'm afraid of what Gnaw-bone might do to me, although I am. I'm afraid of the green girl. It's one thing to think fairies are wicked cool, to own all of Brian Froud's *Faerie* books and see *Fairy Tale* three times and secretly wish you hadn't outgrown your fairy friend. But this girl doesn't look like any fairy I ever imagined. Green leather and dreads—get real! And I'm not really prepared for eyes like living moss and the squirrel curled like a cat in her arms and the sparrow in her hair like a bizarroid hair clip. It's way too weird. I want to run away. I want to cry. But neither of these things seems like the right thing to do, so I stand there with my legs all rubbery and wait for Bugle to show up.

After a while, I feel something tugging at my hair. I start to slap it away, and then I realize. Duh. It's Bugle, saying hi. I scratch my ear instead. There's a little tootling sound, like a toy trumpet: Bugle, laughing. I laugh too, kind of hysterically.

"See?" I tell the green girl and the humongous squirrel and Gnaw-bone. "She knows me."

The green girl holds out her hand—the squirrel scrambles up to her shoulder again—and Bugle flies over and stands on her palm. It seems to me that Bugle used to look more like a little girl and less like a teenager. But then, so did I.

The green girl ignores me. "Do you know this mortal?" she asks Bugle. Her voice is different, somehow: less street kid, more like Mom asking whether I've done my math home-work.

Bugle gives a little hop. "Yep. Sure do. When she was little, anyways. Now, she doesn't want to know me."

I've been starting to feel better, but now the green girl is glaring at me, and my stomach knots up tight. I give this sick kind of grin. It's true. I hadn't wanted to know her, not with Peggy and those guys on my case. Even Elf, who puts up with a lot, doesn't want to hear about how I saw fairies when I was little. I say, "Yeah, well. I'm sorry. I really did know you were real, but I was embarrassed."

The green girl smiles. I can't help noticing she has a beautiful smile, like sun on the boat pond. "Fatso is just saying that," she points out, "because she's afraid I'll throw her to Gnaw-bone."

I freeze solid. Bugle, who's been getting fidgety, takes off and flies around the clearing a couple of times. Then she buzzes me and pulls my hair again, lands on my shoulder and says, "She's not so bad. I like teasing her."

"Not fair!" Gnaw-bone squeaks.

The green girl shrugs. "You know the rules," she tells him. "Bugle speaks for her. She's off-limits. Them's the breaks. Now, scram. You bother me."

Exit Gnaw-bone, muttering and glaring at me over his shoulder, and am I ever glad to see him go. He's like every nightmare Mom has ever had about letting me go places by myself and having me turn up murdered. Mine, too.

Anyway, I'm so relieved I start to babble. "Thanks, Bugle. Thanks a billion. I owe you big time."

"Yeah," says Bugle. "I know."

"You owe me, too," the green girl puts in.

Now, I can't quite see where she's coming from on this, seeing as how she was all gung-ho to let Gnaw-bone have his fun and games before Bugle showed up. Not to mention calling me names. On the other hand, she's obviously Very Important, and if there's one thing I've learned from reading all those fairy tales, it's that it's a very bad idea to be rude to people who wear live birds and squirrels like jewelry. So I shrug. Politely.

"Seven months' service should cover it," she says. "Can you sing? I'm mostly into salsa these days, but reggae or jazz is cool too."

My mouth drops open. Seven months? She's gotta be out of her mind. My parents will kill me if I don't come home for seven months.

"No?" Her voice is even more beautiful than it was before, like a fountain or wind in the trees. Her eyes sparkle like sun through leaves. She's so absolutely gorgeous, so not like anyone I can imagine having a conversation with, it's hard to follow what she's saying.

"I don't sing," I tell her.

"Dance, then?" I shake my head. "So, what can you do?"

Well, I know the answer to that one. "Nothing," I say. "I'm totally useless. Just ask my French teacher. Or my mom."

The beautiful face goes all blank and hard, like granite. "I said Gnaw-bone couldn't have you. That leaves all his brothers and sisters. You don't need much talent to entertain them."

You know how your brain goes totally spla when you're really scared? Well, my brain did that. And then I heard myself saying, "You said I was under Bugle's protection. Just because you're Queen of the Fairies doesn't mean you can do anything you want."

I was sure she'd be mad, but—get this—she starts to laugh. She laughs and laughs and laughs. And I get madder and madder, the way you do when you don't know what you've said that's so funny. Then I notice that she's getting broader and darker and shorter, and there's this scarf over her head, and she's wearing this dorky green housedress and her stockings are drooping around her ankles and she's got a cigarette in one hand. Finally she wheezes out, "The Queen of the Fairies! Geddouddaheah! You're killin' me!" She sounds totally different, too, like somebody's Aunt Ida from the Bronx. "The Queen of the. . . . Listen, kid. We ain't in the Old Country no more. We're in New York"—*Noo Yawk* is what she said— "New York, U.S. of A. We ain't got Queens, except across the bridge."

So now I'm really torqued. I mean, who knows what she's going to do next, right? She could turn me into a pigeon, for all I know. This is no time to lose it. I've got to focus. After all, I've been reading about fairies for years: New Age stuff, folklore, fantasy novels—everything I could get my hands on. I've done my homework. There's a chance I can b.s. my way out of this if I keep my cool.

"Oh, ha ha," I say. "Not. Like that rat-guy didn't say 'how high' when you said 'jump.' You can call yourself the Mayor of Central Park if you want, but you're still the Queen of the goddam Fairies."

She morphs back to dreads and leather on fast forward. "So, Fatso. You think you're hot stuff." I shrug. "Listen. We're in this thing where I think you owe me, and you think you don't. I could *make* you pay up, but I won't." She plops down on the bench and gets comfortable. The squirrel jumps off her shoulder and disappears into a tree.

"Siddown, take a load off—have a drink. Here."

Swear to God, she hands me a can of Diet Coke. I don't know where it came from, but the pop top is popped, and I can hear the Coke fizzing and I realize I'm wicked thirsty. My hand goes, like all by itself, to take it, and then my brain kicks in. "No," I say. "Thank you."

She looks hurt. "Really? It's cold and everything." She shoves it towards me. My mouth is as dry as the Sahara Desert, but if there's one thing I'm sure I know about fairies, it's don't eat or drink anything a fairy gives you if you ever want to go home.

"Really," I say. "Thanks."

"Well, dag," she says, disgusted. "You read fairy tales. Aren't you special. I suppose now you're going to ask for three wishes and a pot of gold. Go ahead. Three wishes. Have a ball."

This is more like it. I'm all prepared, too. In sixth grade, I worked out what my wishes would be, if I ever met a wish-granting fairy. And they were still perfectly good wishes, based on extensive research. Never, ever wish for more wishes. Never ask for money—it'll turn into dog doo in the morning. The safest thing to do was to ask for something that would make you a better citizen, and then you could ask for two things for yourself. I settled on a good heart, a really ace memory, and 20/20 vision. I didn't know about laser surgery in sixth grade.

So I'm all ready (except maybe asking to be a size 6 instead of the vision thing), and then it occurs to me that this is all way too easy, and Queenie is looking way too cheerful for someone who's been outsmarted by an overweight book-worm. Face it, I haven't done anything to earn those wishes. All I've done is turn down a lousy Diet Coke. "Thanks all the same, but I'll pass," I say. "Can I go home now?"

Then she loses her temper. She's not foaming at the mouth or anything, but there are sparks coming out of her eyes like a Fourth of July sparkler, and her dreads are lifting and twining around her head like snakes. The sparrow gives a startled chirp and takes off for the nearest bush.

"Well, isn't this just my lucky day," Greenie snarls. "You're not as dumb as you look. On the bright side, though,"—her dreads settle slowly—"winning's boring when it's too easy, you know?"

I wouldn't know—I don't usually win. But then, I don't usually care that much. This is different. This time, there's a lot more at stake than my nonexistent self-esteem. I'm glad she thinks I'm a moron. It evens things up a little. "I tell you what," I tell her. "I'll play you for my freedom."

"You're on," she says. "Dealer's choice. That's me. What shall we play?" She leans back on the bench and looks up at the sky. "Riddles are trad, but everybody knows all the good ones. What's black and white and red all over? A blushing nun? A newspaper? Penguin roadkill? Puleeze. Anyway, riddles are boring. What do you say to Truth or Dare?"

"I hate it." I do, too. The only time I played it, I ended up feeling icky and raw, like I'd been sunbathing topless.

"Really? It's my favorite game. We'll play Truth or Dare. These are the rules. We ask each other personal questions, and the first one who won't answer loses everything. Deal?"

It doesn't sound like much of a deal to me. How can I know what question a Queen of Fairies would be too embarrassed to answer? On the other hand, what can a being who hangs out with squirrels and fairies and rat-guys know about human beings? And what choice do I have?

I shrug. "I guess."

"Okay. I go first."

Well, sure she does. She's the Queen of Central Park. And I see the question coming—she doesn't even pause to think about it. "So, how much do you weigh, anyway?"

Now you have to understand that nobody knows how much I weigh. Not Elf, not even my mom. Only the school nurse and the doctor and me. I've always said I'd rather die than tell anyone else. But the choice between telling and living in Central Park for seven months is a no-brainer. So I tell her. I even add a pound for the hotdog and the Mr. Softee I ate at the boathouse.

"Geddouddaheah!" she says. "You really pork it down, huh?"

I don't like her comment, but it's not like I haven't heard it before. It makes me mad, but not so mad I can't think, which is obviously what she's trying for. Questions go through my mind, but I don't have a lot to go on, you know what I'm saying? And she's tapping her green boot and looking impatient. I have to say something, and what I end up asking is, "Why are you in Central Park, anyway? I mean, there's lots of other places that are more fairy-friendly. Why aren't you in White Plains or something?"

It sounds like a question to me, but she doesn't seem to think so. "I win. That's not personal," she says.

"It is too personal. Where a person lives is personal. Come on. Why do you live here, or let me go home."

"Can't blame a girl for trying," she says. "Okay, here goes. This is the heart of the city. You guys pass through all the time—like Grand Central Station, right? Only here, you stop for a while. You rest, you play, you kiss in the grass, you whisper your secrets, you weep, you fight. This ground, these rocks, are soaked through with love, hate, joy, sorrow, passion. And I love that stuff, you understand? It keeps me interested."

Wow. I stare at her, and all my ideas about fairies start to get rearranged. But they don't get very far because she's still talking.

"You think I don't know anything about you," she says. "Boy, are you wrong. I know everything I want to know. I know what's on your bio quiz next week. I know Patty Gregg's worst secret. I know who your real mother is, the one who gave you away when you were born." She gives me this look, like Elf's brother the time he stole a dirty magazine. "Wanna know?"

It's not what I'm expecting, but it's a question, all right, and it's personal. And it's really easy. Sure, I want to know all those things, a whole lot—especially about my biological mother. Like more than anything else in the world. My parents are okay—I mean, they say they love me and everything. But they really don't understand me big time. I've always *felt* adopted, if you know what I mean—a changeling in a family of ordinary humans. I'd give anything to know who my real mother is, what she looks like and why she couldn't keep me. So I should say yes, right? I mean, it's the true answer to the green girl's question, and that's what the game is about, isn't it?

There's a movement on my shoulder, a sharp little pinch right behind my ear. I've totally forgotten Bugle—I mean, she's been sitting there for ages, perfectly still, which is not her usual.

Maybe I've missed something. It's that too easy thing again. Sure, I want to know who my birth mom is. But it's more complicated than that. Because now that I think about it, I realize I don't want Greenie to be the one to tell me. I mean, it feels wrong, to learn something like that from someone who is obviously trying to hurt you.

"Answer the question," says the green girl. "Or give in. I'm getting bored."

I take a deep breath. "Keep your socks on. I was thinking how to put it. Okay, my answer is both yes and no. I do want to find out about my birth mom, but I don't want you to tell me. Even if you know, it's none of your business. I want to find out for myself. Does that answer your question?"

She nods briskly. "It does. Your turn."

She's not going to give me much time to come up with one, I can tell that. She wants to win. She wants to get me all torqued so I can't think, so I won't ask her the one question she won't answer, so I won't even see it staring me right in the face, the one thing she really, really can't answer, if the books I've read aren't all totally bogus.

"What's your name?" I ask.

I mean, it's obvious, isn't it? Like, how dumb does she think I am? Pretty dumb, I guess, from the look on her face.

"Guess," she says, making a quick recovery.

"Wrong fairy tale," I say, pushing it. "Come on. Tell me, or you lose."

"Do you know what you're asking?"

"Yes."

There's a long silence—a *long* silence, like no bird is ever going to sing again, or squirrel chatter or wind blow. The green girl puts her fingers in her mouth and starts to bite her nails. I'm feeling pretty good. I know and she knows that I've won no matter what she says. If she tells me her name, I have total power over her, and if she doesn't, she loses the game. I know what I'd choose if I was in her place, but I guess she must really, really hate losing.

Watching her sweat, I think of several things to say, most of them kind of mean. She'd say them, if she was me. I don't. It's not like I'm Mother Teresa or anything—I've been mean plenty of times, and sometimes I wasn't even sorry later. But she might lose her temper and turn me into a pigeon after all. Besides, she looks so *human* all of a sudden, chewing her nails and all stressed out like she's the one facing seven months of picking up fairy laundry. Before, when she was winning, she looked maybe twenty, right? Gorgeous, tough, scary, in total control. Now she looks a lot younger and not tough at all.

So maybe if she loses, she's threatened with seven months of doing what I tell her. Maybe I don't realize what I'm asking. Maybe there's more at stake here than I know. A tiny whimpering behind my right ear tells me that Bugle is pretty upset. Suddenly, I don't feel so great. I don't care any more about beating the Queen of the Fairies at some stupid game. I just want this to be over.

"Listen," I say, and the green girl looks up at me. Her wide, mossy eyes are all blurred with tears. I take a deep breath. "Let's stop playing," I say.

"We can't stop," she says miserably. "It has begun, it must be finished. Those are the rules."

"Okay. We'll finish it. It's a draw. You don't have to answer my question. Nobody wins. Nobody loses. We just go back to the beginning."

"What beginning? When Gnaw-bone was chasing you? If I help you, you have to pay."

I think about this for a little while. She lets me. "Okay," I say. "How about this. You're in a tough spot, right? I take back my question, you're off the hook, like you got me off the hook with Gnaw-bone. We're even."

She takes her fingers out of her mouth. She gnaws on her lip. She looks up into the sky, and around at the trees. She tugs on her dreads. She smiles. She starts to laugh. It's not a teasing laugh or a mean laugh, but pure happiness, like a little kid in the snow.

"Wow," she says, and her voice is warm and soft as fleece. "You're right. Awesome."

"Cool," I say. Can I go home now?"

"In a minute." She puts her head to one side, and grins at me. I'm grinning back—I can't help it. Suddenly, I feel all mellow and safe and comfortable, like I'm lying on a rock in the sun and telling stories to Elf.

"Yeah," she says, like she's reading my mind. "I've heard you. You tell good stories. You should write them down. Now, about those wishes. They're human stuff—not really my business. As you pointed out. Besides, you've already got all those things. You remember what you need to know; you see clearly; you're majorly kind-hearted. But you deserve a present." She tapped her browny-green cheek with one slender finger. "I know. Ready?"

"Okay," I say. "Um. What is it?"

"It's a surprise," she says. "But you'll like it. You'll see."

She stands up and I stand up. Bugle takes off from my shoulder and goes and sits in the greeny-brown dreads like a butterfly clip. Then the Queen of the New York Fairies leans forward and kisses me on the forehead. It doesn't feel like a kiss—more like a very light breeze has just hit me between the eyes. Then she lays her finger across my lips, and then she's gone.

"So there you are!" It was Elf, red in the face, out of breath, with her hair coming out of the clip, and a tear in her jacket. "I've been looking all over. I was scared out of my mind! It was like you just disappeared into thin air!"

"I got lost," I said. "Anyway, it's okay now. Sit down. You look like hell."

"Thanks, friend." She sat on the bench. "So, what happened?"

I wanted to tell her, I really did. I mean, she's my best friend and everything, and I always tell her everything. But the Queen of the Fairies. I ask you. And I could feel the kiss nestling below my bangs like a little, warm sun and the Queen's finger cool across my lips. So all I did was look at my hands. They were all dirty and scratched from climbing up the cliff. I'd broken a fingernail.

"Are you okay?" Elf asked anxiously. "That guy didn't catch you or anything, did he? Jeez, I wish we'd never gone down there."

She was getting really upset. I said, "I'm fine, Elf. He didn't catch me, and everything's okay."

"You sure?"

I looked right at her, you know how you do when you

want to be sure someone hears you? And I said, "I'm sure." And I was.

"Okay," she said slowly. "Good. I was worried." She looked at her watch. "It's not like it was that long, but it seemed like forever."

"Yeah," I agreed, with feeling. "I'm really thirsty."

So that's about it, really. We went to a coffeeshop on Columbus Ave. and had blueberry pie and coffee and talked. For the first time, I told her about being adopted, and wanting to look for my birth mother, and she was really great about it after being mad because I hadn't told her before. I said she was a good friend and she got teary. And then I went home.

So what's the moral of this story? My life didn't get better overnight, if that's what you're wondering. I still need to lose a few pounds, I still need glasses, and the cool kids still hate me. But Elf sits with me at lunch now, and a couple other kids turned out to be into fantasy and like that, so I'm not a total outcast any more. And I'm writing down my stories. Elf thinks they're good, but she's my best friend. Maybe someday I'll get up the nerve to show them to my English teacher. Oh, and I've talked to my mom about finding my birth mother, and she says maybe I should wait until I'm out of high school. Which is okay with me, because, to tell you the truth, I don't need to find her right now—I just want to know I can.

And the Green Queen's gift? It's really weird. Suddenly, I see fairies everywhere.

There was this girl the other day—blonde, skinny, wearing a white leotard and her jeans unzipped and folded back, so she looked kind of like a flower in a calyx of blue leaves. Freak, right? Nope. Fairy. So was an old black guy all dressed in royal blue, with butterflies sewn on his blue beret and painted on his blue suede shoes. And this Asian guy with black hair down to his butt and a big fur coat. And this Upper East Side lady with big blonde hair and green bug-eyes. She had a fuzzy little dog on a rhinestone leash, and you won't believe this, but the dog was a fairy, too.

And remember the trees—the sidewalk ones? I know all about them now. No, I won't tell you, stupid. It's a secret. If you really want to know, you'll have to go find the Queen of Grand Central Park and make her an offer. Or play a game with her.

Don't forget to say hi to Gnaw-bone for me.

DELIA SHERMAN is a writer and editor living in Boston, Massachusetts. She is the author of numerous short stories, and of the novels *Through a Brazen Mirror*, *The Porcelain Dove*, and *The Freedom Maze*. With fellow fantasist Ellen Kushner, she is co-author of a short story and a novel, both called "The Fall of the Kings." She is also co-editor, with Terri Windling, of *The Essential Bordertown*. She is a contributing editor for Tor Books and a member of the Tiptree Awards Motherboard. She prefers cafes to home for writing, and traveling to staying put.

Author's Note:

I grew up in Manhattan just two blocks from Central Park. The tamer playgrounds were my back yard. The wilds of the Ramble were my Forest Perilous. The Boating Pond was my Boundless Ocean. Not long ago, I heard someone say that he didn't believe that fairies would live so close to all that concrete and noise. From my own experience, I knew that he was wrong, and I wrote "Grand Central Park" to prove it. No, I never met the Green Queen personally, but I certainly was conscious of her, and of her court, the dangerous ones as well as the merely mischievous. I still am.

DAPHNE

MICHAEL CADNUM

YOU KNOW HOW the sun is, how he won't shut up on one of those dry, drought-golden days, the vineyards blue-black with fruit, the ox carts groaning by, every human being wishing for a portion of shade.

Apollo the sun god was what you would expect—all smiles, all mouth, too beautiful to look at, and knowing it. Oh, he was good company, dropping by the fields where honest women were herding geese or cranking buckets out of the well, and he'd speak in that voice that was like the sky itself favoring you with its attention.

I had a simple life. My own father was the river god Peneus, and my mother was a former village maiden who, taking her ease by river bathing one hot late summer afternoon, felt the lap and sinew of my father around, beneath, within. Rivers are promiscuous, ardent, and deep. My mother spent years pensive, alone, but sustained by the knowledge that she had once been loved. She raised me to make straw dolls and wax horses, all the petty, pretty toys of girlhood, but never let me forget that I was the daughter of the river—that distant father who never addresses his children but is, at the same time, always faithful to them.

The sun god would amble by and flirt, but I paid him no attention. Young mortal men would come around, too, all blushes and stammers, and I would shake my head and tell them that the wedding candle and the bridal bed held no magic for me. The daughter of the deep current has no great fondness for the merely human breath of any lover, and the prospect of becoming a wife filled me with no happiness.

One day I waded into the river.

I let the current surround and know me. The coursing, seaward longing of my father for the deeper ocean was always his great failing, and his lasting strength. My father pulsed all around my body, both on his way to the salt ocean and steadily in one place at the same time.

Hear me, I whispered.

I heard no answer.

"Oh father, listen to me," I prayed.

The ripples of river water glittered.

I said, "Make me a virgin all my years—make me one who does not tarry with mankind."

And my father spoke at last, in that water-lunged, rotund whisper. You've heard my father speak, soft syllables among the willow branches, muttering whispers in the shadow of the bridge. "Will I not have grandchildren?" he complained. "No wee ones, splashing along my banks?"

I begged him again to bless my maidenhead, and told him that just as Diana the Huntress Immortal was no lover of men, so I, too, would seek a chaste existence. I would enjoy a noble life worthy, after all, of the river's daughter.

This last argument teased the concession from him. The river god is powerful, with his long, grappling arms full-muscled each spring, when the mountains are dark with rain. But the river god is not so mighty he does not feel the weight of the even greater gods, the powerful sea in his abyss, the sun with his yodeling, arrogant look-at-me each day. So with a reluctant but not unkind sigh, he blessed my virginity, and with a loving, guarded murmur added, "Be kind to your mother, Daphne—I still hold her in my heart."

My father—constant, stubborn, fickle, undying. And you ask why I wanted nothing to do with mortal men.

It was not very long before the god Apollo came around as usual, parting the wheat field with his athletic stride, laughing. Tossing back his head and laughing—that god was one great, life-consuming laugh.

But on this day he did not pass me by. Something about me had changed. Perhaps my private vow had altered me, and increased my beauty. The sky was not enough for him, he swore—he desired me.

"Daphne," he said, "let's go see the berries ripen on the bush."

I did not meet his gaze.

"Let's go watch the olive branches get heavy with their bounty," he added, and other such things, all god-chat meaning: let me play in-and-out with you over on the hillside, my dear, and I'll leave you alone and forsaken ever after.

I told him I had taken a vow of chastity.

He frowned as he smiled. "As a divinity, I can dismiss this vow," he said, all teeth and sparkle.

I made no further reply.

"Oh, Daphne, have you not dreamed of being the mother of the sun god's brood?" he asked.

I had nothing to say.

The god would not shut up. He came to see me for days. Each morning he would split the hillsides with his beaming countenance, and each noon he would lay his hot, huge hands all over my body as I carried the bucket from the well, reaching down and feeling me wherever he could, shoulders, brow. But I would not allow him the private favors he sought.

I heard him on his way toward me that hot day. He was more merry than ever. He talked as he came along the winding road from the village, as I was out collecting thyme for my mother's stew. "Wouldn't that head look fine bedecked with a crown?" he sang. "Wouldn't that pair of hips look just right, graced with the girdle of a queen and the silks of a monarch, my comely bride? Wouldn't those lips come alive under the . . ."

But I had heard enough, and casting the sweet-scented herbs to the ground, I walked away. I walked fast.

I hurried.

He followed, never ceasing to talk, his unending spiel enough to wither crops. He described how passionate he had always proved as a lover, how the hills stirred and brought forth forests at his caress, how poppies broke into blossom at his breath.

And who was I? he asked.

Who was I? he said, beginning to grow surly. Who was I, a mere river-godkin's daughter, to turn aside the love of the lord of so much life, and a well-favored, rich-voiced Father of All at that.

Right then I made my terrible error.

I made my mortal blunder.

I began to run.

As I ran, Apollo strode along with me, faster than any greyhound panting after his hare. He circled me as I fled, bounded along, crossed my path, back and forth, mocking, seeking, all but capturing me against my will, as though pursuit made his lust all the keener. In my ignorant virginity I began to weep, my next mistake. My wet tears merely made him laugh.

I ran as no woman has ever run, fled as few mortals have ever flown, down the slope of the river valley, the sun god matching me stride for stride, his sky-warm breath at my shoulder. I reached the side of the river, and called out just as he seized me.

He was very strong.

My voice swept linnets from the willows. It startled harvest mice in their slumber. *Help me, Father.* I heard the god of the sun chuckle at my ear. He said, "What can a mere water godlet do to keep my lust at bay?"

My father did not forget me.

My fingers split. My arms throbbed, and broke wide open. Working fibers snaked down the veins of my lungs. My feet seized and held the bank of the river, a root from my spine to the soil, and down, into the cold stone. Wide into the sky I held my beseeching arms. They branched, and my full-leafed embrace filled the blue from where I panted, a green-pithed tree, rooted to the earth.

Well Apollo loved me then, weeping, feeling the trilling of my human heart within my wooden girth. Because the gods love mortals. They seek our beauty, our courage, our joy. They envy us our hope. We are in our hearts what they can never master, and all the night long the lord of light keened beside me, weeping for the love he would never win.

To this day when a daphne blossoms, or when any tree breaks into leaf, you can feel how the sun is chastened, faithful to the living he can worship but never possess. And as for me—feel no sorrow. When you see the wind stir the greenwood, or when you turn the pages of a book made from a tree's still-blameless flesh, lean close and listen.

You hear my voice.

MICHAEL CADNUM is the author of eighteen novels including *In a Dark Wood*, *Rundown*, and *The Book of the Lion*, which was a National Book Award Finalist in 1999. His most recent novel is *Raven of the Waves*. He has also published two books of poetry, and a picture book for children. Cadnum's short fiction has been published in various volumes of the Datlow/Windling adult fairy tale anthology series and in their children's fairy tale anthology *A Wolf at the Door*. Several of his stories have also been chosen for reprint in *The Year's Best Fantasy and Horror*.

Author's Note:

I've always loved stories of transformation. I wrote about a werewolf in *Saint Peter's Wolf*, and a vampire in *The Judas Glass*—I love writing about people on the verge of becoming something else (including young people in the process of growing up). My favorite classical work is Ovid's *Metamorphoses*, where we find his wonderful version of the Daphne story. This rendition is decidedly my own, and results from my deep regard for the tale. I studied Latin in high school and was not very good at the language, but I love the *Metamorphoses* so much I have translated a little of it just for the pleasure. The lines in this story which describe the chase, just before Daphne turns into a tree, are very much my homage to the original Latin.

Somewhere in My Mind There Is a Painting Box

≈

CHARLES DE LINT

SUCH A THING to find, so deep in the forest: A painter's box nested in ferns and a tangle of sprucey-pine roots, almost buried by the leaves and pine needles drifted up against the trunk of the tree. Later, Lily would learn that it was called a pochade box, but for now she sat bouncing lightly on her ankles admiring her find.

It was impossible to say how long the box had been hidden here. The wood panels weren't rotting, but the hasps were rusted shut and it took her a while to get them open. She lifted the lid and then, and then . . .

Treasure.

Stored in the lid, held apart from each other by slots, were three 8 x 10 wooden panels, each with a painting on it. For all their quick and loose rendering, she had no trouble recognizing the subjects. There was something familiar about them, too—beyond the subject matter that she easily recognized.

The first was of the staircase waterfall where the creek took a sudden tumble before continuing on again at a more level pace. She had to fill in detail from her own memory and imagination, but she knew it was that place.

The second was of a long-deserted homestead up a side valley of the hollow, the tin roof sagging, the rotting walls falling inward. It was nothing like Aunt's cabin on its sunny slopes, surrounded by wild roses, old beehives, and an apple orchard that she and Aunt were slowly reclaiming from the wild. This was a place that would only get sun from midmorning through the early afternoon, a dark and damp hollow, where the dew never had a chance to burn off completely.

The last one could have been painted anywhere in this forest but she imagined it had been done down by the creek, looking up a slope into a view of yellow birches, beech, and sprucey-pines growing dense and thick as the stars overhead, with a burst of light coming through a break in the canopy.

Lily studied each painting, then carefully set them aside on the ground beside her. There was the hint of another picture on the inside lid itself, but she couldn't make out what it was supposed to be.

The palette was covered in dried paint that, like the inside lid, almost had the look of a painting itself, and lifted from the box to reveal a compartment underneath. In the bottom of the box were tubes of oil paint, brushes, and a palette knife, a small bottle of turpentine and a rag stained with all the colors the artist had been using.

Lily turned the palette over and there she found what

she'd been looking for. An identifying mark. She ran a finger over the letters that spelled out an impossible name.

Milo Johnson.

Treasure.

"Milo Johnson," Aunt repeated, trying to understand Lily's excitement. At seventeen, Lily could still get as wound up about a new thing as she had when she was a child. "Should I know that name?"

Lily gave her a "you never pay attention, do you?" look and went to get a book from her bookshelf. She didn't have many, but those she did have had been read over and over again. The one she brought back to the kitchen table was called *The Newford Naturalists: Redefining the Landscape*. Opening it to the first artist profiled, she underlined his name with her finger.

Aunt read silently along with her, mouthing the words, then studied the black-and-white photo of Johnson that accompanied the profile.

"I remember seeing him a time or two," she said. "Tramping through the woods with an old canvas knapsack on his back. But that was a long time ago."

"It would have to have been."

Aunt read a little more, then looked up.

"So he's famous then," she asked.

"Very. He went painting all through these hills and he's got pictures in galleries all over the world."

"Imagine that. And you reckon this is his box?"

Lily nodded.

"Well, we'd better see about returning it to him."

"We can't," Lily told her. "He's dead. Or at least they say he's dead. He and Frank Spain went out into the hills on a painting expedition and were never heard from again."

She flipped towards the back of the book until she came to the smaller section devoted to Spain's work. Johnson had been the giant among the Newford Naturalists, his bold, dynamic style instantly recognizable, even to those who might not know him by name, while Spain had been one of a group of younger artists that Johnson and his fellow Naturalists had been mentoring. He wasn't as well known as Johnson or the others, but he'd already been showing the potential to become a leader in his own right before he and Johnson had taken that last fateful trip.

It was all in the book which Lily had practically memorized by now, she'd read it so often.

Ever since Harlene Welch had given it to her a few years ago, Lily had wanted to grow up to be like the Naturalists— especially Johnson. Not to paint exactly the way they did, necessarily, but to have her own individual vision the way that they did. To be able to take the world of her beloved hills and forest and portray it in such a way that others would see it through her eyes, that they would see it in a new way and so understand her love for it and would want to protect it the way that she did.

"That was twenty years ago," Lily added, "and their bodies weren't ever recovered."

Twenty years ago. Imagine. The box had been lying lost in the woods for all that time.

"Never thought of painting pictures as being something dangerous," Aunt said.

"Anything can be dangerous," Lily replied. "That's what Beau says."

Aunt nodded. She reached across the table to turn the box towards her.

"So you plan on keeping it?" she asked.

"I guess."

"He must have kin. Don't you think it should go to them?"

Lily shook her head. "He was an orphan, just like me. The only people we could give it to would be in the museum and they'd just stick it away in some drawer somewhere."

"Even the pictures?"

"Well, probably not them. But the painting box for sure . . ."

Lily hungered to try the paints and brushes she'd found in the box. There was never enough money for her to think of being able to buy either.

"Well," Aunt said. "You found it, so I guess you get to decide what you do with it."

"I guess."

Finder's keepers, after all. But she couldn't help feeling that this find of hers—especially the paintings—belonged to everyone, not just some gangly backwoods girl who happened to come upon them while out on a ramble.

"I'll have to think on it," she added.

Aunt nodded, then got up to put on the kettle.

The next morning Lily went about her chores. She fed the chickens, sparing a few handfuls of feed for the sparrows and other birds that were waiting expectantly in the trees nearby. She milked the cow and poured some milk into a saucer for the cats that came out of the woods when she was done, purring and winding in between her legs until she set the saucer down. By the time she'd finished weeding the garden and filling the woodbox, it was midmorning.

She packed herself a lunch and stowed it in her shoulder satchel along with some carpenter's pencils and a pad of sketching paper she'd made from cutting up brown grocery bags.

"Off again, are you?" Aunt asked.

"I'll be home for dinner."

"You're not going to bring that box with you?"

She was tempted. The tubes of paint were rusted shut, but she'd squeezed the thin metal of their bodies and found that the paint inside was still pliable. The brushes were good, too. But her using them didn't seem right. Not yet, anyways.

"Not today," she told Aunt.

As she left the house she looked up to see a pair of dogs coming tearing up the slope towards her. They were the Shaffers' dogs, Max and Kiki, the one dark brown, the other white with black markings, the pair of them bundles of short-haired energy. The Shaffers lived beside the Welchs, who owned the farm at the end of the trail that ran from the county road to Aunt's cabin—an hour's walk through the woods as you followed the creek. Their dogs were a friendly pair, good at not chasing cows or game, and showed up every few days to accompany Lily on her rambles.

The dogs danced around her now as she set off through the orchard. When she got to the Apple Tree Man's tree— that's what Aunt called the oldest tree of the orchard—she pulled out a biscuit she'd saved from breakfast and set it down at its roots. It was a habit she'd had since she was a little girl, like feeding the birds and the cats while doing her morning chores. Aunt used to tease her about it, telling her what a good provider she was for the mice and raccoons.

"Shoo," she said as Kiki went for the biscuit. "That's not for you. You'll have to wait for lunch to get yours."

They climbed up to the top of the hill and then went into the woods, the dogs chasing each other in circles while Lily kept stopping to investigate some interesting seed pod or cluster of weeds. They had lunch a couple of miles further on, sitting on a stone outcrop that overlooked the Big Sinkhole, a two or three acre depression with the entrance to a cave at the bottom.

Most of the mountains around Aunt's cabin were riddled with caves of all shapes and sizes. There were entrances everywhere, though most only went a few yards in before they ended. But some said you could walk from one end of the Kickaha Hills to the other, all underground, if you knew the way.

Lunch finished, Lily slid down from the rock. She didn't feel like drawing today. Instead she kept thinking about the painting box, how odd it had been to find it after its having been lost for so many years, so she led the dogs back to that part of the woods to see what else she might find. A shiver went up her spine. What if she found their bones?

The dogs grew more playful as she neared the spot where she'd come upon the box. They nipped at her sleeves or crouched ahead of her, butts and tails in the air, growling so fiercely they made her laugh. Finally Max bumped her leg with his head just as she was in midstep. She lost her balance and fell into a pile of leaves, her satchel tumbling to the ground, spilling drawings.

She sat up. A smile kept twitching at the corner of her mouth but she managed to give them a pretty fierce glare.

"Two against one?" she said. "Well, come on, you bullies. I'm ready for you."

She jumped on Kiki and wrestled her to the ground, the dog squirming with delight in her grip. Max joined the tussle and soon the three of them were rolling about in the leaves like the puppies the dogs no longer were and Lily had never been. They were having such fun that at first none of them heard the shouting. When they did, they stopped their rough-housing to find a man standing nearby, holding a stick in his upraised hand.

"Get away from her!" he cried, waving the stick.

Lily sat up, so many leaves tangled in her hair and caught in her sweater that she had more on her than did some of the autumned trees around them. She put a hand on the collar of either dog, but, curiously, neither seemed inclined to bark or chase the stranger off. They stayed by her side, staring at him.

Lily studied him for a long moment, too, as quiet as the dogs. He wasn't a big man, but he seemed solid, dressed in a fraying broadcloth suit with a white shirt underneath and worn leather boots on his feet. His hair was roughly trimmed and he looked as if he hadn't shaved for a few days. But he had a good face—strong features, laugh lines around his eyes and the corners of his mouth. She didn't think he was much older than her.

"It's all right," she told the man. "We were just funning."

There was something familiar about him, but she couldn't place it immediately.

"Of course," he said, dropping the stick. "How stupid can I be? What animal in this forest would harm its Lady?" He went down on his knees. "Forgive my impertinence."

This was too odd for words, from the strange behavior of the dogs to the man's even stranger behavior. She couldn't speak. Then something changed in the man's eyes. There'd been a lost look in them a moment ago, but also hope. Now there was only resignation.

"You're just a girl," he said.

Lily found her voice at that indignity.

"I'm seventeen," she told him. "In these parts, there's some would think I'm already an old maid."

He shook his head. "Your pardon. I meant no insult."

Lily relaxed a little. "That's all right."

He reached over to where her drawings had spilled from her satchel and put them back in, looking at each one for a moment before he did.

"These are good," he said. "Better than good."

For those few moments while he looked through her drawings, while he looked at them carefully, one by one, before replacing them in her satchel, he seemed different once more. Not so lost. Not so sad.

"Thank you," she said.

She waited a moment, thinking it might be rude of her to follow a compliment with a question that might be considered prying. She waited until the last drawing was back in her satchel and he sat there holding the leather bag on his lap, his gaze gone she didn't know where.

"What are you doing here in the woods?" she finally asked.

It took a moment before his gaze returned to her. He closed the satchel and laid it on the grass between them.

"I took you for someone else," he said, which wasn't an answer at all. "It was the wild tangle of your red hair—the leaves in it and on your sweater. But you're too young and your skin's not a coppery brown."

"And this explains what?" she asked.

"I thought you were Her," he said.

Lily could hear the emphasis he put on the word, but it still didn't clear up her confusion.

"I don't know what you're talking about," she said.

She started to pluck the leaves out of her hair and brush them from her sweater. The dogs lay down, one on either side of her, still curiously subdued.

"I thought you were the Lady of the Wood," he explained. "She who stepped out of a tree and welcomed us when we came out of the cave between the worlds. She wears a cloak of leaves and has moonlight in Her eyes."

A strange feeling came over Lily when he said "stepped out of a tree." She found herself remembering a fever dream she'd once had—five years ago when she'd been snake bit. It had been so odd. She'd dreamt that she'd been changed into a kitten to save her from the snake bite, met Aunt's Apple Tree Man and another wood spirit called the Father of Cats. She'd even seen the fairies she'd tried to find for so long: foxfired shapes, bobbing in the meadow like fireflies.

That dream had seemed so real.

She blinked away the memory of it and focused on the stranger again. He'd gotten off his knees and was sitting cross-legged on the ground, a half dozen feet from where she and the dogs were.

"What did you mean when you said 'us'?" she asked.

Now it was his turn to look confused.

"You said this lady showed 'us' some cave."

He nodded. "I was out painting with Milo when—"

As soon as he mentioned that name, the earlier sense of familiarity collided with her memory of a photo in her book on the Newford Naturalists.

"You're Frank Spain!" Lily cried.

He nodded in agreement.

"But that can't be," she said. "You don't look any older than you do in the picture in my book."

"What book?"

"The one about Milo Johnson and the rest of the Newford Naturalists that's back at the cabin."

"There's a book about us?"

"You're famous," Lily told him with a grin. "The book says you and Mr. Johnson disappeared twenty years ago while you were out painting in these very hills."

Frank shook his head, the shock plain in his features.

"Twenty . . . years?" he said slowly. "How's that even possible? We've only been gone for a few days . . ."

"What happened to you?" Lily asked.

"I don't really know," he said. "We'd come here after a winter of being cooped up in the studio, longing to paint in the landscape itself. We meant to stay until the black flies drove us back to the city but then . . . " He shook his head. "Then we found the cave and met the Lady. . . ."

He seemed so lost and confused that Lily took him home.

Aunt greeted his arrival and introduction with a raised eyebrow. Lily knew what she was thinking. First a painting box, now a painter. What would be next?

But Aunt had never turned anyone away from her cabin before and she wasn't about to start now. She had Lily show Frank to where he could draw some water from the well and clean up, then set a third plate for supper. It wasn't until later when they were sitting out on the porch drinking tea and watching the night fall that Frank told them his story. He spoke of how he and Milo had found the cave that led them through darkness into another world. How they'd met the Lady there, with Her cloak of leaves and Her coppery skin, Her dark, dark eyes and Her fox-red hair.

"So there is a underground way through these mountains," Aunt said. "I always reckoned there was some truth to that story."

Frank shook his head. "The cave didn't take us to the other side of the mountains. It took us out of this world and into another."

Aunt smiled. "Next thing you're going to tell me is you've been to Fairyland."

"Look at him," Lily said. She went inside and got her book, opening it to the photograph of Frank Spain. "He doesn't look any older than he did when this picture was taken."

Aunt nodded. "Some people do age well."

"Not this well," Lily said.

Aunt turned to Frank. "So what is it that you're asking us to believe?"

"I'm not asking anything," he said. "I don't believe it myself."

Lily sighed and took the book over to him. She showed him the copyright date, put her finger on the paragraph that described how he and Milo Johnson had gone missing some fifteen years earlier.

"The book's five years old," she said. "But I think we've got a newspaper that's no more than a month old. I could show you the date on it."

But Frank was already shaking his head. He'd gone pale reading the paragraph about the mystery of his and his mentor's disappearance. He lifted his gaze to meet Aunt's.

"I guess maybe we were in Fairyland," he said, his voice gone soft.

Aunt looked from Lily's face to that of her guest.

"How's that possible?" she said.

"I truly don't know," he told her.

He turned the pages of the book, stopping to read the section on himself. Lily knew what he was reading. His father had died in a mining accident when he was still a boy, but his mother had been alive when he'd disappeared. She'd died five years later.

"My parents are gone, too," she told him.

He nodded, his eyes shiny.

Lily shot Aunt a look, but Aunt sat in her chair, staring out into the gathering dusk, an unreadable expression in her features. Lily supposed it was one thing to appreciate a fairy tale but quite another to find yourself smack dab in the middle of one.

Lily was taking it the best of either of them. Maybe it was because of that snake bite fever dream she'd had. In the past five years she still woke from dreams in which she'd been a kitten.

"Why did you come back?" she asked Frank.

"I didn't know I was coming back," he said. "That world . . ." He flipped a few pages back to show them reproductions of Johnson's paintings. "That's what this other world's like. You don't have to imagine everything being more of itself than it seems to be here like Milo's done in these paintings. Over there it's really like that. You can't imagine the colors, the intensity, the rich wash that fills your heart as much as it does your eyes. We haven't painted at all since we got over there. We didn't need to." He laughed. "I know Milo abandoned his paints before we crossed over and to tell you the truth, I don't even know where mine are."

"I found Mr. Johnson's box," Lily said. "Yesterday—not far from where you came upon me and the dogs."

He nodded, but she didn't think he'd heard her.

"I was walking," he said. "Looking for the Lady. We hadn't seen Her for a day or so and I wanted to talk to Her again. To ask Her about that place. I remember I came to this grove of sycamore and beech where we'd seen Her a time or two. I stepped in between the trees, out of the sun and into the shade. The next thing I knew I was walking in these hills and I was back here where everything seems . . . paler. Subdued."

He looked at them.

"I've got to go back," he said. "There's no place for me here. Ma's gone and everybody I knew'll be dead like her or too changed for me to know them anymore." He tapped the book. "Just like me, according to what it says here."

"You don't want to go rushing into anything," Aunt said. "Surely you've got other kin, and they'll be wanting to see you."

"There's no one. Me and Ma, we were the last of the Spains that I know."

Aunt nodded in a way that Lily recognized. It was her way of making you think she agreed with you, but she was really just waiting for common sense to take hold of you so that you didn't go off half-cocked and get yourself in some kind of trouble you didn't need to get into.

"You'll want to rest up," she said. "You can sleep in the barn. Lily will show you where. Come morning, everything'll make a lot more sense."

He just looked at her. "How do you make sense out of something like this?"

"You trust me on this," she said. "A good night's sleep does a body wonders."

So he followed her advice—most people did when Aunt had decided what was best for them.

He let Lily take him down to the barn where they made a bed for him in the straw. She wondered if he'd try to kiss her, and how she'd feel if he did, but she never got the chance to find out.

"Thank you," he said and then he lay down on the blankets.

He was already asleep by the time she was closing the door. And in the morning he was gone.

That night Lily had one of what she thought of as her storybook dreams. She wasn't a kitten this time. Instead she was sitting under the Apple Tree Man's tree and he stepped out of the trunk of his tree just like she remembered him doing five years ago. He looked the same, too, a raggedy man, gnarled and twisty, like the boughs of his tree.

"You," she only said and looked away.

"That's a fine welcome for an old friend."

"You're not my friend. Friends aren't magical men who live in a tree and then make you feel like you're crazy because they never show up in your life again."

"And yet I helped you when you were a kitten."

"In the fever dream when I *thought* I was a kitten."

He came around and sat on his haunches in front of her, all long gangly limbs and tattered clothes and bird's nest hair. His face was wrinkled like the dried fruit from his tree.

He sighed. "It was better for you to only remember it as a dream."

"So it wasn't a dream?" she asked, unable to keep the eagerness from her voice. "You're real? You and the Father of Cats and the fairies in the field?"

"Someplace we're real."

She looked at him for a long moment, then nodded, disappointment taking the place of her momentary happiness.

"This is just a dream, too, isn't it?" she said.

"This is. What happened before wasn't."

She poked at the dirt with her finger, looking away from him again.

"Why would it be better for me to remember it as a dream?" she asked.

"Our worlds aren't meant to mix—not anymore. They've grown too far apart. When you spend too much time in ours, you become like your painter foundling, forever restless and unhappy in the world where you belong. Instead of living your life, you lose yourself in dreams and fancies."

"Maybe for some, dreams and fancies are better than what they have here."

"Maybe," he said, but she knew he didn't agree. "Is that true for you?"

"No," she had to admit. "But I still don't understand why I was allowed that one night and then no more."

She looked at him. His dark eyes were warm and kind, but there was a mystery in them, too. Something secret and daunting that she wasn't sure she could ever understand. That perhaps she shouldn't want to understand.

"What you do is important," he said after a long moment, which wasn't much of an answer at all.

She laughed. "What *I* do? Whatever do I do that could be so important?"

"Perhaps it's not what you do now so much as what you will do if you continue with your drawing and painting."

She shook her head. "I'm not really that good."

"Do you truly believe that?"

She remembered what Frank Spain had said after looking at her drawings.

These are good. Better than good.

She remembered how the drawings had, if only for a moment, taken him away from the sadness that lay so heavy in his heart.

"But I'm only drawing the woods," she said. "I'm drawing what I see, not fairies and fancies."

The Apple Tree Man nodded. "Sometimes people need

fairies and fancies to wake them up to what they already have. But sometimes a good drawing of a real thing does it better."

"So is that why you came to me tonight?" she asked. "To tell me to keep doing something I'm going to go on doing anyway?"

He shook his head.

"Then why did you come?"

"To ask you not to look for that cave," he said. "To not go in. If you do, you'll carry the yearning of what you find inside yourself forever."

What the Apple Tree Man had told her all seemed to make perfect sense in last night's dream. But when she woke to find Frank gone, what had made sense then didn't seem to be nearly enough now. Knowing she'd once experienced a real glimpse into a storybook world, she only found herself wanting more.

"Well, it seems like a lot of trouble to go through," Aunt said when Lily came back from the barn with the news that their guest was gone. "To cadge a meal and a roof over your head for the night, I mean."

"I don't think he was lying."

Aunt shrugged.

"But he looked *just* like the picture in my book."

"There was a resemblance," Aunt said. "But really. The story he told—it's too hard to believe."

"Then how do you explain it?"

Aunt thought for a moment, then shook her head.

"Can't say that I can," she admitted.

"I think he's gone to look for the cave. He wants to go back."

"And I suppose you want to go looking for him."

Lily nodded.

"Are you sweet on him?" Aunt asked.

"I don't think I am."

"Can't say's I'd blame you. He was a good looking man."

"I'm just worried about him," Lily said. "He's all lost and alone and out of his own time."

"And say you find him. Say you find the cave. What then?"

The Apple Tree Man's warning and Aunt's obvious concern struggled against her own desire to find the cave, to see the magical land that lay beyond it.

"I'd have the chance to say good-bye," she said.

There. She hadn't exactly lied. She hadn't said everything she could have, but she hadn't lied.

Aunt studied her for a long moment.

"You just be careful," she said. "See to the cow and chickens, but the garden can wait till you get back."

Lily grinned. She gave Aunt a quick kiss, then packed herself a lunch. She was almost out the door when she turned back and took Milo Johnson's painting box out from under her bed.

"Going to try those paints?" Aunt asked.

"I think so."

And she did, but it wasn't nearly the success she'd hoped it would be.

The morning started fine, but then walking in these woods of hers was a sure cure for any ailment, especially when it was in your heart or head. The dogs hadn't come to join her today, but that was all right. She could be just as happy on her own here.

She made her way down to that part of the wood where she'd first found the box, and then later Frank, but he was nowhere about. Either he'd found his way back into fairyland, or he was just ignoring her voice. Finally she gave up and spent a while looking for this cave of his, but there were too many in this part of the forest and none of them looked— no, none of them *felt* right.

After lunch, she sat down and opened the painting box.

The drawing she did on the back of one of Johnson's three paintings turned out well, though it was odd using her pencil on a wood panel. But she'd gotten the image she wanted: the sweeping boughs of an old beech tree, smooth-barked and tall, the thick crush of underbrush around it, the forest behind. It was the colors that proved to be a problem. The paints wouldn't do what she wanted. It was hard enough to get each tube open, they were stuck so tight, but once she had a squirt of the various colors on the palette it all went downhill from there.

The colors were wonderfully bright—pure pigments that had their own inner glow. At least they did until she started messing with them and then everything turned to mud. When she tried to mix them she got either outlandish hues or colors so dull they all might as well have been the same. The harder she tried, the worse it got.

Sighing, she finally wiped off the palette and the panel she'd been working on, then cleaned the brushes, dipping them in the little jar of turpentine, working the paint out of the hairs with a rag. She studied Johnson's paintings as she worked, trying to figure out how he'd gotten the colors he had. This was his box, after all. These were the same colors he'd used to paint these three amazing paintings. Everything she needed was just lying there in the box, waiting to be used. So why was she so hopeless?

It was because painting was no different than looking for fairies, she supposed. No different than trying to find that cave entrance into some magic elsewhere. Some people just weren't any good at that sort of thing.

They were both magic, after all. Art as well as fairies. Magic. What else could you call how Johnson was able to bring the forest to life with no more than a few colors on a flat surface?

She could practice, of course. And she would. She hadn't been any good when she'd first started drawing either. But she wasn't sure that she'd ever feel as . . . inspired as Johnson must have felt.

She studied the inside lid of the box. Even this abstract pattern where he'd probably only been testing his color mixes had so much vibrancy and passion. She leaned closer for a better look and found herself thinking about her Newford Naturalists book, about something Milo Johnson was supposed to have said. "It's not just a matter of painting *en plein air* as the Impressionists taught us," the author quoted Johnson. "It's just as important to simply *be* in the wilds. Many times the only painting box I take is in my head. You don't have to be an artist to bring something back from your wilderness experiences. My best paintings don't hang in galleries. They hang somewhere in between my ears—an endless private showing that I can only attempt to share with others through a more physical medium."

That must be why he'd abandoned this painting box she'd found. He'd gone into fairyland only bringing the one in his head. She didn't know if she could ever learn to do that.

She sighed and was about to get up and go when she thought she heard something—an almost-music. It was like listening to ravens in the woods when their rough, deep-throated croaks and cries all but seemed like human language. It wasn't, of course, but still, you felt *so* close to understanding it.

She lifted her head to look around. It wasn't ravens she heard. It wasn't anything she knew, but it still seemed familiar. Faint, but insistent. Almost like wind chimes or distant bells, but not quite. Almost like birdsong, trills and warbling melodies, but not quite. Almost like an old fiddle tune, played on a pipe or a flute, the rhythm a little ragged, or simply a little out of time like the curious jumps and extra beats in a Kickaha tune. But not quite.

Closing the painting box, she stood. She slung her satchel from her shoulder, picked up the box, and turned in a slow circle. The sound was stronger to the west, away from the creek and deeper into the forest. A ravine cut off to the left and she followed it, pushing her way through the thick shrub layer of rhododendrons and mountain laurel. Hemlocks and tulip trees rose up the slopes on either side with a thick understory of redbud, magnolia, and dogwood.

The almost-music continued to pull her along—distant, near, distant, near, like a radio signal that couldn't quite hang on to a station. It was only when she broke through into a small clearing, a wall of granite rising above her, that she saw the mouth of the cave.

She knew immediately that this had to be the cave Frank had been looking for, the one into which he and Milo Johnson had stepped and so disappeared from the world for twenty years. The almost-music was clearer than ever here, but it was the bas-relief worked into the stone above the entrance that made her sure. Here was Frank's Lady, a rough carving of a woman's face. Her hair was thick with leaves and more leaves came spilling out of her mouth, bearding her chin.

Aunt's general warnings, as well as the Apple Tree Man's more specific ones, returned to her as she moved closer. She lifted a hand to trace the contours of the carving. As soon as she touched it, the almost-music stopped.

She dropped her hand, starting back as though she'd put a finger on a hot stove. She looked around herself with quick, nervous glances. Now that the almost-music was gone, she found herself standing in an eerie pocket of silence. The sounds of the forest were muted, as the music had been earlier. She could still hear the insects and birdsong, but they seemed to come from far away.

She turned back to the cave, uneasy now. In the back of her mind she could hear the Apple Tree Man's voice.

Don't go in.

I won't. Not all the way.

But now that she was here, how could she not at least have a look?

She went as far as the entrance, ducking her head because

the top of the hole was only as high as her shoulder. It was dark inside, too dark to see in the beginning. But slowly her eyes adjusted to the dimmer lighting.

The first thing she really saw were the paintings.

They were like her own initial attempts at drawing—crude, stick figures and shapes that she'd drawn on scraps of paper and the walls of the barn with the charred ends of sticks. Except, where hers had been simple because she could do no better, these, she realized as she studied them more closely, were more like stylized abbreviations. Where her drawings had been tentative, these held power. The paint or chalk had been applied with bold, knowing strokes. Nothing wasted. Complex images distilled to their primal essences.

An antlered man. A turtle. A bear with a sun on its chest, radiating squiggles of light. A leaping stag. A bird of some sort with enormous wings. A woman, cloaked in leaves. Trees of every shape and size. Lightning bolts. A toad. A spiral with the face of the woman on the entrance outside in its center. A fox with an enormous striped tail. A hare with drooping ears and small deer horns.

And more. So many more. Some easily recognizable, others only geometric shapes that seemed to hold whole books of stories in their few lines.

Her gaze traveled over the walls, studying the paintings with growing wonder and admiration. The cave was one of the larger ones she'd found—easily three or four times the size of Aunt's cabin. There were paintings everywhere, many too hard to make out because they were lost in deeper shadows. She wished she had a corn shuck or lantern to throw more light than what came from the opening behind her. She longed to move closer, but still didn't dare abandon the safety of the entranceway.

She might have left it like that, drunk her fill of the paintings and then gone home, if her gaze hadn't fallen upon a figure sitting hunched in a corner of the cave, holding what looked like a small bark whistle. She'd made the same kind herself from the straight smooth branches of a chestnut or a sourwood tree.

But the whistle was quiet now. Frank sat so still, enveloped in the shadows, that she might never have noticed him except as she had, by chance.

"Frank . . . ?" she said.

He lifted his head to look at her.

"It's gone," he said. "I can't call it back."

"The other world?"

He nodded.

"That was you making that . . . music?"

"It was me doing something," he said. "I don't know that I'd go so far as to call it music."

Lily hesitated a long moment, then finally stepped through the entrance, into the cave itself. She flinched as she crossed the threshhold, but nothing happened. There were no flaring lights or sudden sounds. No door opened into another world, sucking her in.

She set the painting box down and sat on her ankles in front of Frank.

"I didn't know you were a musician," she said.

"I'm not."

He held up his reed whistle—obviously something he'd made himself.

"But I used to play as a boy," he said. "And there was always music there, on the other side. I thought I could wake something. Call me to it, or it to me."

Lily raised her eyes to the paintings on the wall.

"How did you cross over the first time?" she asked.

He shook his head. "I don't know. That was Milo's doing. I was only tagging along."

"Did he . . . did he make a painting?"

Frank's gaze settled on hers.

"What do you mean?" he asked.

She pointed to the walls. "Look around you. This is *the* cave, isn't it?"

He nodded.

"What do you think these paintings are for?" she asked. When he still didn't seem to get it, she added, "Perhaps it's the paintings that open a door between the worlds. Maybe this Lady of yours likes pictures more than She does music."

Frank scrambled to his feet and studied the walls as though he was seeing the paintings for the first time. Lily was slower to rise.

"If I had paint, I could try it," he said.

"There's the painting box I found," Lily told him. "It's still full of paints."

He grinned. Grabbing her arms, he gave her a kiss, right on her lips, full of passion and fire, then bent down to open the box.

"I remember this box," he said as he rummaged through the paint tubes. "We were out painting, scouting a good location—though for Milo, any location was a good one. Anyway, there we were, out in these woods, when suddenly Milo stuffs this box of his into a tangle of tree roots and starts walking. I called after him, but he never said a word, never even turned around to see if I was coming.

"So I followed, hurrying along behind him until we finally came to this cave. And then . . . then . . ."

He looked up at Lily. "I'm not sure what happened. One moment we were walking into the cave and the next we had crossed over into that other place."

"So Milo didn't paint on the wall."

"I just don't remember. But he might not have had to. Milo could create whole paintings in his head without ever putting brush to canvas. And he could describe that painting to you, stroke for stroke—even years later."

"I read about that in the book."

"Hmm."

Frank had returned his attention to the paints.

"It'll have to be a specific image," he said, talking as much to himself as to Lily. "Something simple that still manages to encompass everything a person is or feels."

"An icon," Lily said, remembering the word from another of her books.

He nodded in agreement as he continued to sort through the tubes of paint, finally choosing a color: a burnt umber, rich and dark.

"And then?" Lily asked, remembering what the Apple Tree Man had told her in her dream. "Just saying you find the right image. You paint it on the wall and some kind of door opens up. Then what do you do?"

He looked up at her, puzzled.

"I'll step through it," he said. "I'll go back to the other side."

"But why?" Lily asked. "Why's over there so much better than the way the world is here?"

"I . . ."

"When you cross over to there," Lily said, echoing the Apple Tree man's words to her, "you give up all the things you could be here."

"We do that every time we make any change in our lives," Frank said. "It's like moving from one town to another, though this is a little more drastic, I suppose." He considered it for a moment, then added, "It's not so much *better* over there as different. I've never fit in here the way I do over there. And now I don't have anything left for me here except for this burn inside—a yearning for the Lady and that land of Hers that lies somewhere on the other side of these fields we know."

"I've had that feeling," Lily said, thinking of her endless search for fairies as a child.

"You can't begin to imagine what it's like over there," Frank went on. "Everything glows with its own inner light."

He paused and regarded her for a long moment.

"You could come," he said finally. "You could come with me and see for yourself. Then you'd understand."

Lily shook her head. "No, I couldn't. I couldn't walk out on Aunt, not like this, without a word. Not after she took me in when no one else would. She wasn't even real family, though she's family now." She waited a beat, remembering the strength of his arms, the hard kiss he'd given her, then added. "You could stay."

Now it was his turn to shake his head.

"I can't."

Lily nodded. She understood. It wasn't like she didn't have the desire to go herself.

She watched him unscrew the paint tube and squeeze a long worm of dark brown pigment into his palm. He turned to a clear spot on the wall, dipped a finger into the paint and raised his hand. But then he hesitated.

"You can do it," Lily told him.

Maybe she couldn't go. Maybe she wanted him to stay. But she knew enough not to try to hold him back if he had to go. It was no different than making friends with a wild creature. You could catch them and tie them up and make them stay with you, but their heart would never be yours. Their wild heart, the thing you loved about them . . . it would wither and die. So why would you want to do such a thing?

"I can," Frank agreed, his voice soft. He gave her a smile. "That's part of the magic, isn't it? You have to believe that it will work."

Lily had no idea if that was true or not, but she gave him an encouraging nod all the same.

He hummed something under his breath as he lifted his hand again. Lily recognized it as the almost-music she'd heard before, but now she could make out the tune. She didn't know its name, but the pick-up band at the grange dances played it from time to time. She thought it might have the word "fairy" in it.

Frank's finger moved decisively, smearing paint on the rock. It took Lily a moment to see that he was painting a stylized oak leaf. He finished the last line and took his finger away, stepped back.

Neither knew what to expect, if anything. As the moments dragged by, Frank stopped humming. He cleaned his hands against the legs of his trousers, smearing paint onto the cloth. His shoulders began to slump and he turned to her.

"Look," Lily said before he could speak.

She pointed to the wall. The center of the oak leaf he'd painted had started to glow with a warm, green-gold light. They watched the light spread across the wall of the cave, moving out from the central point like ripples from a stone tossed into a still pool of water. Other colors appeared, blues and reds and deeper greens. The colors shimmered, like they were painted on cloth touched by some unseen wind, and then the wall was gone and they were looking through an opening in the rock. Through a door into another world.

There was a forest over there, not much different than the one they'd left behind except that, as Frank had said, every tree, every leaf, every branch and blade of grass, pulsed with its own inner light. It was so bright it almost hurt the eyes, and not simply because they'd been standing in this dim cave for so long.

Everything had a light and a song and it was almost too much to bear. But at the same time, Lily felt the draw of that world like a tightening in her heart. It wasn't so much a wanting, as a need.

"Come with me," Frank said again.

She had never wanted to do something more in her life. It was not just going to that magical place, it was the idea of being there with this man with his wonderfully creative mind and talent. This man who'd given her her first real kiss.

But slowly she shook her head.

"Have you ever stood on a mountaintop," she asked, "and watched the sun set in a bed of feathery clouds? Have you ever watched the monarchs settled on a field of milkweed or listened to the spring chorus after the long winter's done?"

Frank nodded.

"This world has magic, too," Lily said.

"But not enough for me," Frank said. "Not after having been over there."

"I know."

She stepped up to him and gave him a kiss. He held her for a moment, returning the kiss, then they stepped back from each other.

"Go," Lily said, giving him a little push. "Go before I change my mind."

She saw he understood that, for her, going would be as much a mistake as staying would be for him. He nodded and turned, walked out into that other world.

Lily stood watching him go. She watched him step in among the trees. She heard him call out and heard another man's voice reply. She watched as the doorway became a swirl of colors once more. Just before the light faded, it seemed to take the shape of a woman's face—the same woman whose features had been carved into the stone outside the cave, leaves in her hair, leaves spilling from her mouth. Then it was all gone. The cave was dim once more and she was alone.

Lily knelt down by Milo Johnson's paint box and closed the lid, fastened the snaps. Holding it by its handle, she stood up and walked slowly out of the cave.

* * *

"Are you there?" she asked later, standing by the Apple Tree Man's tree. "Can you hear me?"

She took a biscuit from her pocket—the one she hadn't left earlier in the day because she'd still been angry for his appearing in her dream last night when he'd been absent from her life for five years. When he'd let her think that her night of magic had been nothing more than a fever dream brought on by a snake bite.

She put the biscuit down among his roots.

"I just wanted you to know that you were probably right," she said. "About my going over to that other place, I mean. Not about how I can't have magic here."

She sat down on the grass and laid the paint box down beside her, her satchel on top of it. Plucking a leaf from the ground, she began to shred it.

"I know, I know," she said. "There's plenty of everyday magic all around me. And I do appreciate it. But I don't know what's so wrong about having a magical friend as well."

There was no reply. No gnarled Apple Tree Man stepping out of his tree. No voice as she'd heard in her dream last night. She hadn't really been expecting anything.

"I'm going to ask Aunt if I can have an acre or so for my own garden," she said. "I'll try growing cane there and sell the molasses at the harvest fair. Maybe put in some berries and make preserves and pies, too. I'll need some real money to buy more paints."

She smiled and looked up into the tree's boughs.

"So you see, I can take advice. Maybe you should give it a try."

She stood up and dusted off her knees, picked up the painting box and her satchel.

"I'll bring you another biscuit tomorrow morning," she said.

Then she started down the hill to Aunt's cabin.

"Thank you," a soft, familiar voice said.

She turned. There was no one there, but the biscuit was gone.

She grinned. "Well, that's a start," she said and continued on home.

CHARLES DE LINT is a writer, folklorist, and Celtic musician who makes his home in Ottawa, Canada, with his wife MaryAnn Harris, an artist and fellow musician. He is the author of numerous mythic novels, many of them set in the imaginary city of Newford. His Newford short stories have been collected in *Dreams Underfoot*, *The Ivory and the Horn*, and *Moonlight and Vines*—the latter of which won the World Fantasy Award in 2000. Other recent books include *The Onion Girl*, *Forests of the Heart*, *Seven Wild Sisters* (with artist Charles Vess), and *Triskell Tales* (with artist MaryAnn Harris), as well as new editions of his science fiction novel *Svaha* and his Newford novel *Someplace to Be Flying*. For more information about his work, visit his Web site at www.charlesdelint.com.

Author's Note:

A couple of my best friends are Karen Shaffer and her husband, Charles Vess. I've known Charles for years—and for years we've been trying to do a larger project together, something more than simply a chapbook with illustrations here, a comic book there.

We finally got the opportunity through Sharyn November at Viking (a children's picture book) and Bill Schafer at Subterranean Press (a short illustrated novel). The two projects are related through the character of Lily; this story takes place in between the other two books. The setting, while ostensibly the hills outside of Newford, (the imaginary city where many of my stories take place) is, in reality, the wooded hills across from where Karen and Charles live in Virginia. The cabin is there, an hour's walk in from the road. The creek is there. The sprucey-pine and beeches.

I don't doubt that the Apple Tree Man is, too.

The title of this story comes from a line in an Incredible String Band song written by Mike Heron.

Among the Leaves So Green

TANITH LEE

"FOR I SHALL wed a fine young knight
   A handsome knight, quoth she—"
sings Bergette as she throws open the wooden shutters.

Ghilane hears her, and knows this means trouble. Oh yes, despite the golden sun now falling in across the floor and bed like spilled honey.

Bergette is Ghilane's sister. Her half-sister. Their mother, the village's easy-woman, went with a woodcutter, and one year later there was Bergette. Then, two years after that, there was the *other* woodcutter. And then there was Ghilane. To the village, both girls are eyesores, the produce of sin. To Bergette, though, Ghilane is worse than that. Bergette was the first. Ghilane's an invader. From the beginning, Bergette has taken her revenge on Ghilane for being born, in one way or another. It used to be slaps and pinches and lies, and the stealing of food. Now it's often more rough—and more gloating—more inventive.

"Get up," says Bergette, turning and kicking at Ghilane. But Ghilane is already away and out of the bed.

They're lucky to have this straw bed up here. Their mother, because of her work, sleeps separately. (Last night the innkeeper was with her. They heard him scurrying off an hour ago, at cock-cry.) Unlike most of the village, neither girl is encouraged to get up too early. It might embarrass some retreating customer.

"And he will dress me in gowns of silk!" sings Bergette. She's sixteen, and black of hair, pale of skin. Ghilane, at fourteen, is the odd one, with her fair brown hair and light brown skin—where did she get those? Each has green eyes though, Ghilane's grape-green, Bergette's like the green of a snake's venom. Both would normally be married off by now, but that won't ever happen, seeing whose daughters they are.

Mother calls them in her demanding, unliking voice.

Bergette laughs, suddenly pushes Ghilane so she staggers, and goes down the ladder to the cottage's lower floor.

Before she follows, Ghilane glances out of the window at the village, an untidy smelly muddle of huts and lopsided houses with a grim stone church. Then she looks up the slope to the forest beyond. The forest which is so unsafe and uneasy, and for which the village is named. "Keep her away from me today," whispers Ghilane to the forest. *"Please."*

They are sent on an errand the moment they've cooked and eaten the lumpy burnt pine-nut porridge.

"Go up to the Widow and get some eggs."

"No," says Bergette.

So Mother clouts Bergette across the face. And Bergette bursts into tears as hysterical and trouble-promising as her singing. What Mother does to her, she will later take out on Ghilane. There really is no escape now.

And why say no? They'll have to do it anyway, both of them.

The reason for the errand is threefold. 1) It gets them out of the house so that their mother can "entertain," or just frowst about, more easily; 2) It gets them into the forest, which is dangerous—full of wolves, wild tusked pig, snakes, sudden traveler-gobbling bogs, and demons—and so is generally avoided by most of the village; besides, the Widow's shack is off the beaten track, so has yet more potential for getting them lost or in the way of a hungry large animal. The idea is, of course, though their mother would *never* admit this, to be permanently rid of them. 3) (Last and perhaps least), it must be the baker who's coming to visit today, because he likes eggs.

As they walk through the village someone throws a stone. It hits Bergette, who turns, ready to kill, but no one is to be seen. Anyway, anyone could have thrown the stone. They all hate the easy-woman and her children—even the men hate them, this side of their house door.

The two girls both know too that a time will come when they won't be able themselves to put off their Turn, as Mother calls it. That is, when they take over Mother's job. Both Bergette and Ghilane choose to ignore this.

On the slope leading up through the coppice woods, into the main forest, Bergette sings again how the knight will court the lady.

Ghilane wants her to be silent so she can listen to the trees and everything that moves among them. But she has the sense not to ask Bergette to shut up.

The coppices are copper-red with buds and green with sap. But the forest, which is full of evergreens, is black and hardly ever loses its shadow. Pines and hemlocks, cedars and firs tower up, and holly trees still dappled with last winter's blood-showers of berries.

The sky is closed away.

Sun gone.

Bergette stops her singing.

"Now, you little pig—"

Ghilane is already running before the clawed hand sweeps her face. (Bergette, if she badly scratches her sister, can now blame it on the holly trees.)

But Ghilane runs fleet as a deer, ducking under the boughs, not stumbling on the great roots hooped up from the forest floor, where mushrooms sometimes grow or patches of briar and bladed grass. Bergette pounds after, not quite so clever at avoiding things.

It gets darker, and darker. The forest is a night-in-day, which now falls.

Oh, they're off the beaten track, well off now. Even the skinny path to the hen-keeping Widow's has been missed.

Ghilane thinks suddenly, madly, as she runs, *Why have I come this way?—I shouldn't have done that*. But where else could she go? It's instinct. She had seen, more than all the other times, near-murder stark in Bergette's white face, her viper-poison eyes, so, like the hunted stag, the ermine, the boar, Ghilane runs to her only hope of safety . . .

Which isn't safety. How can it be?

Not till she reaches the Tree does Ghilane stop, gasping, holding the stitch in her side.

Then, run out, she drops on her knees, bows her head, and waits for Bergette to come and beat her up among the leafy shadows.

The Tree is half an oak. Or rather it's two trees, a hornbeam *and* an oak, which have rooted so close they've grown together and become the Tree.

In all the forest-night of dark, these trees are green already with an early summer not much present in the rest of the woods. The leaves aren't full-blown, but they're still massed all over the two trees, frills of the oak, and the hand shapes of the hornbeam, with its strange yellow sprays like catkins hanging down. The Tree has been able, two in one, to pierce the roof of the forest. And down from there pours a fountain of green-gold sunlight, splashing and sparkling to the ground, where it breaks like scattered flames.

Slowly, despite everything, Ghilane looks up and watches the Tree. She takes in the coiling grapevine which will get purple grapes in fall-of-leaf, and the old honeycomb caught up between two boughs. She sees here, there, where a twist of ribbon has been tied on by others she's never met here. And on an apron-lap that opens from the trunks just at the right spot, offerings have been placed—some over-wintered apples, a crust of a fresh loaf.

All the birds that fly and bell about the forest visit the Tree, but they seldom disturb the offerings. Now they've gone quiet. It's as ominous as when Bergette stopped her song.

And then Bergette is *there*. With one hand she grabs Ghilane's hair and wrenches back her head, and Ghilane screws tight her eyes to save them—

And then, Bergette lets her go.

"What's this weird place?" asks Bergette.

Startled at the interruption to violence, "I don't know," lies Ghilane, who *knows*.

"It's a bad area. Trust you to drag us into it." And she cuffs Ghilane, but forgetfully now.

Bergette's eyes have gone to the altar in the Tree.

"Don't! Don't!" cries Ghilane, as Bergette fists up two of the apples that have been offered to the god of the forest, and begins to bite into them, first one, then the other.

But Bergette just grins, and goes on biting.

They don't often get an apple, or anything nice. Useless Mother has no garden plot, and those that do don't bother to bring anything like that when they "visit."

Ghilane stands up and waits for the god who is sometimes in the Tree to demonstrate his anger.

Why doesn't he do it?

Would Ghilane be glad if he struck Bergette? Oh yes, yes. But even so, Ghilane goes up to the Tree. She leans close as she's done before, and whispers, "Don't be angry. She's ignorant, that's all."

"Am I now." Bergette pulls Ghilane away from the Tree and punches her just above the waist.

While Ghilane lies on the ground, trying to breathe again, Bergette slings the part-eaten apples hard against the Tree's trunk, so they squash.

"Filthy pagan thing!" screams Bergette at the Tree. "What's to be frightened of? What's to give things to? Nothing there."

Then she wheels round and runs off—terrified—into the forest.

Ghilane can't follow even if she'd like to. She isn't lost, anyway, she knows where she is. It's Bergette who is lost.

Ghilane finally gets up and goes back to the Tree.

She stands looking up and up into the cascade of green and gold. Then she touches the bark. "I'm sorry about that. Don't be angry." Then she takes the coin which Mother gave her for the eggs, and puts it down on the altar. "I know money doesn't mean anything to you, but it's all I've got to give." Why—why—does she do this? Ghilane herself isn't certain. Somehow she had a hideous picture of Bergette thrown into a prison for what she's done, and screaming—and despite everything, Ghilane can't stand it. That's just how she is—squeamish and over-imaginative—or compassionate.

The Tree rustles, a long sigh, as if it knows now Mother will also beat Ghilane for having "dropped" the coin and failed to bring home the eggs. But of *course* the Tree knows. The god knows. The god and the Tree know everything.

The Christian priest in the church (who drinks too much beer) lectures them all on how they mustn't believe in *pagan* things, demons and spirits in the forest. The trees are only wood, the wolves are only wolves, and nothing else exists. However, he does tell them to believe in the Devil, who uses their superstition to entrap them. The Devil *is* in the forest, suggests the beery priest, and in their own wicked hearts.

Ghilane, on the other hand, who doesn't believe the Devil is particularly in the forest, believes that other things are.

Having nothing better to do now, she walks between the trees in the direction that will lead her over to the Widow's shack. Perhaps Bergette too may refind the path. And the Widow might let them have an egg for the baker anyway, without payment . . . she sometimes has in the past, when Bergette, who sets some store by money, has pocketed the coin.

The Widow is supposed, by some, to have been the wife of a (now dead) Crusader, who retired to the villages hereabouts for some unknown reason. A most unlikely story, but there *is* something peculiar about her.

She's old and bent, with gnarled brown hands, but she veils her face and hair over as they say women do in the heathen East. Sometimes you catch the flash of her narrow old eyes behind the veil, but not enough to see their color. The rest of her features are invisible.

Her shack is tumbledown and not very clean, and cats live there in quantities, together with a vast, ivy-green toad. They cause each other no harm, strangely, the cats and the toad. Even the hens peck in and out, and sometimes birds from the forest, and the cats just yawn and go elsewhere to tear things apart.

Today, the Widow's out at the front, weeding her garden patch, where she cultivates wild cabbage, celeriac, and a walnut tree. Hens potter round her feet. There's no sign of Bergette.

The Widow straightens from her plants and stands staring at Ghilane through the veil.

"Good morning," says Ghilane. "Do you have any spare eggs?"

"Who bruised your ribs?" snaps out the old woman. How can she know? Perhaps the birds have told her.

"My sister."

"What else?" snaps the Widow.

"She stole the offering to the Tree." (And why say *that?*)

To Ghilane's surprise, the Widow laughs. She says, "No eggs. They haven't laid these past three days."

Ghilane turns to go, knowing now she'll be really thumped and belted, because there'll she be minus coin *and* eggs. The Widow says, "Come in the house."

Also oddly, Ghilane doesn't mind the Widow's shack. It smells of hens and cats (and toad?) but also of herbs and various medicines the Widow makes from nettles and similar things. Light streams in at a narrow window. They sit down on two stools.

"Have *you* made offerings at the Tree?" asks the Widow.

Ghilane hasn't lied to the Widow. Somehow she knows it wouldn't be much use. And the Widow anyway seems to know everything—all this is just a formality.

"Yes."

"What did you ask for in return?"

"Silly things. Not to be hit."

"Didn't work, did it," says the Widow.

"No."

"But you go on thinking there's something in the Tree."

"Yes . . . I just think . . . he's too busy to take any notice of me. But I know—I know he's there."

"So it's a man?" slyly asks the Widow.

"Yes," says Ghilane. "But not a *man*." She goes red and looks away. "I saw him, once."

The Widow seems amused again. "What did you see?"

Ghilane blushes until she thinks her head will burst, but she says, anyway, "It was one early morning. Bergette scalded me, and I ran up there to the Tree, but when I got close, I waited, because there was a wild boar there. Only it wasn't goring at the trunk, just standing still. And then it walked off. And when it did—up in the leaves—sort of *under* the leaves—"

"Yes?"

"Him."

"What was he like, then?"

"Like—" Ghilane can't say, since she has so far nothing to compare him to. If she had, she'd say, "Like a young prince." Or maybe not. Finally she says, "He was handsome, and there were leaves and grapes in his hair, and his eyes were green, and then they were black. And then the wind moved the branches and he was gone."

"I'll tell you," says the old woman, "what you've been doing wrong at that Tree. You haven't been asking for enough."

"*Enough?* But—"

"Listen hard. I'll say it once. Don't ask him to let you off a slap, or make your bruise stop hurting. That's no use. Because if he does it, next minute you'll have another bruise and you'll be slapped again, won't you?"

Ghilane nods, watching the hens.

"So what would you really have, girl, from the god in the green Tree? Think. Think carefully. Then speak it out."

Ghilane shakes back her hair and stands up, and raises her hands. "My life to be changed to something wonderful and new, something different—and far away from them all!"

"Be sure of it," says the Widow.

Ghilane is quite sure. She thinks, *She's a witch, I've always known . . .*

And then she sees straight through the Widow's veil, as if it isn't there.

Ghilane can't scream. She throws herself down on the floor, and the chickens cluck annoyedly. *They* don't worry about the presence of a god who's been around forever, and especially here since the Widow peacefully died at sunset, yesterday.

Bergette had blundered along until she tripped over a great root, and when she sat up, found she'd bruised her ribs and nearly knocked the breath out of herself.

She doesn't know where she is.

She begins to cry, blaming Ghilane for getting her deliberately lost. It's a trick Ghilane's thought up with Mother, who's always hated Bergette and secretly liked Ghilane because Ghilane is almost all one color, honey brown, like a young tree. Bergette hates herself, too, and now she wants to kill someone or something, preferably Ghilane.

Then she looks up properly and the dark forest is all lit with the vividity of noon, the brilliant sunlight crashing down through all the black trees on top of Bergette.

Bergette considers. If the sun's up *there*, when half an hour ago it was over *there*, then that is the east, and she knows that the Widow's shack lies over that way.

In a minute or so, Bergette is limping on—she's hurt her foot too, in the fall. Birds sing, and she hates them and wants to wring their necks. She sees a spotted snake coiled high up, and curses it, and her snake-venom eyes become more venomous, so nasty in fact she can hardly see with them, and so it comes as no surprise when she at last looks round and finds she's now got into a clump of the darkest thickets, ringed by budding ash trees, which in turn seem ringed as if by a wall of thick, sable firs.

Bergette stops again. It was only noon just then, but suddenly she's cold. She shivers, and the firs do the same. As if something unseen is walking across the tops of them.

So Bergette says a prayer. But the prayer won't really come because it's all about being forgiven for her sins, and Bergette will be damned if she'll admit to having any of those right now.

It's all Ghilane's fault, this. Just let her wait—

Bravely, Bergette sings her song, a line or two,

"For I shall wed a bold young knight,
Come from the East, so fine and grave,
And he will dress me in ring of gold,
And I shall be his own true love.

Then he will take me for his bride
And I shall live well as a queen—

(Bergette wants to stop singing now. Finds she can't.)

And like the stars his armor all
Shines in among the leaves so green."

The forest is truly now black as night. Pitch black. A storm must have come up, covering the sky with cloud.

Bergette senses the approach of lightning, thunder—which never happen—but still she crouches down and starts to whimper. Until finally—

"I never meant to take your apples!" cries Bergette.

Too late?

There's someone coming out now from between the fir trees and the ash. Dark as the wood, as the sky. Black of eyes and hair and garments and—oh.

"Oh, it's you," croaks Bergette, as the old Widow-witch comes cranking up to her.

"And is it me?" says the Widow.

And then Bergette knows, with a gush of boiling fear that, no, it *isn't*.

"I never—I never never—"

"But you did."

"I was a fool."

"Yes, you were."

"Don't—don't—only say how I can put it right?"

"Is that all you'd ask for? Ask again."

In her panic, Bergette shrieks, "Set me free! How can I be good when everything's so *bad*? Let my life be changed to something wonderful and new, something different—and far away from them all!" And knows she means this, though why she's said it would almost puzzle her, if she weren't so frightened.

"Where are those selfish beasts of girls?" shouts Mother, stamping about in her horrible dirty stinking house, that can't ever be called a home, even by the mice who have un-rented rooms in the walls. (Let it be said here, not all easy-women are as dreadful as Mother. No, she has developed a special talent for lousiness.)

However, the situation helps. The baker hasn't turned up.

Mother thinks, even so, *she* could have fancied an egg herself, couldn't she?

Those ungrateful parasites—those sluts—put them to work, that's what they needed. Why should she keep them in luxury—their own *bed* and all—she'd never wanted them.

It was the forest's fault. Those two handsome woodcutters. An evil place, the forest, everyone knew it, full of temptations and imps—

Of course, the woodcutters were both village men—another village, she didn't know where it was, they'd neither of them said. Yet, in the wood they hadn't either of them seemed like village oafs. They'd seemed witty and cultured. Especially the first one, Bergette's father. Well, Mother thought disgustedly, she'd almost been in love—twice! And so been careless. Twice.

Bang went the wind, blown down from the woods with its friend, the black sky. It would rain soon, and water would come through the roof.

Oh, she'd tan their hides, both of them, with the leather belt. When they got home.

And looking forward with slight anticipation to this treat—what Life does to Mother she's always ready, later, to take out on Ghilane and Bergette—Mother forgets something. Which is that it's now just possible her *other* (secret) wish—that of losing both daughters—may at last have come true.

When Ghilane wakes up, real night has come, prowling through the forest like a lynx, and she jumps to her feet in fear.

How could she have *slept* after what had happened? Oh, perhaps he made her sleep, the god. Lulled her asleep the way a supernatural being could. Or she'd simply fainted, from the shock. The last thing she remembers is how she stood there and said exactly what she wanted, although she can't actually remember *what* she said. Nor, come to that, what the god looked like—

Anyway. It was a dream. That must be it. She ran up here and found the poor old Widow had died (which is curious too, because Ghilane can't really remember this either, only that she knows about it). And then somehow the god was there, so she must have sat down exhausted among the chickens and dreamed all that about the god.

A shame. It had been a good dream. Alarming but also magical and—well, lovely.

Like the other dream she'd had once about seeing him in the Tree among the leaves.

Ghilane sits thinking about this, until some lights come wending along the path and stop at the door.

Then she glances up and sees ten old women, each one very much resembling the dead Widow, with their faces all veiled, and each one carrying a rush candle that burns with a bluish cats-eye gleam.

This might be upsetting, but isn't really. The Widow was indeed part of a professional Witchery, and her sisters have felt her death and come to bury her in the proper, respectful witch fashion.

They therefore do so. Ghilane, who feels sorry about the old woman—though the witches assure Ghilane the Widow is happy, and even young again, now—helps them. She holds candles, assists with spades, and also gathers in the chickens for the night.

"I'll live here now," says one old woman, who's exactly like the others. Ghilane really can't tell them apart.

Then three of them invite Ghilane to accompany them to their own house, which is apparently far across the forest. They seem to think Ghilane will have witch-power herself. "Something about you," they murmur, staring through and through her with their veiled eyes.

Ghilane knows, whatever else, she can't go home. She's not only not got coin or egg, she's "dropped" her sister as well.

She feels mysteriously drawn to the three old women. She gives in.

They walk all night through the forest.

The trees look like bears in the dark, but the three old women don't seem bothered. The stars cast down their glitterings whenever there's a gap in the branches. Frogs creak from the quags. Once a wolf crosses their path. The old women greet the wolf and the wolf seems to nod, then trots on. A trick worth knowing, if nothing else. (As, come to that, is the trick of walking all day to get to the Widow's, and then all the way back without a real rest.)

Near dawn, they reach an edge of the forest which opens on a wide valley where a river runs. There's a great house down there, a timbered manor, set in walled gardens that have *flowers*.

The three witches blow out their rush candles, (which have sorcerously lasted all this while) as the first pink tarnish of dawn begins in the east over the valley.

Then the witches draw off their veils and some threadbare mittens and their other dark clothes, and under them Ghilane's astonished to see three fine dresses trimmed with embroidery, and necklaces of gold and silver. But most astonished of all to find that, of the three old women, only one's at all *old*, with braided silver hair under a white hood. The other two are younger, one about the age of Ghilane's mother and the other only a few years older than Ghilane.

"There's our house," says the youngest witch. "Do you like it? You do? Then come live with us."

It seems that, like many Witchcries, the members range across all areas of society, from the highest to the most everyday. They don't have any sense of class, however, as they mingle in the forest of the god, the rich women with the women who must pretend to sell eggs for their bread in case they're thought too clever.

And these three seem very much to want Ghilane to be part of their household—not, they explain, as servant or skivvy—but as another daughter.

They ask Ghilane nothing except would she like this?

She hesitates, of course, thinking this is too good to be true. Perhaps it's another dream. Perhaps they're lying and they will ill-treat her.

Then the sun comes up in the east, and Ghilane sees a man riding up the hill to meet the three ladies. He's the manor's lord, got up in his best and very polite to the witches, who are his mother, his wife, and his daughter. It's now fairly obvious, too, that Ghilane is *also* his daughter. His hair and skin are brown like hers. But none of the three witches appear dismayed. And he seems pleased to see her too.

Among the Witcheries, things are different.

So Ghilane accepts her wish come true, and goes down the hill with the ladies, and the lord who isn't a woodcutter, only made out he was long ago, when he was less just than now, and Mother less ugly and harsh.

And what is Ghilane going to, then? To worse unkindness from a jealous stepmother and even more furious half-sister? Judge from this:

Five years on, when Ghilane has been made the lord's legal daughter and is gladsome, healthy, and very well-dressed, she is one day walking in the wood, having also become a full member of the Witchery by then. And she looks up and sees what she thinks is the god again, strolling through the wood. But it'll turn out this time it's only a man, though he is the son of that kingdom's king. So, being now a lady herself, there's nothing to stop Ghilane marrying him. Which she does. After all, it's what young women like Ghilane are meant to do.

Bergette, though.

Oh, Bergette.

Bergette the cruel, claws and fists and kicks and tricks. Bergette with the serpent-poison eyes. Who steals the coins, and steals too the offerings from the altar of a god, in a forest she knows—and she did—in her deepest heart, is the place of that god, or one of them. Stupidity added to viciousness, as so often happens.

Poor stupid, foul, disgusting Bergette, who ought, in the best tradition, to be punished for her endless crimes, just as Ghilane, who's really all right, has been rewarded for her kindness and clear vision.

Well, we've hurried here, you and I, haven't we, almost skipping over Ghilane's much-deserved and nice rest of her life. Sorry for that. But, you see—Bergette, awful Bergette—*she's* the special one.

Yes, didn't look like it, did it? All that underhand rottenness and that inability to see the forest glowing like a rising sun with the presence of the god—

Nevertheless . . .

When Bergette yelled what she really wanted, which was precisely the same (of course) as what Ghilane (and a great many people) really wanted, the most appalling thing in the world happened to her.

Up from the ground sprang vines and creepers and the very roots of the trees, and they caught her fast into themselves, they bound her tight and tighter than the tightest rope.

At first she screamed and fought. But it was no use at all. She couldn't move anymore, and then leaves had wound over her mouth and shut her up, too.

So then she hangs there, trapped in a spiderweb of forest. And the god's also still there, looking at her, the indescribable, beautiful god, but not like that, like a pillar of darkness having only eyes—yet eyes she can't *see*. The voice, though, that Bergette hears.

"Any are welcome," says the voice of the god, "to what lies on my altars, if they have need. The starving fox, the bird, the man, the woman. Any are welcome also to forget me and go instead to another Master, providing that lord is good. There is One. Most are staring in his face and missing him altogether. But you, Bergette, never know to do any of that. Therefore, since you are mine, I shall teach you."

That's what the god says to Bergette, and unlike her sister, she's going to remember it always.

It's the last thing she hears for a while, anyway.

Because next, the snaky creepers and other things are growing again, whirling around and around her, completely covering her, binding her over. Bergette shuts her eyes, thinking now she'll die, so she thinks she has.

And that way, she doesn't see, then, how a great tree is pushing up now out of all the other growth that wraps her, shutting her in like an upright wooden coffin of the finest oak.

Well, after all, that's quite a punishment, wouldn't you say?

In the forest, (across which Ghilane is busy becoming a lord's daughter) early summer ripens to fall. There are green beeches and red chestnuts among the pines and firs. Even the pines and firs are fringed with new green. Birds sing and then grow lazy. Hunting horns sound. Deer rush through and vanish like brown ghosts. Honey drips.

Imprisoned in her tree, Bergette isn't dead.

She's dreaming.

Oh, so many dreams.

First she sees her mother, as she once was, and here's another surprise—Mother is dancing with the witches. She was, then, one of the local Witchery! Mother was also good-looking then, with long, washed hair. Bergette in her dream watches sadly as Mother falls in love with the lord from the manor house, who's come to dance in the witch rituals, but in disguise. And then Bergette's dream takes her back three more years, and Mother is even younger, and falling in love for the first time—with this other one who is a lord, but said he was a woodcutter.

When Bergette in the dream sees this first woodcutter/lord, she sees who her father really is.

Then she realizes he's telling her the story of her beginnings.

For Bergette's father, with his dark, long and curling hair, his eyes now vine-green and now grape-black, is the god-in-green, the Lord of the Wood, the Power of the forests.

Oh, he's much older than how he looks, older even than the oldest forest. Yet, though so old, always young. Yet, too . . . ancient, ancient and young both at once.

As soon as she grasps this, in her enchanted sleep, Bergette begins to trust him.

The stories go on as the dreams go on.

Bergette loves them. She loves being asleep and dreaming them. For the first time in a long while, she's happy.

Outside her strong fortress of bark, fall-of-leaf strips the woodland. The treacherous traveler-gobbling bogs groan with mud. Winter comes and colors everything dead white, but for the blackbirds feeding on the scarlet berries.

Bergette dreams on, seeing other times, other lands and worlds. Bergette is learning such a lot. It's like food and drink to her.

Outside, deer rub their horns on the trunk of the tree. Purple flowers open round its feet, and tawny colonies of mushrooms.

Then summer's back—though it's not the summer we expect, but another summer far off in the future, where now Bergette has come to be.

She opens her eyes.

It's a summer night and the forest smells of pine balsam and wild roses.

Bergette finds she's come out of the tree, she's passed right through its trunk.

For a time, she dances with her shadow—she still casts one, or thinks she does—on the moonlit grass between the trees.

Then a fox arrives, and later two wolves out courting. And an owl sits down in the tree.

Because they're not alarmed by Bergette, she sings them the song her mother had sung over her cradle. The old witch song about a knight from the East, and a lady, and the starry armor in the green leaves. She knows now who the knight is meant to be. It's Father, that's who the knight is.

After some hours, Bergette understands that she isn't as she was. She can, after all, walk into and out of trees—she's already tested this, walked back into her own and out again a couple of times. She looks into a forest pool and sees her long, grape-dark hair, and how her eyes are no longer the green of a snake's poison but of its gliding skin among the vine.

She dances with a wild cat, now.

She chases a marten up a spruce, and plays with it along the whippy boughs—fearless, of course, because even if she falls, it won't matter now; she can't be hurt anymore.

If she thinks about it, she supposes that yes, her life is

changed, wonderful and new and different—and she's far away from them all.

But now, coming and going as she pleases in the forest, she notices the people who come there. Of these, few cut down trees. Most of the villages get their wood from the self-renewing coppices. But the villagers do gather a lot in the forest, fruits and berries, herbs and mushrooms, and reeds from the bogs. Sometimes, Bergette plays little tricks on these gatherers. Nothing terrible. She may move a basket, conceal a fallen glove, then put it back somewhere else, or tie the edge of a cloak to a bush. The people in the forest never see her, but they *sense* her, some of them anyway. Word gets round. "Those imps are mucking about again in the forest." "Stole my knife then stuck it in a clump of violets."

Sometimes too they accuse her of doing things she hasn't, but which someone *has* done . . . That is, someone of her *kind*.

Bergette knows there are others like herself among all the trees. Other brothers and sisters, the sons and daughters of Father. As yet, she only glimpses them—glimmering shadows, breezes blowing by. And for them, she thinks, so far she's the same—just a glimpse. Meetings will take time, but that's one thing she—they—have.

Meanwhile, Bergette begins to see, despite the games she plays, the people of the villages don't seem as wary of the forest as they did, despite what they may say. She becomes curious about this. One afternoon, when the heat runs over everything like slow water, Bergette wanders down to her own village, the place where she was born.

She's stunned.

It's not much like it was.

For one thing, it's ten times the size. The houses are better built too, and there are a lot of gardens. A few pigs wander up and down the streets, but they're fairly neat pigs.

In Mother's revolting house, there now lives a scholar. He has a housekeeper, and everything's immaculate (except the scholar, actually, who's an untidy old soul).

When Bergette gets up to the church (walking all unseen, but sometimes sensed, among the market crowd) she stops, amazed. Because the church has turned into a plant, or vegetable. She can see this at once.

In the summer, the old stone sweats and has a color like the Eastern mineral called jade. But more than this, the whole building has been *carved*. What carvings they are. Stone trees stride up the walls, inside and out, and in among the stone leaves are people of stone and little stone animals. And on the altar, where nothing much stood before, stands a beautiful calm Christ statue, crowned with thorns.

Bergette stays some while in the vegetable church, liking it. When the priest comes through, he's not the drunk one she remembers. He's fat and thoughtful, brown from the sun.

Bergette decides this religion too is, at its true heart, perfectly beautiful. It had only been spoilt a little by fools. The force of an ultimate God pours through the stones, as through the forest. And from this Ultimate spring all and everything, all trees, all carvings, all beasts and men. All gods.

Then Bergette sees, over by the wall, a young man is bending to work on the stone with a mallet and chisel. She knows he's the mason and the sculptor, one of many, maybe, who's carved the church into a sacred wood and shown true God on the altar. Bergette recalls what Father once said to her. She thinks that, though this aspect of God is perhaps the Other One he spoke of, Father too has a place inside the forest of stone.

She whispers in the mason's ear, and he hears her.

And under his cunning hands, the wall carving changes. It becomes a face masked in leaves and which is *speaking* leaves, smiling so they spill, the leaf-words, from its lips—the face of her father.

Then Bergette goes back into the forest, to live forever unlonely, among her brother and sister trees.

Time goes on turning its pages of seasons and history.

One day, a princess comes riding into the May-green wood, which in her language they say is *blue* with leaves, because simply to say *green* doesn't describe such lushness.

The princess and her ladies discard the horses with their grooms and walk off into the depths of the forest.

After they find a place they think suits them, they begin to play like little girls with a gold-stitched ball, throwing it back and forth.

Bergette, sitting up in a cedar, looks over and sees—her *sister*, brown Ghilane, dancing there in a silk gown and rings of gold. A princess! When did *this* happen?

She isn't jealous, you understand; she doesn't hate Ghilane anymore. Why should she? Bergette's almost insanely happy, so there's no room in her anywhere for hate. Besides, she long ago forgave herself, and so forgave everyone else.

But Bergette is, well, fascinated. So she leans down and

snatches the ball out of the Princess Ghilane's brown hands in the instant she throws it.

"It's gone into thin air!" cry the ladies, between thrill and unease. Everyone's always told them these woods are *weird,* which is why they like to go Maying here.

But the princess looks straight up into Bergette's face and seems to *see* her.

"Good morning," says the princess. "You must be the spirit of the tree. The Green Lady."

Bergette understands this; she can speak any language of the world now, just as she understands what the leaves themselves are saying. She smiles, but before she can reply, the princess offers her own name. "I am Princess Ghisella," says the princess.

Bergette remembers. Time isn't as it was, for her. She says, softly, "Not Ghilane."

"Ghilane? Let me think, that was my great-great-great-grandmother's name."

"Who's she talking to? She's gone off her head," mutter the ladies to each other, worried because, if she has, they'll almost definitely get the blame.

But the princess peers on into the tree at Bergette—whom she can apparently see because they're still dimly related.

"Can I have a wish?" asks the princess. Greedily.

Can I grant wishes?

Bergette wonders where her father is. She sometimes senses him passing in the forest, just as ordinary human things sense *her*. But she hasn't seen him for quite some time (centuries in fact). Somehow, that's never mattered. She has instead begun to meet—often by now—with her own kind. Introductions come slowly here, because, once made, they'll last for millennia. She'd like to ask their advice, her kindred, but for once, all she hears is the whispering of the leaves.

So, "What do you want?" inquires Bergette uncertainly of the human princess.

Ghisella squares her jaw—something Ghilane *never* did.

"To be a queen, and the mother of a king."

Bergette thinks (and this really is Bergette, thinking this), *What a shame*.

And she hears herself say, "You won't get that. Why don't you ask for something important?"

But exactly then she sees Ghilane's great-great-great-granddaughter shaking her head angrily, frowning, glaring.

"It's disappeared! All a trick—how dare it?—doesn't it know who I *am?!*"

The ball thuds down on the ground.

But Bergette, who vanished to the princess when the princess became totally stupid, is now leaping laughing over the tops of the trees, and by her, taking her hands, are three or four just like her, their long hair full of leaves. And the whole forest seems to be laughing. And maybe even Ghilane, wherever *she* is by then, is laughing too.

Though obviously, years after, when poor silly Ghisella *is* the queen of a very large country, and her son the king-to-be, she thinks back smugly and says, "I asked this from a wood spirit, whom I charmed with my manner and grace." And everyone nods politely, though by now she's grown graceless and frowsty, like poor old Mother long ago.

TANITH LEE was born in 1947 in London, England. She began to write at the age of nine.

After school she worked variously as a library assistant, a shop assistant, a filing clerk, and a waitress. At age twenty-five she spent one year at art college.

In 1970–71 three of Lee's children's books were published. In 1975 DAW Books published her novel *The Birthgrave*, and thereafter twenty-six of her books, enabling her to become a full-time writer.

To date she has written sixty-two novels and nine collections of novellas and short stories (she has published over two hundred short stories and novellas). Four of her radio plays have been broadcast by the BBC in the UK and she has written two episodes of the BBC cult TV series *Blake's Seven*.

Lee has twice won the World Fantasy Award for short fiction, and was awarded the August Derleth Award in 1980 for her novel *Death's Master*.

In 1992 Lee married the writer John Kaiine, her partner since 1987. They live in Southeast England with one black and white and one Siamese cat.

Her Web site address is www.tanithlee.com.

* * *

Author's Note:

The inspiration came from a long-standing interest in Dionysus who, in ancient Greece, was most decidedly one of the gods of the Wild Wood. Often misunderstood, Dionysus is far more than a wine deity. He is the Breaker of Chains, who rescues not only the flesh but the heart and spirit from too much of worldly regulations and duties. He is a god of joy and freedom. Any uncultivated, tangled, and primal woodland is very much his domain.

As for the sisters and their background, they arrived at once and took over. One of the reasons I like writing such a lot: it's always fascinating to see new places and meet new people!

SONG OF THE CAILLEACH BHEUR

JANE YOLEN

DO YOU SEE her there, her staff in hand,
Calling the deer behind her?
They come like sheep to the shepherd's pipe,
Running on their toes to find her.

Come down frae the hills you wolves, you swine,
Come down frae the highlands and hollows,
Come down frae the snow-capped mountain fasts,
The Cailleach Bheur to follow.

She is the winter, the wind, the snow,
Her breath both warm and chilling.
A single word from her icy lips,
A single kiss is killing.

I kenned her once in the winter tide,
When snow lay on the heather
I saw her dance with the lithesome goats
And the snoutish boar together.

I kenned her wrapped in a winter storm
Like a white shawl on her shoulders,
With icicle drops for earring bobs,
Her hair as grey as boulders.

> She is the winter, the wind, the snow,
> Her breath both warm and chilling.
> A single word from her icy lips,
> A single kiss is killing.

I have heard that upon the May Day Eve,
Her staff will lie under the holly.
Then she will turn to a standing stane,
Like a tall, indomitable folly.

But I dare ye to gae—as I will not
For fear of hurt and dying—
To gambol beside that great grey stane
The winds aboot ye sighing.

> She is the winter, the wind, the snow,
> Her breath both warm and chilling.
> A single word from her icy lips,
> A single kiss is killing.

JANE YOLEN lives part time in Scotland, which only half explains why she wrote this poem.

The author of over two hundred books for young readers, and adults as well, she has won most of the major literary awards, including the Caldecott Medal, the Christopher Medal, two Nebulas, three Mythopoeic Society Awards, a World Fantasy Award, the Golden Kite Award (and two honor books), state awards, ALA Notable Book awards, and ABA Pick of the Lists. Called "the Hans Christian Andersen of America" by *Newsweek* and "the Aesop of the twentieth century" by the *New York Times*, Ms. Yolen is married, a mother of three, grandmother of three, and a dab hand at oral storytelling.

Visit her Web site at www.janeyolen.com.

Author's Note:

Actually, I wrote a short story for this volume which was turned down by the editors. (Or at least turned over to another book they were working on.) So there I was with no more stories in me on the subject, when Terri Windling sent me email about a strange Scottish wood fairy, a kind of winter Highlands mythic creature, the Cailleach Bheur, which she found in Katherine Briggs's *Encyclopedia of Fairies*. Said she, "I thought I'd pass it on in case it sparked any ideas . . ."

P. S. Dear Reader—it did.

Hunter's Moon

PATRICIA A. McKILLIP

THEY WERE LOST. There was no other word for it. Dawn, trudging glumly through the interminable trees, tried to think of a word that wasn't so definite, that might have an out. Ewan had been quiet for some time. He had stopped kicking over rocks to find creepy-crawlies and shaking hard little apples out of gnarly branches onto his head and yelling at her to comelookathis! Now he just walked, his head ducked between his shoulders, both hands stuffed into his pockets. He was trying not to reach for her hand, Dawn knew, trying not to admit he was afraid.

Lost. Misplaced. Missing. Gone astray. They were in that peculiar place where lost things went, the one people meant when they said, "Where in the world did I put that?" She was stuck with her baby brother in that world. It was grey with twilight, hilly and full of trees, and they seemed to be the only people in it. The leaves had begun to fall. Ewan had stopped doing that, too: shuffling through piles of them, throwing up crackling clouds of red and gold and brown. Dawn huffed a sigh, knowing that he expected her to rescue them. She hadn't wanted to take him with her in the first place. She had followed him aimlessly through the afternoon while he ran from one excitement to the next, splashing across streams and chasing squirrels. Now he was tired and dirty and hungry, and it was up to her to find their way home.

Trouble was, home wasn't even home. Here in these strange mountains, which weren't green, but high, rounded mounds of orange and yellow and silver, where rutted dirt roads ran everywhere and never seemed to get anywhere, and nobody seemed to use them anyway, she didn't know how to explain where Uncle Ridley's cabin was even if they did stumble across anyone to ask. It wasn't like this in the city. In the city there were street signs and phones and people everywhere. And lights everywhere, too: in the city not even night was dark.

A bramble came out of nowhere, hooked her jeans. She pulled free irritably. Something fell on her head, a sharp little thump, as though a tree had thrown a pebble at her.

"Ow!" She rubbed her head violently. Ewan looked at her and then at the ground. He took one hand out of his pocket and picked a small round thing out of the leaves.

"It's a nut." He looked up at her hopefully. "I'm starving."

She took it hastily. "Don't you dare."

"Why not? Eating nuts never hurt me."

"That's because you never ate the poisoned ones."

She threw it as hard as she could into some bushes. The bushes shook suddenly, flurried and thrumming with some kind of bizarre inner life. Dawn froze. A bird shot up out of the leaves, battering at the air with stubby wings. It was large and gray, with long, ungainly legs. It fell back to the ground and stalked nervously away, the weirdest bird that Dawn had ever seen.

"What is that?" Ewan whispered. He was tugging at her sweater, trying to crawl under it to hide.

"I don't know." Then she knew: she had seen that same bird on one of Uncle Ridley's bottles. "It's a turkey," she said, wonderingly. "Wild turkey."

"Where's its tail?" Ewan asked suspiciously; he was still young enough to color paper turkeys at school for window decorations at Thanksgiving.

"I guess the Pilgrims ate all the ones with tails." She twitched away from him. "Stop pulling at me. You're such a baby."

He let go of her, shoved his hands back into his pockets, walking beside her again in dignified silence. She sighed again, noiselessly. She was older by six years. She had held him on her lap and fed him, and helped him learn to read, and reamed into bullies with her backpack when they had him cornered in the schoolyard. But now that she had grown up, he still kept following her, wanting to be with her, though even he could see that she was too old, she didn't want her baby brother hanging around her reminding her that once she too had been small, noisy, helpless, and boring. She kicked idly at a fallen log; bark crumbled and fell. She had wanted a walk in the woods to get out of the cabin, away from Uncle Ridley's endless fish stories and her father trying to tie those little feathery things with hooks that looked like anything but flies. But she couldn't just be by herself, walk-ing down a road to see where it went. Ewan had to come

with her, filling the afternoon with his chattering, and leading them both astray.

"I'm so hungry," Ewan muttered, the first words he had
spoken in some time. "I could eat Bambi."

"Bambi" was what their mother said their father had
come to the mountains to hunt with his brother, who had run
away from civilization to grow a bush on his chin and live
like a wild man. Uncle Ridley had racks of guns on his cabin
walls, and a stuffed moose head he had shot "up north."
Painted wooden ducks swam across the stone mantelpiece
above his fireplace. The room Ewan and their father shared
was cluttered with tackle boxes, fishing poles, feathered
hooks, reels, knives, handmade bows and arrows. Dawn slept
on the couch in the front room underneath the weary, distant
stare of the moose. Once, when she had watched the fire
burn down late at night, an exploding ember had sparked a
reflection of flame in the deep eyes, as though the animal
had suddenly remembered life before Uncle Ridley had
crossed his path.

A root tripped her; she came down hard on a step, caught
her balance.

She stopped a moment, looking desperately around for
something familiar. There was a farmhouse on the slope of
the next hill, a tiny white cube at the edge of a stamp-sized
green field. Bright trees at the edges of the field were blur-
ring together, their colors fading in the dusk. The world was
beginning to disappear. Dawn's nose was cold; so were her
hands. She wore only jeans and her pale blue beaded sweater.
The jeans were too tight to slide her fingers into her pockets,

and her mother had been right about the sweater. Ridiculous, she had said, in the country, where there was no one to see her in it, and useless against the autumn chill.

"I think we're close," she told Ewan, who was old enough to know when she was lying, but sometimes young enough to believe her anyway.

"It's getting dark."

"Your point being?"

"Things come out in the dark, don't they? In the forests? Things with teeth? They get hungry, too."

"Only in movies," she answered recklessly. "If you see it in a movie, it isn't real."

He wasn't young enough to buy that. "What about elephants?" he demanded. "Elephants are real."

"How do you know?"

"And orcas—I saw one in the aquarium. And bats—"

"Oh, stop arguing," she snapped crossly. "Nothing in these woods is going to come out in the dark and eat you, so—"

He grabbed for her at the same time she grabbed for him at the sudden, high-pitched scream of terror that came from the depth of the wood. They clung together a moment, babbling.

"What was that?"

"What was that?"

"Somebody's getting eaten. I told you they come out now, I told you—"

"Who comes out?"

"Werewolves and vampires and witches—" Ewan dived against her with a gasp as something big crunched across the leaves toward them. Dawn, her hands icy, hugged him close and searched wildly around her for witches.

Someone said, "Owl."

She couldn't see him. She spun, dragging Ewan with her. A tree must have spoken. Or that bush with all the little berries on it. She turned again frantically. Maybe he was up a tree—

No. He was just there, standing at the edge of shadow under an immense tree with a tangle of branches and one leaf left to fall. He seemed to hover under the safety of the tree like the deer they had seen earlier: curious but wary, motionless, tensed to run, their alien eyes wide, liquid dark. So were his, under a lank flop of hair like the blazing end of a match. He didn't say anything else. He just looked at them until Dawn, staring back, remembered that he was the only human they had seen all afternoon and he might vanish like the deer if she startled him.

"Who," she said, her breath still ragged. "I thought owls said who."

"Screech owl," he answered and seemed to think that explained matters. His voice was gentle, unexpectedly deep, though he didn't look too much older than she.

Ewan was peeking out from under Dawn's elbow, sizing up the stranger. He pulled back from her a little, recovering dignity.

"We're lost," he admitted, now that they had been found. "We walked up a road after lunch, and then we saw some deer in the trees, and we tried to get closer to them but they ran, and we followed, and then we saw a stream with some rocks that you could walk across, and then after we crossed it, there were giant mushrooms everywhere, pink and gray and yellow, and that's where we saw the black and white squirrel."

The stranger's face changed in a way that fascinated Dawn. Its stillness remained, but something shifted beneath the surface to smile. His thoughts, maybe. Or his bones.

He let fall another word. "Skunk."

"I told you so," Dawn breathed.

"And then we followed—"

"My name is Dawn Chase," she interrupted Ewan, who was working his way through the entire afternoon. "This is my brother Ewan. We're staying with our uncle Ridley."

The young man's face went through another mysterious transformation. This time it seemed as though he had flowed away from himself, disappeared, leaving only a mask of himself behind. "Ridley Chase."

"You know him?"

He nodded. He took a step or two out of the trees and pointed. Dawn saw nothing but more trees, and a great gathering of shadows spilling down from the sky, riding across the world. She clasped her hands tightly.

"Please. I don't know where I am, or where I'm going. I never knew how dark a night could get until I came here. Can you take us back?"

He didn't answer, just turned and started walking. Dawn gazed after him uncertainly. Then she felt Ewan's damp, dirty hand grip hers, tug her forward, and she followed.

The moon rose just when it got so dark that the bright hair always just ahead of them seemed about to disappear. Dawn stopped, stunned. It was a storybook moon, immense, orange as a pumpkin, the face on it as clear as if it had been carved out of crystal. Surely it couldn't be the same little white thumbnail moon that she noticed now and then floating above the city, along with three stars and a dozen flashing airplane lights. This moon loomed over the planet like it had just been born, and she, Dawn Chase, was the first human to stand on two legs to look at it.

She felt Ewan pulling at her. "Come on. We're home."

Home under that moon? she thought confusedly. Home in what universe? He dragged her forward a step, and she saw the light beneath the moon, the lantern that Uncle Ridley had hung on the deer horns nailed above the cabin door.

She looked around, dazed like an animal with too much light. "Where's—where did he go?"

Ewan was running across the little clearing, halfway to the cabin. "Come on!" he shouted, and the door swung open. Uncle Ridley stuck his round, hairy face out, grinning at them. The old retriever at his knee barked wildly with excitement.

"There you are!" he shouted. "I knew you'd find your way back!"

"But we didn't," Dawn said, her eyes flickering through the moonlit trees. They cast moon shadows across the pale ground; the air had turned smoky with light. "There was someone—"

"I'm starving!" Ewan cried, trying to wriggle past the dog, who was trying to lick his face. "What's for supper?"

"Bambi!" Uncle Ridley answered exuberantly. That was enough to make the deer Dawn saw at the edge of the clearing sprint off with a flash of white tail. She stepped onto the porch, puzzled, still trying to find him. "Someone brought us home," she told Uncle Ridley, who was holding the door open for her.

"Who?"

"I don't know. He never said. He hardly talked at all. He looked—he was only a couple of years older than me, I think. He had really bright red hair."

"Sounds like a Hunter," Uncle Ridley said. "There are Hunters scattered all through these mountains, most of them redheads. Ryan, maybe. Or Oakley, more likely. He never uses one word when none will do."

"He didn't even let me thank him." She stopped at the threshold, her stomach sagging inside her like a leaky soccer ball at the smell of food. "Where's Dad?"

"He took the truck out to go searching for you. He was pretty worried. There's always some idiot in the woods who'll take a shot at anything that moves. He's probably lost himself now on all those back roads. I told him there's nothing out there to hurt you in the dark. Even the bears would run."

"Bears?"

"But it's best if you don't roam far from the cabin during hunting season. Come in before the bats do, and have some stew."

"It smells great."

He shut the door behind her. "Nothing like fresh venison. Shot it last week, four-pronged buck, near Hardscrabble Hollow."

"Venison?" she asked uncertainly, her throat closing the way it had when he talked about bears.

"Deer."

When she woke the next morning, she was alone. They had all gone hunting, she remembered, even the dog. Earlier, their whispers had half-wakened her. Coffee burbled; the wood stove door squeaked open and shut; bacon spattered in a pan, though it had to be the middle of the night.

"Shh," her father kept saying to Ewan, who was so excited that his whispers sounded like strangled shouts.

"Can I really shoot it?"

"Shh!"

Finally, they had all cleared out, and she had gone back to sleep. Now, the quiet cabin was filled with a shifting underwater light as leaves fell in a constant shower like colored rain past the windows. She lay on the couch watching them for a while, random thoughts blowing through her head. She could eat deer, she had found, especially if it was called venison. She hoped Ewan wouldn't kill anybody. He had never shot a rifle in his life. Uncle Ridley had invited her to come with them, but she didn't really want to be faced with the truth of the link between those wary, liquid eyes and what had smelled so irresistible in her bowl last night. The eyes in her memory changed subtly, became human. She shifted, suddenly finding possibilities in the coming day. She hadn't seen his face clearly in the dusk, just enough to make her curious. The stillness in it, the way it revealed expression without moving. . . . She sat up abruptly, combing her short, dark hair with her fingers. If she stayed in the clearing in front of the cabin, no one would mistake her for a deer, and maybe he would see her there.

She sat for a time on the lumpy ground in the clearing pretending to read, then for another stretch of time on a rock at the edge of the stream that ran past the side of the house, swatting at bugs and watching the falling leaves catch in the current and sail away. She was half asleep in the sagging wicker chair on the cabin porch, feeling the sun pushing down on her eyelids, when the boards thumped hollowly under her. She opened her eyes.

He didn't speak, just gave an abrupt little nod. Even close, she couldn't see the pupils in his eyes; they were that dark. Again she had the impression of expression just beneath the surface of his face, like a smile just before it happened. She straightened in the chair, blinking, then ruffled at her hair and smiled at him. His skin was the warm brown of old leaves, the muscles and tendons visible in his throat, around his mouth. The sun picked out strands of gold in his fiery hair.

"Ryan?" she guessed, remembering what Uncle Ridley had said. "Or is it Oakley?"

"Oakley," he said in his husky, gentle voice. "Oakley Hunter."

"Everyone's gone," she explained, in case he wondered, but he seemed to know; he hadn't even glanced through the screen door. He sat down on the edge of the porch, his movements quiet, neat, like an animal's.

"Dawn," he said softly, and she blinked again. No one had ever said her name that way; it seemed a word she hadn't heard before. "I stopped by to ask," he continued, surprising her farther by stringing an entire sentence together, "if you'd like to take a walk with me."

Her feet still felt yesterday in them, that endless hike, but she stood on them promptly without thinking twice. "Sure."

He didn't take her far, but it was far enough that she was

lost within five minutes. This time she didn't care; she rambled contentedly beside him through the wood he knew, listening to him naming grackles and nuthatches, elderberries, yarrow, maples and birch and oak. She told him about the ungainly turkey; he told her the name of the nut she had thrown at it.

"They only fan their tails for courting," he explained. "Like peacocks."

"How long have you lived here?" she asked. "I mean, your family. You were born here, weren't you?"

He nodded. "There have been Hunters in these mountains for forever."

"Do they ever leave? Or are they all like you?" He turned his dark eyes at her, waiting for the rest of it; she felt the warmth of blood like light under her skin. "I mean—I can't see you taking off to live in the city." She paused, laughed a little. "I can't even see you buying a slice of pizza in the village deli."

"I've eaten pizza," he said mildly. "There are Hunters scattered all over the world." He took his eyes from her face then, but she still felt herself in his thoughts. He drew breath, took another step or two before he spoke. "Every year, in autumn, we have a big gathering. A family reunion. They've been coming for days, now. It begins tonight, when the full moon rises."

"I thought that was last night."

"It seemed that way, didn't it? But one side lacked a full arc. You had to look carefully."

"It was beautiful," she sighed. "That's all I saw."

She felt his eyes again, lingering on her face. "Yes."

"It doesn't seem possible that there could be that many people back here in the hills. Yesterday we didn't see anyone for hours, not even a car. Until we saw you."

"Oh, they're here," he said mildly. "Most of them live in a wood or a forest somewhere in the world. They're used to being quiet. Noise scares the animals and trees; we hate to see them suffer."

"Noise scares the trees?"

"Sure." She looked for his secret smile again, the one he kept hidden in his bones, but she missed it. "You can hear them chattering when they're scared. They get shot, too, along with deer and birds, in hunting season."

"Anything that moves," Dawn quoted, remembering what Uncle Ridley had said. It sounded like a fairy tale: the old trees aware and quaking at the hunters' guns, unable to run, their leaves trembling together, speaking. Oakley had led her into a different wood than yesterday's wood, she realized suddenly. She was seeing it out of his eyes now, a mysterious, unpredictable place where trees talked, and deer lived peacefully among the Hunters. She smiled, not believing, but willing to believe anything, as though she were Ewan's age again.

Oakley gave her his opaque glance. "What's funny?"

"Nothing," she said contentedly. "I like your wood. What do you do, all you Hunters, at the family gathering? Have a barbecue?" She winced at the word after she said it; given their love of animals it seemed unlikely.

But he only answered calmly, "Something like that. After the hunt." She stared at him incredulously; he shrugged a little. "We're Hunters; we hunt."

"At night?"

"Under the full moon. It's a family tradition."

"I thought you said you hated to see animals suffer."

"We don't hunt the animals. It's mostly symbolic."

"Oh."

"Then we have a feast. A big party. We build a fire and eat and drink and dance until the moon goes down."

She tried to imagine a symbolic hunt. "You mean like a game," she guessed. "A game of hunting."

"Yes." He paused; she saw the words gathering in his face, his eyes, before he spoke. "Sometimes we invite people we know. Or friends. We were thinking of maybe asking your uncle. Because he likes to hunt so much. You could come, too. Not to hunt, just to watch. You could stay for the party, watch the moon set with me. Would you like to come?"

She didn't answer, just felt the answer floating through her, a bubble of happiness, completely full, unable to contain a particle more of the sweet, golden air. They wandered on, up a slope, down an old, overgrown road into a dark wood, hemlock, he told her, where an underground stream had turned stones and fallen trunks above its path emerald green and velvety with moss.

She could hear water falling softly nearby. They lingered there, while Oakley showed her tiny mushrooms on the moss, ranked like soldiers, with bright scarlet caps.

"You didn't answer my question," he reminded her, and she looked at him, let him see the answer in her face.

"Yes," she said. Her voice sounded small, breathless among the listening trees. "I'd love to come."

The world exploded around her.

She screamed, not knowing what had happened, not understanding. A crack like lightning had split the air and then a deer leaped in front of her, so close she could smell its scents of musk and sulphur, so close it seemed immense, its hooves the size of open hands, its horns carrying tier upon tier of prongs, some flying banners of fire as though the lightning had struck it, and all of them, every prong, the color of molten gold. She saw its eyes as it passed, so dark she could not see the pupils, only the red flame burning deep in them.

She screamed again.

Then she saw three faces at the edge of the wood, all pallid as mushrooms, all staring at her. Behind her, she heard the great stag as it bounded from the moss onto dead leaves. And then nothing: the wood was silent. The stag left no other sound of its passage.

She heard her father shout her name.

They stumbled toward her, slipping on the moss, Uncle Ridley reaching out to take the rifle from Ewan as he began to run. She couldn't move for a moment; she couldn't understand why they were suddenly there, or where Oakley had gone, along with all the fairy magic of the little wood. Then she saw the stag again in her mind, crowned with gold, its huge flanks flowing past her as it leaped, its great hooves shining, and she began to shake.

Ewan reached her first, grabbing her around the waist, and then her father, holding her shoulders, his face drained, haggard.

"Are you all right?" he kept demanding. "Honey, are you all right?"

"I'm sorry," Ewan kept bellowing. "I'm sorry."

"We didn't see you," Uncle Ridley gasped. "That buck leaped and there you were behind it—thought my heart was going to jump out of me after it."

"What are you talking about?" she whispered, pleading, completely bewildered. "What are you saying?"

"How could you get so close to it? How could it have let you come that close? And didn't you think how dangerous that might be in hunting season?

"It was Oak—" she said, still trembling, feeling a tear as cold as ice slide down her cheek. But how could it have been? Things tumbled in her head, then, bright images like wind-blown autumn leaves: Oakley under the tree, the deer watching at the edge of the wood, the great, silent gathering of Hunters under the full moon, Hunters who loved animals, who hated to see them suffer, who understood the language of trees. She saw Uncle Ridley among them, on foot with his gun, smiling cheerfully at all the Hunters around him, just another one of them, he would have thought. Until they began to hunt. "It was a Hunter," she said, shivering like a tree, tears dropping out of her like leaves.

They weren't listening to her; they were talking all at once, Ewan still shouting into her sweater, until she raised her voice finally, feeling on firmer ground now, though she could still feel the other wood, the otherworld, just beneath her feet. "I'm okay," she managed to make them hear. "I'm okay. Just tell me," she added in sudden fear, "which one of you shot at the deer?"

"It was standing there so quietly," Uncle Ridley explained. "Young buck, didn't hear us coming. Gave us a perfect shot at it. I couldn't take it; I've got my limit for the season. We all had it in our sights, but we let Ewan take the shot. Figured he'd miss, but your dad was ready to fire after that. So Ewan shot and missed and the deer jumped and we saw you."

Her father dropped his face in one hand, shook his head. "I came within an inch of shooting you. Your mother is going to kill me."

"So no one—so you won't go hunting again. Not this season. Uncle Ridley?"

"Not this season," he answered. "And not until I stop seeing you standing there behind anything I take aim at."

"Then it will be all right, I think," she said shakily, peeling Ewan's arms from around her. "Then I think you'll all be safe. Ewan. Stop crying. You didn't hurt me. You didn't even hurt—You didn't hurt anything." He raised his red, contorted, snail-tracked face. You rescued us, she thought, and took his hand, holding it tightly, as though she might lose her way again if she let go, and who knew in what ageless realm of gold and fire, of terror and beauty she might have found herself, among that gathering under the full moon?

Some day, she promised the invisible Hunter, I will come back and find out.

Still holding her brother's hand, she led them out of the wood.

PATRICIA A. MCKILLIP was born in Salem, Oregon, and grew up both in this country and overseas in England and Germany, since her father was in the Air Force. She was educated at San Jose State University in California, where she received a Master's Degree in English Literature. Having sold three young adult novels by the time she graduated, she was able to make a career as a novelist, which she has done since then. One of those novels, a fantasy called *The Forgotten Beasts of Eld*, won the first World Fantasy Award in 1975.

She has written science fiction and fantasy for adults and young adults, as well as a couple of contemporary novels. Her best known include the Riddle-Master Trilogy, which was nominated for a Hugo Award, and *The Changeling Sea*, for young adults (to be reissued by Firebird in 2003). Subsequent novels include *The Tower at Stony Wood*, *Song for the Basilisk*, *The Book of Atrix Wolfe,* and *Something Rich and Strange* (with artist Brian Froud), which won the Mythopoeic Award in 1994, *Ombria in Shadow* and the forthcoming *In the Forests of Serre*.

She lives in North Bend, Oregon.

* * *

Author's Note:

When I lived in the Catskills, I was surrounded by woods, so I am glad to have had a chance to write about places I'd come across in my walks, and various animals I'd seen. No one can ignore deer-hunting season around there. People come up wearing camouflage and orange vests and drive away with dead deer roped to the hoods of their trucks. There are always tales of stray shots barely missing houses or hikers. I wondered what Herne, the ancient guardian of the forest, would make of all this. The idea of the hunters themselves being hunted grew with the story. The red-haired Hunter was based on a young local man whom I met one day in the woods walking with his gun and his dog. He stopped to talk about being surrounded by coyotes once, at twilight, when he was walking alone; they walked with him, as though they recognized him and were keeping an eye on him, for a long time before they faded back into the trees.

CHARLIE'S AWAY

MIDORI SNYDER

UPSTAIRS, LYING ON his bed on Saturday morning, Charlie heard the mail push through the slot in the door and then fall with a heavy thunk on the wooden floors. He listened for the shuffle of his mother's slippers as she went to the door, then her exhaled breath as she bent and scooped up the fallen mail. He imagined her standing in the hallway, a pencil tucked behind her ear, the crossword puzzle under her elbow, scanning the envelopes through her cheap dime-store reading glasses that made her hazel eyes huge and watery.

Charlie knew it would be there. He knew by the sound of the mail as it hit the floor; the weight of the envelope with the letter of acceptance, registration materials, and dorm room assignments. Any moment now, she would call his name. He held his breath and watched the play of shadowy branches on his ceiling cast by the oaks swaying in the spring breeze outside his window.

"Charlie! Charlie, come down here! You got something in the mail," she shouted up the stairs.

"What is it?" he called back, wanting to prolong this moment alone in his room. This moment before the future arriving in a fat envelope announced itself. He lay still, legs stretched out along the bed, sneakered feet crossed at the ankles and his fingers laced together behind his head.

"Charlie, you awake?" his father called. "Your mother's got something for you."

"Just a sec," Charlie answered. The wind outside gusted through the trees and the shadows danced fitfully across the white ceiling. He watched the windswept pattern of charcoal-colored leaves shimmy against the wall. Then reluctantly, with slow deliberate movements, he swung his legs over the side of the bed and left the quiet of his bedroom.

At the top of the stairs he glanced down into the expectant faces of his parents waiting in the hallway. His mother held up a fat brown envelope in her hand like a newly caught fish. Her reading glasses hung around her neck, the pencil resting on her ear. She was smiling, her cheeks flushed. His father stood solidly behind her, hands jammed into his pockets, nervously jingling the spare change.

"Go on then, open it," his mother said as she thrust the envelope into his hands.

Slowly, Charlie opened the envelope. He tried to smile, to feign the same happiness that was radiating in his parents' faces. "Cool," he murmured, rifling through the documents the university had sent him. "Great. I'm in." He refolded the pages with glossy pictures of dorm rooms and campus life, the letter that congratulated him on being one of the lucky ones and stuffed them all back into the envelope. He handed it to his mother, uncertain what to say next.

"We're very proud of you, son," his father said.

"Thanks."

"Don't you want to look it over some more?" his mother asked. "I think we need to fill out some of the housing and financial aid forms right away."

"Later," Charlie said evasively, "I'll look at them later. I told Nina I'd meet her almost twenty minutes ago. She'll be pissed if I don't show up soon. Besides," he added seeing the disappointment in his mother's eyes, "I want to tell her the good news."

"All right." His mother relented and smiled. She touched his arm, and he could feel her hesitate between hugging him or letting him go. "Later, then," she said withdrawing her hand.

"It's great news, Charlie," his father repeated.

"Yeah. Really great," Charlie said. He kissed his mother quickly, the scent of coffee and graphite on her cheek and turned to leave. "Gotta go." He grabbed the door and jerked it open forcefully. He could feel the panic bubbling in his chest, a chilly hand constricting his throat even as he stepped out into the fresh air. Any minute they would ask him what was wrong. Any minute they would get angry, hurt, because he couldn't tell them, couldn't explain the numbness that overwhelmed him when he thought about leaving for college in the fall.

He walked down the street, his gaze following the tree line of the oak woods that fell away behind his house. It was strange to have such a piece of wild wood left in the city, but it had been the reason his parents had bought the rambling old house, which had needed work, lots of it, when they moved in. The roof leaked and the gutters were clogged with leaves, seedlings, and old sparrow nests. The pipes banged, hissed, and coughed up rusty water every time someone tried to take a bath. Worn gray and orange splotched linoleum had covered the hardwood floors, which slanted enough in the hallways that Charlie had set his marbles rolling on their own races. But a glance outside made one forget all the problems with the house.

From practically every window, one could see the ancient and stately oaks, the broad-lobed leaves spreading a canopy of green over the yard. Among the dark trunks and leather-brown leaves were the occasional maples, their red foliage blazing in the fall. Small stands of birch waved delicate leaves of silvery green in the summer that turned to butterfly yellow in the cool autumn air. One gnarled oak in particular had been Charlie's refuge. The trunk swelled with rounded burls and the bark was shaggy with a blue-gray beard of lichen and feathery patches of staghorn moss. Wedge-shaped mushrooms, fluted like ears, spiraled around the base. One branch, seared black by lightning, had partially split away from the trunk and lay against the ground. Charlie used the fallen limb as a step to climb higher into the upper reaches of the ancient tree and disappear for a while from the world below.

Charlie kept walking, trying not to look at the young oak standing alone in a little clearing of mowed grass. But it was no use. Every time he passed it, he glanced at it and remembered, with a dart of pain.

Compared to many of the trees, the oak was young, slender, the branches light and uplifted. The wind worried the soft green leaves, and dense clusters of new acorns bounced at the tips of the branches. His baby sister had been born in the house, and as a toddler, Celia had claimed the sapling oak as her own. She wrapped her arms around it, sang to it, sat beneath the small circle of its shade and played with her dolls and stuffed rabbit. Though Charlie was older by three years, she would let him join her, her face solemn as she served tea in acorn caps or plastered sticky maple seeds to his ears and nose.

The summer she was four she began to sleepwalk. They heard her wandering in odd hours of the night and rose to retrieve her from the kitchen, where she would be standing still asleep, jiggling the back door knob, or from the study struggling to open a window, or from the front hall pressing against the locked door. "It'll pass," the doctors said. So they locked the doors, made sure the windows were shut and slept fitfully, listening for the sounds of her feet in the night.

It stopped in the late fall almost as abruptly as it had started. She slept the night without stirring, a thumb in her mouth, the toy rabbit in her arms. Charlie, used to waking, still got up in the night and went to look at his sister. She was annoying, but he loved her. She was short and stocky, a head wreathed in dark auburn curls that bounced when she ran. Her cheeks were full and always streaked with dirt, her nose a rounded button over a pale pink mouth. She guffawed from deep in her belly, and Charlie loved it that he was the one who could most easily make her laugh. He'd check the window, draw the covers higher over her shoulder and return to his bed.

So how did it happen? He must have asked himself that question a million times in the last ten years. And still he had no answer. It was winter, just after Christmas, the days short and dark. The snow had fallen steadily for a few days. The night before her fifth birthday, it had finally cleared and became cold and crisp. He remembered seeing the bright moonlight casting a silver light over the woods outside Celia's window. She was there sleeping, the rabbit in her arms and he had returned to bed. But in the morning he knew something was wrong. He felt the cold draft that brushed a hand over his face, rifled his hair. He woke shivering beneath the comforter and went to Celia's room.

She wasn't there. The covers had been thrown back revealing the indentation of her body in the rumpled sheets. He ran through the hallway, down the stairs following the cold breeze. He called for his parents as he saw the front door wide open, snow drifting in from the porch. How had she unlocked it? The key still hung high on the hook near the doorjamb. He threw on his boots and a coat over his pajamas and ran outside. He could hear his parents shouting, calling her name, his mother's voice frantic in the still morning.

His breath had curdled into milky steam as he ran, searching for her outside, his boots crunching the dry snow on the pavement. And then he stopped, seeing her, a fallen leaf in a green nightgown, curled at the base of her oak tree. He went to her, terrified by her stillness. He called her name but there was no answer. He touched her sleeping face, rimed with frost. It was stiff and cold, ice crystals on her lashes, her lips blue around her thumb.

That was a long time ago. Yet, standing in the spring sunshine Charlie shuddered with the chill and made his feet move quickly down the street. It had taken forever for his mother to stop weeping. For his father's stone face to soften beneath the mask of stifled grief. And for the unbearable loneliness of his own heart to stop aching in Celia's absence.

"You're late," a girl called from across the street.

Charlie looked up and gave a Nina a lopsided smile that was meant as an apology. She waited for him, balled fists resting on her hips, the red lipstick mouth pursed. She tossed her head, flicking her long hair angrily over her shoulder.

The pit of Charlie's stomach squeezed pleasantly as it always did when he caught sight of Nina. He crossed the street to her, feeling his grin widen at her pouting face. She was almost taller than him, her shoulders surprisingly broad for a girl, her waist narrow above the smooth slope of her hips and long legs. She was on the swim team and her blonde hair had faint greenish chlorine-dyed streaks. She wore a blue T-shirt that pulled tight across her breasts and a pair of jeans worn low on her hips, displaying a slice of bare skin above her belly. A warm flush stained his neck, and Charlie tried to rub it away as he approached her.

"Don't be mad," he murmured. He circled his arm around her waist, pulled her close, and kissed her lightly. The lipstick tasted of cinnamon. She smelled peppery and creamy, a mixture of chlorine and bottles of lotion smoothed over the water-soaked skin.

"You're always late, Charlie," she complained with a laugh and draped her arm over his shoulder. She caught a handful of his chestnut hair in her fingers and tugged gently.

"It wasn't my fault," he replied and kissed her again.

"It never is."

"No really," he lied, looking earnestly into her clear blue eyes, the color of the municipal pool she swam in every morning. The "urban mermaid," he had called her once after workout, looking for the webs between her white wrinkled fingers. "My parents wanted to talk. I got my acceptance today from Brown University."

"Awesome," Nina said. "Congratulations. That is so cool."

"Yeah, I guess," Charlie answered.

"You guess?" she repeated, frowning. "You're going right?" she asked. "Tell me you're going."

He slipped his arm from her waist and sat down on the stoop, leaning back on his elbows, his legs stretched out in front of him.

"What's the matter? You don't seem very happy," she asked, sitting down beside him.

"I don't know," Charlie said with a shrug. "I guess, I guess I thought I wouldn't get in and then I'd go to school here. You know, with you. I could live at home. My parents would probably like that."

"Yeah, they probably would," Nina said dryly, "you being the perfect son and all. But is that what you want, Charlie? Do you really want to stay here? I sure as hell don't," she added vehemently. "I'm holding out for that swimming scholarship to Florida State so I can get away from home."

"Away from me?" he asked a little hurt.

She gave him a pained grin. Then bending low, the curtain of her hair shielding them, she kissed him, softly at first and then more forcefully, her tongue slipping between his teeth. She snaked her hand up under his shirt and laid her warm palm against his bare chest. He tried to do the same to her, his fingers reaching under the tight T-shirt, but she stopped him and pulled away from the kiss with a breathless giggle.

"Not here, you goof." Her eyes glanced over the top of his head. "My mom's watching out the window." She looked earnestly at Charlie again. "Don't you see? That's why I need to go away. To be my own self for a change. To figure out who I am. I love 'em but I can't stand my parents looking over my shoulder all the time. Don't you feel the same?"

Charlie shrugged again. "Yeah, maybe," he answered softly and looked away. It wasn't her fault that she didn't understand his life. Nina had four brothers, one older and three younger. None of them had died. It wasn't up to her alone to make her parents happy. To keep them preoccupied so they wouldn't remember the child they had lost. The obligation he owed them. Suddenly he felt his throat constrict again, renewed panic thread his pulse. He needed to get away. "Listen, I just came to say I couldn't hang out today. I promised my mom I'd do some errands for her," he said inventing his excuse.

"But you said you'd come with me to practice. And then we're supposed to meet Elliot and Katie at the movies."

"I'm sorry. But I gotta do this instead."

Nina stood brusquely and brushed fallen maple seeds from the backs of her jeans. "Yeah, sure," she said, her voice chilly. "It would've been nice if you could've let me know sooner. Or at least got here on time. You know, I do have a life too."

"I'm really sorry. Can I call you later? Maybe I can catch up with you guys at the movies, later?"

She gave him a measured stare, then swept her hair off her shoulder with a single irritated gesture. "Yeah, maybe."

She went back into her house and left Charlie sitting there wondering if he shouldn't ignore his panic, ring the doorbell, apologize for being a jerk, take her out somewhere with their friends, eat, laugh, celebrate like normal kids did when they got good news. But that was the problem, wasn't it, he thought as he dragged himself up from her stoop. He couldn't bring himself to realize that it was good news. He knew it was what was expected of him, but the thought of leaving was like a vague black hole in front of him, a chasm he didn't know how to cross, or even if he wanted to cross.

Charlie shuffled toward home, hands in his pockets. The air was warm, the loamy scent of damp earth exhaling from the woods. The green leaves, newly unfurled and dappled with sunlight were soothing to look at. Branches whispered verses as they rubbed together in the slight breeze, and the leaves rustled a gentle applause. Charlie turned off the sidewalk and pressed himself between the low shrubs of dogwood, wild honeysuckle, and brambles until he was standing surrounded by the dark columns of the trees, the high canopy of leaves sheltering his head from the open sky. He held up palms, gathering in the muted sunlight sieved and stained green through the filament of leaves. He moved easily through the trees, a fish in water, a bird through bush, touching the familiar trees, and inhaling the sweet fragrance of rising sap. The sounds of the city disappeared and there was a hushed silence in the woods.

But he remembered those other silences. When Celia died, the silence in the house had been thick and suffocating as wool, broken only by the soft murmur of his mother's crying. His father ground his jaw, lips pressed tightly closed, fists clenching the usually jingling coins in his pockets. The loss of his sister and his parents' anguish had weighed on Charlie so heavily that he imagined he carried the burden of it strapped across his back everywhere he went. It had been his fault that she had slipped away. He should have heard her; known the moment the door was opened and she had wandered out. But he hadn't and so it was up to him now, the only child left to fill the gaping hole of his sister's absence. In the days and months after the funeral, he expanded, recreated himself huge and loud, pliable; stretching and accommodating, fitting himself into every corner of his parents' lives, stroking away their fears and disrupting the muffled silence with noise enough for two children.

And it had made him stronger, Charlie thought drifting between dappled patches of sunlight and green shadow. The responsibility wasn't so heavy anymore, but second nature now. He could hold his parents' lives, their wants and needs, like two polished stones in his hand. He knew them so well, his mother's anxious hovering, her love dense and sweet as fruitcake, his father's feigned gruffness that turned tender in brief hugs. They had survived this loss because he had willed it for them. And he had survived because he had found a place in which he could temporarily forget his own grief.

Walking into the woods to the lightning-blasted oak, Charlie would climb the stairway of branches high into the leafy canopy. The dusky fragrance of the trees in the summer reminded him of his sister's scent, the sharp green of new leaves the color of her eyes. Cradled in the supple branches he could remember without sorrow her sturdy arms reaching for him, her plump hands holding his as he swung her in circles. Only in the woods could he find the sense of her again, only in the cross-hatchings of branching shadows on his ceiling could he imagine her child's face once more and tamp down, deep inside of him, the loneliness that gnawed at him.

But the future was coming, and he wondered how his parents would manage when he was gone. Who would hold the silence at bay? Who would carry them, like the polished stones, from day to day, as he did?

Charlie reached his oak tree, ran his hand along the flank of the blasted branch, now alive with a carpet of emerald moss. He stepped on the branch, feeling it give under his weight and then seeming to lift him again into the arms of the higher branches. He rested midway up the tree in a crook between two stout limbs. He was sweating a little, his face hot as he leaned his back against the tree and closed his eyes.

If only he could stay here. Forever. Keep this peace, this sweet silence that wasn't dense with need, but buoyant and comforting. Not have to worry about his parents' lives, not have to feel this overwhelming responsibility, the need to atone for the loss of his sister, nor the swallowed sorrow of her death. The tree swayed in the wind and Charlie opened his eyes with a smile. He climbed higher until he had reached the upper branches, long slender limbs arching out over the ground to intertwine with the limbs of its nearby companions. Charlie grabbed two branches, held on tightly and let his body and feet dangle in the air. He bounced lightly, the freedom of weightlessness in the gusting wind, suspended between earth and sky, only his grip on the slim branches keeping him from falling. He stayed there, swaying, until his arms ached, the muscles begging for release. Then reluctantly, his feet found a perch and with a heavy sigh he began to scramble down toward the earth again.

"Hey Charlie," a husky voice called above him. "Come away with us." Bits of bark, tiny dried twigs, and laughter drifted down through the leaves.

Surprised, Charlie nearly lost his footing. He clung to the tree trunk, his head craned upward, peering through the tangle of branches.

"Who is that? Who's up there?" he called.

"Come away, Charlie. You belong to us!"

Slowly, Charlie began climbing upward again, his eyes searching through the green foliage. Something darted between the branches, a sudden flash of rusty red, like the flutter of bird wings. A child's face appeared between the leaves and grinned from ear to ear and then quickly disappeared again.

Charlie climbed faster, burning with curiosity.

"That's it, Charlie, come away with us," another voice called from the canopy.

Charlie hauled himself hand over hand into the upper reaches of the trees, the branches growing thinner and more delicate. It was a ladder of green wood reaching effortlessly into the sky, the leaves like hands pressing against his thighs, the small of his back, brushing him higher into the vaulted ceiling of branches and leaves. And as he climbed, still more voices joined in, a chorus of children, women, and men, calling out greetings, welcomes, and urging him to climb ever faster. Charlie climbed until his arms grew weary and the muscles of his thighs trembled with the strenuous effort.

And all once, he discovered that he could climb no further. The branches flattened into a broad floor of matted leaves. He pulled himself up onto its leafy surface and rolled over on his back, his chest heaving, his eyes wide with astonishment.

A bowl of clear blue sky was above him, broken by arches of blooming dogwood, rowan trees that dangled orange berries, silver aspen, and dark brooding yews. The sunlight slanted across the curved sky and a pale moon like a drop of milk nestled on a green horizon. Children stared down at him, their faces brown as polished wood, their cheeks tattooed with whorled patterns. They were mostly naked, bracelets of seeds on their bony wrists, a twist of grass tied around a stick thin finger. One girl wore a pair of red wings tied across her shoulders. A boy next to her, his hair a thatch of furry snarls, wore a necklace like an owl's ruff beneath his pointed chin. His large, tawny eyes blinked slowly at the sight of Charlie sprawled over the floor of leaves.

"Charlie's away!" the girl in red wings trilled over her shoulder.

Charlie sat up and raked his fingers through his hair, catching fragments of twigs, moss, and bark tangled in the curls.

"Where am I?" he asked.

The children clapped their arms over their stomachs, doubled over and laughed.

"The Greenwood," a soft voice answered behind him.

Still sitting, Charlie turned and saw an older woman standing, swaying as the floor of matted leaves lifted and fell with the wave of winds beneath it. A girl waited beside her, berry-colored lips pressed into the hint of a smile. He scrambled to his feet, hands held out to steady himself on the sea of leaves.

"Who are you?" he asked.

The older woman smiled, her teeth white in the olive-colored skin. Across the broad plane of her brow she wore a crown of oak leaves dotted with clusters of tiny gold acorns. Thick ropes of raven and gray-silk hair coiled around her neck and fell in long plaits down her back to her feet. A scar of knotted flesh puckered the skin of her neck, spilled over one squared shoulder and left seams on one of her breasts lying flat against her chest. The scarred flesh eased away just below the faint outline of her ribs. A thin sheath of green fabric wound around her hips, clung to the long thighs and floated above her knobbed ankles. She inclined her head as she spoke to him.

"I'm known by many names, Charlie, most your mouth cannot say. But you may call me the Greenwoman, and I will answer to that."

"How do you know me?" he asked awed.

"You have climbed my arms many times seeking refuge. My ears have heard your whispered cries. There is little of your life that I don't know, Charlie. But come, don't be afraid. Feel welcomed here. Refreshed. It is your home too. Let my daughter set your mind at ease."

The girl stepped forward, took Charlie by the hand, and easily pulled him to his feet. Her grip was firm, her palms cool and moist. She smiled broadly, her round face framed by a heavy mantle of auburn hair. Tiny green fans of maple seeds were trapped in the curls, and she wore a crown of twisted coils of fox grape.

Charlie stared at her, something lighting up a long forgotten corner of his mind. He knew her. Knew her face, the tilt of her chin when she looked up, the keen gaze of her green eyes, and the bossy way she grabbed his hand and pulled him after her.

"Come away, Charlie. Let me show you our world. You know our foothills, the lower reaches where man and bird can find their rest. But travel now with me across the broad green road and I will show you our domain. This is the Greenwood, Charlie, born of the first seeds, erected from the first root of the Tree of Life. From here all things are joined. Like you and me."

"Wait," he said, slipping his hand free from the girl's grasp. He sat down on an arched branch and wrenched off his sneakers, suddenly wanting to feel the green path beneath his naked soles. The coolness of the matted leaves sighed against the skin of his feet. He felt strange, like something slowly unraveling. He realized he was unafraid standing in the liquid gold sunlight, the girl waiting for him, her figure supple as a stalk. He relaxed feeling his hips balance over the gentle swells of the rolling green path. "What's your name?" he asked the girl.

"Like the Greenwoman, I have many. But you can call me Dunia."

"Dunia," he repeated. "Do you know why I'm here?"

"You desired it," she replied, with a little shrug. "To come away from the world. From the sorrow that weighs you down like stones in a seal's pocket."

"Am I free from that then?"

"For a while." She added, "whether you stay or not depends on you." She held out her hand again and Charlie grasped it and followed. With every step he took, he felt himself grow lighter, until he imagined himself weightless, his feet thin sheets of paper floating over the green path.

* * *

That day and the next and the next until he lost track of time altogether, Charlie walked with Dunia down the green path of matted leaves, sometimes beneath the open sky, sometimes crossing beneath a shelter of arched limbs. They slid down the rain-wet slopes of ironwood and ash, fanned themselves with switches of maple, and drank the dew that collected along the veined ribs of oak leaves. Around him, Charlie heard the voice of the Greenwood come alive with birdsong, the scrabbling claws of small animals, the rasp of insects, and the whispered incantations as bodies slipped from the skin of tree trunks, joined them on their journey and then faded back into the green light of the woods. He slept beneath the open sky, the wheeling stars needles of light, his bed a web of branches padded with moss. Dunia talked, sang, teased, and dragged him running at times over the greensward. When hunger took them, they descended to low branches that dangled out over ice-cold springs. With a hand to steady himself, Charlie squatted beside Dunia on the branch and lowered his head into the bubbling water. He ate tart watercress, his chin stained green from the juice, and handfuls of withered blueberries stolen from lumbering bears. Their hunger satisfied, they returned to the green road, their arms reaching deftly for the branches that guided them upward through the trees to the high canopy.

It was easy here. He never thought of his family. Every step he took, he drifted farther from the anchor of his parents. He understood now how heavy those stones had been, how he had carried them unknowingly bent by the weight. He had never looked up or forward, only down. But now the yoke of grief, of unspoken guilt and shame fell away, abandoned and forgotten in the everlasting green of his journey. He found the open sky, and watched the hawks soar over the edge of the green horizon.

Charlie borrowed feathered wings from a thrush and darted through the trees. In the shinning black armor of a beetle he nestled in the hollows of rotting logs. And in the brightness of the day, Dunia beside him, his feet skimmed effortlessly over the canopy of leaves high above the world below.

Then one day Dunia, dashing ahead of him, stopped, a hand to her mouth. Charlie ran to her and saw the tears like quicksilver on her flushed cheeks.

"What is it?" Charlie asked.

"Look," she pointed.

And Charlie saw where the Greenwood fell away into a ravine of gray slag, heaps of coal and rutted crevasses of black mud, littered with rusting trucks, the skeletal remains of an old car, a bent bicycle, a broken toilet. Small mountains of lumpy garbage bags split their seams and children were rifling through the contents, hunting for cans. Crows cawed defiantly, their talons tearing open the bags, sharp beaks scavenging the contents. A woman in a long black sweater with a ragged hem trudged across the slag, a clear plastic bag full of smashed cans slung over her shoulder. Behind her, a filthy child dragged a heavy pail of pilfered coal.

"What is this place?"

"The end of the Greenwood. Every season there is less of our domain. Come away, Charlie. This is too painful to look on."

Charlie watched the child struggling to keep up with his

mother. She stopped and waited for him, her body all angles like the rusted metal hulls of the abandoned trucks. The child set the pail down and, fists to his eyes, he started to cry. The woman waited, shifted the bag of cans higher on her shoulder, silently contemplating the bawling child. Charlie wanted to leave, to turn away but his eyes remained fixed on the gaunt woman. He inhaled and held his breath, a stirring of hope in his breast as she set down the bag and tenderly bent toward the child. She knelt and held him close. The child's cries quieted, the small arms circling her neck.

Dunia pulled on his hand and Charlie followed, back the way they had come along the green road. But for the first time in many days, Charlie remembered who he was. He looked at his hands, the fingers stained green. He thought of that mother and her child, of what he had seen. Touch. A gesture of love, a reprieve even in that grim, dark place. It was all Charlie had wanted ten years ago. But he had hid his tears, silenced his cries, too ashamed to ask for comfort. A dagger of fresh pain lanced Charlie's chest and he felt the weight suddenly return to his bones. His legs crashed beneath the surface of the leafing path and he fell feet first, arms thrashing, snapping the thin branches along the way. Dunia plunged in after him and nimble as a squirrel, she bolted down the tree trunks, reaching out to snatch at Charlie's flailing hands. His feet kicked wildly like a swimmer in the foaming leaves.

"Charlie," Dunia screamed and reached for him, over and over again, missing him, grasping only the tattered leaves.

Charlie stared wide-eyed as he fell and the square blue patch of sky directly overhead disappeared as the green path closed over the tear in the road. He was falling fast, his skin scoured by the broken twigs as he crashed through their feeble embrace. Dunia darted between the branches, fierce as a cat trying to stop him from falling.

The leaves thinned and suddenly the branches grew dense and broad. He landed on one, was hit hard in the pit of his outstretched arm and ribs. For a moment he stopped falling, lay balanced over its beam, stars exploding violently in his head, nausea roiling in his stomach. He started to slide off its surface and his hand scrabbled along the coarse and brittle bark trying to find a handhold. Then Dunia was at his side, grabbing him by the shoulders and pulling him safely into the crook of the tree.

Feeling a solid branch beneath him again, Charlie hunched in her arms, panting in terror, aware of the thousand cuts and bruises he had experienced in the rush of his descent. He could feel Dunia's heart beating furiously as she held him pressed to her chest.

"What happened?" he asked, dazed.

"You remembered," she said.

"I have to go home," Charlie answered weakly.

"Yes."

And then tears trickled from his eyes, the salt stinging the cuts on his cheeks. Sobs rolled up from the hollow of his empty stomach, and he felt his heart crack, sheared like the branches breaking with his fall. He had been free and now he feared the weight again, dreaded the responsibility, the years of his own muffled, silenced grief. How would he explain all this to his parents?

"I can't," he said, his head held between his hands.

"Come, Charlie. The Greenwoman will help you," the girl answered and with a hand to steady him, they moved slowly and carefully downward through the layers of tree branch.

It was dusk in the world below when Charlie, weary and aching, laid his hand to a familiar branch. He looked below him and saw the long, outstretched arm of the oak blasted by lightning resting against the ground.

"Wait here," Dunia said. "I'll be back."

Charlie closed his eyes and laid his head on his drawn-up knees. His skin burned, raw from the thrashing leaves, but exhaustion released him to sleep.

He woke, much later in the night, someone calling his name from far below. He didn't answer but listened in the darkness to the voice that spoke to him. It was his mother, her voice insistent, sad, and yearning like the cry of doves.

"Charlie, Charlie, are you there? I know you're there. She told us we would find you here. She told us it was time to talk. You don't have to answer, son. All I ask is that you listen."

Charlie sat up and looked down through the dark webbing of branches. His parents were there, his mother sitting on the low branch and his father standing beside her, a hand resting on her shoulder.

"Before you were born," she started, "your father and I used to walk often in these woods. We always knew this was a special place. So when the house came up for sale, it could have been a shack for all we cared, just so we could live here, close to the woods. Perhaps you can understand that now. How special it is."

She waited as if hoping for a word from him. But Charlie kept silent.

She continued. "When you were about three, a terrible spring storm blew in, pitching lightning everywhere. A lot of trees were struck, including this one, this branch nearly torn from the trunk. We saw the smoke from our windows and then thought no more of it as the pouring rain seem to douse the fires. But later that night as the rain lashed the windows, an injured woman came to our back door." In the dark Charlie heard his mother's voice falter for a moment. "She was certainly strange looking. But worse, she was badly burned, the skin seared and blistered down one side of her body."

Charlie straightened his back with interest, remembering the Greenwoman and the scarred flesh that knotted her skin.

"Your father and I let her into the kitchen. But we were at a loss as to how to help her. She sat down at the table and insisted she didn't want doctors or hospitals. She'd heal herself she said. But she needed one thing from us. She had watched us living here on the edge of her world and she knew we could be trusted to help her. The blast had nearly killed her and it would take time, too much time to heal. She had a seedling, not yet ready for the soil, that needed growing. Would I help her?"

Charlie moved down closer, listening intently to his mother's tale. He could see her now in the faint moonlight, her rounded shoulders hunched, her hands folded in her lap.

"I said yes, not imagining what she asked of me. Hold out your hands she said and I did. She cracked open a green acorn between her fingers and shook the nut into my palms." His mother's voice trembled again in the dark. "It was full of light, a sliver of a green star. She told me to swallow it and I did. I didn't hesitate. Not for one second."

"Then she took my hands, looked deep into my eyes and said, 'I'll come back when the time is right to claim my own. For this act of generosity, may you always know the Greenwood and may you and yours be as kin to us.' Nine months later, your sister Celia was born."

Charlie clutched a twigging branch so tightly it snapped.

"It was my fault really. When the time came I couldn't let her go. By then I loved her as though she was my own daughter. But the call of the Greenwood was too strong and she began to wander, fighting to go back. I should have told you Charlie," she whispered fiercely. "But I didn't know how. Not until now, that is. I'm sorry, son."

"Charlie, I need to tell you how it was," his father broke in.

Charlie saw his father standing, his hands in his pockets, head craned upwards.

"When your sister was born, just after New Year's, a man came to the door." Then his father gave a dry laugh. "Well, a sort of man. There were deer horns, here," he motioned to his forehead, "and he wore a cape made from deer hide, tied on with vines. He came to see the baby and to ask a favor. Celia was healthy, a great set of lungs and a big eater. You remember?"

Charlie nodded. At least that part had been true.

"Well, the horned man was satisfied at what he saw. Then he gave me a sapling and told me in the first thaw to plant it and see that the child spent time there. So I did. It's that oak, over in the corner of the yard, where she always played. It was her tree, in more ways than one, I guess. It's her life rooted there. She grows as it grows. Do you understand?"

Charlie nodded silently, hearing again the murmured

words as the bodies slipped from trunks and traveled in the Greenwood.

"We were to let her go back to the woods when she was ready. But when that happened, your mother couldn't let go. And I'll admit, I had trouble too. We held on, and every night your sister, driven by instinct tried to go home. It was wrong of us, I know. But we loved her and we feared for you. That you would be lonely when she left."

"I was," Charlie said softly to himself.

"One night I got up to check on Celia and I saw the horned man waiting out in the deep snow in the yard. He was just standing there, staring up at me, his face as lost as mine would probably be if I knew I had lost you to someone else. I went to your mother. We had no right to keep her, I said. And after a lot of tears, she finally agreed. So that night, I unlocked the door and went back to bed. I let her go home. I know you blamed yourself when it happened and I tried to let you know it wasn't your fault. It was never your fault. She just needed to go home." He paused, and Charlie saw the moonlight spilling over his father's worried face, eyes searching the trees. "And what about you, son? What about you, Charlie? Are you ready to come home?"

"Not yet," Charlie answered aloud. He scrambled up the rough bark of the tree, across the wide-swept branches and jumped into a second, taller tree. He climbed, reaching hand over hand, his mind racing back to all the years he'd spent carrying the responsibility of Celia's death. He was angry and confused. For ten years he had watched over his parents, for ten years he had shaped every waking moment of his life to their needs. He thought about his parents' confession and it shocked him that their lives, which he believed he had shaped and sculpted, were not his creation. He didn't really know them and that surprised him.

Pausing to catch his breath high in the arms of an old maple, Charlie closed his eyes and remembered his little sister sitting beneath the slender oak, smiling at him as she brushed the auburn curls out her eyes. "Dunia," he said, recognizing her face now. His sister was here in the Greenwood. "Dunia!" he called aloud. Then, "Celia! Where are you?"

"Not far away," she answered close by him in the dark. "I've never been far away, Charlie. As close as the shade of the oaks." Her face appeared between the branches, her hands white in the moonlight where they circled the limbs.

"I thought you had died. I saw your body," Charlie said. "There was funeral, a casket."

"It was a husk; the shell of the acorn. I had already returned to the sleeping heart of my tree. The horned man, my father, left the husk for you and your parents that they might know of my passing into the Greenwood. Without that, he feared you would grieve my disappearance. It was to console you, Charlie."

Charlie leaned his back against the trunk, the bark scratching his neck. "Why didn't anyone tell me sooner?"

"I tried, Charlie. The Greenwoman tried. Every time you climbed into her arms she tried. But you wouldn't listen. You spelled yourself into a knot so tangled that none of us could find the loose end to pull apart again. That is until a month ago," she added, "when you wished at last to join us."

Charlie startled in shocked surprise. "A month? I've been in the Greenwood a month?"

"Yes. It's almost the start of summer."

"But my parents! They must have freaked," Charlie said, his stomach turning. "How could I do that to them?"

"They knew you were here. They worried. But they weren't afraid," Celia answered. She angled her way through the branches and joined Charlie on a higher branch.

"How did they manage without me?" he asked, puzzled.

"Come and I will show you." Celia took Charlie's hand and once more led him high into the trees, tripping softly over the branches, weaving her way through the dense clutter of twigs. And then she pulled Charlie close beside her and parted a heavy curtain of leaves. Charlie leaned forward and looked in the living room window. They were sitting together in his father's large, overstuffed chair, his mother curled up on his father's lap, his arm sheltering her. They looked at each other tenderly, resigned. Charlie saw his father brush away his mother's graying hair, tuck it behind her ear, and then kiss her softly. Seeing them face to face, their arms a closed circle around each other, Charlie sensed for the first time in his life that his parents had a life without him. He had always believed that he rested on their shoulders, their eyes focused on him, their hands reaching out to steady him. And now in this lamplight circle of intimacy, he realized there was a place between them where he did not exist.

"Do you see it, Charlie?" Celia asked.

"I do," Charlie answered and sighed deeply. They didn't need him as much as he thought, as much as he feared. They had each other. He wasn't hurt or angry, just relieved. His shoulders sagged wearily as though the weight had slipped from them once and for all.

"Charlie, you will always be my brother," Celia said, holding his hand. "But it's time you were away. The seed must drop from its tree, must split the husk and find new soil."

"I hear you, Celia." He smiled at her in the dark. "You always were a bossy sister."

Celia laughed and Charlie's heart ached to hear the low guffaw rumbling up from the depths of her stomach.

"In the morning I'll go. But I want one last night to sleep here in the Greenwood."

"Sleep then, Charlie. And know that the Greenwood is always home to you."

Charlie closed his eyes and inhaled the sweet fragrance of the trees, the musty loam of damp soil and new mushrooms springing up in the gathered dew. Laying his head on the long stretch of a branch, he heard the soft murmur of the Greenwood's heartbeat pulsing slowly through the veins of the tree. The wind gusted, swayed the branches and rocked him into a deep sleep.

In the morning Charlie woke, feeling the heat of the sun through leaves, the gold light flaming the insides of his closed eyelids. A thrush trilled an alarm, the wings beating through the leaves.

"Charlie, wake up!" a girl's voice called from below.

He rubbed the daze of sleep from his eyes and looked down. He saw the flicker of pale blonde hair.

"Charlie, it's me, Nina. I know you're there, you goof. Your mom told me the whole story when I got really pissed off because she wouldn't let me talk to you. Everyone at school thinks you've got mono. I've been playing along, bringing home your homework and even doing some of it for you. But it's time now. Come home."

"Did you get your scholarship to Florida State?" Charlie asked, slowly lowering himself down through the tree branches.

"Yes. And I accepted."

He could see her now, standing in the green light of the wood, murky as a pond, her arms akimbo, her head looking up at him like a mermaid at last returned to her watery element.

"I'll miss you," he said, crouching in the crook of the tree.

She smiled at him, and tossed back her blonde hair. Leaves cast a stippled shadow over her white T-shirt, cupped her breasts, and shivered over her bare thighs. She tugged the legs of her shorts down.

"You look good for somebody living off leaves for a month," she said. "Kinda got that nature boy thing going on. Very sexy."

"I said I'll miss you," he repeated.

"And I'll miss you, you goof," she repeated. "But look, Charlie, this is our last summer together before we go away, before we become someone else, meet someone else, and grow up into something else. But right now, this summer, we can still have fun, still be free, still be who we are, not what we will be. Let's enjoy ourselves, Charlie. We'll hang out, lie around in the sun, and neck a lot. You'll be my first, Charlie, and even though we go away to college and meet other people, you will be always my best and sweetest memory and you won't be able to go to a pool without remembering me and getting turned on. These last few months, Charlie, they're all ours, a bridge between one place and another, between our old lives and the new one we have to reach for. Come on, Charlie, come down." A blush pinked her smooth cheeks, her eyes earnest and hopeful.

Charlie climbed down the branches, hesitated for a moment on the blasted branch lying outstretched on the ground. Nina was waiting for him, grinning, her smooth skin slick in the soft green shadows. He glanced up into the dappled branches above and saw the slow spiral of maple seeds twirling down through the slanting light, a few at first and then a shower of seeds.

He laughed, recognizing his sister's silent prodding. He nimbly leapt off the branch, his feet finding the solid earth once more. He stepped with a rolling gait like a sailor back from a long sea voyage into Nina's open arms. He felt the heat of her breasts as he embraced her tightly, breathing in the scent of chlorine and the musk of her summer sweat. She tilted back her head, her hands stroking the back of his neck and he kissed her, grateful for the taste of cinnamon. They parted, breathless, their faces moist and soft.

Charlie took Nina's hand and they walked together out of the Greenwood, the spinning maple seeds twirling green and gold in the falling shafts of sunlight.

MIDORI SNYDER has published numerous fantasy novels, including *The Innamorati*, winner of the Mythopoeic Award in 2001, *The Flight of Michael McBride*, which combined Irish folklore with the legends of the American West, and a high fantasy trilogy, *New Moon*, *Sadar's Keep*, and *Beldan's Fire*, set in the imaginary world of Oran. She has a new novel, *Hannah's Garden*, forthcoming from Viking, about a young violinist and her trickster relatives. Snyder lives with her husband and daughter in Milwaukee, Wisconsin, and when she isn't writing or teaching English, she plays second mandolin with the Milwaukee Mandolin Orchestra, the oldest such orchestra in the nation.

Author's Note:

The source of inspiration for my Green Man story comes from a wonderful Irish epic called "Sweeney in the Trees." Sweeney, a soldier of great renown, is cursed with madness when he kills an unarmed priest in battle. The mad Sweeney drops his weapons and scampers like a terrified bird into the trees, where he survives, traveling over the leafy tops of Ireland's ancient forests. Every once in a while he descends, meeting with other madmen and hermits to eat watercress and drink cold spring water, and to share their mutual tales. Though Sweeney is cursed, removed from the comforts of human society, the trees and bushes magically sustain him until slowly, he becomes a part of the forest, half wild bird and half mad poet. Sweeney's tale, sadly, is tragic compared to Charlie's, but I liked the idea that the Greenwood was a fertile, imaginative place where one could temporarily escape life's burdens and be changed. I wanted Charlie to have such a moment, free from grief, to skim the tops of the trees like Sweeney, and to experience in that newfound "lightness" the possibilities for his future that he had denied.

A World Painted by Birds

KATHERINE VAZ

ONE MORNING A man danced in a public fountain. He was happy. He and his wife were about to have their first child. The man splashed water on some soldiers, even though they ordered him to stop.

That night, he vanished from Rio Seco and was never seen again.

His wife knew that if she screamed, she might also join the Disappeared People. She swallowed her shrieks, and they knifed their way into the baby she carried inside her.

At his birth, her son gave off the loudest cries of anyone ever born.

His name was Hugo Costa. When his mother hugged him, she felt the sorrow rippling below his skin. His red hair made her think, *His brain is on fire.* She painted a portrait of her missing husband, curled up next to it, and died of heartbreak.

Hugo was taken in by a Musician who taught him to play the violin. People always sighed at its music and said, "That is so sad but so beautiful!" When he turned eighteen, he stood outside the mansion of the General and played "Ode to Joy," which was against the law.

He played for the people who painted their houses purple and yellow—they disappeared in the night.

The Musician who raised Hugo came out to stop him—but then he stepped back to admire Hugo's courage.

His notes soared in honor of those who wrote poems of protest against the General—they, too, joined the Disappeared People.

His tears flowed for the Gardener of Rio Seco, who had disobeyed the law by planting flowers. (Plants like to climb walls, and they stick out their tongues and hold up their scarlet skirts.) The rumor was that he had escaped to the forest before they could drag him to the detention camp on the other side. It was a prison where people were put if the General did not like them.

Lucia del Mar went to her balcony. She had never heard music so explosive. Bright colors were not allowed, but the hair of the violinist was the shade of a blood-red rose, and the sunset brushed him in gold. She wept. Long ago her parents had disappeared for kissing in public, and she had been put in the General's house, thanks to her talent for creating lace. (A forbidden activity, since lace is very lovely, but the General's Wife had a weakness for it.) Her green eyes wept out a green river that cascaded from the balcony.

The green river of her eyes ran to him, to pool around his feet.

His blue eyes were pouring out a blue stream. It ran into the green river from her eyes. That was how Hugo and Lucia first touched each other across the distance, and they smiled to see that they had painted the blue and the green of themselves in great, wet strips across the dull landscape.

Hugo gazed at her. Now he would be banished or killed, instead of having the chance to love her. But he knew this: While the ants danced on his skeleton, they would be like tiny black notes playing a xylophone of bones, and the music he would sound out from the dead would be: Joy! Joy! Joy!

Word reached Lucia that the General had decided to forgive Hugo if he became his personal musician and learned military marches (which are terribly wrong for a violin). Hugo was locked into a house on the General's estate. When the Musician who raised Hugo came to protest, he was driven away.

Hugo's music echoed inside Lucia, who had nerves like a violin's strings—thin and trembling. The shine on her long, black hair was like the shimmer that stays on a pearl, even when it is snatched from its home in the sea. Her feet were large, and she had a habit of whistling badly, but these things made her worthy of being loved. A goddess might be adored for a moment, but only a real person can speak forever to the rest of us.

"I am in love," Lucia said aloud. Her words were carried to him—a Valentine stitched into the air. When she awakened, she said, "Hugo." Already just saying his name was the same as proclaiming her love.

She strained to hear his music entertaining the General. How brave Hugo was—and she would be brave, too. She started making lace pieces, big as curtains, that told stories, dangerous ones. Her mother, who had been a fine lace-maker in the days before beauty was outlawed, said to her once, "Listen, Lucia. The delicacy of what we do is what makes us strong."

Lucia got out the lace-making bobbin that had belonged to her mother. It was a stick with a hollow carved in it, like a cut-out window. Inside was a toy-sized bobbin, painted to look like a slender girl. This type of lace bobbin with a treasure tucked inside a hollow is called a "mother and babe." Thread was wound around the stick so that it could be easily used. Lucia's mother had said, "Remember that I am always with you: We are mother and babe."

Lucia let her green tears splash onto a lace picture of two people kissing.

She stitched a scene of the Gardener who had escaped to the forest.

She showed Hugo's father splashing in a fountain.

Spinning out lace goods as fast as a spider, Lucia wove herself into her work. The love inside her leaked into the thread. Suddenly Rio Seco got inflamed. Anyone who touched Lucia's lace touched the wild heart of her and caught her fever.

A woman wearing a lace collar made by Lucia del Mar began dancing in public! She narrowly escaped arrest.

The man who raised Hugo coughed into a lace handkerchief and burst into song.

A child who received some lace angels asked, "Mama, can't we plant sunflowers?" until his frightened mother hushed him.

Now we all know that when a girl falls in love, everyone rushes in to tell her that she's wrong, wrong, wrong, she doesn't know anything about love. These people come out of the woodwork! Their big faces are so eager!

The Cook in the General's house said to Lucia, "Love means that the other person does things for you. Does he bring you soup?"

"He sends his music to me," said Lucia.

Hugo's music was filled with sorrow for the people in the detention camp, and the notes he played every night were carried to anyone who would listen. He created a picture of the suffering people. Lucia sat very still so that she could hear the music filled with all that sadness, and it made her want to take it out of the air and show it to everyone. When she finished a lace picture of people screaming in the camp, she threw it onto the back of a horse galloping toward the public square.

The General's Wife burst into Lucia's room and shouted, "You've gone too far!"

Lucia controlled her trembling. She looked calmly at the General's Wife, who was sharp-featured, the way most liars are. It is impossible to tell a lie and not have it take a slice from the skin, sharpening the nose, tightening the mouth. Each time the General's Wife drank whiskey in secret, she added a brush of varnish, death-colored, to the backs of her eyes.

Whenever the General's Wife stole kisses with the Colonel, it put faint lines on her skin. Instead of telling the General to stop sending people to the other side of the forest, she was content to live in his nice house. Instead of telling the General that she loved the Colonel, she waited to see what one or the other of them could give her.

"I'll miss you after they drag you away," said the General's Wife, unable to look Lucia in the eye. "I'm sorry but—what are you doing?"

Lucia was spinning a lace daisy, soaked with her frantic love for Hugo.

Seeing the lace flower, the General's Wife felt her love blossom for the Colonel, for Lucia, for love that tires of hiding.

"They plan to come for you at ten o'clock," said the General's Wife abruptly. "Every night at nine, the soldiers lock the door to Hugo's house. When they leave, I'll go myself and unlock it."

"I won't forget your kindness," said Lucia. She tried to peer into the eyes of the General's Wife, but they were flat, whiskey-colored.

Lucia ran under cover of night to Hugo's house, bringing only her mother's bobbin and a supply of thread. Her hand dripped with sweat as she tried the latch. She threw open the door, and Hugo put down the plate he was washing. His red hair and blue eyes made him seem like all of fire and all of sky. He put his violin into its case, and he took her hand. The moon shut out its light to let them escape to the forest at the border of Rio Seco.

Entering the world of the thick firs was like being in a sound chamber made of plants. There were two silences, stacked one on top of the other. The dome overhead was green-black. Fireflies arrived like fairy-sized lanterns to flicker over Hugo and Lucia. Hidden animals hummed a serenade. She rested her head against his chest, the music of his heartbeat spooling around her mind. He whispered, "Think of me at six-thirty every morning. That's when the two hands on the clock are joined as one."

"Think of me at six-thirty every morning," she replied. "That's when night and day are joined as one." They fell into an embrace until morning, six-thirty, when they leaned their heads together to think of everything joined as one. The bodies of the fireflies, going off and on, seemed to go light, then lighter—until they were merged with the light of dawn.

Lucia found a stream and exclaimed, "Hugo! Look!"

Fish scales were sewn to leaves, to make mirrors in the trees.

Moss was sewn onto bees to make buzzing, floating islands.

"It's true, then, what I heard," said Hugo. Vultures had reported to the General that the Gardener was trying to create a new world. He was grafting strange forces together, and he was threading vines under the forest. When he figured out how to make a parachute, he would harness it to the vines, and his own small country would sail away from the earth. Lucia whispered, "I'll make a lace parachute. Let's find this Grafter, this Gardener."

Lucia walked quickly; Hugo walked slowly. Lucia with her worries; Hugo with his calmness. Lucia with her bad whistling; Hugo correcting her tunes until she shouted, "Stop!" They were getting to know each other.

Why are habits endearing when first glimpsed, but irritating in such a short while? What if you make each moment with someone feel like your first? (They are *always* first moments, since no moment is ever the same as the next.)

Hugo and Lucia sat down and laughed. Their pounding hearts gave them their reminder to love each other: Doesn't the heart perform the same task over and over, stubbornly repeating itself, washing blood in its chambers minute by minute, without end? Isn't it wonderful?

Mushrooms were sprouting. When Hugo pulled one from

the earth, the stem grew longer, and what looked like a gray stone emerged and turned into—an elephant!

"Thanks," said the elephant, sitting elegantly on a rock, brushing dirt off the wrinkles in her hide. "The Grafter attached us to mushrooms to hold us up. Our trunks water down the fire at the center of the earth. It's quite hot."

Lucia pulled a mushroom—and pulled—and out burst another elephant, its trunk gushing. "Whew," he said. "It's hell down there."

Hugo played "The Baby Elephant Walk" on his violin, and the animals danced, trampling grass and orchids. They trumpeted and shot water out of their trunks. Lucia grabbed the paws of a fox to waltz under the spray.

"Such a lovely red coat you have!" said Lucia.

"You should see the birds near the Grafter," said the fox.

"Hang on!" bellowed an elephant, lifting them onto his back. He grasped a vine to use as a tow-rope, and they flew as if they were skiing.

When they reached a glen, they stopped and blinked hard.

Birds that they had seen in forbidden books—parrots, parakeets, toucans, macaws—drifted and left ribbons of blazing colors in the sky. The Grafter had figured out a way to turn birds into paintbrushes! Wherever they flew, their feathers stroked crimson, cobalt, primavera green, violet, and mandarin orange in great washes that hung a bit, then melted into the sky, leaving it tinted before the colors faded— and then came other birds sweeping across, leaving new banners in the air, perhaps of lemon and saffron and topaz and every grade of yellow, to hang for a moment like colored smoke. Hugo pointed with excitement: The trees caught bits of the colored banners that floated off the flight of the birds, and they hung like bright rags from the branches. Filling the streams were fish with lavender heads and spotted tails. Lucia gasped to see them leap from the water and pop their scales off their bodies, and squirrels, wolves, and deer fit the scales over their eyes to use as goggles so that they could swim. The Grafter had planted the wolves' howl into the fish, so that a salmon swiped a pink rainbow band over the water while it jumped out to bay at the moon. A parakeet's song was married to a tree, which trilled, "Oh, how high can I go?"

The Grafter had attached tomatoes to narrow tubing, in case any plants needed red infusions.

He had grafted morning dew to a picture of a Disappeared Person so that he would never stop weeping.

"If we've found the Grafter's home, why can't the General?" said Lucia.

"Ah!" A voice echoed through the trees. Some twigs on the ground twitched and took the shape of a man's hand. Hugo pulled into view a tall, thin creature made of twigs. A green fog settled onto his frame, and hazy green arms and legs and a face took shape. Leaves sprouted into a tunic, and spiders were knitting a webbed robe. The spiders dangled off the ends, clinging for dear life, because this green-fog man waved his arms as he exclaimed, "Don't you see? Don't you hear? Oh, wait! You don't have your forest-eyes *or ears* yet, do you?"

He pointed upward. He had stretched the stars into a fleet of eardrums to collect every plot in the General's house, every whisper in Rio Seco.

"My fish and birds listen to the heavenly ears, and we are

warned before he comes. We made the mistake of trusting the vultures."

"I'm getting my forest-ears," said Hugo. "What's that moaning?"

"The cries of those locked in the camp," said the Grafter quietly.

Hugo sank onto the ground. The cries made an underground river that flowed outward, trying to reach through the forest back to Rio Seco. Hugo recalled the father he had never met. Where was his resting place? He missed the wonderful Musician who had taken care of him, too—was he safe?

When Lucia stroked Hugo's red hair, his burning thoughts passed through her skin. That is finally what love does: It lets us read the insides of people to save them the pain of speaking. She grieved for everyone's lost sons, daughters, husbands, wives, friends. Why had she been selfish, planning to fly away in a new world with only herself and Hugo?

The Grafter was desperate to rescue the prisoners. He had grafted vines to thorns, hoping to cut through the barbed wire around the camp. But sweet vegetation is helpless against such sharpness.

A huge padlock was on the gate. He once sent porcupines to pick the lock with their quills, but the guards shot every one of them.

His underground elephants volunteered to surge under the camp and blast it sky-high, but the bars went too far into the earth.

"Wait a minute," said Hugo. "Did you say the camp has a padlock?"

"A very big one," said the Grafter.

"Would a very big padlock need a very large key?"

"I would think so."

"Oh!" said Lucia. She was not only beginning to read Hugo's mind. She was beginning to hear the notions in his head before words were formed.

"The General wears a large golden key around his neck," said Hugo, gripping Lucia's hand.

Overhead, the birds never stopped painting the sky with their bodies. Despite her fear, Lucia ached with pleasure. Pink with green! Disorderly bands of orange with rippled chartreuse! Who ever heard of such pairings! She would fight for a world like this.

"When the army finds us," she said. "We'll tear the key off the General's neck."

"Yes," said the Grafter. "This time, we won't hide." When the General was within range, the Grafter would hurl a vine to capture the key.

"Very dangerous," said Hugo.

"Extremely," said the Grafter, and the green fog of his skin paled.

Spiders knit a canopy to shelter them. Lucia worked bobbin and thread, hooking out the start of the parachute. There was no time to waste. Hugo and the Grafter helped. The stars flickered, as if they, too, were nervous. The deer used periscopes—the eyes in peacock feathers grafted to branches—to look past the trees toward Rio Seco. Robins and cardinals brushed the air red as flames, as if to announce: *Step into our fire. Hand over the key.*

As night fell, Lucia asked the Grafter for his story.

"The soldiers ripped out my garden," he said, "but my brain kept sprouting gardenias. My body turned into my dreams. I became twiglike from so many dried-up memories of people who were gone, and I kept my tears to myself so that I seemed surrounded by a fog, and I wanted to explode into greenness whenever I walked past those plain houses with their sad people. When I planted a bird-of-paradise, they dragged me away, but the forest opened before me like my soul. It was easy to vanish inside its greenness, because it was my dream. The trees lifted me to safety, since I was already a man who was half a plant. When the birds greeted me, all I had to do was graft onto them the shades I had trapped inside me, and I could paint the sky."

Lucia reached through the green mist of the Grafter's hand until she touched the bones made of twigs.

The hours ticked along until a fox streaked to their canopy at dawn and gasped, "There's a reward for your capture!"

Lucia's legs felt as breakable as twigs.

The Grafter used a periscope to observe the vultures hovering over the army, which stretched as far as he could see, kicking through the streams. The General was in the lead, on horseback. Gold gleamed around his neck. "There it is," said the Grafter, forming a vine into a lasso.

A glint of swords from the army hit the fish-scale mirrors hanging on the leaves. Streaks of light zapped the trunks of trees, cutting open trapdoors. Out sprang gremlins that looked like frogs made of rotting wood pulp. They shed beetles as they ran at Lucia and Hugo, who grabbed mushrooms to fling elephants at them. Half of the wood gremlins got crushed, and the other half got infuriated at the idea of anything trying to crush them.

The Grafter used a vine to hoist himself and Lucia and Hugo to the high branch of an evergreen. The gremlins clamored around the base of the tree.

"Hold on!" shouted the Grafter, throwing a lasso toward the General.

A sword chopped the vine in two as it hit the General's neck.

"I'll try one," said Hugo, fashioning a new lasso as Lucia tied one herself and so did the Grafter. They would all try at once.

The General rode closer. Looking through a periscope, Lucia saw the brown spots on his bare head, and she thought: *People like the General get pictured as gods or monsters, so we think we're helpless against them.* And who was in the back flank of the first guard? The General's Wife and the Colonel. Lucia's breathing quickened. The General's Wife had helped her once before.

Hugo and Lucia gripped their lassoes and when the General was in their sights, the gold key reflecting the light, the Grafter yelled, "Now!"

Three lassoes spun out from their hands. The vultures grabbed Lucia's vine and almost pulled her from the tree, and the elephants started a stampede against the army. Many of them fell. The horses shied up and whinnied, unable to ride past the mountains of dying elephants, and the birds darted so fast to distract the soldiers that they smeared the air with the colors of heat, reds and yellows and oranges, but the vultures attacked them. "No!" screamed Lucia, horrified to see the birds being cut in two. The Grafter gripped another vine and chanted, *I'll get the key, I won't give up*, and Hugo broke off a branch to pound away the wood gremlins who had clawed their way up, while foxes shot out from the underbrush and died under the horse's hooves.

Flying opossums swarmed toward the treetop, screeching, swinging their ratlike tails. They attacked Hugo first. Lucia was bitten as she punched at them. They dug their claws into Hugo's shirt, giving snorts of pleasure. The General stopped his horse to enjoy the show, and while the Grafter was distracted, knocking the flying opossums off Hugo, a soldier threw a rope and pulled the Grafter to the ground. As his fog-body sank into the grass, the soldiers tore the leaves of his tunic. Lucia was hitting at opossums and throwing pinecones to get the soldiers off the Grafter, but the soldiers laughed. They chopped the Grafter to bits as if they were cutting up kindling, throwing a leg in one direction and the pieces of his arm in another, and they scattered his green hair. When the Grafter was killed, the opossums carried Hugo out of sight as he called out, "Lucia! Escape!"

Lucia grabbed a vine, and as a soldier was climbing the evergreen to get her, too, she swung over the left flank of the army and landed near the horse of the General's Wife and said, "Madame! Oh, please."

The Colonel rode to her side. The General glanced at them over the legion of soldiers, but he was more interested in having his horse trample the pieces of the dead Grafter.

"Let the prisoners go, bring Hugo back, let us create a forest in the Grafter's memory," Lucia said. "Please. You saved me once before."

"What's she talking about?" said the Colonel. He was as handsome as a lion—grand but dangerous.

"Save you? I did no such thing," said the General's Wife, and a dent appeared near her jaw, a cut of flesh.

The Colonel grabbed Lucia by her long dark hair.

"Madame," said Lucia. "Save our greatest violin player. I'll give my life in exchange for his." Lucia twisted her head, despite the Colonel's grip, to look at the General's Wife.

"I want the reward money," said the Colonel. "A violinist—who cares?"

They come to us all, those few moments when we can say, "This is when I decided the entire course of my being." The General's Wife's could choose Hugo, or the promise of the Colonel buying her gifts.

Lucia had a moment come upon her, too. She could say to the Colonel, *I know about your affair with the General's Wife. I will announce it so that the General hears it.* She got ready to yell, but she stopped. She was incapable of betraying anyone, even someone who deserved it.

The General's Wife smiled. Lucia recoiled to see the cracks opening on the face of the woman for whom she had made countless lace gifts.

Having made her terrible decision to do nothing but see her lover collect a reward, the General's Wife belched out several toads, and the Colonel, laughing, coughed up some rats.

But Lucia was meant to be free. She was a teller of stories in lace. Spiders are also weavers and storytellers, and they emerged from the churned-up earth to wind her in a cocoon. Before the astonished eyes of the General's Wife and the

Colonel, the tarantulas sat on the cocoon and waved their stingers and pretended to plunge them into Lucia. She lay very still.

"Well," said the Colonel. "That's the end of her, too."

"How awful," said the General's Wife, her voice shaking. That is the trouble with people who are partly good and partly bad. They think it is enough to feel bad and apologize for their weaknesses.

"Everything will be forgotten soon enough," said the Colonel.

Lucia did not dare breathe. The spiders dragged away her cocoon, and she did not move for a long time, until the land was mute.

It felt like days before she broke through her winding sheet. Gremlins pranced around fallen branches. The foxes limped; the trees were chalky, as if shock had drained them of chlorophyll. Under a birdless sky, Lucia walked to the fir tree where the Grafter had met his end. She tried to patch twigs together, but nothing held. Sprigs from his hair crumbled in her hand. She ordered herself to be strong. The Grafter would want her to free the prisoners—and now that included Hugo. She lay on the earth as if it would whisper about him—and, surprise! Musical notes—faraway and indistinct, but true notes, real ones—trickled through the ground.

Hugo was playing his violin, forced to entertain the soldiers at the camp. Her refrain became: *My body will play the songs he sends! His music will pluck my veins, and that will keep me alive.*

She often put her ear to the ground, to follow the trail of

notes. Sometimes a clattery, odd music added a harmony. She did not know what that was. She knew only that she must go forward, through the lifeless forest.

A fox brought her honey and colorless berries.

"Hello, my friend," she said. "What happened to your pretty coat?"

"Gone away," said the fox.

"Where is Hugo?"

"Gone away," said the fox. "Why don't you tell everyone how much has disappeared?"

She got out her bobbin to sew a lace picture of the battle. The spiders lent her thread when she ran out of her own. If she was captured, she would leave the truth behind. The Colonel was wrong: Nothing would be forgotten. Every night she folded her lace picture up like a knapsack and wrapped her arms around it, and the spiders protected her.

At six-thirty every morning, thinking of Hugo kept her sane. Otherwise her loneliness would have no curve of beginning, middle, and end. But how much time had passed? Three days? Two weeks? Where was the other side of the forest? The clattering noise grew louder as Hugo's music grew fainter.

One day she heard only a short measure of sound.

"Hugo!" she cried. "Don't give up! I'm on my way!"

Then a day arrived of only a few scattered notes.

The hour came when she put her ear to the dry earth, and there it was—quavering toward her, the last, weak note of a violin. She spun a lace net to catch that note and held it against her thudding heart. Grafted to her, kept alive by her heartbeat, the note made her weep. Her tears dampened the bed of the forest, and dragging herself forward, she cried a green river from her green eyes. It spread into tributaries. Dead seeds cracked back to life; plants pushed to the surface. Water seeped back into the trees. A fox lapped at the green river and his coat glowed, but Lucia crawled onward, sobbing, wanting only to keep alive Hugo's last note. She heard the clattering again. What *were* those things jutting out of the forest's wet floor? Bamboo? Saplings? They were now poking out of the moist ground, set loose by the water of her tears.

She stopped and lifted her head. "Hugo?"

A blue river was pouring toward her through the trees.

"Hugo!" She flung herself into the blueness rushing to meet her greenness. The rivers converged into one long blue-green waterway. She swam in it, legs kicking and arms flailing, her lace story folded inside her dress.

Two gray birds dipped into the river and flew into the sky, where they retouched it with blue and green.

She rode the water to the other end of the forest, where a blank vista was blocked by a prison. But over its walls, gushing around its padlock and barbed wire, blue streams cascaded. She bobbed in the water while the earth stormed and shifted. Rising out of the swampy ground were neither saplings nor bamboo, but skeletons. That clattery music was from those who had died in the camp, their bones rattling the land. The bones knit together along the riverbanks into a lacework of the dead who began to roar, and the roar brought up more green shoots that snaked like sea serpents—like living thread stitching through the cloth of the earth and digging under the sunken bars of the prison.

Lucia thought her eardrums would shatter. The landscape convulsed in one world-stopping scream.

It was the Grafter. The Grafter was among the furious dead. She had watered his chopped-up pieces with her tears, and the cuttings of the Grafter had been resown and had attached themselves onto living matter, and all this time he had been burrowing forward, out of the forest, below the camp. He had wrapped his arms around the foundation and was shaking it. His battle cry was commanding the vines to help him uproot the prison.

The earth tilted and showed itself remade as the face of a shrieking green man. The Grafter had taken over the whole visible world. His open mouth was an ocean, his beard and hair were the forests, his eyes were volcanoes.

He threw the prison off his face as if it were a mosquito on his nose. Elephants tossed the guards into space. Anyone that the Grafter did not want clinging to him he flung off, sneezed off, onto the sharp points of the stars.

Thin bodies fell out of the upended prison, to the safety of the blue-green water or the trees that were now the whiskers of the Grafter. Hugo tumbled out with the other prisoners. Lucia saw him clinging to a fern—part of the Grafter's mustache—and she swam to a riverbank and climbed out and ran along throbbing ground that was now the skin of the Grafter.

Hugo's face was stained with trails of blue. When she collapsed with her arms around him, they clung together, too tired to speak.

The General's Wife ran to the Colonel, but he said, "Go away!" She raced outside and sap gushed from the trees to trap her like an insect. The Colonel met the same fate—caught in amber-colored sap, thrown past the moon.

The General was pecked to death by his own vultures and

pitched toward Saturn, where he spun alone, the gold key twisting on his neck.

The swords and guns of the army—what good were those against the Grafter bellowing them into oblivion?

When the world righted itself, Lucia gazed into Hugo's eyes: All of sky, all of ocean. "Lucia," he said, because just saying her name was the same as saying, "I am in love." She touched the new face of the land and said, "Grafter, can you return? Shall we finish the parachute and sail away?"

"No." His sigh made the planet rumble. "Thanks to your tears, I've grown into the entire world, my dearest. It's not so bad to be here with the dead. We can help them go on living, if we remember them."

The earth had become so spongy from so many tears that it was easy for skeletons to dislodge themselves. They returned to Rio Seco with their stories: One had been killed for writing a play! One had died in prison for questioning the politics of the General!

The Musician who raised Hugo embraced him and said, "I knew your music would rescue us all."

On a clear morning, Hugo was startled by the ghost of his mother gliding toward him, arm in arm with the ghost of his father.

A skeletal couple touched Lucia's shoulder, and she said, "Kiss me, Mother. Kiss me, Father."

Blue and green birds stuck out red tongues and stared with their yellow eyes. With blue, red, and yellow, every possible color can be made.

The elephants cried, "There's aquamarine! A banner of violet! Rose!"

Tan. Black. Ochre. Cream.

The Grafter stayed busy. His roots visited the barren lands until Rio Seco was bursting with gardens.

"I'm going to think of you every hour, not just six-thirty in the morning, if you don't mind," said Lucia to Hugo.

"Not every minute?" said Hugo.

She laughed. "Not every second?"

Lucia, among the roses, among the lilies and the gladiolas, spent many years listening to the ghosts of the Disappeared. She told their histories in lace and tossed the finished pieces into the sky for the birds to paint with their bodies. Hugo invented a violin music that shaped the air into tunnels for the birds to swoop through. It was a time of stories, and of memories putting the flesh back onto bones. Who could dream of sailing away? The Grafter freely offered bouquets from his enormous green face. And the world painted by birds made both the living and the dead feel joy to come from such an earth.

K*ATHERINE* V*AZ* is the author of *Saudade,* a selection in the Barnes & Noble Discover Great New Writers series, and *Mariana,* translated into six languages and selected by the U.S. Library of Congress as one of the Top Thirty International Books of 1998. Her collection *Fado & Other Stories* won the 1997 Drue Heinz Literature Prize.

Her short fiction has appeared in numerous literary quarterlies, and she occasionally reviews for *The Boston Globe.* "The Kingdom of Melting Glances," her first children's story, was published in *A Wolf at the Door,* another anthology edited by Ellen Datlow and Terri Windling. Vaz's fiction often draws upon the author's Portugese-American background.

Author's Note:

My father's family is from the island of Terceira in the Azores, and he told me about a famous legend from the biggest of the islands, São Miguel: One day a shepherd with blue eyes was told he could not marry the princess he loved. She loved him, too. She came to him weeping so terribly that she cried a green lake out of her green eyes. He cried a blue lake out of his blue eyes, and they each jumped into the lake made out of the other's tears and disappeared. Those two lakes, brilliant green and brilliant blue, side by side, are still visible today on the island of São Miguel, often covered with a sea fog that makes the story seem completely alive and mysterious. The "Grafter" figure is my tribute to the incredible gardeners of the Azores, who put together plants so magically.

I have made an entirely new story out of those details.

GROUNDED

NINA KIRIKI HOFFMAN

MY MOM SPENDS a lot of time with dying people. She's a hospice nurse.

She's had this job my whole life. It used to scare me—maybe because I knew it scared Dad. Maybe that's one of the reasons he left. If you watch people die every day, doesn't it depress you? Do you look at everyone you meet and imagine their death?

Two years ago, when I was twelve, Mom took me with her to work. Not all the time, only when I wasn't in school and she had permission from her clients. That was when I learned not to be scared of Mom's job.

By the time Mom visits, people know they're dying, that there won't be a miracle or a way out.

Mom's job is to make people comfortable. She makes sure their pain meds work. She helps people figure out what un-finished business they have, and what to do about it. Some-times she just sits with them and holds their hands.

I tried to play those visits on the piano. I managed some of the mood, but there was a lot I didn't get. I wrote down my half-pieces. My piano teacher said there was something there, but it wasn't finished yet.

My mom is really good at her work. Last year, though, she started coming home from work feeling burnt out. She'd lost too many people.

Then she found a new boyfriend.

She met him online. She came home tired every night, grabbed the laptop, sat on the couch, logged on, and bang, she was gone, off someplace where only she and Vernon Denys existed. I was alone except for keys clicking. I could play the piano as loud as I liked or watch anything I wanted on TV; she wasn't even in the room.

Sometimes while Mom typed she smiled. Sometimes she laughed, and sometimes she sighed. She hadn't smiled much since Dad left two years ago, until she started typing to this guy.

She got dreamy-eyed even when she wasn't online. She started a lot of sentences with, "Vernon says," or "Vernon thinks," which could have been terminally irritating, except I liked what Vernon said and thought.

Vernon sent presents: A miniature rosebush. Cedar and sage incense. One of those tabletop fountains, only this one looked like somebody had actually made it instead of it being mass-produced—it had polished rocks in it, red and green jasper, black obsidian, brown and white flint, rose quartz, and in the center, a piece of brown, gold-flecked pottery with a leafy face on it.

Mom had never been good with houseplants, but Vernon told her how to take care of the rosebush, and it thrived. Its flowers started out red, then changed: orange, yellow, pink, white.

One day I came home from school. I saw the rosebush, smelled a trace of last night's cedar incense, heard the fountain murmuring in the living room. It occurred to me that our house looked, smelled, and sounded different now. A guy I didn't even know had changed the way we lived. This spooked me.

But I liked that sight and smell and sound.

For a while, Vernon called on the phone. I talked to him a few times. He listened to me and wanted to know what I thought. I liked talking to him, but I was skeptical, too. He was a psychologist, and I figured he had to know how to make people think he was really listening to them; it was his job.

Still, it was nice for Mom to have somebody listening to her.

She and Vernon shared phone calls that lasted hours, but then they scaled back to typing at each other, for two reasons, I guess; one, to save Mom money on her phone bill, and two, because Mom captured the typed conversations and read them over and over.

Five or six months after Mom and Vernon started typing to each other, Mom decided she and I were flying to California for spring break to meet him and his kids. "Fiona," Mom said to me, "Vernon and I are getting married, if it's okay with all of you. This trip is so we can find out about each other."

Vernon had two kids, Tam, a boy my age, fourteen, and Holly, an eight-year-old girl.

"Have you even exchanged jpegs?" I asked Mom. We didn't have a digital camera, but some of the kids I knew at school did. I'd suggested before that Mom have my friend Scott take a picture of her and upload it so she could send it to Vernon. Mom had laughed and vetoed that idea. "What do you really know about him?"

"It doesn't matter what he looks like. I know I love him. We've talked more since we met than your dad and I talked in twelve years of marriage." She studied my face and smiled. "Okay. You think your mom is a fool. I don't confirm or deny it. Let's go check everything out, Fiona. If you can't stand the Denyses, Vernon and I won't take the next step now. I'll stick with my long-distance relationship until you go away to college. It's only four years."

"You're that sure?"

Mom grinned.

I watched the weather channel to find out what to pack for a trip to California. We still had snow in Idaho, which mean the ninety-mile drive to the Spokane airport on Mom's bald tires was going to be slow-going misery. But heck! Spring break in California! My friend Amy thought I was so lucky.

As I packed summer shirts and the scary bikini I got last summer but never had the courage to wear, I thought about my dad.

He and my stepmom and my baby half-sister lived ten minutes away from me and Mom. What if Mom married Vernon and we moved to California? It would make my two weekends a month of visitation a lot harder to manage. Maybe they'd just stop.

I didn't know if Dad cared about staying in touch with me. He usually brought work home on the weekends I spent at his house, so I ended up doing things with his second wife, Ginny. She was only ten years older than I was, and she had never figured out how to relate to me. Sometimes I was snotty and hideous to her. She responded by whining.

She was supposed to be the grownup.

Once she had the baby, she didn't pay any attention to me at all, except to teach me how to take care of little Catrina and ask me if I wanted to babysit. Which, depending on how broke I was and how much she was paying, I sometimes did. One thing my baby sister had going for her, she was really sweet.

Okay. California. It had to be better than Idaho. For one thing, no snow in the winter. I also—based on my one trip to Disneyland right before my parents' marriage broke up— knew California stores were better than the ones in our mall. Though the Denyses lived in the mountains somewhere be- tween Santa Cruz and San Jose, not exactly in a town. Still. . . .

On the plane I started worrying for real. Here we were, heading for California to meet strangers. I checked Mom out. She had lots of untamed frizzy black hair, and she sure wasn't built like a model, although she had really gorgeous dark brown eyes. She was short, and fat, and freckled all over. She was wearing this red dress that was a little too tight over her stomach.

I was so scared for her.

I mean, she was in love with this guy, and he said he was in love with her, and they'd never met. Wasn't this just like the setup for some horror movie where we ended up dead because we had too much faith in some unknown person's word?

Then, of course, there was me. Taller than Mom already, and thin in every way, even the bad ones; my best feature was my hair, which was thick and dark and wavy, not frizzy, and long enough to hide in. But Mom made me braid it on the plane so my face would show.

When I woke up that morning I had no idea what to wear. I tried on three things, and then Mom said we had to leave for the airport right away. So I ended up in black jeans, a black long-sleeved shirt, and hiking boots. I looked like a walking stick. Way to make a first impression.

This was, of course, a zit day.

We landed at the San Jose airport, and there was no snow in sight. But there was this gorgeous fake-looking family waiting, with a sign that said MEG & FIONA, and the man held bouquets of iris and freesia and sprays of menthol-smelling leaves I later learned were eucalyptus, of which there's a lot in California. Everybody in the Denys family was movie-star, magazine-model gorgeous. Vernon was muscular and clean-jawed, and he had all this curly brown hair, not like Dad, who was losing hair and adding stomach. Tam had crisp blond hair and slanted green eyes to die for, and Holly had long golden hair and eyes just like Tam's. They had toothpaste smiles that made you wonder when the press would show up.

It was creepy.

My heart raced because I thought, oh no, Vernon will take one look at Mom, whom I love with most of my heart, and pretend he's waiting for someone else.

But that totally didn't happen. He saw us and smiled, and the closer we got, the wider his smile.

So I checked out the kids.

They grinned like we were the ice cream truck driving up to their front door on a hot day.

More horror movie warning signs.

Then Mom hugged Vernon, and Vernon hugged her back, and then he handed me flowers and took my hand and said how happy he was to meet me and stared into my eyes like he was telling the total truth. And I believed him.

I thought: Oh, no. This is actually going to happen.

I thought: Well. Maybe it'll work.

Then we picked up the luggage and stepped out into the legendary California sunshine and smog, and I realized that, of course, a long-sleeved black shirt was not the thing to wear here.

We climbed into a white minivan and drove to the Denyses' house to look at our possible future.

The drive up was scary. I mean, we were in a city when we started, and we drove past all kinds of interesting shopping opportunities, but then we were on a freeway, and we drove farther, and ran out of stores and gas stations and strip malls and into a piney forest, and then we got off the freeway and took narrower and narrower roads.

I was from Idaho. I had already lived at the edge of the universe. What if there was nothing interesting within walking distance of the house? It was two whole years until I could drive.

We drove off the road onto a long skinny driveway which took us higher into the mountains, deeper into the forest, and farther from everything else.

Then the driveway ended, and there was the house, strange straight slabs of honey-colored wood, gleaming glass, trees pressing in around it, and a tumble of rocks and shrubs in front, redwood forest close all around.

They had their own fountain. Or creek. Or waterfall, or

pond. I guess one of each. As you approached the house, you looked to the right, and there was this rocky cliffy thing right next to the house, with water spilling down it, in some places trickling, and in some places waterfalls. At the bottom of the cliff was this pool, with all kinds of fuzzy-headed water plants and lily leaves growing in it. From the edge of the pool a little creek ran past the house, over really pretty stones, some of them as shiny as glass and some sandy. An arched bridge led from the driveway across the creek to the front door, and then the creek ran into another pond, this one round, with a fountain in the middle.

If they were going to have waterworks, why couldn't they be like normal Californians and have a swimming pool?

I felt like we had dropped off the map of the known world.

Vernon and Tam took our bags. I checked Mom's expression. She looked excited. Okay. No help there.

Then we went inside, and I thought, maybe we don't need a town. This place is huge enough to have everything in it.

Weird architecture. Wood everywhere, big giant windows so you couldn't get out of the sun if you tried, strange skylights and roof angles and ceiling heights, and plants all over. Some of the plants were so big they didn't leave much room for people.

The entry hall was huge, and split-level, and jungly. There was this smell, water, leaves, flowers blooming, and dirt. Glassed hallways led away in two directions. In front of us across the entry hall, two steps down took you into a big living room. Pale carpet, stone-topped tables, lots of space and light and distance. And, of course, plants.

"Shoes off, please," said Vernon, setting the suitcases

down and slipping out of his loafers. His kids had already taken off their shoes and stored them in this little shelfy thing to the side of the sunken entryway, pulled out pairs of slippers and slipped them on.

My face heated. Boy, if we had to do this every time we came into the house, it was going to get old fast. I stooped and untied my hiking boots, kicked them off. Holly gave me a pair of pink scuff slippers. I wondered if anybody else's smelly feet had been inside them, but they looked new. I put them on. Mom stowed her shoes neatly in the compartment thingie and glared at me until I put my boots away too. They were too big for the shelves, so I put them on top.

Then Vernon led us on a tour.

He had a whole wing of the house where people came so he could counsel them. Like, a waiting room with magazines, and an office where they had sessions, and a spare bathroom we weren't supposed to use. There was all this artwork, too, pictures that grabbed your attention and took you to other worlds. This wing had its own outside entrance. Vernon showed me the door between this part of the house and the rest. "When this door is shut, it means I'm working, and nobody should come through here unless there's an emergency involving fire or blood," he said, but he smiled while he said it.

Then we checked out a wing of the house with bedrooms, one of which was apparently mine, since Tam put my suitcase in it. I had this feeling that Mom had told Vernon way too much about me. The room was decorated in blue and pale tan and some gold, and there were a couple of small statues from India on the furniture, gods with six or eight arms and interesting dance poses. On the dresser sat a gilded Buddha.

My favorite color was blue. I'd been studying Eastern Religions.

"Like it?" Holly asked.

"Yeah." In a way I wanted to hate it. Everything was happening too fast.

"My room's across the hall." Holly pointed to a carved wooden door. "Tam's is around the corner, and the bathroom's over here."

We all went to check out the bathroom. It was awesome—big and carpeted, with a shower *and* a bathtub, and I had my own towel rack, with a set of blue towels—a bath towel, a hand towel, and a washrag. How classy could you get? Tam's towels were gray and Holly's were red.

My stomach lurched a little.

We headed farther into the house, and there was the master bedroom. Vernon put Mom's suitcase there. Which I thought was extremely weird, since this was the first day they had met each other face to face. Shouldn't Mom be in a guest room?

I tried not to look, but I couldn't help noticing that the bed was huge. A family of five could sleep on it and never bump into each other. My face overheated again, and I was glad when we moved on.

We passed a library, an office complete with a computer desk, which I guessed was where Vernon had sat while he was Instant Messaging to Mom, a couple more guest rooms, another bathroom. How big *was* this place? Big enough to get lost in! I didn't know anybody in Idaho who had a house this big.

We went back to the living room. Where was the entertainment center? Did they have a PlayStation? Was there even a TV? Did these people have cable? Premium channels? Any channels at all?

Vernon said, "Here's the new piano we got for you, Fiona."

And there it was, around a corner, in an alcove of its own: a Story & Clark upright, varnished the color of weak tea.

Mom had already told me that if she and Vernon decided to live together, I couldn't move my old piano, which was as ugly as dirt and weighed about eight hundred pounds. It was a weird square piano that was hard to keep in tune. It had come with our Idaho house when Mom and Dad moved in, before I was born. Nobody could get the piano out; they figured people had built the house around it. Nobody played it, either, until Mom and Dad thought it would be cute to get me piano lessons when I was about six.

I used to hate to practice, but something happened a couple of years into my relationship with the piano. The piano started talking to me. I got this sense of power from it. It told me we could do things together. Then I got so I could hear a song on the radio and play it. That was a rush; music couldn't get away from me. Once I heard it, I owned it.

Of all the things and people I was maybe going to have to leave behind in Idaho, the piano was what I worried about missing most.

So it was significant that Vernon had bought a piano for me before he even knew me.

On the other hand, his psychology practice had to be doing pretty well for him to afford this fabulous house on practically the most expensive real estate in the world. So what was one piano more or less to him?

If it was a bribe, it was a really beautiful bribe.

I sat on the piano bench, glanced at Vernon. He nodded. I slid the key cover back and looked at the keys. This was not a brand-new piano. The keys had yellowed with age, but they weren't chipped on the edges the way the keys were on the practice pianos at school. I placed my hands two octaves apart and set my fingertips down. Silky smooth ivory, yum, and lovely ebony. I played Hanon's Keyboard Exercise #2, which is not an exciting piece of music, but it lets you hear a lot of different notes in the course of it, since it moves up and down the keyboard.

Something inside me swelled up, pushed against my throat. The sound was beautiful, the action perfect. I finished the exercise and let my fingers choose what came next. They picked Chopin, one of the waltzes. I dropped into the altered state where music takes me.

A while later I stopped playing and blinked. I knew a few things then. One, I could be bought. Two, I could move here as long as the piano was here, because while I was playing, I lost track of everything else: no worries. If I could achieve that state here, I would be all right, no matter what else happened.

Only, would they be able to stand it, the potential new family? Not everybody loved music.

I glanced around. Tam and Holly sat on this big puffy couch next to a giant philodendron. They both stared at me, their mouths open.

Mom and Vernon sat on a loveseat, their hands tangled in each other's.

It occurred to me that Dad hadn't asked me to play for him

since he left to marry Ginny. He hadn't even come to my recitals. Out of town those weekends. But Ginny had come.

"Um," I said. "Sorry."

Vernon shook his head. "Don't apologize for that. It was beautiful. Please play whatever and whenever you like."

Tam jumped to his feet. "Can you teach me to do that? Dad just got the piano two days ago, and I tried it, and it didn't sound like that at all! Could you show me—"

"Me too," Holly cried.

"It takes a while to learn." I left the unspoken question in the air: would we have a while?

I stood up. I was afraid I loved the piano too much. "Where's the kitchen?"

We went down yet another hallway.

The kitchen was big like the rest of the house was big, with a giant steel refrigerator, hanging copper-bottomed pots, a wide butcher-block table, a six-burner stove, and two ovens, microwave and regular. I opened the fridge, and Mom said, "Fiona!" So I shut it, but not before I saw there were no soft drinks, no Kool-Aid, not even any milk.

"It's all right," Vernon said. "I want you to feel at home here. Tam, show Fiona where we keep the snacks."

This was when the true horror of living with the Denyses hit me. Their idea of snacks was totally uncivilized. Carrots? Celery? Apples? Oranges? Fat-free microwave popcorn?

I was *so* glad I had brought a stash of Snickers and Reese's peanut-butter cups.

"Which reminds me," said Vernon. "After you guys get settled, we'll go to the grocery store and pick up whatever you want to eat. I realize we may have different ideas of what makes good food."

Another objection to our possible future sidestepped. This guy was good.

I got Holly to show me how to get back to my room, then unpacked, changed into a blue T-shirt, and snooped around. The drawers of the desk and dresser were empty until I put things into them. The closet held hangers and nothing else. The windows showed forest. There was a birdbath out there under the trees, but no lawn anywhere that I had seen from all those windows. And no pool either, unless there was more of the house and yard than I had seen already. Which wouldn't surprise me.

I went across the hall and knocked on Holly's door. She let me in. Her room was done in brown and red, with colorful pictures painted on bark hanging on the walls, and squat stone statues from other countries perching on the furniture. There was forest out her windows, too.

However. Not a Barbie in sight. It made me wonder; I mean, I had only retired my doll collection to the attic two years ago, and I still thought about them. Holly didn't even have a teddy bear on her bed.

"So, what do you guys do for fun?" I asked my potential sister as I sat on her bed.

"Hike. There are trails out back, and lots of great places to drive to if you like hikes. Read. Go to the beach. Monterey has this great aquarium. We can take you there this week. In the summer, Daddy leads family retreats in the woods, and we get to go on those. Also, I paint." She knelt in front of her desk, opened a deep drawer, and pulled out this silver box, like a briefcase but bigger. "Do you like to paint?"

"I suck at art."

Her grass-green eyes widened. "Oh, no, Fiona. Nobody sucks at art. Maybe you just haven't had the right teacher."

Uh oh. Condescension alert. And from an eight-year-old. Where did I go from here? Sideways. "So, what happened to your mom?"

She bit her lip and worked on the clasps of her silver box. She slanted me a glance. "She died a couple years ago."

I waited a second, then said, "What happened?"

She sucked air in through her teeth. "Cancer."

"I'm sorry." Because of Mom's work, I knew a little about how awful that could be, or how well it could go. I didn't know which kind of death Holly's mom had had, and I didn't think I should ask until I knew her better, if then.

She gripped the clasps on her box. "Daddy didn't stop it," she whispered.

"Sometimes there's nothing you can do." I wished Mom was with us. She knew how to talk to people about this stuff.

She stared past me, her eyes narrow. "She wanted to leave," she whispered. "I heard them one time when they didn't know I was there. Daddy told her he could give her the green, but she said she just wanted to rest, and he should let her go." She glanced at me with wet eyes. "How could she leave us?"

"Death happens. You can't stop it." I thought about Mom's client Peggy. I saw her twice before she died. She was one of the nicest people I had ever met. So calm. So not afraid. Why?

She had touched my hand on the second visit. Her fingers were thin as sticks with plastic wrap stretched over them. Her eyes were full of shadows and light, and her smile was peaceful.

The day Mom told me Peggy died, I thought I saw Peggy walking away from me on the street. I don't know how I knew it was her. Maybe because I was thinking about her, and Mom said she had died well. She had a full head of brown hair, not the stubble I had seen her with. She turned and waved to me, and I saw a distant house through her. Then she faded.

Holly shook her head. "Daddy could. She wouldn't let him."

"Holly—" I held out my hand.

Holly looked up suddenly, blinked, shook her head. Her blinding smile flashed, and she opened the clasps on her box. I dropped my hand to the bedspread.

She lifted the box's lid, revealing a compartmented interior full of tubes of paint. She slid some flat canvas-covered boards from brackets in the box's lid and held one up to show me.

It was a picture of a tree, or maybe a person, vivid, green, leafy and branchy, twisted and strange and powerful. It had eyes, and it stared straight into mine. I couldn't look away.

"Do you like it?" she asked me after I tried to win a staring contest with a painting.

I shook my head.

Holly sighed and put the picture down. "That's my best one."

I shook my head again, trying to wake up. "Huh?"

"You don't like it."

"Like it? It's fantastic. You did that? You're amazing."

"Really?" She smiled. "Do you want it?"

"Holly—" I couldn't let her give me presents. Not when I didn't know how this was going to turn out.

Her smile crumbled.

"Sure, I want it," I said. "I just thought—it's too good to give to some stranger."

"But you're not a stranger. You're going to be our sister."

I bit my lip. "How can you be sure? What if it doesn't work out between our parents? What about us? What if we hate each other?"

"But I don't hate you. Do you hate me?"

"No, of course not. I don't even know you."

"Don't you know right away if you're going to hate somebody?"

"No." It took me a while to hate someone. First they had to do something hateful and hurtful and mean. Usually after I liked them and thought they were my friend.

Holly sat on the bed and gripped my hand. Hers was cool and a little sticky. It was weird for her to just grab me like that. I wanted to pull away, but I waited. Maybe she had been brought up with different manners from mine.

She turned my hand over and traced some kind of sign on my palm with her fingertip. My hand prickled, and I had the taste of honeydew melon in my mouth, which confused me. Holly looked up at me. "It'll be okay." She sounded way too sure of herself for an eight-year-old.

Tam knocked on the open door. "Hey? You hungry?"

I licked my lips. I still tasted melon. My stomach growled way louder than I was comfortable with.

Tam laughed. "Come on down to the kitchen. Dad's making lunch."

A guy who cooked? Culture shock again. Sometimes I thought one of the reasons Dad remarried right after he left Mom was because he couldn't find his way around a kitchen and would have starved to death without someone to cook for him.

Naw, scratch that, it was backwards. Dad left Mom because he already knew and wanted Ginny. Sometimes I almost hated him.

Holly picked up the painting and darted across the hallway to put it in my room. We all headed for the kitchen.

I heard Mom laughing, and Vernon's voice. A popping, sizzling sound, something frying, and the smell of something good.

I paused in the living room. Everything was rushing by me again. A pang of homesickness tightened my throat. Everything I knew was so far away, even Mom, somehow.

"What are you worried about, Fee?" Tam asked.

I blinked. My friends at school called me Fee, but Mom never did. How come Tam knew my nickname? "What's Tam short for?"

"Tamarisk."

Okay, what the heck did that mean? Oh, well, as long as he was answering questions, why not try some of the big ones? "Why does your dad like my mom?"

"Your mom is great. How could anybody not like her?"

"That's not what I mean." I took a couple breaths. Could I actually ask the questions I hadn't even let myself ask in the privacy of my own head?

If I didn't ask now, I would drive myself crazy. "Yeah, everybody likes Mom, but nobody else asked her to marry him. Look at this place. You guys have everything. You live in California. There must be scrillions of women around here who would drop everything if your dad looked twice at them. How and why did he come looking for Mom? How'd he even find her?"

Tam shrugged. "It doesn't matter where you live on the World Wide Web, only what languages you type in. People find each other. But if you really want to know, you should ask Dad."

Holly took my hand. Hers was cool and still sticky, and I felt that weird prickling in my palm again. "Come on, Fee." She tugged me toward the kitchen, and as I followed, my questions washed away. I felt like I could follow Holly anywhere and be happy.

"I don't know if you'll like this, Fiona," Vernon said when we walked through the kitchen door. He was stirring something in a big black frypan on the stove, and Mom stood beside him, holding plates. "It's vegetarian stir-fry. If you can't stand it, we have peanut butter and jelly and bread. What do you think?"

"It smells great." It must have soy sauce in it; it smelled like Chinese food, which was one of my favorites. Holly drew me over to the kitchen table and sat me down. I felt weird and twitchy, but I didn't know why. Part of me was happy, and the rest was trying to wake up.

She patted my shoulder. Happiness surged up. "Want some apple juice?" she asked.

"Sure," I said.

She went to the fridge and got out a pitcher, then took glasses down from a cupboard.

Tam sat down next to me and took my hand. What was with these hand-grabbing people? I wanted to ask that out loud, but the words wouldn't come. He stared at my palm the way Holly had, and like her, he wrote something on my hand with his index finger. This time the prickles in my hand were almost like needle stabs. The taste in my mouth was tangerines. My melon-Holly mood vanished.

"What are you doing?" I whispered.

"Getting to know you."

That didn't make sense. "How come it hurts?"

He stared into my face. "Does it? I'm sorry. I didn't mean—" He raised my hand and kissed the palm, and I felt strange, but better.

Then I felt swamped in confusion. No boy had ever kissed any part of me before. No one I knew had even mentioned some boy kissing their hand, not even Amy, who said she had French kissed Zack Dolby once.

Was Tam hitting on me?

It was true we hadn't met before, but weren't we, sort of, almost related?

I looked for Mom. Had she seen? What would she think?

She had her eyebrows up, and she was definitely staring our way.

I jerked my hand out of Tam's. His turn to look confused. Four expressions crossed his face, none of which I could read.

Then Holly brought juice to the table, and Vernon dished up the stir fry, and Mom passed out the plates, and Tam got napkins and chopsticks for everybody, after asking me and Mom if we liked to use them. We ate and talked. The food was really good—green peppers, red peppers, onions, soy sauce, this stuff called tempeh I had never had before, sliced water chestnuts, and mushrooms.

I finished first and watched the rest eat. I felt comfortable here.

* * *

In the afternoon, we went to a supermarket. It was twenty miles away, and it had the most beautiful produce I had ever seen. Everything looked like art: a pyramid of green peppers, a galaxy of oranges, crisp leaf lettuces arranged in a bouquet, fresh herbs in bunches. The store bakery sold ethnic breads, beige, black, brown, covered with sunflower seeds or corn meal. The shelves were loaded with things labeled "organic" and "natural." I could not find a single product made by Hershey or Mars or Hostess.

Tam grabbed a box of licorice buttons, opened it, and fed me one. I mean, he put it in my mouth. I was weirded out by this. I didn't even like licorice, and he hadn't asked.

Then I fell into the flavor. I spent the rest of the shopping trip in a haze as I sucked on the licorice button. It was soft and tasted black, but not like your usual Twizzler, more strange and sharp, strong and somehow primitive.

It wasn't until we got back to the house that I realized I hadn't chosen a single grocery. Mom and Vernon had asked me if what they were choosing was all right, and I just kept saying "Sure."

The last nubbin of licorice on my tongue vanished as we unloaded the car and took groceries in, and then I got mad.

"What did you do to me?" I asked Tam. We were in the entryway kicking off our shoes. Mom and Vernon and Holly had already unshoed and headed for the kitchen.

He pulled the box of licorice out of his shirt pocket and shook a button out, but I hit his hand and he dropped it. "Quit that!" I stooped and grabbed the little black dome.

"What is this stuff? How can they just sell it in a market? Is it some kind of drug?"

He put one in his mouth. "It's just candy."

"Don't give me any more."

"Didn't you like it?"

"It made me zone out. I hate that. *You* made me zone out. Why? How?"

Tam picked up two bags of groceries and walked away from me.

I went to the piano and pounded out some Scarlatti, the one with all the double-handed octaves in a minor key. What did these creepy, beautiful kids want? What was their father doing to my mother?

What were we doing here?

When I finished crashing around on the piano, I looked up. Vernon sat in a nearby chair.

"Let's take a walk," he said.

We sat down side by side in the front entry and put our shoes on. I didn't know where Mom was, or where Tam and Holly were. I didn't care.

We crossed the bridge and went around the house to a trail that led off into the trees. The trail was carpeted with short tan needles, and the trees were tall and quiet, with dark furrowed bark that went up and up before the feathery dark-needled branches drooped from the trunks. The woods were cool and shadowy, and the ground felt soft. Our footsteps made very little sound.

We walked a long way without saying anything. The forest was so quiet—occasionally a bird called somewhere in the distance. We passed a stream so small it hardly trickled out loud.

Vernon stopped when we came to a fallen tree. Sunlight shone down through the hole in the canopy the tree's falling had left behind. He went to the tree and stroked its trunk, like someone smoothing wrinkled bedcovers, then turned to me. "Want to sit?"

I sucked on my lower lip, then went and sat on the trunk. The bark was craggy, but the tree was so big around that it made a good seat. The air smelled like pine needles.

Vernon sat beside me.

We listened. Birds, a hush of breeze wavering the branches above us, the knock of a woodpecker somewhere.

"Why us?" I asked, eventually.

Then I looked at him.

He wasn't there.

A branch spiked up from the trunk of the tree beside me, wide around at its base as a person. Twigs spread out from its top, and each one had a different kind of leaf on it, some feather-shaped, some like maple leaves, some needled, some like arrowheads or oak leaves or teardrops.

I jumped down and ran into the trees. I hid behind one whose trunk was ten feet thick. My hands shook.

I leaned against the tree until I stopped shaking, then peeked around it. Vernon sat on the trunk. It looked like he had never left. The weird branch was gone.

I hid behind the tree, trying to make sense happen in my head. All I could come up with was: I was alone in the forest with Something Else, and I didn't know what it wanted.

I glanced around. I couldn't remember what direction we had come from. Soft needle-padded trails wound away be- tween ferns and sorrel and rhododendron bushes in lots of directions. If I hid here, would Mom ever find me? Would anyone?

Eventually, I walked back to the fallen tree. I stared into Vernon's face. "What do you want?" I wailed.

"I didn't mean to scare you. I will never, ever hurt you, Fiona."

"I don't understand any of this."

He held out his hands to me.

I thought about his kids, how they touched me and it changed me inside somehow. They touched my hand and my mouth knew something strange had happened. Nobody back in my real life could do a thing like that.

I licked my upper lip, and put my hands in his.

No tingling. No strange tastes. His hands were warm, nothing more.

"Are you going to hurt my mother?"

"No. I love your mother."

We stared into each other's eyes. In the shadows under the trees, his eyes were honey-brown with green flecks.

"I'd like to show you my work," he said. "Is that okay?"

"I don't know. What is it? I thought you talked to people."

"There's more to it than that." He slid off the tree trunk and held out his hand again. I hesitated, then took it. He led me over to a tree. He pressed my palm to the bark of the tree and said, "Feel."

I felt rough wood against my hand, almost shaggy. I could see spiderwebs in the fissures of the bark, and ants crept over it. I smelled afternoon-sun-on-forest.

Vernon laid his hand on mine. "Feel," he whispered. And then—

It was like music. I dropped down into a different place, and I could feel that inside the tree, things flowed, ran, changed, water and sap, light fizzing into green, roots plunging down, flavors of the soil, sense of sun and shadow, breeze and stillness, and the years—years and years and years, one wrapped around the next, weather graven into them, rains and droughts and the fresh embrace of fog, nights and days, summers, winters, under it all Earth, above it all Sky, and the eternal giving of Sun.

Vernon lifted his hand from mine, and I collapsed down from a hard stretchy tree-self into a small, soft-outside human.

I leaned against the tree, pressed my cheek to it. Still, faintly, I could sense life flowing through it. The bark felt warm.

After a little while I straightened and studied the forest. The trees seemed different, individual and alive, ancient, somehow friends. There was this undertone. When I held my breath, I could hear threads of music all around me.

"What?" I murmured.

"People lose touch."

I sat on the ground and dug my fingers down through the pine needles into the soft dirt. I could almost taste it with my fingertips.

Vernon dropped beside me. He dug his fingers into the soil too. His hands looked gnarled and hard and brown.

I lifted one hand and reached out to touch the back of one of his.

Bark.

He smiled at me. "People lose touch," he said. "Especially in Silicon Valley, where they spend so much time in little windowless rooms staring at computer screens. Some people are searching for a way to get back in touch, and others can be called back. That's my work. Give them roots, get them grounded."

I sighed and put my hands on my knees. "What does that have to do with Mom?"

"Sometimes I touch something special. Meg is special." He scooped up a handful of earth, held it cupped in his palm. He glanced around, picked up a little round pinecone, shook a seed out and poked it down into the earth, covered it. Then something baby and green speared up out of the dirt. Gently he joined the earth in his hand with the earth under us, without disturbing the new shoot. He frowned at it. "I can call them here," he whispered. "Meg is my other half. She can let them go."

He smiled, his eyes soft and distant. "I had forgotten that part of the cycle until I found her. Together, we . . ." He smiled again and shook his head. "Together."

I twisted my hands inside each other. I stared at the little plant, trying to put everything together. Mom spent so much time with the dying, and Vernon spent his time bringing things to life. I touched the tip of the new green shoot. It was so soft I could barely feel it.

I couldn't get the ends to match up. Vernon was some kind of plant person. And yet—"You found Mom on a computer."

Vernon laughed. "I know. I help people who lose themselves inside machines, and I lost myself inside a machine and found life." He shook his head, smiling. "Life reaches out in new ways. There are always surprises."

I pulled my knees up to my chest and gripped my ankles.

Vernon sat back, his hands shifting from bark to skin. "Meg and I can wait to live together until you're ready. Do you want to go home?"

"Home," I said. My room back home had one little window, and it looked out on the parking lot in back of the Safeway.

Dad was there, and Ginny, and Catrina, and my very own square piano, and my friends from school. Everything I knew was there.

I touched the tree again, sensed the life rustling under its skin.

There were trees along the streets at home, though the town I came from sat in the middle of rolling pea and lentil hills, land furred with crops and not wilderness. If I went home, would I be able to touch the street trees, sense what moved through them?

If I stayed here, and Vernon helped me touch things, what else would I learn? What different kinds of music would I hear?

But—"Tam and Holly did things to me."

Vernon's face sharpened. "What?"

I thought it through. It sounded stupid, but I said it out loud anyway. "They wrote things on my hand and made me taste strange things. Then Tam gave me a piece of candy, and it made me stupid."

He frowned. "They shouldn't have. I'll talk to them, tell them to stop that. They did it because they don't want you to leave."

I thought of the second time Holly touched me, how she

led me to the kitchen table and sat me down like I was a doll. If she kept touching me, would I do what she wanted? Would I forget what I wanted?

I leaned forward against my knees, rocked, chewed my lip. "Vernon? I don't know what I want. Nobody at home can do that kind of stuff to me, and I didn't like it when Tam and Holly did it. I know I want them to stop. If they don't stop, I want to go home. But you and Mom—"

"It's no problem for us to wait, Fee. I've waited a long time already, and I don't mind waiting longer." He rose, held out a hand, and helped me to my feet. "That's not the issue. You have to feel safe. No one should touch you without your consent. They know that. I'll remind them. You don't have to decide anything until you're sure."

We walked back to the house amid murmuring trees. I took Vernon's hand. He smiled at me.

The forest was full of music. I knew the direction to the house; I knew things about the forest, which trees were healthy, which felt sick; I knew how the land lay even in places I hadn't walked.

As we approached the house, I sensed something else, a chorus of different voices. The house plants, lively and wild. I stopped.

Vernon stopped.

"I hear them."

He cocked his head. "You opened your ears in the forest. Do you want them closed again?"

I went to the nearest window and stared at the jade plant on the other side of the glass. It sang a song of water-fat sun-bright contentment. Beyond it, a potted palm mourned and asked for water.

The house was alive with plant conversations.

"Not yet," I told Vernon.

We rounded the house and went in the front door. I kicked off my shoes and raced to the piano, then played the music of the trees until my fingers had it memorized. Something . . . something. . . .

With my right hand, I added a phrase about Vernon startling a seed to life. With my left hand, I played Mom's face as she sat at Peggy's bedside, listening to a story about Peggy's granddaughter. The two phrases were so different from each other. At first they crashed into each other. I staggered them, a beat, two beats, three beats apart, and then something happened; they clicked together like puzzle pieces.

I played the forest. I played pea and lentil fields. I played Mom and Vernon and mysteries until I was used to the sound of them together.

I played Mom wondering how she could keep doing her job when she was sunk too deep into death. I played Vernon giving her the green, fresh energy to take back to her work. I played Mom giving Vernon shadows to go with his light.

I played a theme for me, and one for Holly, motherlorn and sister-seeking, and one for Tam, more of a question mark because I had so little sense of who he was. That part of the music clashed and didn't work out so well, so I went back to the Vernon and Mom themes, with forest and water, treesong and sunlight, late night and the fresh silence after breathing stopped woven in.

It sounded right. I could work on the other stuff later.

I stopped. I turned. Everyone was there: Mom, Holly, Tam, and Vernon. Holly's hands were clenched into fists, and she was breathing through her mouth. "Please," she whispered.

"That's it," Tam said. "That's—huh? What was that, Fee? It was like my heart beating. Can you teach me that?"

Mom smiled, bewildered.

Vernon stood just behind me. His eyes glowed. I turned and swung one leg over the piano bench. He leaned over and hugged me, and I hugged him back.

NINA KIRIKI HOFFMAN has written and sold more than two hundred short stories and a variety of books, including the novels *The Thread That Binds the Bones, The Silent Strength of Stones, A Red Heart of Memories, Past the Size of Dreaming,* and the forthcoming *A Fistful of Sky.* Some of her short stories have appeared in Bruce Coville's anthologies.

She also wrote and sold four middle-school books. Her ghost story novel (still undergoing the titling process), a prequel to *A Red Heart of Memories,* will be published by Viking sometime in 2003.

Her short stories and novels have been finalists for the Nebula, the World Fantasy, and the Endeavor Awards. *The Thread That Binds the Bones* won the Bram Stoker Award for first novel, and her short story "A Step into Darkness" won a Writers of the Future Award back in 1984.

She lives in Eugene, Oregon, with cats, friends, and many creepy toys.

Author's Note:

I have always been drawn to forests, but I must admit that they also scare me, especially after dark. My few camping experiences have been exercises in passing the night without sleeping. I also dream of a forest spirit whose motives and goals are deeper than understanding, but whose general leaning is toward the light.

While I was working on "Grounded," my mother and I watched *On Our Own Terms: Bill Moyers on Dying*, a four-episode PBS series about people who are facing their deaths with courage and curiosity, strength, fear, open eyes, and acceptance; and also about the doctors, nurses, and social workers who help the dying face death. Their stories were inspiring.

There is so much mystery in the darkness, under the leaves, inside the bark, and down in the dirt.

It doesn't always have to be scary.

OVERLOOKING

CAROL EMSHWILLER

IF YOU WANT to hug a tree, here's the perfect place for it. They all belong to us, and we wouldn't bother, but we don't mind if *you* do it. There's no better ones than these to hug, stunted, weathered, half dead. They're more used to hardships than any of us, so, good to hug them.

We're crepuscular. And grayish, which makes us hard to see. We're wide awake when you're tired.

You bring dogs to sniff us out, but we outwit them. If caught, which is rare, we lie about ourselves. We pretend we're *you*.

When it's cool we wear squirrel hats and jackets. From a distance, you think we're those wild furry people you keep talking about, but those wild people are of another sort entirely. But if you think we're them, all the better.

In certain spots, way up here, there are more of us than of you. You come in small groups or alone. It's *us* you're looking for. Sightings? If we want you to have them, then you'll have them.

But we watch *you*—follow you, here and there; set up blinds you think are piles of brush. We use your own field glasses. (You often lose them. When we come out to clean up after you, there they are. Sometimes cameras, too. We don't use those. How would we get film developed way out here? Though sometimes we play a joke on you and take pictures of each other and then leave the camera back where one of your kind will find it, develop it, and wonder: Who are these odd people making funny faces?)

We giggle when we see you, crunch, crunching around, your big feet on dry leaves, or slipping on wet moss. We giggle when you think you've caught a glimpse of us. *That's* not us.

Lately the woods are full of you—*and* tin cans *and* plastic water bottles, sunglasses. . . . There's hardly a place to sit alone and contemplate anymore. And God forbid (your God) that we should stand, anymore, at the top of anything, silhouetted against the sky!

Don't think we don't have weapons. Silent ones, unlike yours. You don't know you're hit till you're hit, and you never know which direction it came from. Crossbow with darts. So silent, we can shoot and miss more times than several and *you* don't know you're being shot at until you're shot.

As to *your* weapons, we make sure our babies' first words are, "DON'T SHOOT."

I'm the mother. I don't mean really. I mean I'm the oldest and wisest. I lead my group around at an arthritic limp and everybody calls me Maaaaaaaah. I haven't had any other name since . . . I can't remember when. If I approve of something, then that's what happens.

When one of us gets hurt it's me they call. They know, by now, that I know about all there is to know around here.

In order to avoid *you*, we have nothing to do with the highest and therefore most popular mountains. What difference does it make, high or a little bit less high?

But we've captured one of you.

I was sitting here reading from your manuals about us. Most of the books insist we *do* exist. A few say maybe. Some say we don't. There are many of you who swear you've seen us and have pictures to prove it. They're lying and the pictures are fakes. Others write about how those people are crazy. We're like flying saucers, maybe yes, maybe no. Except it's not exactly us they write about. It's those others who live farther back. It's said those others are so cold they sleep with rattlesnakes to keep them warm. We don't believe that any more than we believe *we* don't exist.

You say we're seven feet tall and fuzzy. *That's* not us.

So I was sitting here in my favorite shady spot reading when they brought one of *you* in. An old man almost as old as my own old man got to be. I wondered why they'd bring a grown man up home this time of year. Our women are running around as if it was mating time. All because of this poor old man. It's the gang caught him. They'll do anything just to be different or to shake their elders up.

I like the old man's looks. Gray haired like us and nice and bony. Younger men are too baby-faced for my taste. I never liked that look even when I had a baby face myself. Such faces are all right for the young but softness of that sort is scary in a man when one must trust one's life to him. Mostly it's our men who keep *you* from us. They will sacrifice themselves if need be.

You can see on his face that this man can't figure out if we're us or his kind. I suppose we look odd. (*You* never look odd to us. We've seen you much too often.)

This man has the usual paraphernalia: camera, backpack, field glasses, big notebook full of notes and maps. He must be here on purpose. In his backpack, food, including three little easy-open cans of apricots. I sample one right away. Since I'm the maaaaaah, I have the right.

I ask the gang, "Why have you brought this one up here among us? If you don't know that's got to be the end of him, you should go down with the fathers and stay there."

"He knew."

"He didn't, but now he does."

"He did, too."

"There's nothing to know."

But then I see he's hurt. His arm hangs in an odd way and he's holding on to it.

"We didn't do that. He had that already."

I don't trust those young ones. They're at a bad age. Well, but they usually tell the truth.

"Bring him here and hold him down."

(Up this close those young ones smell bad. It's a sign of maturing.)

I put my foot in the man's armpit, grab his wrist and pull and twist and pop his shoulder back in place. I bandage him so it won't move.

If he didn't look good to me, I wouldn't have. . . . Well, yes, good looking or not I would have. Would I do less for a wounded turkey vulture than for this man? I nursed a vulture all spring. Everybody knows that.

I give this man broth. I don't tell him what's in it. We know *you* better than you know us. Best he not know. To him it'll taste as buttery as snails.

"I'm Maaaaah," I say.

Right after, when he says his name, I don't listen. Why know a thing like that when . . . well. . . .

I've been inside your cabins lots of times—even when you were there. Sometimes, as I walked right past you, I could hardly keep from laughing out loud at how you didn't even know I was in your shadows. I made myself peanut butter sandwiches. I drank your milk. There was one particular cabin—large for a summer house. It was all woody inside. Smelled of cedar and pine. Big woodpile outside. . . . (You never miss what wood we take.) Usually your cabins have chandeliers made from wagon wheels and horseshoes, but here there was a cut glass chandelier, small though; in the cabinet were teacups with gold on them, on the table, silver candlestick holders. I really did want one of those. Each held three candles and had silver leaves all up and down it. I went up to our home and thought about it for a couple of days, and then I came back down and took one. After all, there were four. After all, I'm the maaaah.

I could have made this man soup from *your* supplies because, once your campers get started, you don't realize how heavy your packs are and how tired you'll be, and how you'll lose your appetite because of altitude. You hide things along the trail that you think to pick up on the way home. We watch from our watching spots, thinking: Ha, ha, you'll search and search and wonder how you could have forgotten so soon and only a couple of days later. You even wrote where you hid it in your little book on flowers or the little one on birds or the little book where you write about this trip you're taking right now, and you still can't find that food.

(Why do you leave your food so as to cut down on the weight and not your books? More often we find glasses and cameras than we find those little nature books or your notebooks.)

By now this man will be wondering, where are those furry ones? You're *always* getting us mixed up with them.

I say, "I can take you where you want to go."

But he has to rest up a bit first so I can still sit here in my shade listening to the ravens. It's the stone that doesn't roll, that sits as I do, that gathers moss. That accounts for my greenish tinge.

I say, "You can catch a glimpse of them."

Now look at this. Already he's clumping around, snooping, peering but seeing nothing, standing right on our vegetables. Of course our gardens don't look like gardens to *you*, they just look like the normal forest floor. (Our walls look like just more greenery or random piles of sticks. You walk right through them. This man already has done it several times.)

But our rattlesnake is waiting there, in the garden.

I should have listened when that man said his name. I hadn't thought there'd be any need to call him.

I say, "I'll go with you and lead the way."

(I'll go with him even though the gang thinks he's theirs.)

This year those young ones won't wear hats. Even in the rain. (They chew your used-up gum. Smoke your cigarette butts. They want to try everything.)

I do love that gang. I love the overgrown, the clumsy and wild and insecure and smelly. Or, on the other hand, I love the stunted, the dry, the half dead. This old man has eyes as gray as shadowy water.

What attracted me right away were his stringy muscles, the hair on his arm, that wispy mustache, mostly white. What attracted me was how he laughed when he tried on our hats.

There has to be a reason why he came. What if he's tired of being one of *you* all the time and would rather be *us*?

Helicopters come, flying low. They keep searching back and forth. They're noisy. Even the noisy gang doesn't like it. Even this man doesn't like it. If he wanted to, he could show himself and get himself rescued. I couldn't stop him.

The gang goes out and cavorts around in plain sight. We're as pale as the slatelike fragments of limestone we sit on. We wear cobwebs. They make us wispy and dim. We can disappear right before your eyes.

Since the man isn't showing himself, he might as well look out over those fuzzy others in their habitat.

"In situ," I say. "Just look over, don't go down. You have to promise not to."

I give him a lesson for the journey as I've already done, and many times, to the gang. "Some mosses you can eat, and some pine needles. You can eat the roots of Solomon seal if you don't mind a little—quite a bit, that is—of grit. You can eat ants. You can roll in dust as a sunscreen, or plaster on mud."

He's taking more notes. (I *do* love the way all of you cling to your notes and your bird books.)

When I was young I once showed myself right in the middle of the trail. I just stood there, all greenish and gray. It was to one of you about my own age, climbing up, geologist's hammer hanging on his belt. I liked his looks though I couldn't see much under his hat. Well, I liked his *legs*, strong and brown and covered with curly golden hairs.

I stood in a spot where the sun streamed, one of those shiny golden streaks, down, just on me. I wanted to be his vision of a forest nymph of some sort, and that he'd never forget me, but he looked at me, staring so, that I got scared and skipped away, not as gracefully as I'd hoped. It turns out I'm the one has the memory forever. That man might have been this man right here.

There was an episode in a cabin, I the succubus. It was dark but not completely. There was a moon, gibbous of course. I'm not sure who the man was but it might have been this one. (I caught a glimpse of legs with curly hair.) I was no more than a shadow in a shadow, but I was hoping there was a glistening around my edges.

At first he didn't want to but I don't think he was frightened. He resisted. Just in case, I had feathers in my hairdo and a bag of wild strawberries. I whispered things. I sucked.

Then after twisting about a bit, one position and another, I lay under, as a succubus should.

Once he got started, I lost count of how many times. After all, he was a mountain climber and in perfect shape as all those who come here usually are. I felt he loved me. Too bad I hadn't seen his face, neither then nor on the trail in the shadow of his hat.

Misty or Dandy, I forget which, could be his own son.

We begin the journey to the looking-over site.

I flit and flutter, slither and slide. My old man used to say I was like a hummingbird or a butterfly. I wonder if this old man can see that? We always think of you as not noticing much.

He takes my picture.

He says, "I've always believed in you creatures. When I looked out the windows of my cabin, I saw shapes dancing. I locked my doors. Even so I saw, in the corners, shadows that seemed on top of shadows. Now and then I missed a package of frozen green beans." (Maybe *I* took those beans.)

Flit and flutter, skip and slide and so forth. . . . I wanted to be, "shrouded in mystery," as you always say we are, but I was thinking too much about how I looked flitting. I'm the one who stumbles. I had not thought such a thing would ever happen. *You're* usually the ones who fall. I scrape myself, top to bottom. I hurt my good leg. I tear my grays.

That man picks me up. His arm, my leg. . . . We'll have to help each other. At least it's *my* forest.

* * *

So, and with many hardships along the way, including the aforementioned, having climbed up and over from one valley to the next, having slept in a hollow with leaves over us, having chewed on wintergreen, having eaten whole meals of nothing but chanterelles, we arrive at the looking over point.

I dress him in a stick hat and a few vines. He'll look like that candelabra of mine (or perhaps it's his), leaves all up and down him. He gets his camera ready and we enter the blind. I push a peephole for him and one for myself, and we look down on the fuzzy ones' habitat.

Cottages of stone and wood, gardens with little flags to label the vegetables, birdbaths, goldfish ponds, here and there a ceramic rabbit. There's an iron deer.

I say, "There's a deer," and, "Here they are, the furry ones. Don't they look nice, all glittery in their golden coats?"

Except they're not there. He'll think I made this all up.

I say, "Their little ones are *so* cute."

He's got his field glasses out now. He says, "Where? Where?"

"You can't see it from here, but their eyes are green."

Why am I saying all this, *I'm* the romantic notion. *I'm* the hope. *I'm* the story. He's been writing me down every day. We're the wish-you-existed-after-all people.

I think he's going to go on down even though he promised not to. I don't think I'm strong enough to keep him from it.

I say, "We're as important to the forest as these fuzzy ones. If we weren't here some other creature would have to take our place. Put that in your notebook."

But he's going on down.

* * *

Of course the gang has followed us. There's not a place they don't roam (or anybody they don't follow), outskirts of towns, back yards, mountain tops. . . . Those young ones not only won't wear hats. This year they expose their navels. They cut cute little three-inch holes in their shirts. Where did that idea come from? As if it has to come from anywhere. Those young ones think all sorts of things. But it could be worse.

We try to keep them out of danger, but they don't listen. I used to be that way myself. They're at an age when they're easily mortified. Just as I used to be, and they never apologize.

However it's when your little kids get lost in the woods that our young ones show their best side. First they take them by the hand and lead them to a place full of flowers. Then they feed them berries. After that they take them to where *you* can find them and they sit with them until you do. Or, if you don't come, they bring them home to us.

He says, "Well, where are they?"

I say, "But it's *you*, the mysterious ones and you don't even realize it. Perhaps it's even *you*, the ones important to the trees. You hug them and kiss them. You sit in the tops to protect them. Sit sometimes for *months*. What could be more like us than what *you* do?"

But he's crawled out of the blind. He's standing up in plain sight, field glasses at his eyes, camera dangling.

"Why don't you sit and contemplate for a few minutes. Give them time to manifest themselves. There's one now. Over to the right, halfway behind the rosebush." (There isn't.)

I could have sneaked away and gone down there myself in one of our fur suits, but I forgot to bring one.

I have my crossbow and a dozen darts. I told him the dangers are few, but one never knows. I said, "No harm in being ready."

We always aim for the lower leg.

Then, there they are at last, the fuzzies! A dozen. Of course it's our young ones. I can practically see who's which by the way they cavort. Dandy, the thinnest and oldest, doing his usual leaps over hedges. They're doing everything right, climbing fruit trees, digging in the marigolds. . . .

Except my finger's on the release already. There'll be just a little swishing sound. I let go right where I aimed, into the big muscle of the lower leg. Those darts are small and sharp. At first he doesn't know what happened and then he's on the ground. Not so much because of pain. *Yet.* But because his leg gave way. He thinks it collapsed by itself.

It's too bad, but I don't think he even had a chance to take one single picture of the furry ones. (Nobody would have believed the pictures anyway.)

Does he realize I'm the one who shot him?

I throw the bow into the brush. Best to pretend I don't know he's shot.

There's no blood. There never is.

He's examining his calf. He's going to pull the dart out.

"Don't do that! . . . till I get my bandages ready."

He won't be able to go much of anywhere, especially not in a hurry.

Those young ones finally realize what's happened. They come up to us, still wearing their fur suits. Dandy is the first to get up here. He's more or less the leader. I suppose exposed belly buttons was his idea.

Oh, for Heaven's sake, they've even done that to their fur suits—cut little holes. They love to take chances.

I say, "He got shot."

"We didn't do that." They all say it, practically in unison.

"Well. . . . I suppose not."

It's *so* easy to put the blame on them. They expect it, too. All I have to do is keep my mouth shut.

"Make one of those little stick stools. Four of you to carry him and two can help me. Then, when we get to the edge, you know what to do."

And they do it. Showing their navels and all. And with clicks and clucks and lots of giggling. They don't even realize, but when have young ones ever?

There's this longing in you. *All* of you. Even if you were sure we didn't exist you'd still hope. We intend to live so as to fullfull *your* dreams and expectations—be of some worth to those of *your* ilk. Who would there be to sneak and follow? Come upon you suddenly. Who would live at the corners of your lives? Who would there be to be us if not us?

You stop and listen. *All* of you do. Every snap and rustle has a meaning. You look. You turn around fast to see what's behind you.

You want to believe in us and we—*I* especially—want to be believed in. It's always been my main goal.

* * *

That man went over with his field glasses and camera and notes and birding book and tree book, even one leftover can of apricots.

I wish I knew which cabin used to be his.

I wish I knew his name. I should have listened when he said it.

I wanted to keep him but of course that was never possible.

Well, at least we didn't break any of our own rules. At least I don't have to know what happened. I mean, not *exactly*.

CAROL EMSHWILLER was a winner of the World Fantasy award in 1991 for her collection *The Start of the End of It All*. She has received a National Endowment for the Arts grant and two New York State grants. Her short fiction has appeared in many literary and science fiction magazines. Her story "Yukon" was chosen for a Pushcart Prize and then was in the Best of the Pushcart Prize collection titled *Love Stories*. Her novels include *Carmen Dog, Ledoyt,* and, most recently, *The Mount*. She teaches fiction writing at New York University's School of Continuing Education. She grew up in Michigan and in France.

Her Web site address is www.sfwa.org/members/emshwiller/.

Author's Note:

I'd like to dedicate this story to Molly Gloss. I wrote it after reading her novel *Wild Life,* though my story came out entirely different. Everything Molly Gloss writes turns me on. I think we have the same love of wild places and of people enduring hardships. I loved her *Jump-Off Creek*. I only found out about it when I was almost finished with my *Ledoyt*. After I found it, I read it three times and yet I didn't read the last twenty or so pages for a long time because I didn't want to ever be finished with it. The only other book I did that with was Jung's autobiography. I wonder if I ever did finish that. I did finish Molly's.

FEE, FIE, FOE, ET CETERA

GREGORY MAGUIRE

JACK THE LESSER. As a name it had originally meant smaller, younger, quieter. But he had grown into his name, or rather, he had failed to grown in conformance with it. When his older brother, the first Jack, had begun his expeditions in social climbing, as you might call it, Jack the Lesser was still squatting among the lettuces, trying to marshal ladybugs to walk in single file, to strut, to polka. The ladybugs remained magnificently oblivious to Jack the Lesser's improving lectures, and flew about the unweeded garden with their usual abandon. Perhaps they were conducting missionary work so secret that not even they could divine its final aims.

Their mother had an ax to grind, figuratively as well as literally. In all of Kingland scarcely could be found a peasant less resigned to her station. Born three-score years earlier, she'd been nicknamed Filthy Tilda due to the state of her binding rags. As she'd grown though, with a drive unusual in a peasant, she'd mastered the vocabularies of the educated palate. So she could discourse about, and languish in need of, say, a saucily disposed Chateau Chillinger Haut '47, meaning the vintage of that favorable year that had been derived from the vines planted upslope of the pearlstone streambed. But Filthy Tilda had to settle for swill, and swill it was. Potato peelings steeped in briny water, treated with a few raw carrion berries to make it potable.

Jack the Lesser, arguably moronic, took little notice of his mother's airs, deprivations, and grievances. He had a slack grasp of the monarchical system, and could not see in the mutterings of Filthy Tilda anything approaching conspiracy to overthrow the King. But when Jack the Greater—as he was called only in contrast to his younger brother—when Jack the Greater disappeared up the trunk of that mighty muscled column, the authorities suspected treason, opaque in its strategic cunning, and rounded up Filthy Tilda and Jack the Lesser before daybreak.

"Name."

"The name of what?" said Filthy Tilda.

"Your name, mudwife. For the constabulary's records."

"Donnatilda, of Damp Meadows."

"Filthy Tilda," muttered the scribe as he wrote.

"If you knew what I was called, you need hardly have asked. My given name is Donnatilda, anyway."

"Your son's name?"

"Ask him yourself."

The scribe did so, sighing. "Name?"

"This ladybug is Beryl, and this one is is Pockle," said Jack the Lesser, "and this one is Clive Staples."

"Put those back in your pocket. I need your name."

"Oh, Jack. Jack the Lesser."

"Lesser than filthy? I doubt it."

"Lesser than more. I ain't much. Don't complain though."

"The less said, the better," said Filthy Tilda sharply. "'The Lesser' is a pet name. Leave it be."

"And the rest of the family."

"Gone to the Great Beyond," said Filthy Tilda, not as disingenuously as all that.

The scribe said, "Any statements to make?"

Filthy Tilda tilted her chin and pursed her lips. Her eyes were agate. "Any statements?" said the scribe to Jack the Lesser wearily. "Have to ask. It's the job."

Jack spoke into his vest pocket. "Any statements?" and concluded, at the sound of silence, "They're shocked speechless."

Emerging from the gloom when the scribe had closed his volume and trundled off, the Captain of the Guards said, "Do you know why you're under arrest?"

"Excessive charm?" said Filthy Tilda, venomously.

The Captain was a seasoned agent and did not wither under sarcasm. "You are suspected of plotting treason against the Crown. The stalk that has been cultivated in your cow pasture is a gross incitement of passions and an exhortation of republican sentiments."

"How can you call it a cow pasture? The cow was lost in a bad exchange long ago," said Filthy Tilda. "Dear dim Jack the Lesser traded her for a bean. We cooked it for four days and it was still as hard as stone; useless. Like your heart. As for our turning to a cash crop in our time of poverty, can this be considered a crime? We must live in order to pay taxes to the Crown, after all, or how would you feast so well at Broad

Betty's tavern?" She could smell smoked oysters on the Captain's breath.

"A *crop*," said the Guard. "A single plant? Don't joke with me."

"You've seen it? Well, you can hardly miss it. In the instance of a variety such as that, yes, a crop. The single sprout takes all our management. But I don't see how this should cause agitation to the throne or the court."

"Your neighbors protest you've been singled out for special government agricultural aid, and their jealousy and suspicion arouses the mob passion for justice."

"If there were any special aid to be had, we'd welcome it. My son and I spend our every waking hour drawing buckets from the well to keep that thing from withering. If you could spare a phalanx of crisply dressed dragoons to form a bucket brigade twice a day, His Majesty's humble subjects could find the chance to pause and breathe for a moment now and then. Isn't that the proper use of government?"

"Don't be saucy. We're going to have to send you into the cells until we decide what to do about your plant. What do you call it, anyway? What sort of plant is it?"

"What a well-attended Captain of the Guards, who doesn't recognize a bean plant when he sees it!" shouted Filthy Tilda. Jack the Lesser looked up in alarm. "You've been too long away from real life, fellow, if you can't identify the basic stuff of the vegetable plot!"

Guards hauled them off, gently enough, and turned them into a cell with a single cot. Jack the Lesser sat on the floor with his back against the wall. His mother fell into a deep sleep at once. The ladybugs came out to smell the night air and flew off through the bars of the window.

* * *

Having had a run in with a goose as a child, the Captain had a secret fear of farm animals. He was pleased to know that the family didn't keep fowl, and that the last livestock had been sold. So though the hour was still late, he set out to see the aberrant growth for himself, close up.

As he paced the distance, along a route first cobbled, then rutted, and finally overgrown with tall grasses, he considered the state of the Crown. Agricultural treason was a somewhat ridiculous charge, but of late things had been less than stable at the court. Perhaps the King, in trumping up charges of sedition, was seeking to divert public attention from his mismanagement of the treasury. Filthy Tilda and her idle sons had provided a perfect foil. The Captain did his home-work: A little judicious listening to the chatter around Broad Betty's inn table had revealed the neighborhood's general sentiments about the family, which weren't warm. Tilda and sons had paid no taxes for several years—people of that sort could be said to be the real reason the treasury was being milked dry—and when the aberrant vegetable apparition had sprung up in their useless barren meadow, word had been passed to the King's advisers and come back again to the Captain: *Secure that family and make sure the public hears about it.*

With her everyday expression betraying greed and resent-ment, Filthy Tilda would not quickly inspire her neighbors to clamor for her release. Of this the Captain was fairly sure. But the lad seemed blameless enough, only dull as ditch-water. He seemed to live in a magic land of his own making, with that congress of bugs in his sleeve. A simpleton like him would have been unlikely to forge strong friendships among the brawny stupid lads of the surrounding farms. So there seemed little chance of strenuous objection about their being detained pending the registration of charges before a magistrate in the morning.

Still, thought the Captain a bit wistfully, someone might object. Someone should. There always ought to be someone who notices the disappearance of neighbors.

As he approached the district known as Damp Meadows, the astonishing bean plant seemed less a silhouetted embellishment against the sky and more a change in climate. A heaviness in the air, a clammy sort of coolness. The odor of huge waxy bean flowers was repellant. A few had dropped already and the Captain had to maneuver about them. If his sense of scale wasn't too far off, the beanpods themselves would be the size of small canoes.

He reached the base of the plant. It was as broad around as the central tower in the palace. The skin of the stem was smooth—unnaturally smooth; it gave him the shivers to feel it. Any plant this large was supposed to be a tree, and trees had bark: cracked, striated, shagged. This surface was smooth, glossy, slightly warm, as much like human skin as anything else. He withdrew his hand in amazement and a faint sense of excitement.

Rearing back, he noted how the stalk twisted ever so faintly; sending out leaves, shoots, tendrils, growing even as he watched—or so he imagined. The thing was a menace, but a captivating one. Its root system must stretch for miles already. There was no need to call up a bucket brigade. This thing had no use for human tending. Filthy Tilda and her stupid son were kidding themselves if they thought they had any hand in how it thrived so mightily.

From what rare bean can such a thing grow?

When Jack the Greater returned that morning, hauling a pot that steamed and bubbled with a different variety of victual every time you removed its lid, his mean-spirited mother was not there to receive it. So he ladled himself a portion of milled oats with milk and apples, and covered the pot, and then opened it again to find several quarts of fresh-brewed coffee, sweetened with refined sugar and lightened with cream. Following this he worked his way through a mound of fennel-and-garlic pork sausages, then several dollops of eggs made with fresh mustard and tarragon leaves, and though he thought he smelled something faintly syrupy, like buckwheat pancakes, he left the pot alone after that and went to find his mother and brother.

It was unlike them to wander off. Where would they go? The only cow had been sold. Jack the Greater did not care to venture far from the hovel—he knew the family wasn't much liked in the neighborhood—but he could think of little else to do without his mother to chastise him or his brother to berate. Several dozen ladybugs on the doorsill were carefully lined up to spell the word HELP, but Jack the Greater couldn't read, and he stepped on half of them as he wandered in and out, bored and—for once—filled to satiety.

After a while he relieved himself behind the old pig shack and did up his trousers. Then the urge took him over again and he was drawn to the trembling promise; and hand over hand he began again to climb.

* * *

The Magistrate filed charges of sedition with intent to overthrow the throne, and by noon the town criers were studying the text so they could report the news with a semblance of accuracy. Filthy Tilda and Imbecilic Jack! *Stalking the King!* The sleight-of-word would attract eager listeners on street corners and in pubs, who might tip if the news was juicy and they'd had ale enough to behave stupidly.

Jack the Lesser was chagrined. Only two ladybugs had come to see him. Berrybright and Wilhelm. He watched them do a pas de deux in his honor, and tried to interest his mother, but she was irate at what she could hear through the barred windows of their cell and she wouldn't attend to the ladybugs at all.

"Stalking the King! Are they mad? I've never laid eyes on the blessed gentleman!" She was keeping her language respectful in case there were eavesdroppers about. "This is a huge mistake! Were the King's minions as sensible as the good Majesty must be, they would know I've nothing but awe for the power of the throne!"

The palace was only a few moments from the prison. A dog nosing his way from jail to jardinière would follow this menu of smells: human offal in the open drains of the prison facilities; wet paving stones; clots of horse manure; splashes of old sour ale and splashes of old sourer vomit; planking over a recessed gutter with a reek of standing water, as the gutter flowed poorly when at all; paving stones again, swept free of interesting litter; a lane of cobbles leading in a broad path along an iron fence much tagged with dog pee; a scatter of hydrangea petals on brick; a colder skid of gray marble, shiny as if in the act of reflecting the gray sky. Then the dog's nose would bump up against the wrought iron gates leading into the palace gardens, whose impeccable lawn hosted a fleet of white peacocks. Its borders were not so much riotous with color as downright giddy; its ornamental shrubbery was cut in the fanciful forms of naked satyrs, coy dryads, mermaids and phoenixes and acrobatically inclined bears.

The dog, like the peasants, would be restrained by the elegantly twisted iron. However, a delegation of ladybugs would scarcely notice the matter and could make their loopy way right through, even to the marble windowsills of the King's music chambers, if they were so inclined.

Within such a chamber, with its hangings of yellow silk, its yellow parquet floors, its plush plum-colored ottomans and sofas, the King of Kingland wandered, humming a melody. His was a nasal voice, unmemorable in the speaking mode and unforgettable, sadly, in the singing mode. Though hardly a despot, indeed more distracted by the affairs of governing his subjects than obsessed about them, he did insist on giving annual public concerts to show off what his music teachers, with understandable lack of precision, called his improvement.

"Dum diddle diddle fiddle fee," he intoned, moving his index finger up and down as if to remind himself in which direction the melody was intended to turn. "The words come later when the tune kicks in, dum diddle diddle fiddle fee fee fee. For a fee, just a little, or for free free free, I will hum diddle diddle, little me!"

"Darling boy," said the Queen Mum, busy with tatting, "there's some sort of annoying pest in the room making a dreadful noise."

"You're shameless cruel, Mother; I've always said it and you can't deny it." He was cut to the quick.

"Oh, for once I'm not talking about you, though I hate to have missed the opportunity," she said, for she was cruel and she liked to be so. "I mean there's a bug or something flying about, clicking its wings and making the most tremendous row."

"Where?" said the King, who did not care for bugs of any sort.

"Well, it fell on my needlework for a moment, I think, and then pushed off and went over on your side of the room. It's my belief that the poor thing was trying to smash itself brainless to get away from the sound of your little song."

"What sort of a bug?"

"A stinging one, or a pinching one, or a tickling one, or the sort that whines in the general neighborhood of the ear trumpet, or lays eggs in your hair, as far as I could gather. One whose nasty ways are set off by the sound of tuneless doggerel."

"Very sweet, Mother." The King sat down and drew his knees up under his chin, and circled them with satin-sheathed arms. "You've ruined my rehearsal."

"You were rehearsing, were you? I had thought you were performing glottal surgery on yourself through some brave new technique of adenoidal hypnosis."

A ladybug settled on the antimacassar and made his way along to the King's shoulder. In the King's peripheral vision it was like a spot of blood, rolling slowly toward him. Angry at his mother, he reached out and smashed the bug into a pulp, then flung the starched cloth out the window into the bushes. "What do you make of the giant vegetable growth down in Damp Meadows?" he asked, to change the subject. "If you stand here and strain just a bit, you can see a leafy sort of tasseling leaning against the sky. Do you know, the top is completely lost in the clouds?"

"I don't strain for anything," said the Queen Mother. "Unseemly."

Thanks, perhaps, to his sizeable and nourishing meal, Jack the Greater was lighter on his feet than usual. A good thing, too. He needed the speed and all the strength he could muster. Swinging with one hand he scrambled down the stalk. His other arm was folded like a clamp across the breast and neck of the angry goose. Jack's leggings were bloody and shredded; the bird had a capable beak, able to scissor, tweak, pinch, and poke. Jack flung the bird on the ground, half hoping he might brain her, reduce her to a feathery factory specializing in golden eggs, a factory without an attitude. But the bird sprang up like a splash of white venom, lunging and lunging; Jack had to retreat to the cottage. He availed himself of a savory cassoulet bubbling away in the pot while the goose honked her imprecations and fouled the footpath leading toward the mighty base of the stalk.

But after a while she found a damp heap of old moldery straw in a corner of the yard, and by the time evening arrived she had delivered herself of several hours' worth of muttered curses as well as a single luminous egg of gold, sitting in its floppy translucent sac. The goose rubbed the goo off her tail-feathers, ate a few ladybugs malingering about the place, and when she wandered off to take the air, Jack took the egg.

It slid easily enough out of its sacking, which was no more than a kind of loose net. He weighed it in his hands. You'd have guessed an army of Doytchish jewelers had spent weeks polishing it with chamois cloths. Jack, not much given to fancifulness, leaned in and looked at how the curved surface of the egg distorted the reflections. If he leaned his forehead nearer, he could see himself with a much more prominent brow, bespeaking a lofty mind; if he cocked his head back and looked down through slitted eyes, his stub nose took on a patrician slope, his weak chin a noble prominence. The light of the evening sun, breaking through the shifting leaves of the stalk, caught on the egg, making brazen embers of his eyes. They looked like the eyes of a fellow who had ideas.

And maybe his forays abroad were expanding his horizons, as forays were said to do. For Jack the Greater had an idea, suddenly. If the goose could be cozened into performing this simple task on a daily basis, Jack could pay backtaxes.

With a strong tendril of beanstalk Jack made a necklace for the goose, and tethered her to the handle of the magic cooking pot. Then, a golden egg in each pocket threatening to pull his tattered trousers right off his slender hips, he set off to the City. What would his horrible mother say, to learn that her ne'er-do-well son had solved the family budget problems!

At the office of the Tax Collector tongues were silenced, doors were opened, and Jack was ushered deep into sumptuous interior rooms of the sort he had never glimpsed before. When summoned, the Chancellor of the Exchequeur came running from his ablutions with his buttons incompletely fastened. He paused and gaped at the egg of gold. In the silence of the Chancellor's reverence, Jack the Greater heard the town criers broadcasting news of the arrest of his mother and brother.

He arranged with the first egg to pay all outstanding debts to every government office. With the second he paid the bail on his relatives, and when the family was reunited at home, enjoying a smart little scupper of champagne followed by a pasta dish steaming with Parmeshanee and the most rare and precious lake oysters, Jack the Greater told them tales of his adventures in the Afterlife.

Then, for a time, was Filthy Tilda reborn as La Tilda. The goose obligingly brought forth another golden egg every few days. Within a week the family members were arguing over whether to shift their domicile, and if so, to which toney address. La Tilda favored a tall townhouse on one of the city's more prestigious squares, where in elegant gowns she could be seen sweeping in and out of the doorway. Jack the Greater, eyeing the beanstalk, wanted to be someplace out of its shadow, away from the crush of rotting vegetation should it ever begin to fall of its own weight. He considered the highlands, the Cobalt Coast, the Herring Isles. But Jack the Lesser said he would miss his ladybug friends, especially Karl, Albert, and Sigmund, with whom he pretended to have long philosophical discussions.

For scut work, La Tilda hired a local maiden named Rindabella and renamed her Rotten Ronda.

* * *

The King, as expected, won first place in the Amateur Singing Competition.

"Divine!" said some.

"Captivating!" said others.

"Sounded like a cow in an abattoir," said La Tilda.

"Shh!" said those around her.

"I'm not indulging in poetic nastiness," said La Tilda. "How many of you have ever escorted a cow to the abattoir? They make a certain *noise*. Don't credit me with rudeness. I'm merely making an informed comparison."

But she made it loudly enough that news of her opinion reached the King's ears, as well as his mother's. The King blushed and didn't comment. The Queen Mother tried to control a smirk, but failed.

"Money does that to one, lifts the muddy out of the gutter and plants them in your parlor," she said. "Isn't the Crown rapidly going bankrupt, Bedwad? Perhaps you're not taxing this La Tilda enough."

Jack the Greater wasn't as great as all *that*, thought Rotten Ronda, looking fondly at the lump in the hay next to her. Wonder how his brother would be? Wonder how they would be together?

The goose waddled over and deposited an egg in Rotten Ronda's lap. She would have pocketed it, had she been wearing clothes with pockets; she would have tucked it into her bosom had her bosom not been liberated from its binding. So as Jack the Greater snored off his little death, she kicked the egg under the straw for retrieval later on. Then she lay back and closed her eyes, the better to enjoy the tickling perambulations of three ladybugs who were out for a stroll on her left breast.

Through a crack in the boards, Jack the Lesser watched with immodest jealousy. That his ladybugs should take such license! What on earth were they up to? Well, they were up to the nipple, and the nipple was up to something, too. He looked away.

When Rotten Ronda and La Tilda, woman to woman, exchanged words about the relative crudeness of the Jacks, they both laughed with the soft gusto reserved for connoisseurs. Then La Tilda fired Ronda for not knowing her station.

"Fie on you," said Ronda. "Fie, fie, fie."

Jack the Lesser watched her pack up what passed for a reticule—a fallen leaf from the beanstalk twined round three times with a good stout vine runner—and then he watched her leave. She did not look back. "Good-bye," he called. The ladybugs tried to distract him from his sorrow by doing a little dance. "Oh, stop it," said Jack the Lesser. "I'm not in the mood."

Moses, Bathsheba, and Arthur C. Clarke continued to do something approximating a conga line. Or perhaps they were coming down with a virus.

Ronda told the Queen Mother, "My name is Rindabella of Damp Meadows. I know some things you should know."

"Bedwad, stop that caterwauling and come here," snapped his mother.

"If you're trying to marry me off to that foul creature, I'm not interested," he replied, not looking up from his music sheets.

"He's hopeless as well as rude," said the Queen Mother.

"He's a king," said Ronda, and shrugged her shoulders. She took out the golden egg. "There's more where this came from."

"What an unusual talent," said the Queen Mother. "Bedwad, get over here at once."

"I didn't produce it," said Ronda, and then kicked herself. She'd just lost a possible invitation to join the the Royal Family through the financial plan called matrimony. "But I know where they can be had."

"For what?"

"For a price."

"Like your freedom and your life?" said the Queen Mother. "Otherwise it's the dungeon, the guillotine, various slow-working poisons that induce pain in your limbs even after they've been severed from your torso. Think it over."

"Sounds like a fair deal," said Ronda, sighing. "There's a goose, you see."

Lonely for a thrill, and being uninterested in the wispy lisping maidens his mother was busy shopping for on his behalf, Jack the Greater made a final trip up the beanstalk. When he returned, carrying a harp under his arm, the harp was carrying on in fluting tones, rather too loud to be considered sweet. A contingent of soldiers at the base of the beanstalk was waiting to arrest him.

"What's the charge?" said Jack.

"Withholding payment of taxes!" said the Captain of the Guards.

La Tilda screamed, "That Rotten Ronda squealed about our goose! It's been impounded by the Treasury!"

"Ah, Ronda," said Jack the Greater, sighing. "You shouldn't have fired her, see?"

"She's a slut and a tramp! She's sold us out! I'll rip out her eyes when I see her! From this day forward I have no other foe!"

"Foe," sang the harp, a bit maliciously, it seemed. "Foe, foe, foe."

"Leave it to me," said Jack to his mother. "I'll bargain our freedom again by presenting this harp to the King as a token of our remorse and affection. Meanwhile, where's the moron gone?"

"He's taken his bugs to church for a blessing. He thinks they're about to commit mass suicide or something."

"Into the tumbrel with you," said the Captain of the Guards apologetically. The harp sang on.

Annoyed at his mother, the King accepted the golden harp in exchange for the freedom of La Tilda and her son. "We have nothing else to give you," said La Tilda. "We're back to mud." But she knew the pot that presented them with ample and deluxe victuals was still on the premises back home. Maybe they could start a tavern.

They were hardly at the wrought iron gates when they heard the harp begin to trill out songs of revolt, anthems of sedition. "Is that *La Marseillaise*?" asked La Tilda. "Mercy, it possesses a clear and a penetrating timbre, that harp. Good riddance to it."

The soldiers caught up with them before they'd even reached the house and imprisoned them again for inculcating treasonous musical literature in the harp they'd donated to the King.

"Don't be too worried," said Jack the Greater. "More trouble is on its way. There's a giant upstairs bound to be able to hear that noisy harp. He'll be down the stalk in a flash and then that feeble King won't know what's hit him."

The harp took a rest from time to time. In the intervals, Jack the Greater and La Tilda could hear the executioner sharpening the ax that would be used to cut off their heads.

"Do you think Jack the Lesser might rescue us?" said La Tilda, picking a ladybug off her shoulder and crushing it between her fingers.

"We lose our heads at four o'clock," said Jack the Greater.

He was hard at work, was Jack the Lesser.

"Now, friends," he said, "I know you're suffering from a sense of mass inferiority. The presence of this beanstalk in our midst has made you question your very stature in the universe. Some of you have become dissatisfied, and others, apathetic. But if we all work together we can effect great changes. Everyone line up and ring the stalk at my shoulder height. Come along, Eudora. Don't dawdle, Jane. You too, Winona. On the count of three."

As he counted three, so did the clock towers in the town. There was an hour left before the beheading of his closest kin. "Now, chew as if your lives depended on it," he said. And seventy-four ladybugs set to work, gnawing through the beanstalk. The sound was something like *fum fum, fum fum*.

At five minutes to four the executioner split the hair of a chihuahua with the tip of his ax. The two segments peeled apart beautifully, with rococo balance and symmetry.

"Ready," said the executioner.

"Ready," said the Captain of the Guards. "I regret all this business, you know."

"This land is your land," sang the harp. It had been hidden in the highest tower but the more anyone tried to suppress its sound, the louder it got. From way up there it sounded something like a muezzin. Jack the Greater, being brought out of the cell into the ravishing sunlight, thought glumly that the giant might be able to hear the noise that much the better. But the giant had big thick limbs and he was not much of a self-starter, like Jack the Lesser. It might take a month before the noise penetrated the giant's thick skull and a thought resulted: I could climb down the beanstalk and get my harp back, and my goose and my pot while I was about it.

"Any last wishes?" asked the Captain of the Guard.

"I should like Bedwad the King to watch the crime he is about to commit upon my person," said La Tilda. "Also a glass of Dom Basilisk, chilled, with bitters."

"A kiss from Rotten Ronda," said Jack the Greater. "And everyone watching. I'll show you how to grow a stalk, you toadies."

"Requests denied," said the Captain. "Mount the scaffolding, please."

They did. The clouds overhead busied themselves with other matters, to turn the sun's attention elsewhere, or so Bedwad's poetic fancy put it, for he *was* actually watching from behind the drapes in his room. But it wasn't the clouds, really; it was the huge canopy of green leaves that hung over much of the land now, like a grapevine hanging from an invisible trellis. The leaves shook and the sound of their huge flanks against each other was like the voice of avalanches a valley or two over.

"Fee, fie, foe, fum," said God.

"I'm having a religious experience, first time in my life," said La Tilda. "Imagine. Well I suppose it's to be expected, my deathbed and all. Yes, God?"

"Fee, fie, foe, fum," said God.

"I know that voice," said Jack the Greater. "Where have I heard that voice before?"

"Fee, fie, foe, fum," said God.

"Would make a catchy lyric," said King Bedwad of King-land.

"Fee, fie, foe, fum," said God.

"If that's God, He's remarkably one-note about it," said the Queen Mother.

"Fee, fie, foe, fum," said God.

"I like a God with a big voice," said Rotten Ronda, rubbing herself here and there.

"Fee, fie, foe, fum," said God.

"I like a girl who knows what she likes," said the Captain of the Guard, noticing Rotten Ronda for the first time, and smiling at her.

"Fee, fie, foe, fum," said God.

"I smell the blood of a Kinglishman!" screeched out the Harp. "You fools, run for your lives! Scram, skedaddle, head for the hills! It's Big Daddy, and he's no jolly green giant!"

"Fee, fie, foe, fum," said God, and the ladybugs completed their task as the clocks in the church towers struck four.

Down came the beanstalk, with a sound as of a meteor rucking up angel's acres of starry meadow. Jack the Lesser looked up and saw the world turn green, and stood back as the stalk danced on its severed stem, and begin to slip sideways.

"I did what I could, Melba," he said to a ladybug on his nose.

The giant died in the crash, of course, and it took more than a year for the Comrades of Justice to clear away the rotten vegetation. Tourism shrank to an all-time low that year, and the bodies of the King and his Mother were burned in a pyre of peapods.

The singing harp was thrown to the bottom of the sea, where, when the tide was low, it could sometimes be heard chortling chanties or bawdy barroom songs.

By executive fiat of the Prime Executor of State, at the wedding of La Ronda and the Captain the goose that laid the golden eggs was served in a caperberry aspic. The meat of the fowl was stringy and dry and there wasn't enough to go around.

As for the brothers Jack, they remained in the house with their mother. The magic pot refused to work for its living and would not serve up meals to the newly forming middle class eager to spend disposable income in restaurants. But La Tilda and her boys did not go hungry, and that was something. They always took a special pleasure when the pot decided to surprise them with heaping slabs of succulent goose in caperberry aspic.

The various golden eggs remained in the hands of scoundrels who had lifted them from the Treasury on the day that the Crown collapsed and the People's Republic of Kingland was formed. No one wanted to admit to having taken part in

the looting and the pillage of the Palace, so harboring the egg
as a family heirloom became a very private badge of honor.

Many years later, after silent weeks dawdling on her deathbed, La Tilda sat up and told her sons with fiery clarity, "Fee,
fie, foe, fum. I have had my vision. The view of the other side
is clear to me now. Very soon the first of those golden eggs is
going to hatch. And when it does. . . ."

But she fell back on the sacking that made for her head a
rough pillow, and her lads, greater and lesser, had to wait for
fate to happen, just like the rest of us.

GREGORY MAGUIRE is the author of several novels for adults, including *Wicked: The Life and Times of the Wicked Witch of the West, Confessions of an Ugly Stepsister,* and *Lost.* He has written more than a dozen novels for children, among them the popular Hamlet Chronicles series. A resident of Massachusetts, Mr. Maguire teaches creative writing and lectures as a critic of children's literature across the nation.

Author's Note:

The appetite to retell stories, to ring changes on them, is a huge and unslakable one. On either side of any story—including the personal narrative of one's life—looms the uncharted terrain of the unknown. I think that writers revisit favorite material and embellish what the canonical text has reported in order to distract themselves from that urge to see on either side of their own blinkered existence, an urge that can never be satisfied.

Of the story about Jack and the Beanstalk, what always interested me as a child was the notion of how our world would look from the clouds. With such a vantage point—such a camera angle—how much could be seen, how much more could be understood, than we crawling ladybugs on the ground might ever know! The giant, in a sense, had the place usually reserved for an omniscient narrator. From his cloudy terraces he might see and understand everything. Sadly, the giant in the original tale was not known for his curiosity, so he took no pleasure from his vantage point. When I began to write "Fee, Fie, Foe, et Cetera," I had thought I might take the giant's point of view. But in fact, omniscient narration takes a little fun out of telling a story. If the giant, with his god's-eye view, can't figure out what is going on because he's too dull to notice or care, perhaps the writer should stay down and crawl with his subjects, too, and find out moment by moment, paragraph by paragraph, how things turn out.

As with my novels *Wicked* and *Confessions of an Ugly Stepsister,* I tried to add to the story of Jack and the Beanstalk without contradicting any of the sequence or known characteristics of the original characters. I prefer to add and to embellish rather than to change the template.

JOSHUA TREE

ᔌ

EMMA BULL

MY NAME IS Tabetha Sikorsky. Yes, that's usually spelled "Tabitha," but spelling has never been my mom's hot subject. I'm not sure what my dad's hot subject is, but I hope it's wood shop, since he's now living in Phoenix nailing roofing on tract houses.

That beats the hell out of being a manicurist in the middle of the desert in the most horrible town in the world. Which is what my mom is. Which makes me the daughter of a manicurist in the middle of, etc., etc. No comment on where that falls on the beats-the-hell scale.

I'm sixteen. The school district thinks I'm seventeen (when they think of me), because my mother faked my birth certificate to get me into kindergarten when I was four. Kindergarten is free day care. It wasn't till third grade that I realized my real age wasn't a secret of Defense Department proportions, and Mom and I wouldn't go to jail if it came out that she'd forged my birth certificate. But it was still a while before I stopped getting dizzy and sick to my stomach every time someone asked, "And how old are you, sweetie?"

I don't want anyone to think my mom doesn't love me. I've seen her with people she's said "I love you" to, and I figure she does a better job of loving me than she does with most of them. She just has a short attention span. I bet I was 24/7 interesting when I was the new Cabbage Patch baby, but now I'm only intermittently riveting. I try not to use it up.

We live in a town that wouldn't exist if it weren't for the Marine base. They put military bases in the middle of nowhere because real towns wouldn't take that crap. In our case, they put the base in the center of hundreds of miles of desert and let a town happen around it, like a parasite. That's us: Tapewormville.

If you're just driving through, it probably looks like a thriving little burg. Look! They've got a 7-Eleven *and* a Circle K! If you stay, you have time to notice that the successful businesses deal in the following: barbering (there are more MARINE HAIRCUTS signs in town than stop signs) liquor (drink here, or take-out); fast food (pizza delivery is big); strippers; and auto body shops. The body shops are because, after coming into town to drink and watch girls take off their tops, the Maggots try to drive back to the base. It's not just an economy, it's a whole ecosystem.

Not that the only people on base are the Maggots. The officers are mostly older, married with kids, even. Even Marines grow up eventually. Still, it's like living in an occupied country. I read someplace that people in Guam want the U.S. military base out of there, but they're afraid the economy would tank. Well, here we are: Guam with no ocean.

Normal towns have plenty of laundromats and supermarkets and clothing stores and stuff. Not base towns. The base has its own washing machines. It has a mess hall and a commissary. Uniforms come with the gig. And for everything else, like videos and cigarettes and magazines that aren't *Soap Opera Digest,* there's the PX. So that leaves the townies' needs, which can be met by one scabby Wal-Mart twenty miles away.

It's probably pretty clear that I'm not a base kid. I was born a townie, and I'm scared shitless that I'll die one. I'm more scared of that than car wrecks, earthquakes, or AIDS. This is the kind of town you can't possibly stay in all your life. So why are there so many people here who've done exactly that?

That's the real reason the town hates the base. On base, people get reassigned, moved around, resign their commissions.

They can leave.

Which raises an interesting question: To get out of this town, do I have to join the Marines?

I'm writing this because Ms. Grammercy gave us an over-the-weekend assignment for Junior English: write our autobiographies. She had to explain to the back of the room what "autobiography" means. Okay, that's not fair. I already knew, and Maryanne Krassner probably knew, because she reads them if they're by actors. But I could see the rest of the townies in the back two rows hearing "autobiography" and thinking, "Cars?"

I thought it was a bullshit assignment. We're in high school. How much autobiography are we supposed to have? But I've sort of gotten into it.

To encourage our creativity (she actually said that) Ms. G. gave us a list of questions we could start with. Here they are:

1. What is your name?
2. How old are you?
3. Who are your parents? What do they do?
4. Do you have brothers or sisters?
5. Where were you born? What is your hometown like?
6. What career do you want to pursue?
7. What is your favorite kind of music?
8. What person has had the most influence on your life?
9. What problem in the world is most important to you?

Here's what I wrote to turn in:

> My name is Tabetha Sikorsky. I'm seventeen years old. My mother's name is Cheryl and she's a manicurist. My father's name is Arthur and he does construction in Phoenix. My mother and father are divorced. I don't have any brothers or sisters. I was born here. It's small but okay. I would like a career at a store maybe a record store. My favorite music is Eminem. The person who had the most influence on my life was Ms. Keating my 3rd grade teacher because she was smart and still pretty. I think the problem in the world that's most important to me is pollution.

I think it's a masterpiece. Especially considering what I had to work with.

I picked Eminem from an unbiased study of the T-shirts in Mr. Kuyper's geography class. Two Jennifer Lopez, one U-2, two Bone Thugs 'n' Harmony, three Led Zeppelin (and isn't that sad?), four Eminem. The Ms. Keating thing I just thought was funny. As for the world problem—oh, excuse me, "the problem in the world"—how am I supposed to pick one? Global warming, poverty, war, torture, nuclear waste disposal, the whole damn government, everybody else's government. I was sitting next to the trash can, and I had an inch left before the margin, so I settled on "pollution." If you cross the margin lines on your notebook paper, Ms. G. takes points off. It's as if we're figure skaters and she's the Russian judge.

I take it back about not being able to write your autobiography at sixteen/seventeen. I just realized I know everything that will happen in Ms. G.'s class on Monday. I'll pass my homework over Luis Perez's shoulder, and he'll make a big deal of reading it and laughing before he passes it up. (I was going to write that I wanted a career as an exotic dancer, but then I remembered Luis. He stifled my creativity.) Piper Amendola will toss back her Pantene Pro-V hair and hand in twenty typed pages with the comment that she found the assignment "really useful and interesting." Ms. G. will tell the front of the room that they're all clever and going to heaven or college, whichever comes first, and the back of the room that we don't seem to be trying.

And if I know what will happen Monday, why shouldn't I know what will happen next month, in ten years everything right up to when I die? I can write my whole life story now. But some things are too big a waste of time even for me.

Monday went as predicted, except I forgot to mention the hangover from Janelle's birthday party. I knew I'd have one; I just forgot to mention it.

The party Janelle told her stepmom about was on Saturday. But Sunday we went over to Little Mike's rec room for the real thing.

When I was a kid, and I thought about what I'd have when I got my own place, it looked a lot like Little Mike's. It's embarrassing to write that. Black-light posters, for godsake. A couple crisscross strings of Christmas lights "for atmosphere" (of what? Trailer-park holiday cheer?). A black vinyl couch that makes fart sounds when you move around on it, no matter what you're wearing. A red shag carpet that smells like dog pee when you're close enough—like when you sit on the floor (I only did it once). And the incense, of course. "African Love." I think he bought it at a truck stop.

But Mike's okay. He's always up for hosting a party, as long as you give him money for the beer. If you want pot, though, you have to bring your own. He doesn't want to violate his parole. I don't have the heart to tell him that supplying alcohol to minors has got that covered already.

I really thought I'd get through Sunday night without a crappy moment. TLC was playing loud on Mike's stereo, my third beer was in my hand, Janelle was sitting beside me singing along, Barb and Nina were dancing and pretending they didn't notice the guys watching them.

Then suddenly, boom. Everything sucked. I have no idea what set it off. Nina was shaking her big butt and her big boobs, and I could tell that in her head she looked like Lisa "Left Eye." But she really just looked sloppy and sad. Barb's water bra bounced up and down, and the guys watched like the young males in the herd watch the female who's going into heat, planning to be first with the most when she's ready (in this case, after one more beer).

Suddenly everyone in the room seemed to be on the fast track to pregnancy, jail, or a seasonal job on the line at a fruit packing plant. Including me.

I looked at Janelle, and she wasn't singing along anymore. For a second I thought maybe she felt it, too. The crappy mood almost lifted. Then I realized what was actually up with her face, and helped her outside to puke.

Little Mike's place is at the edge of town. His backyard is basically miles of sand, rocks, and mesquite. There's even a Joshua tree right behind the garage, a pretty sickly-looking one (though how can you tell with Joshua trees?) with its two branches twisted like rejects from a grade-school pipe-cleaner project.

I held Janelle's hair out of her face while she did the deed. Janelle never just throws up and gets on with her life. It's a big production number that goes on forever. The motion sensor light over the back door had turned off by the time she got serious about it.

Janelle sounds like she's dying when she pukes, so I tried to distract myself, but the desert in the dark doesn't provide much material. I pretended the tree was a psycho killer with two heads sneaking up on a houseful of naughty, naughty teenagers. A psycho killer with shaggy, spiky hair. Stupid hair. Stupid psycho killer, making your big move on a bad hair day. Don't you want your picture in the paper?

Janelle and I became best friends in fifth grade. Actually, we became twins. I stole Mom's paring knife, and we cut our thumbs and pressed them together in a sacred ritual in Janelle's garage. We wore the same clothes, loved the same bands, crushed on the same TV stars, had the same opinions—I bet it drove everyone nuts.

We recruited Barb and Nina to the posse the next year. It was girl heaven. Sleepovers at my house, when my mom would give us manicures at the kitchen table. Parties at Nina's, whose dad works in the bakery at Costco. Afternoons riding Barb's uncle's horses. Saturdays when we'd dress up in clothes Janelle's stepmom was giving away and pretend we were making a music video.

It was at Nina's quinceañera that I first made a joke that Janelle, Barb, and Nina didn't get. It didn't happen again for a while, but that was the first one.

I handed Janelle a couple of tissues and let her swish her mouth out with my beer (then let her keep the bottle). "Thanks, Beth," she said, "you are the best friend ever. I just really love you."

I don't know why, but the puker/hair-holder relationship generates these feelings of intimacy. It wears off in about an hour, or sooner if you screw it up.

"Do you ever think that growing up isn't as good as it was supposed to be?" I said.

Our moving around had turned the light back on, so we could even see each other. Her face was still blotchy and pale, and the dark liner around her lips was smeared. "What?" she said.

"When we were little kids, it just felt like we were on this big adventure. Now it's like we're on a guided tour of a landfill. Do you know what I mean?"

She frowned. "If you don't want to be at my party, you don't have to stay."

"It's not the party! But don't you ever feel like there's something really important out there, that we aren't getting?" You'd think I'd have learned to cut my losses by now.

"Oh, God, Beth, I get enough Jesus crap from my step-mom." She took a big swallow of beer and said, "I'm going back in."

Of course, I did, too. Everything was swell. I had another beer, and we were all laughing and happy. Wahoo.

Here's what I think I'm having trouble with: this *is* what happiness is. When I was a kid, I thought I'd just get happier and happier as I got older, and have more things to be happy about. I based this theory on observation of select adults. The problem with my results is that I couldn't tell the difference then between happy and fake-happy. Now I know you pretend to be just frigging ecstatic over everything, maybe because you're so glad it's not worse. Pleased to meet you! means, Thank God you're not a cop! or, I love this car! means, At least it's not a '78 Datsun with bald tires and bad hoses!

But sometimes I can still have these moments of total happiness. And I feel as if every time I pretend to be happy, I'm scaring that real happiness off.

I rode my bike home from the party. Randy Nesterhoff offered me a ride, but the car smelled like Southern Comfort from six feet away. I'm stupid, but at least I'm selective about it.

I don't know why I'm still writing this shit down. If I wanted to keep a diary, this wouldn't be the way I'd do it. And for sure no one is ever going to see this. Unlike the master-piece version, which I turned in Monday morning. (Got it back today. C–, with my carefully omitted commas written in, in red. Got to give Ms. G. something to do.)

Maybe what I'm doing, writing this, is what Piper's crew do when they're crammed in front of the girls' room mirror before first period (and just incidentally, hogging the sinks). "Eeuw, is that a zit?" "Is my hair too straight?" "I just got this lip gloss, is it, like, okay?" I'm holding up these words to my face so I can check myself out. Looking for normal in there somewhere, or even a good sort of abnormal.

Piper and Co. take that whole "the few, the proud" thing pretty seriously—their folks are officers, so they're sweetly condescending to the base kids whose fathers are mere grunts, and treat the townies the way the Spanish missionaries treated the Indians. Make yourselves useful and don't talk back, or we'll shoot you. I'm pleased to say that Piper hasn't once figured out a way I can be useful to her.

Bigots are people who say, "I don't hate all [fill in the blank] people. Why, some of my best friends are [ditto]." I'm proud to say I'm not a bigot. None of my friends are kids from the base.

As far as I know, the only good thing that ever came off that base was Steve. Mom dated him ("dated" meaning "slept with") for nine months, when I was twelve/thirteen. He didn't treat me like an adult, exactly. It was more that I was a real person to him, not someone he had to impress on the way to impressing Mom. He figured out that I really wanted a mountain bike, and gave it to me for my birthday.

Then he got transferred. I didn't find out for almost a year that he asked Mom to marry him when it happened. He wanted to take us with him.

Obviously, we didn't go. Mom had a huge fight with him instead. Don't ask me to explain that.

He's in Saudi Arabia now. Another desert.

I think sometimes I should do with Piper what the Indians did with the missionaries. Be polite but stupid to her face, and sabotage the hell out of her when she's not looking. But I can't keep my mouth shut. Today she and Kristin Gold and Amber Janeke were hanging around Piper's locker, which is annoyingly close to mine. I passed them on my way to get my geography book, and Piper said, "Do you smell something?" Smothered laughter from Kristen and Amber.

So I stopped. "Probably," I said. "Your locker door's open."

It took her a second to get it. By that time I had my locker open and my book out. (Being fast on your locker combination is a survival skill.) I smiled at her, slammed the door, and hauled it for class. I was so proud of that one that I raised my hand when Mr. Kuyper asked where Mongolia is. Adrenaline is a dangerous drug.

And of course, I came back after class and found the entire contents of my locker on the hall floor. Note to self: check door after slamming to ensure latching has occurred.

There are at least two sets of Rules for Life, as far as I can tell. There are the ones that get you picked up by the cops or taken to the assistant principal's office if you break them: Don't leave school grounds, don't spray paint stop signs, don't drink, don't drop firecrackers in the toilets.

But there's a different set that you really can't break if you don't want your life to suck relentlessly. At the head of the list, Rule Number One: Don't get noticed. As long as you stay exactly the person everyone thinks you're supposed to be, you're

fine. Piper can answer questions and get A's on homework because that's who she's supposed to be. I'm supposed to be
somcone else. Usually I have that person nailed. But sometimes I lose perspective and do something inconsistent.

Then I have to put my crap back in my locker, get my gym
shoes out of the toilet, prove to Janelle that I'm not dissing
her party, and give the wrong answer to a question I shouldn't
have stuck my hand in the air over anyway. But that's fair.
High school exists to teach you the rules, and I figure I'm getting a solid B average.

Ring ring! Life changes. How can you not love telephones?
For better or worse, *ring ring!* and presto, there's something
different in your ear from what you were doing or thinking a
second ago. Even if it's about replacement windows or something.

But it might not be. What if it's NASA, and they want you to
know the shuttle is making an emergency landing, and it looks
as if touchdown is going to be somewhere around your bathtub, and you might want to evacuate your neighborhood?

Raves are not on the list of approved uses for national monu-
ments, I bet. But it's tough to police a national monument
that's hundreds of thousands of acres wide, full of blind
canyons and dry washes. What makes Joshua Tree a monument, anyway, like the Lincoln Memorial? And why is it a national monument *and* a national park? Who decides this stuff?

Anyway, now Saturday night is spoken for.

Mom answered the phone, so after I hung up, she had to
know who it was. It's hard to explain a phone call from a
stranger who asks for you by name, then only has fifteen sec-

onds of things to say. I told her it was the library, and a book I'd reserved was in. Thank god she has no idea when the library closes.

Mom shares the school district's expectations for her daughter. I think that's because the school district is her most dependable source of information on me. We aren't home together much. It makes the library excuse risky, though, since she has no idea how much I read, and based on my grades, I shouldn't know when the library's open, either.

"What book?" she asked.

I was in the middle of dialing Bob Esquivel. I turned the phone off and tried to look dazed while I figured out an answer.

I guess Mom and I really haven't seen much of each other lately, because I was surprised at how tired she looks. There are two deep lines between her eyebrows and this heaviness around the corners of her mouth, as if she's been having a bad day for the last 365. When I was really little and Dad still lived with us, she had cheerleader hair, blonde and thick and long. When people talk about hair like ripe wheat, I figure that's what they mean. Now her hair looks more like dry grass before the fall wildfires, the life sucked out.

"Just a book for school," I said, then, thinking of Mr. Kuyper, "about China."

"Don't they have the right books in the school library? You'd think they'd have what the teachers are teaching, for godsake."

"It's not like you're paying extra, Mom. The library's free."

"Nothing's free. Those books cost tax money."

What do you say to that? Better books than a bomber?

Maybe I looked a little too stupid, because she stomped out to the kitchen.

She cheered up after she found out there was lasagna in the fridge. It's weird—cooking is the only thing I'm supposed to do well that I'm actually good at.

And I cheered up because Bob was home and up for Saturday night.

I don't know how they do these things in cities, but out here, if you want to find the party, it helps to have a global positioning system. Seriously. Bob Esquivel's the only other person in town I know who likes to rave. He has a GPS and a dirt bike, and a profile like Keanu Reeves. He graduated last year, and the high school halls are dark and drab since then. Okay, they were dark and drab before that, but for some of us, birds sang and the ceiling rained flowers if he met our eyes as we passed on the way to class. The "us" did not include Janelle, Nina, and Barb, who thought his hair was too long.

Raving is one of the things I don't have in common with those guys. The first rave I ever went to, Janelle went, too. After fifteen minutes, I was bouncy and breathless and felt like a little kid who'd just discovered a fully-equipped secret fort. Janelle hated the music, thought all the people were freaks, and was afraid to touch anything for fear of getting AIDS or TB. Janelle believes everything she reads on the Internet.

Given that I'm not exactly the life of the party at parties, I suppose it's weird that I'd drag my ass into the desert in the dark to hear some DJ spin for a bunch of X-heads wearing glow-necklaces.

Well, surprise.

The way to get through normal life is to pretend it isn't getting to you. If you let on that you're hurt, the other animals will turn on you and tear you to pieces. Don't attract the attention of predators.

But in the dark in the desert, with a pile of speakers the size of our house kicking out the groove, and everyone around me faceless and trancing, it's different. Then I can scream loud as I want, and sometimes everyone around me does, too, as if for once I'm not the only one who wants to scream. I can stamp as if everything I hate is down there in the dirt and I can smash it to bits. I can jump up and down and flap my arms like a nut, just because maybe the DJ will see the top of my head and then I can imagine the groove is just for me.

Most of all, when I'm out there banging up against dozens of strangers and sharing their sweat, I'm alone. Yes, alone. So I'm safe. I'm free.

I should have mentioned the park earlier. I usually think of this place as being divided into two cultures, the base and the townies. But it's really three parts, and the third one is the park. That's a whole different culture.

There's the rangers, who live here but not quite *here*—I don't know how to explain it. Then there are day visitors, campers, backpackers, rock climbers, driving through town on Highway 62 in shiny SUVs and rental cars. Lots of Eddie Bauer and Northface logos on clothes, lots of bright-colored nylon gear. They stop for breakfast at the Lucky Lizard or La Boule (the only places in town with real coffee, and I'm counting our house) and fill 'er up with premium, but that's it for their contact with the other two cultures.

If this were the Middle Ages, we'd be the peasants, and the Marine base would be the landowners. The park would be the Church, with its own walls and special rules, and the monks being contemplative in their monastery. With pilgrims in really nice wagons.

The Marines ship people out, the tourists come and leave. But the peasants are forever. The only escape the park offers is the occasional rave, and that's like getting drunk—it's temporary.

It's a really good temporary, though.

How can you do something so crappy to your kid as to move her to a new school in spring of junior year? I guess the Marines don't exactly ask first, but wasn't there an aunt she could have stayed with?

Naturally, Ms. G. stood her up in front of the class and introduced her, as if this were third grade. I don't remember her name—I was too busy feeling sorry for her, and being mad at myself for wasting time feeling sorry for her.

She looked like David Bowie dressed up like Audrey Hepburn. Little black sheath dress, bangle bracelets, big sunglasses pushed up into her hair, which was white-blonde and short and stuck up. Fishnet stockings (tramp!) and Converse hi-tops (weirdo!). She looked out over the rest of us with these huge round brown eyes, like a deer who has no idea that that thing in your hands is a shotgun.

Sure enough, when the bell rang, Randy Nesterhoff sauntered up to where New Girl was stuffing her books into the biggest purse in the world. "Man, you don't have any tits at all, do you?" he said. His buddies snickered behind him.

She looked up and kind of blinked her eyes wider—it's not easy to describe. "Neither do you," she said.

"Yeah, well, I'm a *guy*."

Her eyebrows went up. "You are?" She shouldered the monster purse and walked out. Randy's crew laughed and Randy turned purple.

Me, I was revising my opinions about deer.

The second incident, at lunch, was even more interesting. Amber and Piper had set up the ballot box for Junior Formal king and queen at the end of the cafeteria line, so there was no dodging it.

"Did you vote yet, Beth?" Amber cooed as I went by with my tray. The way she asked made it a joke. Only not funny.

"You should vote for yourself," Piper added. "Then at least you'd get a vote."

Somebody behind me said, "What was your name again? Piper?"

I had to turn and look. It was New Girl.

Piper opened her mouth, but New Girl finished, "No, I must have misheard. I mean, you're a girl, not a light plane."

For a second, I adored New Girl. Then she turned to me and said, "And you don't look like a Beth."

It's one thing to step into the searchlight yourself. Dragging someone else in with you is rude. "My parents couldn't spell 'Goddess,'" I said, and bolted for the table where Janelle and Barb were sitting.

They asked me about New Girl. God knows, they couldn't help but notice her. I just said she was in my English class.

But I thought about it for a long time. New Girl is an equal-opportunity insulter: Randy the townie and Piper the officer's brat both got a faceful. She doesn't care if she sticks out like the proverbial thumb, and she has no clue about the class structure.

Obviously, Dead Chick Walking.

I don't know how to tell this. I don't even know if it happened. But if it didn't happen, what did?

I'm really careful about what I drink at a rave. Beer out of a bottle, watch it being opened, then don't let the bottle out of my sight. Keg beer, watch the cup all the way from the tap to my hand, and then don't let the cup out of my sight. Never hard liquor, because the bottle stays open too long. What did I say earlier about only being selectively stupid? You never know when somebody'll decide to spring enlightenment on you unannounced.

I have to cover that because that's the first thing you'd think—it's still what I think, except I know it can't be true. Unless I drank so much that I don't remember being stupid— eating a brownie or drinking out of someone's canteen. But I wouldn't do that. I'm always careful.

Okay, this is making me cry. And the tears really sting, which makes me feel sorry for myself, so I want to cry even more. Stupid, stupid, stupid. But I feel like I was abducted by aliens or something, as if there was a piece of my life when I lay bare-assed under a big light and everyone stared at me *only I can't remember it*. Instead there's this thing I do remember that can't have happened.

Must not be crying next time Mom comes in.

Mom stayed home from work to take care of me. She hasn't done that since I was in third grade. She's taking the emergency room nurse's instructions pretty seriously. She pops in to check the Gatorade level in my glass, and no matter how much I've drunk, she makes me drink more, and then she refills it. You'd think I'd be peeing like a horse. Shows how dried-out I am.

She came in when I was writing. I told her this was homework. That was the first time she sounded pissed off since it happened. She said, "The school won't expect you to do your damn homework with your brains cooked out." I remember it exactly because I liked the image. My skull like a busted pressure cooker, and all my nutritious brains coming out like steam.

I wouldn't hurt as much if I'd lie still, but if I don't write this, I think it instead, and it goes round and round until it's a little brain tornado. At least if I write it down, it seems like it goes in a straight line. And on one of these Gatorade runs, Mom will tell me to quit or else, so I want to do as much as I can before then.

She was so scared in the emergency room.

It was a great party Until. Riding there with my arms around Bob's waist—I feel stupid about it now, but I thought, Tonight he'll see me dancing, and he'll be really into me. We'll dance together like Belle and the Beast, alone in the desert and as the sun comes up he'll kiss me. It makes me feel crappy just to write it, but I have to.

We got to the last set of coordinates, which turned out to be an alley between two long rockpiles, and followed the line of tiki torches stuck in the rock cracks over our heads. At the end of the alley I could feel the space open up, as if there wasn't anything for my body's sonar to ping off of. The sky was like a black sequined dress—no moon, but all the stars in the universe, gathered to watch.

The party was marked off by a huge circle of torches ten feet high. Outside the circle, I couldn't see a thing. I knew there was a lot of *there* out in the dark, but I couldn't tell if the desert went up or down on either side, or just lay flat forever. The DJ stand was at one end of the circle, with its red work lights and secret movements—not whole people, just parts moving in and out of the light. There must have been a hundred people in the circle, being restless and noisy.

We stepped out of the alley and an organ chord swelled up from everywhere. The whole circle went dead quiet. It was like the party had been waiting for us.

Bob went to find the beer. I wanted to follow him, but that chord began to throb, right in time to my heart. I ran toward the torches. The chord turned into the intro to an old Prince song, with the DJ scratching it so it had a new rhythm. Then he let the song go.

I let me go. I was sweating like a hog in about a minute, when he started cross-fading between Prince and the Ramones. Someone near me started to laugh, as if they'd got a joke.

He spun up some Moby after that, and I danced till my legs felt wobbly. Then I found the kegs and got a big red plastic cup of beer. It was thin and acidy, but it was like cold lemonade after dancing. I chugged it.

I like remembering the beginning of the night. I just want to write about dancing and getting my buzz on, and the cool things I saw in the circle. I did see cool things, like the woman who'd glued rhinestones to her arms and chest and face in patterns until she was one shining diagram, and the guy who'd smeared the stuff inside the Cyalume Light Sticks on his hands and was drawing patterns in the dark as he danced. There were a bunch of people in masks made of leaves and feathers, dancing together, and when the torch-light shone in their eyes, it was like seeing a coyote watching you through the bushes. They were cool enough that I figured they'd come in from L.A.

I danced and drank until I didn't feel either cool or uncool. The point wasn't see-and-be-seen. The point was to be there, part of this mob in the dark. I felt as if I had to be there, or there'd be a break in the circuit, that the juice wouldn't flow. If I stopped dancing, there'd be a rolling blackout. If I stopped dancing, even the DJ wouldn't be able to mix. I was invisible, unnoticed, but connected and necessary.

But I did stop dancing, didn't I?

I went for beer—and there was Bob. He was shiny in the torchlight, and his shirt was unbuttoned. He looked like a big, sweaty romance novel cover. "Beth," he said. "You look way hot."

I pretty much stopped breathing. "So do you."

"Yeah." He grinned and flapped his shirt. He meant temperature-hot. I replayed the conversation—okay, then so did I.

"You know, I really like you," he added.

I was drinking beer. It slopped over my upper lip, down my chin, and onto my tank top. "I like you, too," I got out past the back of my hand as I wiped my face.

"I like that shirt. You should wear more clothes like that."

It was just a tank top. I wanted him to like me, not my clothes.

"You should wear it without a bra, though. If you wore tight clothes, guys would notice you more."

Okay, he'd found the Ecstasy. Sure he liked me—right then, he liked *everyone*. But maybe he liked me a little bit more. . . ?

"Hello, Goddess," said a voice off to my right. It was New Girl.

"Huh-uh," Bob said. "This is Beth."

New Girl shook her head. She looked even more deerlike in the dark, with her eyes black and shining. She'd stuck a line of sparkly bindi down her cheek below one eye, like tears. Her hair in the torches made her head look like a little moon. She had on a black sleeveless T-shirt with a glitter snake on it.

"You can't be a Beth. What's your real name?" she asked. She didn't look at Bob.

"Tabetha," I said.

"Excellent! The Goddess Tab, who dances in the desert to bring secrets to the surface!"

"Ooo-kay. Way too much X." I turned to get away and drink my beer. Inside my head I was yelling "Follow me!" at Bob. Instead, New Girl followed, and Bob trailed after.

"No X. I don't do that stuff. It's too embarrassing afterward," said New Girl. "It makes me tell people I can't stand that they're wonderful human beings."

My sentiments exactly, but I wasn't going to tell her so. "What the hell is your name?" I asked.

"Alice. The female incarnation of the Hanged Man from the tarot. A woman on a perilous quest of self-discovery down the rabbit hole of life."

I actually opened my mouth to blow her off when I realized that I was hearing the kind of thing that I think but never say. "Is it really Alice?"

"Uh-huh. Is it really Tabetha?"

"Yeah."

"Well, then we know each other's true names. And you know what that means."

And I actually did. Jesus, nobody else in town would, but I did. All those years of reading weird shit, and it finally seemed as if it had a point.

That's when Bob said, "You talk really strange. Either of you give blow jobs?"

I don't know what I was about to say or do before Bob's little conversation starter, but suddenly I was scared of whatever it was. Real terror, like I'd almost walked in front of a speeding car and barely jumped back in time. I don't remember what I said, but I chugged my beer and headed straight for the center of the circle where it was darkest.

Even that was no good. If something got slipped into my beer, it must have been before that, because suddenly I didn't feel safe. The whole mob was watching me, waiting for me to do something I wasn't supposed to. But what was I supposed to? No matter how loud the music was, every noise I made was louder. When I moved, I was in someone's face. I wasn't connected anymore. And "darkest" wasn't dark enough to hide in. I had to get away.

I shoved out of the dancers, past the torches, and stumbled over rocks and tufts of grass. Then I just kept going. After a minute my eyes adjusted to the starlight, as much as they ever would.

Everything was horrible. Bob wasn't going to kiss me under the sunrise. I was the slut with beer on her shirt who'd maybe do him because it wasn't as if guys liked me. And Alice New Girl had seen the whole thing.

That's when I put my foot in a hole, twisted my ankle, and fell down. Another wake-up call. I just sat there and cried like a jerk.

I had to go back to the circle. To being who I'm supposed to be—too stupid to bruise, too dumb to imagine, hard and happy and in hiding. I'm the tortoise, pulling my body parts back under cover, saying, Who, me? Oh, I'm just a rock.

Of course, I couldn't find the circle.

They'd made it hard to find, because if you could see it from anywhere, then so could the rangers. But I couldn't hear it, either. I'd gone a lot further than I thought.

I got scared. That's what screws you when you're lost in the desert. I should have stayed where I was till morning. I could have been right next to a park road. Instead I went stumbling through the dark.

I remember the sun coming up. I was in the middle of a plain, and the plain had Joshua trees all over it, spaced out like an orchard without rows. Real trees, maybe thirty or forty feet high, not like the crummy little tree behind Mike's garage. Every one had a big crown of twisty branches, but there was no shade. When the wind blew, it hissed through the leathery knife-blade leaves, but nothing moved.

Rock piles stuck up around the plain. I couldn't tell how far away they were. No road, no trails. Not even footprints.

I just kept walking. I didn't know what else to do. Little lizards slid off rocks when my shadow fell on them. Ravens flew over, making ugly laughing sounds. A rabbit with black ear tips crossed in front of me and didn't even look at me. A coyote sat and scratched his ear with a hind leg, then trotted off between the rocks. It got hotter and hotter. I remember noticing I wasn't sweating anymore.

Now comes the part I remember that didn't happen. I don't know when, except that there was still enough light to see by.

I thought it was a tree. I saw its feet first, and they were twisted and dry and dark like juniper roots. Its legs were like the trunks of the big Joshua trees, corky-looking bark where the old leaves have fallen away. Above that, dry leaves hung on it like brown daggers overlapping. Only its head and hands were green. Knobs of green sword leaves like the ends of the Joshua tree branches. Mistletoe was scattered around its head, the dark red strands like tiny bones. It had a face, but it was made of leaves, so I almost had to imagine it, like seeing pictures in clouds. That bent leaf in the middle is the nose, that line of leaf-ends there, that's the mouth. And those deep pits between the leaves are where its eyes would be.

Inside my head I was flailing and screaming, but my body wasn't doing anything. I think I was either passed out or close to it. It was like having a bad dream—you want it to go away, but it doesn't occur to you that you can do anything about it.

It bent over as if it was trying to look into my face. I guess I must have been sitting or lying down. Maybe. It had to bend practically in half. Then it picked up a rock and cut its hand open.

That sounds nasty, but it was just interesting at the time.

It cut a long gash in the bark of its palm. Water, or maybe sap, oozed up out of the cut and filled its cupped hand. It stuck its hand out under my nose.

Now I understand about animals being able to sniff out water. The water smelled like being alive. Everything else in the world was dying, in different ways and at different speeds, but that water was alive forever.

So I drank it. I was so thirsty I'd stopped feeling it, but all of a sudden I couldn't get enough to drink. (So much for Miss I'm-careful-what-I-swallow. But since it couldn't have happened, does that time count?)

And that's it. I don't remember anything else, even in little confetti bits like I remember the rest. There's just nothing between that and when I woke up in the morning at the edge of the park where the all-terrain vehicle freaks go to play. Some vroom-vroomer saw me sit up on my sand dune and nine-one-oned.

I have a hideous sunburn (blisters in places) and I'm massively dehydrated. But I overheard the doctor tell the nurse he thought I was lying about being out there for two nights and a day. I wasn't messed up enough. And for sure I was lying either about where I started or about being on foot, because it was twenty miles from there to the place I was found.

Sure, whatever. I'm lying. That works for me.

Our dog died when I was eleven/twelve. Oh, boo hoo, right? Well, yeah—he was a great dog, and I'd grown up with him. But what was important, because I hadn't expected it, was the way it changed things between Mom and me. We did a lot of talking in between the crying, about important stuff. I don't know why grief made us feel as if it was safe to take the lids off. But it turned a crappy experience into a pretty good one, and for a while, we were closer than we'd been since I was tiny.

My point is, sometimes truly crappy experiences have a crowbar effect on the rest of your life. Everything shakes loose. Then you can let it go back to the way it was, or you can step in and make something happen, something that might be permanent.

Janelle, Nina, and Barb came over yesterday after school. You'd think I had cancer. Lots of hushed voices and sentences trailing off. Of course, me being lost in the desert is about the most interesting thing that's happened to any of us for years, so I understand that they'd want to get some mileage out of it. It made me feel like a museum exhibit.

Then Barb and Nina had to go babysit Nina's brothers. So I told Janelle about Bob at the rave.

"So did you do it?" Janelle asked.

"Do what?"

"Blow him. You *didn't*?" She squeaked that last bit. "Beth, I thought you were into him!"

I couldn't think of a thing to say. No joke, no verbal shrug, no cover story, nothing.

"Oh, god." Janelle looked disgusted. "He was supposed to say, 'I love you. I've always loved you.' Right?"

"Of course not!" Well, yes. Was that wrong? If it wasn't wrong, why had I denied it?

"Hel-lo! Guys have to know there's something in it for them. It's just, you know, biology. You love them before the blow job, and they love you after."

"Don't you ever both love each other at the same time?"

Blank stare from Janelle.

It was worse than not speaking the same language. At least with languages there's a chance you'll have a word for the concept.

I told her I was tired. Actually I was kind of sick to my stomach. She suddenly remembered to talk as if I was dying. And brain damaged. "You take care of yourself, hon. Okay?" Then she left.

That was when I had my big revelation. I didn't want to be just like Janelle anymore. I *couldn't* be. I wasn't built with the right parts or something. I guess I'd hoped that, if I stuck with her, she'd want to be more like me. But what was there about me that screamed "role model?"

Being like Janelle wouldn't save me from my life. And being like me wouldn't save Janelle. The people from the *Titanic* might have found some floating debris to hang onto, but they were still in the middle of the North Atlantic.

I said it was a revelation. I didn't say it made me insanely happy.

After dinner (frozen pizza—I'm the cook, after all), Mom came to my bedroom door and said, "There's a girl who says she's in your English class and has your homework assignment." She was half-frowning—not angry, just trying to figure out how she felt about this. "Alice somebody?"

Oh, god. Alice New Girl, witness to my shame, calling to find out if I had committed seppuku like a smart person. Well, I had to face the world eventually. Make like a rock, I told myself. "Sure. Where's the phone?"

"She's not on the phone," said Mom. "She's here."

I had only seconds to get my ducks in a row. All I could do

was tug the sheet up straight and make my face blank. In that last moment I saw my bedroom as others see it: the matching furniture bought during my ten-minute girlie phase in fifth grade, now with the white laminate chipped off the corners. The dark blue mini-blinds with the puffy valance (Wal-Mart!) that grotesquely needed dusting. Clothes tossed everywhere. Invalid crap on the nightstand.

Alice came in. She wore black capri pants and a red bowling shirt with "Stan" embroidered over the pocket, and had the giant purse over her shoulder. Her face was world-class blank. "Hi," she said.

My mom took that as some kind of signal, because she left. Alice instantly closed the door and plopped down on the floor beside the bed. "Oh, jeez, Tab, you look *awful*! I'm so sorry. I tried to follow you at the rave, but I lost you in the dancers. Then I went back and tried to get that idiot guy to help me find you, but he was so full of Happy-Shiny he couldn't find his own head. How do you feel?"

Like I'm in the path of Hurricane Alice, I wanted to say. "Okay, considering."

"Considering that you could still be out there, bleaching like a cow skull?"

"With the ravens picking out my eyes," I said, just to see if she'd be grossed out.

"And the kangaroo rats stealing away your hair to make their nests," she said gleefully.

I tried not to grin. "The search party would never find me, but I'd be all around them."

"Part of the desert forever!" Alice finished. "It sounds like a song."

"Or an *Outer Limits* episode. You brought my English homework?"

She made a spitting noise. "That was just an excuse. I'm grounded. Nothing else would have got me past the parental units, short of climbing out a window." She looked at the wall over my head. "Where's that?"

When I did my frantic life-flashes-before-my-eyes view of the bedroom, I'd forgotten the tree picture over the bed. It's a blown-up color photo I got at a church rummage sale, nothing fine art about it. In the picture, a path climbs a hill in the foreground, around these big oak trees and a couple of good-sized rocks, then curves out of sight.

When I first saw it, I had this *hunger* to get into the picture, to follow that path. I can still stare into it and imagine walking around those rocks, into the shade of the trees, and seeing what's on the other side of the hill.

"I don't know where it is." Then I amazed myself, because my mouth opened again, and out came, "It's a picture about possibilities. About wanting. The path always goes out of sight." I didn't just figure that out, but I hadn't planned to tell anyone. Now to see what Alice would do to my exposed throat. . . .

Alice looked very serious and intense. "What do you want when you look at it?" she asked.

I didn't feel like I could lie. I'd started this, after all. And the tree picture is one of the few things I'd grab if the house caught fire. I shrugged (which reminded me about the sunburn). "I don't know. I just want."

A big grin spread across her face. "Yes! Just like 'Malibu'!"

"What?"

"Hole! Courtney Love! On *Celebrity Skin*. . . . You haven't heard it?"

She grabbed up the giant purse and pulled out a portable CD player. At first I thought there were morning glories glued all over it. Then I saw some of them were scuffed, and I realized they were painted on. Amazing.

Alice handed me the headphones. "'Malibu' makes me feel the same way. Like there's a road in front of me, and I have to find a way to get on it and see where it goes, or I'll go nuts." She looked up to make sure I had the phones on and pushed PLAY.

Wistful, jangly, beautiful guitars in my ears, and a girl singing, talking right to me. I mean, *spooky* to me—the voice wanted to know how I'd gotten so screwed up, and how I'd held it together in spite of it. And then it said, Hey, meet me halfway, *chica*, and the two of us can maybe save your stupid life, okay?

Even with the sunburn, I got goosebumps.

When the chorus started, Alice sang along, as if she knew without listening exactly how long the first verse was. Then she grabbed the phones off my ears.

"Hey!" I said.

"I can't not listen to it. We need a boom box."

I pointed to my desk. She jumped up, found mine (under a pair of jeans), and put the disk in. The song started over, and Alice bumped the volume up.

"Play it again," I said when it stopped.

After a couple more plays, we were singing along with Courtney as loud as we could. About a place where the ocean would wash away all the bullshit. A place to live, not just survive.

"Have you ever been?" Alice asked.

"What, to Malibu?" I laughed. "No chance."

"But it's only three hours away! Well, L.A. is. When my dad told me we were coming to California, I went nuts. But it seems like nobody here has ever been to L.A. . . . ." Alice grabbed her spiky hair and pulled it. "Three hours away there are great bands and dance clubs and juice bars and history and art and *the ocean*, and we're missing it! There are surfers and pelicans and movie stars!"

"All in the same place?" I asked, trying not to laugh.

"Yes! And you and I have got to go."

It wasn't like with Janelle, when I knew I was trying to fit my sticking-out pieces into the empty spot in the puzzle. It was as if I'd had a dream every night that I couldn't remember, and Alice had remembered it for me.

I know where that path in the picture comes out. On the other side of that hill is Malibu.

Mom must have heard us singing and shrieking, because she came in and said I had to rest.

"I'll bring your homework tomorrow." Alice winked.

"Don't forget your CD." I really didn't want to remind her.

"You can borrow it," she said.

Mom came back after she shooed Alice out. I asked, "Have you ever been to the ocean?"

She stared at me for a second. "No."

"Alice and I are going."

"Oh? When's that happening?"

"I don't know yet. But we will."

She gave me such a funny look, as if I'd surprised her, as if she felt sorry for me. Or for her. But she just said, "Drink your Gatorade."

I've listened to the whole album about a dozen times already.

Today I told Alice what happened when I was in the desert. She's the only person I've told. It was like having to be honest about how I felt about the tree picture: either I wasn't going to say anything about what happened after I ran off, or I had to tell her the whole thing.

I was afraid she would be different when I came back to school. I had visions of her being tight with Piper, pretending I'd become See-Through Girl. I know all about survival tactics, after all.

And, okay, I was afraid of the way I'd be—that I'd go back to sticking with Janelle and our posse. Because I *do* know about survival. I didn't know if I could resist that yummy, cozy, supposed-to-be hiding place.

But it was as if Alice and I were wired up like Secret Service guys. We could watch the crowd for snipers while we had each other's backs. I've started raising my hand in class. I just laughed and walked away when Amber called me "Gross Peeling Thing." I'm not alone, like the tree behind Little Mike's garage. I'm a forest, like the trees in the park.

The park is why I had to tell Alice. "Let's go out there this Saturday," she said today after sixth period.

"Why?" The bottom fell out of my stomach.

"Joshua Tree is a big deal. I read about it. It's this amazing ecosystem that doesn't exist anywhere else. And so far I've only seen it in the dark."

"It's the desert. There, I saved you so much time."

"Tab!" Then she looked at me with her eyes squinched up. "Is this anything I should know about?"

Even when I was behaving like a psych case, she didn't insist I tell her my deepest, darkest secrets. So of course I had to.

I told her about the creature in the desert, about waking up on the other side of the park, and the doctor saying I was lying.

Alice didn't say anything right away. I got scared. "It was probably heatstroke," I added, and heard the flatness in my voice.

She shook her head. "I don't think so."

That scared me even more. "Why not? It was heatstroke, LSD, or I'm insane! What do you mean, 'I don't think so.'"

"Remember your lips?"

I was about to yell at her, but she looked so serious.

"Lips dry out worse than any other part of your face, because they don't have any oil glands," she went on. "When I came to see you right after it happened, you looked like you'd just come off a barbecue grill. But your lips didn't. They weren't even dry."

I think every hair on my body stood straight up. "When I drank out of its palm—"

"You put your mouth in the water."

This Saturday we're spending the day in the park. We're going to bike in, and pack a lunch and huge amounts of water. Alice has a guide to the birds and animals and plants, and the plan is to see how many we can check off.

It's funny, but I'm not worried about seeing the Joshua tree thing again. I think if something like that happens to you, you get one shot. You can do what you want with it, but that taste of live magic is one per customer.

Now that I'm not trying to be who I'm supposed to, I've started to wonder about the rest of the world. Is everybody wearing a disguise with the zipper stuck? Are all the supposed-to-bes big fat lies? If so, how about the desert? I know what it's supposed to be: no water, no life, everything poisonous, pointy, or otherwise out to get you.

I was supposed to be a loser. Maybe the desert and I have something in common.

Can't wait to talk this over with Alice.

EMMA BULL's first novel, *War for the Oaks*, is a cult favorite among fans of urban fantasy, and was recently reissued by Tor Books. Her third novel, *Bone Dance*, was a finalist for the Hugo, Nebula, and World Fantasy Awards, and was the second place Philip K. Dick Award novel. She collaborated with Steven Brust on a historical fantasy, *Freedom and Necessity*, and is working on another collaboration set in Arizona in 1881, called *Territory*. She and her husband, Will Shetterly, sold a screenplay for an animated science fiction film and have had two live-action feature scripts optioned. Emma's current band, the Flash Girls, released their third album, *Play Each Morning, Wild Queen*, in 2001.

Her Web site is homepage.mac.com/emmawill.

Author's Note:

When Terri and Ellen invited me to write a Green Man story, I thought I'd do something with the desert. After all, everybody loves the rain forest, but the desert still doesn't get the respect it deserves. Having decided that, my brain pretty much filed the subject in the "dealt with" folder. I forgot all about it.

A month or two later, I was in my favorite coffee house when a stranger complimented me on my T-shirt. It was my Green Man Press shirt, from the company Charles Vess runs, with a beautiful big Green Man face silk-screened on the back. The stranger and I started talking about Green Man myths, and this great book on the subject he'd just found, *Green Man,* by William Anderson and Clive Hicks. A couple of days later, back at the coffee house, he lent me the book, and XTC's *Apple Venus One* CD, with their "Greenman" song on it.

When I got home, I found an e-mail from Terri and Ellen reminding me about the anthology. All right, all right, I said to the universe. I get the message. I'll write a story.

Tab started dictating her autobiography to me pretty much right away. Well, it seemed like she was dictating it. Sometimes characters pop into my head so clearly that I feel guilty taking credit for making them up. I got so involved in Tab's story that I found out more of it than I could use here. So eventually this may be the beginning of a novel.

The Green Man is a symbol of rebirth in nature, and, from carvings in the churches of Europe, the rebith of the soul. Through Tab's story, I realized that he can also be part of the rebirth of the self. Like forests and grasslands, people can suffer fire and drought. They forget why they're here, what they really love, what's important to them. The Green Man says that everything regrows, that it's never too late to figure out who you are and why, and do something about it.

ALI ANUGNE O CHASH
(THE BOY WHO WAS)

❧

CAROLYN DUNN

*TWO BOYS WERE hunting. One was of the Deer Clan, who
make songs of light and send them stars. The other was of the
clan related to the Hawk, the messengers, the ones who stay
silent and speak only when the world must be spoken to.*

*They had been hunting a long time, singing the charm songs
they had been taught, the songs to hunt for or to woo a deer.
They had seen the antlers hiding in shadow, hiding in sunlight,
along the oily leaves and sweet-scented magnolia, along the
light pathways in darkness of the fireflies and hidden in soft
wood, water, damp bark. They heard the deer sing, and could
have sworn it was the voice of a woman.*

The darkness is kind; it does not say the words the light
must always repeat. Stories told in darkness are always safer
than ones told in light. Spirits cannot always see so good in
the dark, but in the light everything is up for grabs. Inside of
the house of The Boy Who Was they tell a story about a
woman who went to the water, came home, and was never

the same again. I will never be the same again. My words bleed their lies, and I will always be one with the water, kin to the darkness, calling the stone river home, deep within those recesses of memory that I can never shake.

His touch at first was cool, damp. I remember him before he went there to the water, before he had left Wolf Town and went in. He would look at me from the secret place behind his eyes when he thought I was not looking. A flash of darkness under a daylight sky, a look that would hold me well within him, and I would sigh, smile in that way that he knew he had won.

Ali Anugne O Chash, the one who would become The Boy Who Was, they say was the tallest of the tall, the bravest, the most handsome, and I thought so too. My sisters and cousins would speak his name in hushed tones, turn their faces to the ground when he would walk by, turn their heads and pretend to not see him. Not I. I was bold, they said, because my mother had strong charms and sang protection over me. Because she had dreamed I would be taken by the Long Hairs but she had kept me from their claws. This made me bold. Made me look people in the eye. Made me laugh and smile when the Peace Chief spoke, her eyes arrows my way. Gave me the backbone to look into the eyes of the tallest, most handsome, strongest warrior of the Deer Clan, with my club foot and bent leg.

And he had chosen me, Iyi Tanakbi, a girl of modest means, not the wealthiest of the clans or the most beautiful, but my hair did shine and my eyes were dark, ringed with silver, like the moon's shadow, in spite of my club foot, my slow walk, my small leg. Hidden in the small shadows and dappled light among the shade trees, I would watch the young men in the circle of men smoking their pipes, fathers standing over them as they stripped the oak of its bark to smooth, damp and clawed surfaces, make the sticks that would bring them fortune, call in the deer, gamble for love, for money, for women. And I, Iyi Tanakbi, would be his downfall.

The two men, barely out of their youth, turned to one another, and began to sing their hunting songs louder. Surely, this was no male deer, but with antlers? They had become separated from the rest of the hunting party and knew they would be lost at once if they did not perform the ceremony for hunting the deer. One reached for the dark earth and put it to his face, singing a charm song all the way. Brother deer, *he sang,* sister fawn, blood of my blood, there is nothing to fear from me. Let my arrows be strong, may they find your heart. Do not fear.

The other, with steady hands, made fire.

What becomes of his man-name does not matter, the memory of who he was, the nights dreaming of the warmth of his touch cannot say what he was to me, and I can no longer see that part of him. The name he had then is dead to me, and in its place, in his place, is the touch of the cool, damp clawed bark, smooth laden skin and touch of ice that he has become. I no longer speak this name, and it is not the name with which I speak to him now. Ali Anugne O Chash, they whisper behind their hands. The Boy Who Was.

The day I was born my father sang songs into the night, as my mother's silence frightened him. No other child of hers had been brought into the world without restlessness and fear of the life that would fall from her. No other child of hers came into the world singing. No other child of hers was lame, born with the leg turned in and the foot shorn off. She had dreamt of this time, dreamt me into being, formed me through her words and her songs and my father's pipe, but she would never see me as I was, the broken leg, the bent hip, the club foot. No other child of hers would fall from her body, eyes ringed with the moon, wide open, challenging with my stare. Only those born with their eyes open tempt the Little People to come round, for they are the ones who are bold, the ones the Little People like to keep for themselves. My mother would not tempt the *Hutuk Awasa* with her screams, for they would see me as their own and take me away, take me to the place where water, earth, and sky meet in the holes in the ground and water bubbles forth, singing its own song, and air rising to the top. She banished all sign of water when the pains first came upon her, sent away the men as well as her sisters, and kept closed mouthed, so that no one would hear her scream, cry out, as wave upon wave shook my life out from within her and forced me to the shore. I would not cry out as well, but when she lifted her shaking hands to me, my eyes were what caught her first. She would never let the *Hutuk Awasa* have me, never let them see me, and my father's singing would keep them away.

The fire rose, an ascent of prayers to the darkening sky. A cool wind rose off the river and soon seeped into the cracks between clothing of the hunters. The fire was warm, but their bellies were empty. As the one who sang the charm song con-

tinued his prayer, the other looked and saw, in a clearing near the water, three small eggs. Cracking the eggs into the fire, he cooked them and prepared to divide them with his companion. "Where did these come from?" asked the one who sang the song.

"They were here, at this camp," said the one who had cooked.

"Who has laid them?" asked the one who sang.

His companion replied, "They were here in camp, waiting for us to eat."

"I will not eat what I do not know," said the one who sang.

His companion was hungry and set to eat the eggs. On the first bite, the eggs slid down his throat and into his empty belly. They were light as air, and tasted of smoke and fire and water and life. They filled him, and he craved more.

They say the one born with the crooked leg fears no one, and I was no different. Don't step over pools of water, my mother would say. I laughed. I am the yellow bird, *hoshi lugna,* I fly over and the ones who are underneath love me. No harm comes to me. Even the yellow bird with the lame foot can fly. She can hunt with the men, lead them to the deer. Fly away. Earthbound, water laden, she can still fly over the underneath, the land of the water people, land of the *Hutuk Awasa,* the little ones who come and steal children, steal hearts, turn them cold, spit in the faces of their mothers, pour ash from hot coals in the hair of their fathers. I am one club foot ahead of them. My legs are longer and my stride does not matter when the yellow bird wings take flight.

* * *

The one who sang stoked the fire. "The deer will surely show himself tonight," he said, "and I must stay and watch for him. You sleep."

And his companion did, and all night he dreamt of water and wood. In his dream, his hands and feet would not move. He woke, feverishly, his companion keeping watch over him. "My hands . . ." he whispered, and could not move them.

Once I saw one of them in the woods. Them. The Little People. In a clearing of oak, tracking the men as I did, as they gossiped their *kabucha* plays, I turned and stepped over a log. Too late, I saw the shimmer of sky beneath it. I stood still, did not move, became stone. The *Hutuk Awasa* would not see me if I did not stray. If you step over the shadows, they awaken, look for the one who wakes them, take your soul, whisper evil thoughts in your ear, cause you to spit in your mother's face, rub ash in your father's hair. But if they do not see you, they will look for you but never find you.

I saw her antlers first, the wildness of her hair, the moon in her eyes, the trees in her walk. Antlers rising from the pool beneath the stump, and I saw her eyes, looking into me, but she could not see me. Her fingernails, filled with black mud, dragged on the ground, the sound causing me to shake, but I ground my teeth to stand against the cold. Her hooves beat a dance on the wooded earth as she moved like a deer across the stump and toward the river. I saw her antlers dance in the shaking light and I knew she would search for me until she found me, her breath cold against my neck, dragging me down with her back to the cold, wet underground sky. *Hutuk*

Awasa. My teeth were like stone. I would never belong to her. I prayed the men would not find her and me together and know it was I who released her.

The boy who would become The Boy Who Was reached me first. I heard my brothers' voices shaking off the trees, the moss, the russet earth. They were singing a hunting song and my own voice had left me, chasing the deer. He reached out, touched my hair, touched my heart. "Iyi Tanakbi," he whispered. My name had never become so much of me until that moment, until he spoke it aloud in the voice of stars, the sound like water over stones. My heart leapt to my mouth and I opened. I cracked beneath the sound, became liquid. His skin did not touch mine, but with his words the world between us stopped, and I was his. "Iyi Tanakbi." The first wave lulled me into his embrace. The second tempered me to his touch.

"The Woman Who Is the Deer," I said, my voice steady, my moonlit gaze locked in his watery eyes, "she emerged from this place."

Only his voice mattered. Only his touch without skin, breath of heartbeat, words of love, became real. "Iyi Tanakbi." His lips found mine, sliding against cool water and damp oak.

Nashoba, his brother, was the next to arrive. Yuka Keyu, my brother, was the third. The boy who would become The Boy Who Was turned his head away from me and toward the river. "She has seen the deer," he said, "there."

And he ran further into the woods, my brother following. Nashoba, staying behind, turned and looked at me, his eyes sending me home. He would not know, he could not have known, that it was I who freed her. I would never tell him. I would never tell anyone, save for the one who would know my heart.

The one who sang moved closer. "You should not have eaten those eggs," he said, concerned for his friend. "You are having trouble now. Go to sleep, and soon you will awaken and the illness will pass."

And sleep he did, but his dreams were even more fitful and frightening. In his dreams, his feet and legs were numb, and he could not move. When he woke, his fevered cries brought the alarmed attention of his companion. "It is the eggs," his friend said. "Go and sleep the sickness away."

And he dreamt again, of the world beneath this one, of a world of coldness and dark, of vast underground tunnels that led from this world to the world of the spirits. And he was frightened because he could see into both worlds, and he knew that something was happening to him, something that had been set into motion that he could not control.

He woke, unable to move. His hands and feet had grown together, seamless. His friend looked upon him in horror. "Go to the village, and find my family," the one who ate the eggs implored his friend, "and they will help me."

The one who sang ran through the woods and came to the village. He rounded up his friend's family as well as his own, ran back to the place by the river that he had left. All that remained was the skin shed by a snake and a trail leading to the river.

He had shown me kindness, where no one else would. He had shown me tenderness, his touch cold, his eyes dark as the whirlwind. They told me I could no longer speak his name, but I screamed it from the top of my voice until the bottom of my voice was no longer. They said that Iyi Tanakbi, the bent leg, the crooked step of the Bird Clan, lost her mind and grieved for Ali Anugne O Chash as if he still lived. They said she wandered the shores of the Pearl River searching and searching and would die there, searching for Ali Anugne O Chash. Her fingernails had grown long and ragged, filled with silt as she dragged the mud for her lost love, the one who had gone into the river a man, tallest of the tall, and become the Water Panther, never leaving.

My mother insisted I marry immediately. They were afraid I would speak his name and he would return for me, but if I married another, his claim to me was no longer valid under our law. A warrior was chosen from the Wolf Clan, a son of the Peace Chief. I was sullen. I was lost. I was not even allowed to speak his name. My mouth opened and his name tumbled from my tongue, but before he could be free my mother clamped her hand upon my mouth, my sisters wrestling me to the ground, my brothers sitting upon me so I could not move.

The moon around my eyes grew wider until I agreed to their demands. I would marry this man from the Wolf Clan. I would be silent and never speak the name of the man I loved again. I allowed my mother to trim my nails, allowed my sisters to shell comb my hair, allowed my brothers to smile in appreciation, allowed my father his horses. And when their backs were turned and the moon around my eyes had waxed, I took my chance.

I tore my hair and went to the river. All of this had been set into motion because I, a foolish and rash girl, had not looked to see the pond and my feet and I'd stepped over it, waking the deer who crawled out from the whirlwind water and entered the world in a thunderstorm. And my brother and the one I loved had chased her into the woods, and only my brother returned. And Ali Anugne O Chash was The Boy Who Was because I had made him so.

His voice stirs softly upon the water grass, the edge of a stream. Everywhere I hear him, feel his heart beating, feel his breath upon my skin. I stand at the river, dropping tobacco, crushed mint, magnolia, cedar, and sage. I do not listen to the warnings of my mother and my sisters. I wander singing my own songs, songs not of our language but in the language of our enemies. I am bold. I laugh, skip over water as if taunting them to take me. They will not. For I am too foolish to be ever lost to the *Hutuk Awasa*.

At night in the woods I dance naked with no fire. Even the *Anpanshe Falaya*, the Long Hairs, the ones who do harm, fear me. Even the deer who became a woman will not approach me, for grief binds the *Hutuk Awasa*, keeps them close to the world they so want to live in but cannot or they will die. I have set her free, woman who is a deer, and the spirits know that if they take me I will destroy them all.

And I hear his voice. *Iyi Tanakbi*, a whisper of breath from a breeze upon the water, *Iyi Tanakbi*. . . .

I stand over the water, stretch my arms wide.

The creek dances at the touch of my toes, stirring at my bare feet. Only now do I stand tall, my clubbed foot and my crooked leg moving of their own accord. I grow taller, more beautiful, as the water dances around my misery. *Iyi Tanakbi*. . . .

His hands roam the hollows of my ankles, ice at his touch. My feet are rooted straight, sinking in the mud as the water moves up my calves to the place where my knees join. *Iyi Tanakbi.* . . .

His skin is slippery, cool, hard, and smooth as he moves up my leg, the curve of my thigh, the swell of my hip. I do not cry out. Instead I look to the starless night sky under shimmering, swirling water, and looking up I can no longer see myself but drown in his kisses, his touch, the tongue that flicks between my lips as he drags me under.

CAROLYN DUNN is a wife, mother, daughter, journalist, teacher, poet, fiction writer, and catechist born in Southern California. Her work has appeared in the anthologies *The Color of Resistance, Reinventing the Enemy's Language,* and *Through the Eye of the Deer,* and Kenneth Lincoln's *Sing with the Heart of a Bear: Fusions of Native and American Poetry.* Her poetry has been collected in the volume *Outfoxing Coyote,* and she is co-editor of two anthologies of Native American fiction: *Through the Eye of the Deer* (with Carol Comfort) and *Hozho: Walking in Beauty* (with Paula Gunn Allen). Currently pursuing a Ph.D. from Saybrook Graduate School in San Francisco, she is a member of the all-woman Native drum group the Mankillers, whose CDs are *All Woman Northern Drum* and *Comin to Getcha!;* as well as of the indigenous rock band Red Hawk.

Author's Note:

For over ten years now, the Deer Woman spirit has been nagging at me to tell her story. She is one of the Little People, as we call them in the southeastern Native nations: Choctaw, Cherokee, Creek, Seminole, Chickasaw. The Little People are our fairies and sprites, who are not necessarily good or evil, but have been known to bend the rules a little bit.

Deer Woman's stories are about power and knowledge,

and how to use that power and knowledge in the correct way. She is a spirit from whom we learn how to maintain harmony and balance in our relationships, especially in marriage and other committed relationships. Deer Woman teaches us that too much of a good thing can be harmful, and that we must maintain a balance of everything in order to remain healthy.

"Ali Anugne O Chash (The Boy Who Was)" is based upon a traditional Mississippi Choctaw story that my late mother-in-law, Juanita Anderson, used to tell. It is a story of transformation in many ways, a story of obsessive love and woman's power that come together at one moment in the distant past to unleash the power of the Deer Woman upon the world.

Non-Indians tell us these stories aren't true. Does Ali Anugne O Chash exist in this earth below the muddy waters in Mississippi? Did Iyi Tanakbi pine for him so much she was swallowed into the water to join him forever? Maybe not. But let me tell you, there are people who have seen the Water Panther and his wife firsthand. Many of them are my family. And they keep telling the stories so we won't ever forget what is really truth and what maybe isn't. And maybe that is just what the spirits want us to hear.

REMNANTS

KATHE KOJA

IT'S THE FIRST thing you see, when you come to my house: A thicket, a picket, a fence of wine bottles, soda bottles, jars of mustard and jam. I wash them all first, don't think I don't, wash them clean and green and brown and clear, wash them so they sparkle in the sun. When it's sunny. Sometimes it rains, rains all night and the glass and the plastic get wet, run threads of water down to the sidewalk, down the cracks in the concrete like little rivers half-dammed by cigarette butts, the plastic tops of take-out coffees, the odd dull shine of a coin, run till everything is mud and the rain stops and the sun comes out again.

I don't save the coins I find; I don't need money. What I need is *material,* stuff to make things out of: like the bottles, or my hanging forest of beautiful plastic bags—do you know I have over one hundred kinds of plastic bags? From over one hundred different stores? I know, because I counted. I even made a list: bags from K-Mart, and Costco, and Schiller's, and Sav-Mor, Speedy's and Quikky's and Reddy-Rite-Now. . . . One hundred stores! Who could go to so many places, buy so many things? Who would want to?

They make a secret sound, my bags, ripped and slit and hung like leaves from the branching arms of coat racks and fence posts and ladders missing rungs, like tree trunks propped and leaning, or braced like scaffolding against the house—this used to be a house, you know. Not a nice one; I can still remember living here, or someone did, I'm not sure who, but there were bedrooms, two bedrooms and a bathroom with a toilet, and a kind of front room where people sat and there was TV. And a kitchen. I won't forget the kitchen, the stink and scald of it, the chipped metal teapot, the white bleach scour of the sink. . . . It's buried in my forest now, that sink, filled with rocks and concrete chunks and dirt, all the shovel could carry, all I could lift before my arms couldn't hold any more. I filled it up good and covered it over, and then covered *that* with plastic, a wrinkled tarp as blue as the sea that murmurs with a sound like waves when you step over it; a safe sound.

Not that it's all safe here; that's not the point. But it's *good*, you know? A good place, a place where you can just . . . be, just stand and think, or watch the whirligigs, you know what a whirligig is? I make them out of plastic jugs, tinsnip patterns of milky white, or the dull silver of aluminum cans. Real metal, iron and like that, is too heavy, it can't really spin, and whirligigs need to spin, to move when the wind does, around and around so fast you can't tell what's there beyond the movement, as if speed herself were twirling on the tiptoe end of a pole.

I fixed them up high, where the wind is, way up on the

peaks of the house. It was hard to get up there—and harder to get *down,* oh my, with no one to hold the ladder, I just hung there and hung there and *hung* there until that meter reader came. She was so nice. . . . But I knew when I made them that that's where they were meant to go, where they belonged. It's important for things to be where they belong, don't you think? The whirligigs on the roof, the sink sunk deep into the ground, and me here, working in my own front yard.

I like everything in my yard: the bottle fence, the Mirror Pond, the zoo where I keep the lawn animals—deer, ducks, flamingoes, I even have some plastic dogs. But my favorite place of all is the bag forest. Sometimes I call it Sure-Would Forest, like I sure would like to live out there if I didn't have to go to sleep inside. It's all so *pretty,* especially when the wind blows: the new bags firm and crackly, puffing outward like sails, the old ones fluttering, tattered and soft like ragged flags. People think a plastic bag lasts forever, but you know it really doesn't; it breaks down. Like plastic bottles get more brittle; like whirligigs spin themselves apart. Like I told the ladies, the DPW ladies: it's all just entropy. Isn't that a nice word? I invented it. *En-tro-pee.* It means "grow up."

At first I thought they were giants, those ladies, their shadows standing over me while I planted Popsicle sticks in the dirt. (Have you ever tried it? It really works.) Then I thought they were, you know, princesses or something, the one lady with her headful of beautiful black braids, the other with her shiny gold glasses, it seemed like things that princesses would wear. And who else but magic princesses would appear like they did, out of nowhere, just all-of-a-sudden there on the sidewalk? *My* sidewalk, where hardly anyone ever comes?

But when they started to talk—actually only Black Braids ever talked, Gold Glasses just stood there—I knew pretty quickly what they really were: DPW, Department of People Watching, they said they'd been watching me a long time. Watching the house, and the bottle-fence, and the bag-forest, watching it all come together and grow. And questions, oh boy, she must have asked me a thousand questions, like who I was and how long had I been there and who else lived with me in the house. I said if they'd been doing all that watching how come they didn't already know? but she just kept on asking, little lists coming out of her pockets, flap pocket jacket like a magician's top hat and finally, "There've been complaints," Black Braids said, like that was somehow my fault, how could it be my fault? I *never* complain. The sink taught me that. "We've gotten quite a few calls about your property. The most recent one was from, let's see, a meter reader."

I didn't say anything.

"It's not only an eyesore," Black Braids said, "it's a sanitation issue. For the neighborhood, but for you, too. According to this report," another flap pocket, another piece of paper, "inspectors have been out here twice before. Do you remember talking to them at all?"

"No," I said. Behind me the bags rustled, a soothing sound; it made me smile so I said it again. "No."

Gold Glasses took a piece of paper from her pocket and gave it to me; I gave it back. Black Braids said, "We don't want to—" something "—you," some word I didn't know. "We only want to help."

"If you want to help," I said, "start planting." I really meant it, I wasn't being a smarty, I don't like it when people are smarties to me. But the DPW ladies got mad, I could tell. They didn't take the Popsicle sticks, they tried to give me some letters or pamphlets or something, and when I wouldn't take them Gold Glasses put something right on the house: a big red sticker, dark red like a fire, like a fresh new scar, and "We'll be back," Black Braids said, and something about the way she said it—not ugly, but like a promise, a hard promise you mean to keep—made me think of the sink, and thinking of the sink right away made *me* ugly and so I started yelling, I didn't mean to but I did, yelling swear words too which is not nice and I know it but I did it anyway, yelled them all the way down the sidewalk and up to the DPW car, a car too new to be parked on this street, new blue car that pulled away fast, jerk of speed like a carnival ride, where your head rocks back, and you laugh. . . . But the ladies weren't laughing, and neither was I; I might have been crying, I'm not sure. There was stuff on my face, I had to go in the house and wipe it off and once I was in the house I *did* cry, the kind of crying you do when you know no one can hear, my head pressed against the wall where the phone used to be, *we've gotten quite a few calls about your property* . . . calls? from who? I don't have any neighbors, not anymore. Maybe it was a lie; they're allowed to tell lies, those kind of people, did you know that? DPW and cop-type, social worker, testify-in-court people, they're allowed to lie as much as they like.

On the dark red sticker it said BOARD OF HEALTH and then some other stuff I couldn't read. I admit, I sort of liked the sound of that: the Board of Health, like a big strong piece of wood sanded smooth and honey-brown. But this was a different kind of board, the people kind, the kind that means someone's going to do something to you that you're not going to like. So I had to think.

I can figure things out, I can put any kind of stuff together, but thinking is hard for me. So the first thing I did was bring my zoo inside. I didn't have tags or licenses for any of them so it was better they be out of sight. It made the bedrooms kind of crowded but I liked the company, and maybe one of them would give me a signal, some sign to tell me what to do. The dogs were best for that, and the deer, the smart little ones with the antlers. . . . But by the time it was dark they still hadn't told me anything.

So I did what I always do when I feel bad: I went to Sure-Would Forest, to stand in the night and the breeze, listening to the bags and the way they sound like whispering, a hundred voices whispering, telling strange and quiet secrets to each other in the dark. I felt the hairs on the back of my neck moving along with the whispers, like plants underwater, pulled by tides and currents that no one can see, they're just *there,* like the night air, like the Forest; like me. It made me feel strange and secret too; it made me happy, in that funny way you're happy in the dark. But I still didn't know what to do about the bottles, about the DPW and the Board of Health.

Maybe there was nothing I could do.

So I went back in, out of the night of secrets, and brushed my teeth with my fingers, and climbed into my sleeping bag next to the deer and the dogs. And right away I had the dream again.

I am standing on something soft, like a mattress, like quick-sand, something that sags and shifts when I try to move. And

from way up above, past the high lip of a cliff, comes garbage.
Bags and chunks and thunks of garbage, raining down like gi-
ant bullets on me: rotten oranges, filthy socks, wet newspaper
and styrofoam and cracked plastic cups, it falls forever and the
smell is awful *but what really scares me is that there's no end*
to it, no escape, it just keeps falling and I know if I don't get out
of there it's going to bury me, cover my head so I can't breathe,
already it's up to my waist but the ground's so soft I can't move,
can't get away, it's coming faster and faster and it's bigger *now*
too, it's warped lawn chairs and blown car tires and wrecked-
up old computers, refrigerators without doors, cars too rusted
to drive, everything's bigger than me and it's falling faster, it's
going to bury me for sure, I open my mouth to scream but

   but I

wake up, my own breath a shout, a scary sound—and as I
sit up, right away I feel it, cold and wet all around me, I peed
the sleeping bag—and now I'm really scared, because that's a
bad thing to do, a baby thing, *dirty garbage baby*, oh God I
know what happens next

   dirty garbage babies belong in the SINK

so I *run*, run right out of the house like I used to do, flee to
the heart of my forest where I Sure-Would like to stay forever, safe forever under the flutter of the bags, their soft
sound now a million mother's voices, good mothers, godmothers, fairy godmothers who in their million voices all say,
now, the very same thing

   come with us

in the safety of the trees, where everything is just the way
I left it, the way I made it, everything is mine and everything
is safe, the garbage isn't garbage anymore because I fixed it,

cleaned it, made it fences and ponds and beautiful trees, beautiful trees

come with us

the godmothers and me and the plastic animals, the flamingoes and the ducks and the sitting-down dogs, all of us escaping into the trees, where we drink from the Mirror Pond and listen to the leaves, and watch the whirligigs dance in the breeze that blows forever, the breeze that tells secrets, and hears them, and heals

come with us, the forest says

and I just do.

They're right on time, the DPW people, Black Braids in the new car and two men, work men in workmen's uniforms, driving a truck: they have rakes, and brooms, and heavy gloves; they have plastic bags. Black Braids sits watching and drinks from a paper cup of coffee; the men have no coffee, the men have to get to work.

They leave my Popsicle sticks untouched, the animals are safe inside, but everything else . . . I stand there watching as they pull out, one by one, each bottle in the glass-bottle fence, still the whirligigs, uproot my trees, throw my bags away into another, bigger, bag. "One hundred bags," I say, only to myself but the workmen hear me, one of them stops for a minute and "You shouldn't live in all this trash," he says, slow and kind, like he knows me and is worried about me. Sweat on his face, his gloved hands at his sides. "It's not healthy, you know? We'll clean it up some, give you a nice fresh start."

I already had a nice fresh start, but I don't say that; he's trying to be nice, he *is* nice so "Thank you," I say, and move out of their way, go stand back by the truck until they're all done, until Black Braids comes out of her car with a piece of paper, she doesn't even bother to speak to me, just folds and tucks the paper in the door . . . and then they're gone, Black Braids in her car, the men in the truck with all my things, everything piled away like nothing, like trash; I almost think I can hear the bottles clinking at me, jam and spaghetti sauce, *good-bye, good-bye*—

—and I cry a little, I can't help it, even though I know it never does any good to cry: the truck still turns the corner, my yard is still ruined, everything I worked so hard on is still gone. But even as I cry my hands are already getting busy, tugging and nipping at the heavy plastic, the thick clear gorgeous plastic of the workmen's garbage bags. The back of the truck was full of them, long bags to make long leaves like, like palm trees, I've never had palm trees before. I don't know what the deer will think, but the flamingoes are going to love them.

KATHE KOJA's novels include *The Cipher*, co-winner of the Bram Stoker Award, *Skin*, and *Kink*. Her debut YA novel, *straydog*, was recently published and she has just finished *Buddha Boy*.

Several of Koja's numerous short stories have been published in the Datlow/Windling Adult Fairy Tale series and several have been chosen for Year's Best anthologies. Some of her short fiction has been collected in *Extremites*. She lives with her husband, artist Rick Lieder, and her son Aaron in the suburbs of Detroit.

Author's Note:

The forest—its mystery, its safety, its embrace—is sometimes where we make it. And sometimes what we throw away is what we need the most.

THE PAGODAS OF CIBOURE

❧

M. SHAYNE BELL

ON A DAY of the summer Maurice nearly died, his mother carried him to the banks of the Nieve River and his life changed forever. He was ten years old then. It was a warm day around noon in June of 1885. A gentle breeze blew off the bay, and from where they sat Maurice and his mother could smell the salt of the sea. His mother believed such breezes could heal.

"When will Papa be here?" he asked his mother.

"Any day," she said. "His letter said he would come soon."

"Will he bring a doctor to bleed me?"

"Hush," she said. She brushed the hair across his forehead. "No one will bleed you in Ciboure, Maurice. I won't let them."

Maurice leaned against his mother and slept for a time in the sunlight. When he woke, he wanted to walk along the river. Yes he had a fever, and yes he did not feel well, but he wanted to walk upstream. He felt drawn to something in that direction, curious about what might lie just out of sight. His mother watched him totter along. "Don't go too far," she said, glad that he felt well enough to do this on his own but anxious that he not hurt himself.

Maurice worked his way slowly up the riverbank. He picked a reed and swished it at the grasses ahead. The grasses gave way to flowered bushes, and the land rose gently to a forest. The water of the little river gurgled over rocks as it rushed clear and cold down from the Pyrenees.

Not far into the trees, in a wide glen, Maurice came upon the walls of an abandoned pottery. Five hundred years earlier this workshop had sold sparkling dinner plates and soup bowls to Moorish and Christian princes. After the region had passed to France, its wares had been treasured in the palaces and mansions of Paris, Lyon, and Marseilles. But most of the wealthy family who owned the pottery had been guillotined in the Revolution. The few survivors had not returned to open it again.

The roof was now caved in. Windows in the stone walls were sunny holes. Maurice stood on his tiptoes and looked through one of the windows. He saw grass growing where workers had once hurried about polished floors.

Maurice walked around the ruined building and stopped in surprise. Three high mounds down by the river glittered in the sunlight as if covered in jewels. He had never seen anything like it. Among the daisies and the wild roses and the lacy ferns sunlight gleamed and sparkled on what looked from a distance like gems. It was as if he had wandered into a fairy treasury.

"Mother!" he called because he wanted her to see this. "Mother!"

But she was too far away to hear. Then he decided to be quiet: if there were jewels on those mounds he did not want to attract anyone else walking in the forest. He would fill his pockets first, then he would lead his mother here. If he had found jewels, they could buy a seaside mansion and he would get well and his father would come to live with them. They would all be happy again.

He walked slowly down to the mounds. His feet crunched on the ground, and he realized he was walking on broken china and glass. When he got to the mounds, he could see that that was what sparkled in the sunlight—broken dishes. The mounds were the old trash heaps of the pottery. There would be no fortune here.

Maurice scooped up a big handful of the shards, careful not to cut himself, and he carried them to the river. He held them down into the water and let the water wash away the dirt that had blown over the shards all these years. After a moment he shook out the water and spread his handful of broken china, wet and glittery, on the riverbank. Some shards were edged with a gold rim. One had a black fleur-de-lys entirely complete. Three pieces were from a set of blue china so delicate and clear he could see shadow through them when he held them up to the light.

Maurice was tired and hot. He sat breathing heavily for a time. When the breeze moved the branches overhead, sunlight sparkled on the broken china that had washed into the shallow riverbed. Maurice liked this place. Even if there were no jewels, it was nice to dream about being rich. It was nice to dream about being well again. This was a place that invited dreams.

He sat quietly—just long enough for the things that had gone still at his approach to start moving and singing again. First the birds, then the butterflies, then Maurice saw clusters of pieces of china moving slowly over the ground: one cluster, then another, then more than he could count. They moved slowly between the flowers and around the stands of grass.

Maurice sat very, very still. He did not know what was making the pieces of china cluster together and move. He shivered, but he did not dare run. He watched very carefully, hardly daring to breathe. Sometimes only three shards moved together. Sometimes a handful. The pieces that moved were bright and clean, and the sharp edges had all been polished away. One small clump of six snowy-white shards came upon the pieces Maurice had washed. It stopped by one of the blue ones, and drew back as if amazed.

It was then that Maurice heard the singing. It was an odd music, soft and indistinct, and he had to struggle to hear it at all. The simplest birdsong would drown it out. But the white china shards tinkled as they moved, and amidst the tinkling a high, clear voice sang. He thought the music sounded Chinese.

Other clusters of shards hurried up—pink clumps and white clumps and some with each shard a different color or design. With so many gathered around him Maurice could hear their music clearly. Somehow, surrounded by music, Maurice forgot to be afraid. Creatures that made music would not hurt him, he thought. They seemed to debate in their songs the merits of each piece he had washed. Maurice slowly reached out and picked up the white shard with the black fleur-de-lys. He set it down by a small cluster of terra-cotta shards and thought it made a fine addition.

All movement and song stopped. The clusters sank slowly to the ground. No one walking by would have noticed them or thought them special at all. Maurice put his hand back in his lap and sat still. He wanted them to move once more. He wanted them to sing.

It took some time for it to happen again. After the birds had been singing by themselves for a long time and when the butterflies were fluttering about Maurice's head, the terracotta pieces slowly drew themselves up into a terraced pattern, the larger pieces on the bottom, the smaller on top. It held the fleur-de-lys shard in the middle, as if it were a shield.

You look like a pine tree, Maurice thought.

But the more he looked at it, the more he realized it looked like a Chinese temple. He knew then what these creatures were. "Pagodas," he whispered. "Pagodas!"

His mother had told him stories about the pagodas. She'd said they looked like little Chinese temples. They were creatures made of jewels, crystal, and porcelain who lived in the forests of France. If you were good to them, they could heal you. He had thought the stories mere fairy tales.

He looked at the glittery river and the sparkling mounds and then at the shining shards around him. "Please heal me," he whispered. "I want to get better. Please help me."

He did not know how it would happen. He thought that maybe he should touch one of them. Some power might flow into him and make him well if he did. He reached out and gently touched the terra-cotta shards.

They sank down at once. He picked up each piece, then put it back in its place. He saw nothing among them. He found no hint of what a pagoda inside its shell of shards might look like. "Please help me," he whispered. "Mother's doctors can't, and I don't want Papa's to bleed me again."

Nothing around him moved now. When he heard his mother calling, he stood up very carefully. He did not want to step on the pagodas. He took off his shoes and planned each footstep before he took it. He tried to walk on grass and flowers, not the broken china. He hoped he had not hurt a single pagoda.

His mother met him at the steps of the pottery where he sat lacing his shoes. "You have been gone a long time," she said. She looked around as she waited for him. "Oh, this is pretty here. The trash heaps glitter so. You shouldn't walk barefoot to the river, Maurice—you could cut your feet on the glass!"

"I was careful, Mother," Maurice said.

She smiled and took his hand. They walked home slowly. She did not have to carry him.

That night, while the fever made him wobbly, Maurice pulled the box that held his favorite things out from beneath his bed. Inside were all the letters from his father carefully tied with a red ribbon. He set them aside. There were the thirteen francs he'd been able to save, wrapped in a note to his parents asking them to divide the money. He set that aside as well. There was the bright red, white, and blue pouch that held the set of seven tin soldiers his grandmother had sent him from Switzerland.

And there was his kaleidoscope. It was his most treasured possession. It was a shiny brass tube filled with mirrors. A person looked through one end to see the glorious patterns; the other was a chamber that could be screwed off and opened. Into that chamber Maurice would put pieces of broken glass and the beads and the strips of colored paper and string that made the intricate images in the kaleidoscope. The most common objects could become beautiful there. He could change the images whenever he wanted, and he and his mother had spent pleasant hours walking along the roadsides looking for broken, colored glass small enough to fit inside. He unscrewed the chamber and picked out three bright blue glass shards and one crystal bead. He took the tin soldiers out of their pouch and laid them in a row along the bottom of the box. Then he put the pieces of glass and the bead in the pouch.

He would take them to the pagodas, he thought. Maybe if he gave them something they would help him.

In the morning, his nose would not stop bleeding. He kept old pieces of rag stuffed up his nose and his mother made him lie down, but every time he removed the rags, his nose would bleed again.

"Will Papa come today?" he asked.

"He may, or he may arrive tomorrow morning. It won't be long."

Maurice thought about that. He wanted to see his papa. He felt better when his papa held him. But he did not like the doctor his papa took him to, and neither did his mother. The good doctors, as his mother called them, had said to keep him comfortable and to give him medicines to take away the pain. The doctor Papa had found believed he could cure Maurice if he bled him. Papa had had to hold him down while the doctor had cut his arm and let his blood drip into a

bowl. It had made him dizzy and sick, and he had embarrassed everyone by crying. It was why his mother had taken
him away from Paris to his grandmother's house in Ciboure.

"Can we walk to the river again?" he asked.

His mother laughed, but then she looked out the window
and put down her sewing. How many mornings would he
want do to something like this, she wondered? A nosebleed
was manageable.

She packed them a lunch and extra rags for his nose. They
walked slowly to the river. Maurice could not wait to be gone.
After eating a few bites, he stuffed some of the rags into his
pockets and started for the trees. His mother was glad to see
him take exercise, but she could not help herself. "Be careful,
Maurice," she called.

The day was chill, and Maurice wore a heavy sweater. He
took off his shoes when he came to the old rubbish heaps. He
stepped very carefully down to the river, careful not to crush
clumps of china shards and careful not to cut his feet. He
started to be able to distinguish the shards that made up a
pagoda's shell: they were the shiny and polished ones, the
ones with bits of color, not the ones caked with mud or dust.

He inspected the ground before he sat down, and he sat
where he had sat the day before. He listened, but he heard no
Chinese music. "Pagodas?" he whispered. "Pagodas?"

Nothing stirred. He looked around and saw a few clumps
that he recognized: the terra-cotta shards, still with the black
fleur-de-lys; the light pink shards; clumps that were all white.

"Don't be afraid," he whispered. "I've brought you presents."

He took the pouch out of his pocket and opened it in his
lap. He took out one of the pieces of blue glass and set it by

the nearest snowy white clump. He wasn't sure, but he thought it might have shivered ever so slightly at his touch. He waited for a time, then he set the crystal bead by the terra-cotta shards.

Slowly, shard by shard, the terra-cotta pieces rose up. He watched the bead roll along the different shards, passed from one to another until it stood balanced on the very top.

Other pagodas began to move then. They rose up and gathered warily around Maurice, keeping their distance. He could hear their tinkly music again, and all at once he understood part of what they were asking him.

"I'm Maurice," he said. "My name is Maurice Ravel."

They sang at him, and he imagined that they were telling him their names. He had never heard one of those names before. He thought the terra-cotta shards were saying "Ti Ti Ting."

"You *are* all Chinese!" he laughed.

Then he started coughing, and he could not stop coughing for a time. Most of the pagodas sank down to the ground while he coughed. But not Ti Ti Ting. It edged a little closer.

"Can you help me?" Maurice asked it. "Can you make me well? Tell me what to do, and I will do it."

All the shards grew quiet. The music stopped completely.

"I know my presents are not very valuable, but it was all I could think to bring you today."

Nothing happened. The pagodas did not tell him anything more then. After a time, Maurice could see pagodas moving all around him. The mounds were covered with them. He could see places where they were digging into the mounds— mining, he imagined, for shards to weave into their shells. In other places, they were forming what looked like protective walls four or five inches high with sharp-edged pieces of china poking out from them. He wondered what small enemies they could fear? Whatever it was, they were going about their business unconcerned with his presence.

When he heard his mother calling, he made his way barefoot back to the steps of the pottery. His mother met him there.

"Is your nose still bleeding?" she asked.

Maurice took out the rags, but no blood followed. He threw the rags aside, and he and his mother walked home.

His nose did not bleed again that day.

Before bed, his grandmother brewed him a tea from herbs she had sent for from Spain. A priest in San Sebastian had blessed the tea, and his grandmother had even paid to have the priest touch the cross of Saint Teresa of Avila to the little packet. His grandmother was sure the tea would cure Maurice. He drank the whole cup to please her. It did not taste bad.

His mother brought out her silver-handled brush from her bedroom and started brushing his grandmother's hair. She did this every night before they went to bed. He liked to lay his head in his grandmother's lap and watch her face while his mother brushed her hair. She would close her eyes and hold herself very still and lean her head back into the brushing. Sometimes Maurice fell asleep while he watched his grandmother, and his mother would have to wake him to take him to bed. He did not fall asleep that night. He lay awake on his grandmother's lap till his mother finished brushing, then she led him to bed.

"Tell me about pagodas," he asked as his mother tucked the blankets around his chin.

"Oh, they are magic creatures!" she said. "They live in crystal and porcelain cities hidden in the forests. Few people see them or their cities these days. But when I was a little girl, your grandmother told me about an evil man who had found one of their cities not far from here. He tried to steal their jewels, but the pagodas attacked him with their crystal swords. He ran away, but bore the scars on his hands and feet the rest of his life. Because of those scars, everyone in Ciboure knew he was a thief so they could watch out for him."

She stood up to go.

"Can pagodas heal people?" Maurice asked. "You told me before that they could."

She looked at Maurice, then she sat down on the edge of his bed and held his hands. "Sometimes in your sleep you can hear them singing," she said. "They weave healing spells in their music. I hope you hear their music tonight, Maurice. I wish we had pagodas in the back garden. I'd set them on your windowsill and let them sing to you all night."

When his mother had gone, Maurice touched his nose. It still was not bleeding, though it had bled most days since winter. He thought of the walks he could take now on his own, despite the fevers.

The pagodas were helping him. He was sure of it. If he could stay here long enough, they would cure him.

Maurice slept soundly but heard no music. He woke to the sound of his parents arguing softly in the kitchen. His father had come. Part of him wanted to jump out of bed and run to his father's arms, but he did not do that. Instead he lay listening to what his parents were saying. He could not hear the words clearly. He got out of bed and crept to the door. He heard his father say "doctor" and "bleeding." Then, "I want him to get well too! He's my son."

"I won't let anyone bleed him again!" his mother said.

"Does he still bruise easily? Does he still have fevers?"

"Yes, but—"

"Then Dr. Perrault knows how to help him! He uses ancient treatments for fevers and swelling, nosebleeds and abnormal bruising in children. I trust his techniques more than herbs and priests' blessings."

"Maurice is improving here. What Mother and I are doing is helping, though whether priests' blessings have anything to do with it I don't know. He is strong enough now to take walks every day. He sleeps through the nights. How could he ever sleep in Paris with all the street traffic?"

"You are wearing yourself out," his father said. "You can't do everything for him. None of us knows enough, Marie."

"I know enough not to hurt him."

"The other doctors we took him to had given up—they said to just keep him comfortable. At least Dr. Perrault had reason to think he could save him. Don't you think we should try, Marie? Don't you think we'd wonder the rest of our lives if we didn't try?"

Maurice had heard enough. He stood and opened the door. He looked out at his parents sitting at the big wooden table in front of the fireplace. His grandmother was still locked in her bedroom.

"Maurice," his father said. He stood and hurried to his son. Maurice did not want his father to touch him, but his father knelt and hugged him close. "Look at you!" he said. "So brown from the sun. Our neighbors in Paris will think I've adopted a peasant boy when I bring you back home."

"I don't want to go back to Paris," Maurice said. "Don't take me there again."

"Never go back to Paris? Who could say such a thing? Our home is in the greatest city in the world."

"I love the forest here, Papa. It's magic."

"All forests are magic," his father said.

His mother was setting out dishes for breakfast, and when Grandmother came out they all sat at the table. There was cheese and fresh bread, strawberries and milk.

"Don't ever take me back to Paris," Maurice said before any of them could take a bite.

His mother and father looked at each other. They all ate in silence for a time.

His father cleared his throat. "When do you set out on your walks, Maurice?" he asked. "May I go with you today? I want to see this magic forest of yours."

Maurice felt he had no choice but to take him. At noon that day, they set out. Maurice was nervous. He did not want his father accidentally stepping on the pagodas and crushing them. He decided not to take his father to the mounds of broken china. They would stop at the old pottery or even before they reached the trees. He'd claim to be sick, and his father would have to take him home.

His father carried a basket with a lunch in one hand, and he held Maurice's hand in the other. They passed his grandmother in her garden. She straightened up at their approach and bent her back.

"What a lovely summer this is," she said. "I find practically no slugs in the vegetables. The lettuce is free of slugs, and I found only one in the strawberries last week. Now if I could just keep the birds away."

"I'll make you a scarecrow when we return," Maurice's father said. "That should help."

She smiled and turned back to her hoeing. Maurice and his father walked to the river. Maurice was not very hungry. "You should eat to build up your strength," his father said. "Here, take more of this rabbit breast. Meat will make you strong."

"Yes, Papa," he said, and he did eat the meat. It was salty and good.

"Are those trees the forest you walk to?" his father asked, pointing.

They were soon among the trees and at the ruined pottery. They walked slowly. Maurice's legs hurt, and he was not making that up. "Can we just sit here for a time?" Maurice asked, and they sat on the steps.

His father rubbed Maurice's legs, then he put an arm around Maurice's shoulders and hugged him close. "I—" he started to say something, but he stopped. He looked away. He just held Maurice.

Maurice looked down at the mounds. They glittered, but his papa said nothing about that. Maurice looked all over the ground for the pagodas, but he saw none. That didn't surprise him. They would have taken cover at their approach.

But there were things moving on the nearest mound. Dark things. Maurice sat up straight. His father kicked at something at their feet, and Maurice saw that it was a shelled slug. It lay for a moment in the dirt where his father had kicked it, then it started crawling toward the mounds.

"Are those slugs on that mound, Papa?" Maurice asked.

His father looked where Maurice was pointing. "I think so," he said. "How odd. I've never seen them gather like that." He stood to walk over to the mound.

Maurice grabbed his hand. "Don't, Papa!"

"It's just slugs, Maurice."

"We have to be careful where we walk. We could crush things and not mean to."

"The slugs? You grandmother would be grateful if we stepped on them."

"No, you don't understand. If we walk over there, let me show you where to step."

His father sat down beside him again. "So the magic begins here, does it? What is it we're trying not to crush?"

His papa had a merry smile. Maurice knew that Papa thought this was a game he had made up, but Maurice didn't care. He had to get over to the mound to see what was happening.

"Take off your shoes and step where I step," Maurice said.

They unlaced their shoes, and his father followed along behind him. Maurice worried about his father's bigger feet, but he saw no pagodas along the way that his father might step on. None of the shards they passed were washed and polished.

The nearest mound was a frightening sight. It was covered in shelled slugs. They heaved themselves about it in a dark mass sometimes three or four deep.

"Testacella," his father said, "carnivorous slugs. They eat earthworms and other slugs. No wonder your grandmother's garden is free of slugs. If these testacella migrated through this region on their way here they would have cleaned out all the other varieties in their path."

Maurice was looking for the pagodas. Where would they have gone to escape this blight of slug-eating slugs?

"I've never seen so many in one place," his father said. "I wonder if it's their mating season?"

Maurice felt a growing panic inside him. He knew it was selfish to think only of himself, but if the slugs had done something to the pagodas or if they had driven them away and he could not find them again he would never get well.

"They seem to be trying to reach those other two mounds, but something is holding them back," his father said.

It was the pagoda walls. Maurice understood now what the pagodas feared and why they had had to build walls. But what did the slugs want here? Where were the pagodas?

Then he saw the terra-cotta shards with the black fleur-de-lys scattered on the ground on the wrong side of the wall. Three slugs were nosing among the pieces. "No!" Maurice screamed.

He started for Ti Ti Ting.

"Come back, Maurice!" his father said. "You'll cut your feet!"

But Maurice did not cut his feet. He stepped on the grass and the flowers and the slugs. He was glad to crush the slugs underfoot. He threw the three slugs on Ti Ti Ting into the river and knelt to pick up the pieces of the pagoda.

"What is it?" his father asked softly. He was standing next to him.

"A pagoda," Maurice said. He could barely talk. He would not cry, he told himself. He would not let himself cry in front of his father.

His father knelt down next to him. "What was the pagoda?"

Maurice held out the terra-cotta shards in his hands for his father to see. He picked up the piece with the black fleur-de-lys. "I gave it this piece," he said. "And I gave it a crystal bead. I can't find the bead."

"There it is, by your right foot." His father picked up the bead and handed it to Maurice.

"I watched them building these walls," Maurice said, nodding at the low walls in front of them. "I didn't know why they were doing it."

"Your pagoda was a brave one then. He was fighting outside the walls."

Maurice saw some of the pagodas he recognized lying on the ground on the safe side of the walls: the pink one, the white one with the piece of blue glass he had given it, clumps of multicolored shards.

"We have to go, Papa. They won't stand to fight if you are watching."

His father stood. He picked up a handful of slugs and threw them into the river.

Maurice stepped forward and set the pieces of Ti Ti Ting down by the other pagodas. Maybe they could do something for him. He wiped his eyes and watched for a moment, but none of the pagodas stood up. He wished he could make them trust his papa and get up to help Ti Ti Ting or at least get up to fight the slugs.

"They've breached your wall over here," his father said. "Let's get the slugs that have crawled onto that mound."

"It's not my wall," Maurice said.

"The pagodas' wall, I meant," he said.

Maurice went after the slugs that had crossed the wall. They were nosing down among the pagoda shards on the ground in the area. They *were* eating them! Maurice knew as he stepped along that he was probably stepping on pagodas, not just slugs. He didn't know what was worse: his crushing weight or the carnivorous slugs. He threw handful after handful of slugs into the river. His legs hurt and his arms hurt, and his nose started bleeding again.

"Maurice," his father called. "Let's go home. You've done all you can do to help here."

They sat on the steps of the ruined pottery and pulled off their slimy socks. "Just throw them away," his father said. "No one would want to wash them."

They rubbed their feet on the grass, then pulled on their shoes. Maurice had to turn his head so blood wouldn't drip onto his shoes while he tied them. He found the bloody rags he had thrown away days before and stuffed them back up his nose. He could see more slugs in the grass making their way slowly toward the mounds.

"The pagodas were helping me, Papa. They were healing me."

His papa considered that for a moment. "I'm sure they were," he said. "We all want to help you. Your grandmother tries with her priests. Your mother gives you good food, rest, and quiet. I would do anything for you too, Maurice. I've tried. I'm sure the pagodas did what they could."

He took his son's hand and led him away. When they came to the road, he had to carry Maurice.

* * *

But Maurice decided he had not done everything he could to help the pagodas. He lay feverish in his bed and listened to his parents talk quietly at the table. His father was trying to convince his mother to go back to Paris in a week or so. He knew what would happen there. Never mind Dr. Perrault and the bleeding. He knew what would happen to him without the pagodas.

And the pagodas themselves needed help. He could not let the slugs eat them whether they helped him or not. No one would believe him about the pagodas, of course. They thought he had made it all up.

After his parents and his grandmother had gone to bed, and after he had listened to his father snore for some time, Maurice crept out from under the covers. He had kept on his clothes and covered up before his mother had come to tuck him in, so no one had guessed that he was still dressed. He pulled on a sweater. He picked up his shoes, opened the bedroom door, and looked around the main room. No one was up. He walked barefoot to the kitchen and set a chair carefully by the cupboard. He stood on the chair and opened the top cupboard. He took out his grandmother's sack of salt. He would give her some of his money later to pay for it. Slugs hated salt. He'd use it to drive them away from the pagodas.

He closed the front door quietly behind him and set out down the road. There was a bright moon, and the road shined clearly ahead. He had to rest by the river, but soon he was at the ruined pottery.

It was darker there among the trees. The wind sighed in the branches. It felt different being among the trees at night. Maybe the slugs had changed the feeling of the forest, Maurice thought. He hurried up to the mounds. The slugs had breached the wall again and had covered half of the second mound. He looked frantically about for the pagodas, but saw none. He looked for the pieces of Ti Ti Ting, but they had been moved from where he had set them. The pagodas he had lain Ti Ti Ting next to had all moved somewhere else, too.

He looked around for the pagodas. "Don't be afraid," he called. "It's Maurice. I've come to help you fight!"

He started scattering salt onto the slugs at his feet. They curled up quickly into little balls at the slightest touch of salt. He took a handful of salt and threw it onto a mass of heaped slugs higher up the mound by the opening of what Maurice had thought was a pagoda mine. The slugs writhed and rolled around when the salt touched them. They would pull back into their segmented shells, then stick all the way out, then pull back inside. How the salt must hurt them, Maurice thought, but he had to try to help the pagodas. There was no stopping now.

"Where are you?" Maurice called to the pagodas. "I have only one bag of salt. Show me how best to help you before it's all gone."

Then he saw a pagoda, one of the white ones—the white one with the piece of blue glass. It was standing just around the edge of the second mound. It held up the piece of glass as if in salute. But then Maurice saw that it was pointing. He looked and saw a huge mass of slugs slowly crawling over the wall and swarming over the depression between the second and third mounds.

Maurice had an idea what they were swarming over— what they were eating there!

"I'm coming!" Maurice called.

He surprised the slugs from behind. He scattered salt over the slugs massed at the wall and left them writhing there. He started scattering salt on the huge heap of slugs in the depression, but there were so many. He picked up handful after handful and threw them into the river, then he scattered more salt.

He saw more pagodas, the pink ones and the white ones and all the multicolored ones. They were standing in a defensive line at the base of the third mound—and they did carry crystal swords! Maurice saw them glitter in the moonlight. The swords were as thin as needles. He watched them stab the slugs in the mouth with them. They would wait till a slug loomed over them, its mouth gaping open, then they would strike with their swords and pull back quickly. The slugs would snap about and try to bite them, but some fell over and did not move again.

The pagodas were stabbing through the mouth into the brain, Maurice realized.

He did not see Ti Ti Ting.

"Ti Ti Ting!" Maurice called. "Ti Ti Ting!"

But he could not see him.

"Did the slugs kill him?" he asked the other pagodas, but they did not have time to sing answers to his questions.

Maurice kept scattering salt and throwing slugs into the river. He started to conserve the salt. He threw only slugs he hadn't salted into the river. The pagodas advanced on the slugs he had salted, and they could easily dispatch them with their swords as they writhed about in salty agony. Maurice threw unsalted slugs until he had to rest. He sat down on a part of the third mound free of slugs and free of pagodas and changed the rags in his nose. His nose was bleeding steadily. He tried to stopper it up tight, though he knew the blood would soak through the rags and start dripping onto his clothes again.

He wanted to sleep. He was tired. He was feverish. But there were more and more slugs.

Then he saw Ti Ti Ting. He was drooping in a depression of the third mound. Maurice stood up to look down into that area. There were other drooped pagodas there, and some just lying on the ground. Three intact pagodas were singing to the hurt ones—he could hear the music softly. They were trying to heal their friends.

"Get well Ti Ti Ting!" Maurice said. "I know what it feels like to be sick. Get well!"

Ti Ti Ting stood a little straighter and looked at Maurice. He seemed to be trying to tell him something, but Maurice could not hear what it was. Maurice reached out and touched Ti Ti Ting softly, then he hurried off to scatter more salt.

When he ran out of salt, he filled the bag with slugs and emptied it into the river then went back for more. He dropped unsalted slugs onto the salted ones, trying to get twice the use for the salt. He worked for hours it seemed. The night grew darker, as it does before dawn. All the wind hushed. Maurice and the pagodas had cleared the slugs from the depression between the second and third mounds. Pagodas were manning their wall again. Others were securing the second mound and the wall there, and some were advancing even on the first mound.

Maurice could do no more. His arms ached, and his legs

ached so badly that he had to sit down. He lay back for a moment to slow the blood dripping from his nose.

He watched the pagodas. They were still fighting hard to save themselves, but Maurice thought they had the advantage now. He and his grandmother's salt had changed the outcome of the battle.

He knew he should be getting back before someone missed him. "Good-bye pagodas!" he said. "Good-bye Ti Ti Ting. I'll try to come back before we leave for Paris."

None of them noticed him now. They were all too busy. Maurice was tired and cold, but he decided to lie there just a little longer till maybe his legs felt a little better. He was not sure he could walk all the way home just then.

He woke with a start. Pagodas stood all around him, singing. There were more pagodas around him than he had ever seen. Ti Ti Ting stood right by his head.

The battle was over.

Maurice felt so at peace surrounded by the music he did not move. His head felt different somehow, clearer, not feverish. His nose had stopped bleeding.

A soft morning light burnished the glen and the mounds. A gentle breeze blew east off the bay. Yet it was so quiet he could hear the pagodas' music clearly.

They were singing for him.

Maurice closed his eyes. His legs did not ache. His nose throbbed, but it was not bleeding. He felt certain his body was healed. "Thank you," he whispered.

It seemed that Ti Ti Ting was singing thank you in return.

* * *

He woke again when he heard his mother and father calling his name. It was full light now. The pagodas had moved away. He could see them on all the mounds, even the first. He saw only dead slugs. He stepped carefully away from the mounds and walked steadily up to the pottery steps. He lay there waiting for his parents.

"Maurice!" he heard his mother call. "Maurice?"

"I'm here, Mother," he called.

He saw her running up the path. Soon he was in her arms, and Papa and Grandmother were there, too.

"I'm better now," Maurice said. "The pagodas sang to me last night. I went to sleep hearing them sing after we defeated the slugs, and I feel better now. They helped me."

"Oh, Maurice," his mother said.

But Maurice was right. He was still weak, and he had to work to regain his strength, but his nose did not bleed again. His legs did not bruise abnormally again. The fevers did not return. His grandmother thought her priests and their blessings had done it. His mother thought it had been all their tender care, and maybe a miracle. His father did not care how it had happened, just that his son was well again.

On their last day in Ciboure before returning to Paris, they all picnicked by the river. They let Maurice walk alone up to the old pottery.

He went straight to the mounds. The pagodas were there. None of them sank down at his approach. He looked around for Ti Ti Ting and found him standing guard on the repaired wall. Maurice knelt in front of him. He opened his tin soldier pouch and scattered the broken pieces of a dish his grandmother had dropped the day before. "I brought you presents," he said.

The pagodas all gathered around. He set down a big bag of salt in front of them. "You know how to use this," he said. "I'll bring you more next summer when we visit Grandmother."

The pagodas started singing. Maurice listened. He tried to catch a melody he could remember and hum, but it was all too different. The music seemed so foreign to him then. But Ti Ti Ting seemed insistent about something. Maurice leaned down to listen to what he might be saying. Maurice listened and listened—and suddenly he understood. Ti Ti Ting was telling Maurice that he would understand their music in time, that Maurice would write down some of it and present it to the world. They knew this about him: that Maurice would become a composer who would give beautiful music to a world that needed beauty.

Maurice sat up and laughed. "Oh, I hope so!" he said. "That would be such fun."

They said their good-byes, and Maurice made his way up the path. He met his father standing in shadows under the trees at the edge of the glen. He had an odd look on his face. Maurice just smiled and took his father's hand as they walked back to the others.

In the coming years, Maurice always took salt and bits of broken china to the pagodas when they visited his grandmother. His illness never returned, and he grew into a strong young man. In time, all the world knew the name "Maurice Ravel" because of the beautiful music he wrote. He remembered what Ti Ti Ting had told him, and when he could finally make sense of it, he used some of the pagoda music in his *Mother Goose Suite* and a ballet before that and a set of piano pieces before that. The music delights audiences to this day. Maurice hoped it might heal some of them.

One day, a letter arrived from his grandmother. She told him that a corporation had bought the ruined pottery with plans of establishing a shoe factory on the site. Maurice rushed to Ciboure. The men loading his trunks onto the train wondered why he took so many empty trunks, but when he returned they were not so empty. Maurice bought a house in the forest of Rambouillet outside Paris, and over time he purchased all the land around it. The neighbors wondered at the many happy parties the Ravel family held among the trees there, at all the tinkling lights and the Chinese-sounding music.

Maurice always donated to charities helping children with leukemia. From time to time he let his friends bring their children to his estate, if they were sick. They'd take them home well again weeks later.

The Ravels keep that forest estate to this day. It is a wild, brambly place with secret, flowered glens. No one will ever build on that land.

Other things have built there.

M. SHAYNE BELL has published short fiction in *Asimov's, Fantasy and Science Fiction, Interzone, Amazing Stories, Tomorrow, Science Fiction Age, Gothic.Net, SCI FICTION,* and *Realms of Fantasy,* plus numerous anthologies, including *The Year's Best Science Fiction, The Year's Best SF #6, Starlight 2, Future Earths: Under African Skies, The Best of Writers of the Future,* and *Vanishing Acts.* His short fiction is collected in *How We Play the Game in Salt Lake and Other Stories.*

Bell is author of the novel *Nicoji,* and editor of the anthology *Washed by a Wave of Wind: Science Fiction from the Corridor,* for which he received an AML award for editorial excellence.

M. Shayne Bell lives in Salt Lake City. His Web site address is: www.mshaynebell.com.

Author's Note:

This story began for me when the local classical radio station played something I had never heard: Maurice Ravel's suite *Ma Mère l'Oye.* The announcer explained that even though the piece in the suite titled "Laideronnette, Empress of the Pagodas" sounds Chinese, it actually has nothing to do with China: it's about *pagodas,* creatures of crystal, porcelain, and jewels that inhabit the forests of France.

When I heard that, I knew I had a story.

Finding details about the pagodas and Ravel's early life both proved difficult. The French writer Marie-Catherine d'Aulnoy first wrote about pagodas in the seventeenth century, but little more about them has been translated from the French. So little is known about pagodas outside France, in fact, that they are not even listed in most of the world's encyclopedias of mythical creatures.

Most biographers of Ravel gloss over his early life and start with his years at the Paris Conservatory. He is sometimes mentioned as having been sickly and frail as a boy. His father was Swiss and his mother came from a Basque village sharing a border with Spain. That both his mother and his father loved and supported him in every way possible is unquestioned.

So I built my romance on the life of Ravel from those few details. I tried to bring the love he knew as a boy into the story. I tried to bring some of his music. And I brought the pagodas, lovely creatures that they are, out of their ancient forests.

Although most of the story fictionalizes the early life of the musician, the Ravel family really does still own Maurice's estate in the Rambouillet Forest outside Paris.

Green Men

BILL LEWIS

GREEN MEN GRIN and gurn
from blackened beams
that creak and groan
as ancient houses dream
and are swayed by
wind in branches
long since snapped.
Foliate faces flower and the
memory of an antique hour
unwinds beneath
a carpenter's craft;
masons, too, saw their shape
sleeping in the stone.
So all is forest then,
vegetable, mineral, flesh, bone.
The world tree becomes
the column of my spine;
eyelids leaves of oak;

fingers ash and pine.
I am lost within a wood
that is lost within me.
Green men grin and gurn,
for no one knows more than they
what is and is not tree.

$BILL\ LEWIS$ is a poet, storyteller, and performance artist from a rural working-class background in Kent, England. His collections to date include *Rage without Anger, The Wine of Connecting, The Intellect of the Heart, Shattered English, Leaving the Autoroute,* and *Beauty Is the Beast.* He is a founding member of the Medway Poets group and the international "Stuckists" art movement, and has traveled extensively through Europe, North America, and South America giving performances and readings. In America, his poems have appeared in various journals and *The Year's Best Fantasy and Horror* volumes. He also teaches in adult education centers, schools, and prisons, committed to bringing poetry and art to people from all walks of life. Bill Lewis lives in Chatham, Kent.

Author's Note:

Many of my poems are mythic in nature, and the Green Man is an image I've always found compelling. This particular poem was inspired by carved wood figures and faces on the buildings of Canterbury. I've often wondered what parts of these buildings, which are largely Elizabethan, might have been made of recycled materials originally belonging to much older dwellings. The village where I grew up in Kent had a medieval church containing bits of wood and decoration dating back to Roman times. My father used to point this out: the pagan past propping up the Christian present.

THE GREEN WORD
꒰

JEFFREY FORD

ON THE DAY that Moren Kairn was to be executed, a crow appeared at the barred window of his tower cell. He lay huddled in the corner on a bed of foul straw, his body covered with bruises and wounds inflicted by order of the king. They had demanded that he pray to their God, but each time they pressed him, he spat. They applied the hot iron, the knife, the club, and he gave vent to his agony by cursing. The only thing that had prevented them from killing him was that he was to be kept alive for his execution.

When he saw the crow, his split lips painfully formed a smile, for he knew the creature was an emissary from the witch of the forest. The black bird thrust its head between the bars of the window and dropped something small and round from its beak onto the stone floor of the cell. "Eat this," it said. Then the visitor cawed, flapped its wings, and was gone. Moren held out his hand as if to beg the bird to take him away with it, and for a brief moment, he dreamed he was flying out of the tower, racing away from the palace toward the cool green cover of the trees.

Then he heard them coming for him, the warder's keyring jangling, the soldiers' heavy footsteps against the flagstones of the circular stairway. He ignored the pain of his broken limbs, struggled to all fours, and crept slowly across the cell to where the crow's gift lay. He heard the soldiers laughing and the key slide into the lock as he lifted the thing up to discover what it was. In his palm, he held a round, green seed that he had never before seen the likes of. When the door opened, so did his mouth, and as the soldiers entered, he swallowed the seed. No sooner was it in his stomach than he envisioned a breezy summer day in the stand of willows where he had first kissed his wife. She moved behind the dangling green tendrils of the trees and when a soldier spoke his name it was in her voice, calling him to her.

With a gloved hand beneath each arm, they dragged him to his feet, and he found that his pain was miraculously gone. The noise of the warder's keys had somehow become the sound of his daughter's laughter, and he laughed, himself, as they pulled him roughly down the steps. Outside, the midsummer sunlight enveloped him like water, and he remembered swimming beneath the falls at the sacred center of the forest. He seemed to be enjoying himself far too much for a man going to his death, and one of the soldiers struck him across the back with the flat side of a sword. In his mind, though, that blow became the friendly slap of his fellow warrior, the archer Lokush. Moren had somehow forgotten that his best bowman had died not but a week earlier, along with most of his other men, on the very field he was now so roughly escorted to.

The entirety of the royal court, the knights and soldiers and servants, had gathered for the event. To Kairn, each of them was a green tree and their voices were the wind rippling through the leaves of that human thicket. He was going back to the forest now, and the oaks, the alders, the yews parted to welcome him.

The prisoner was brought before the royal throne and made to kneel.

"Why is this man smiling?" asked King Pious, casting an accusatory glance at the soldiers who had accompanied the prisoner. He scowled and shook his head. "Read the list of grievances and let's get on with it," he said.

A page stepped forward and unfurled a large scroll. Whereas all in attendance heard Kairn's crimes intoned— sedition, murder, treachery—the warrior himself heard the voice of the witch, chanting the beautiful poetry of one of her spells. In the midst of the long list of charges, the queen leaned toward Pious and whispered, "Good lord, he's going green." Sure enough, the prisoner's flesh had darkened to a deep hue the color of jade.

"Finish him before he keels over," said the king, interrupting the page.

The soldiers spun Moren Kairn around and laid his head on the chopping block. From behind the king stepped a tall knight encased in gleaming red armor. He lifted his broadsword as he approached the kneeling warrior. When the deadly weapon was at its apex above his neck, Kairn laughed, discovering that the witch's spell had transformed him into a seed pod on the verge of bursting.

"Now," said the king.

The sharp steel flashed as it fell with all the force the huge knight could give it. With a sickening slash and crunch of bone, Kairn's head came away from his body and rolled onto the ground. It landed, facing King Pious, still wearing that inscrutable smile. In his last spark of a thought, the warrior saw himself, a thousandfold, flying on the wind, returning to the green world.

All but one who witnessed the execution of Moren Kairn that day believed he was gone for good and that the revolt of the people of the forest had been brought to an end. She, who knew otherwise, sat perched in a tree on the boundary of the wood two hundred yards away. Hidden by leaves and watching with hawklike vision, the witch marked the spot where the blood of the warrior had soaked into the earth.

Arrayed in a robe of fine purple silk King Pious sat by the window of his bedchamber and stared out into the night toward the tree line of the forest. He had but an hour earlier awakened from a deep sleep, having had a dream of that day's execution—Kairn's green flesh and smile—and called to the servant to come and light a candle. Leaning his chin on his hand and his elbow on the arm of the great chair, he raked his fingers through his white beard and wondered why, now that the threat of the forest revolt was eradicated, he still could not rest easily.

For years he had lived with their annoyance, their claims to the land, their refusal to accept the true faith. To him they were godless heathens, ignorantly worshiping trees and bushes, the insubstantial deities of sunlight and rain. Their gods were the earthbound, corporeal gods of simpletons. They had the audacity to complain about his burning of the forest to create new farmland, complained that his hunting parties were profligate and wasted the wild animal life for mere sport, that his people wantonly fished the lakes and streams with no thought of the future.

Had he not been given a holy edict by the pontiff to bring this wild territory into the domain of the church, convert its heathen tribes, and establish order amidst this demonic chaos? All he need do was search the holy scripture of the Good Book resting in his lap and in a hundred different places he would find justification for his actions. Righteous was his mission against Kairn, whom he suspected of having been in league with the devil.

Pious closed the book and placed it on the stand next to his chair. "Be at ease, now," he murmured to himself, and turned his mind toward the glorious. He had already decided that in midwinter when what remained of the troublesome rabble would be hardest pressed by disease and hunger, he would send his soldiers into the maze of trees to ferret out those few who remained and return them to the earth they claimed to love so dearly.

As the candle burned, he watched its dancing flame and decided he needed some merriment, some entertainment to wash the bad taste of this insurrection from his palate. He wanted something that would amuse him, but also increase his renown. It was a certainty that he had done remarkable things in the territory, but so few of the rulers of the other kingdoms to the far south would have heard about them. He knew he must bring them to see the extraordinary palace he had constructed, the perfect order of his lands, the obedience of his subjects.

While he pondered, a strong wind blew across the fields from out of the forest, entered the window by which he sat, and snuffed the flame of the candle. At the very moment in which the dark ignited in his room and swiftly spread to cover everything in shadow, the idea came to him. A tournament—he would hold a tournament and invite the knights from the southern kingdoms to his palace in the spring. He was sure that his own Red Knight had no equal. The challenge would go out the following morning, and he would begin preparations immediately. The invitation would be so worded to imply that his man could not be beaten, for he, Pious, had behind him the endorsement of the Almighty. "That should rouse them enough to make the long journey to my kingdom," he whispered. Then he saw the glorious day in his imagination and sat for some time, laughing in the dark. When he finally drifted off to sleep, he fell into another nightmare in which a flock of dark birds had rushed into his bedchamber through the open window.

The witch of the forest, doubly wrapped in black, first by her long cloak and then by night, crouched at the edge of the tree line, avoiding the gaze of the full autumn moon, and surveyed with a keen eye the field that lay between herself and the palace. She made a clicking noise with her tongue, and the crow that had perched upon her shoulder lit into the sky and circled the area in search of soldiers. In minutes it returned with a report, a low gurgling sound that told her the guards were quite a distance away, just outside the protective walls. She whistled the song of a nightingale, and a large black dog with thick shoulders padded quietly to her side over fallen leaves.

She pulled the hood of the cloak over her head, tucking in her long white hair. Although she had more years than the tallest of trees looming behind her had rings, she moved with perfect grace, as if she was a mere shadow floating over the ground. The dog followed close behind and the crow remained on her shoulder, ready to fly off into a soldier's face if need be. The same memory that gave her the ability to recall, at a moment's notice, spells containing hundreds of words, all of the letters in the tree alphabet, the languages of the forest creatures, and the recipes for magical concoctions, worked now to help her pinpoint the spot where Moren Kairn's blood had soaked the earth three months earlier.

When she knew she was close, she stopped and bent over to search through the dark for new growth. Eventually she saw it, a squat, stemless plant, bearing the last of its glowing berries and yellow flowers into the early weeks of autumn. She dropped down to her knees, assuming the same position that Kairn had the day of his execution, and with her hands, began loosening the dirt in a circle around the plant's thick base. The ground was hard, and an implement would have made the job easier, but it was necessary that she use her hands in order to employ the herb in her magic.

Once the ground had been prepared, she started on a circular course around the plant, treading slowly and chanting in whispers a prayer to the great green mind that flows through all of nature. As she intoned her quiet plea in a singsong melodic voice, she thought of poor Kairn and her tears fell, knowing she would soon join him.

From within her cloak, she retrieved a long length of rope woven from thin vines. Taking one end, she tied it securely around the base of the plant. With the other end in hand, she backed up twenty paces and called the dog to her with the same whistled note she had used earlier. He walked over and sat, letting her tie that end of the rope around his neck. Once the knot was tight, she petted the beast and kissed him atop the head. "Stay now, Mahood," she whispered and the dog did not move as she backed farther away from it. Then she took four small balls of wild sheep wool from a pouch around her waist. Carefully, she stuffed one into each of the dog's ears and one in each of her own.

The moon momentarily passed behind a cloud, and as she waited for it to reappear, the crow left her shoulder. Eventually, when the moon had a clear view of her again, she motioned with both hands for the dog to join her. Mahood started on his way and then was slowed by the tug of the plant. She dropped to her knees, opened her arms wide and the dog lurched forward with all his strength. At that moment, the root of the plant came free from the ground, and its birth scream ripped through the night, a piercing wail like a pin made of sound for bursting the heart. Both witch and dog were protected from its cry by the tiny balls of wool, but she could see the effects the terrible screech still had on Mahood, whose hearing was more acute. The dog stopped in his tracks as if stunned. His eyes went glassy, he exhaled one long burst of steam, and then sat down.

The witch did not hesitate for a heartbeat but began running. As she moved, she reached for the knife in her belt. With a smooth motion she lifted the exposed root of the plant and tugged once on the vine rope to warn Mahood to flee. Then she brought the knife across swiftly to sever the lead, and they were off across the field, like flying shadows. She made for the tree line with the crow flapping in the air just above her left shoulder. The bird cawed loudly, a message that the soldiers had heard and were coming on horseback. The hood fell from her head, and her long white hair flew out behind her, signaling to her pursuers.

When she was a hundred yards from the boundary of the forest, she could hear the hoofbeats closing fast. The mounted soldier in the lead yelled back to those who followed, "It's the crone," and then nocked an arrow in place on his bow. He pulled back on the string and aimed directly for her back. Just as he was about to release, something flew into his face. A piece of night with wings and sharp talons gouged at his right eye. The arrow went off and missed its mark, impaling the ground in the spot where the witch's foot had been but a second before.

Mahood had bounded ahead and already found refuge in among the trees of the forest. The crow escaped and the witch ran on, but there was still fifty yards of open ground to cover and now the other horsemen were right on her heels. The lead soldier drew his sword and spurred his horse to greater speed. Once, twice, that blade cut the air behind her head and on both passes severed strands of her long hair. Just when the soldier thought he finally had her, they had reached the boundary of the trees. He reared back with the sword to strike across her back, but she leaped before he could land the blow. The height of her jump was miraculous. With her free hand, she grabbed the bottom branch of the closest tree and swung herself up with all the ease of a child a hundred years younger. The other soldiers rode up to join their companion at the tree line just in time to hear her scampering away, like a squirrel, through the dark canopy of the forest.

The black dog was waiting for her at her underground cave, whose entrance was a hole in the ground amidst the vast stand of willows. Once safely hidden her den, she reached beneath her cloak and pulled out the root of the Mandrake. Holding it up to the light from a burning torch, she perused the unusual design of the plant's foundation. Shaped like a small man, it had two arms extending from the thick middle part of the body and at the bottom a V shape of two legs. At the top, where she now cut away the green part of the herb, there was a bulbous lump, like a rudimentary head. This root doll, this little wooden mannikin, was perfect.

She sat on a pile of deerskins covering a low rock shelf beneath the light of the torch. Taking out her knife, she held it not by the bone handle but at the middle of the blade, so as to have finer control over it. The technique she employed in carving features into the Mandrake root was an ancient art called *simpling*. First, she carefully gouged out two eyes, shallow holes precisely equidistant from the center of the head bump. An upward cut beneath the eyes raised a partial slice of the root. This she delicately trimmed the corners off of to make the nose. Next, she made rudimentary cuts where the joints of the elbows, knees, wrists and ankles should be on the limbs. With the tip of the blade, she worked five small fingers into the end of each arm to produce rough facsimiles of hands. The last, but most important job was the mouth. For this opening, she changed her grip on the knife and again took it by the handle. Applying the sharp tip to a spot just below the nose, she spun the handle so as to bore a deep, perfect circle.

She laid the knife down by her side and took the Mandrake into the crook of her arm, the way in which one might hold a baby. Rocking forward and back slightly, she began to sing a quiet song in a language as old as the forest itself. With the thumb of her free hand she persistently massaged the chest of the plant doll. Her strange lullaby lasted nearly an hour, until she began to feel a faint quivering of the root in response to her touch. As always with this process, the life pulse existed only in her imagination at first, but as she continued to experience it, the movement gradually transformed from notion to actuality until the thing was verily squirming in her grasp.

Laying the writhing root in her lap, she lifted the knife again and carefully sliced the thumb with which she had kneaded life into it. When she heard the first peep of a cry come from the root child, she maneuvered the self-inflicted wound over the round mouth of the thing and carefully let three drops of blood fill the orifice. When the Mandrake had tasted her life, it began to wriggle and coo. She lifted it in both hands, rose to her feet and carried it over to a diminutive cradle she had created for it. Then looking up at the crow, who perched on a deer skull resting atop a stone table on the other side of the vault, she nodded. The bird spoke a single word and flew up out of the den. By morning, the remaining band of forest people would line up before the cradle and each offer three drops of blood for the life of the strange child.

King Pious hated winter, for the fierce winds that howled outside the palace walls in the long hours of the night seemed the voice of a hungry beast come to devour him. The cold crept into his joints and set them on fire, and any time he looked out his window in the dim daylight all he saw was his kingdom buried deeply beneath a thick layer of snow the color of a bloodless corpse. During these seemingly endless frigid months, he was often beset by the thought that he had no heir to perpetuate his name. He slyly let it be known that the problem lay with the queen, who he hinted was obviously barren, but whom, out of a keen sense of honor, he would never betray by taking another wife. The chambermaids, though, knew for certain it was not the queen who was barren, and when the winds howled so loudly in the night that the king could not overhear them, they whispered this fact to the pages, who whispered it to the soldiers, who had no one else to tell but each other and their horses.

To escape the beast of winter, King Pious spent much of the day in his enclosed pleasure garden. Here was summer confined within four walls. Neat, perfectly symmetrical rows of tulips, hyacinths, roses, tricked into growth while the rest of nature slept, grew beneath a crystal roof that gathered what little sunlight there was and magnified its heat and light to emulate the fair season. Great furnaces beneath the floor heated the huge chamber and butterflies, cultivated for the purpose of adding a touch of authenticity to the false surroundings, were released daily. Servants skilled in the art of recreating bird sounds with their voices were stationed in rooms adjoining the pleasure garden, and their mimicked warblings were piped into the chamber through long tubes.

In the afternoon of the day on which the king was given the news that the first stirrings of spring had begun to show themselves in the world outside the palace walls, he was sitting on his throne in the very center of the enclosed garden, giving audience to his philosopher.

On a portable stand before him lay a device that the venerable academician had just recently perfected, a miniature model with working parts that emulated the movement of the heavens. The bearded wise man in tall pointed hat and starry robe lectured Pious on the Almighty's design of the universe. The curious creation had a long arm holding a gear train attached to a large box with a handle on the side. At the end of the arm were positioned glass balls, connected with wire, representative of the Sun and Earth and other planets. Pious watched as the handle was turned and the solar system came to life, the heavenly bodies whirling on their axes while at the same time defining elliptical orbits.

"You see, your highness," said the philosopher, pointing to the blue ball, largest of the orbs, "the Earth sits directly at the center of the universe, the Almighty's most important creation which is home to his most perfect creation, mankind. All else, the Sun, the Moon, the planets and stars, revolve around us, paying homage to our existence as we pay homage to God."

"Fascinating," said the king as he stared intently at the device that merely corroborated for him his place of eminence in the far flung scheme of things.

"Would you like to operate the device?" asked the philosopher.

"I shall," said the king. He stood up and smoothed out his robes. Then he advanced and placed his hand on the handle of the box. He gently made the world and the heavens spin and a sense of power filled him, easing the winter ache of his joints and banishing, for a moment, the thought that he had no heir. This feeling of new energy spread out from his head to his arm, and he began spinning the handle faster and faster, his smile widening as he put the universe through its paces.

"Please, your highness," said the philosopher, but at that instant something came loose and the entire contraption flew apart, the glass balls careening off through the air to smash against the stone floor of the garden.

The king stood, looking perplexed, holding the handle, which had broken away from the box, up before his own eyes. "What is this?" he shouted. "You assassinate my senses with this ill-conceived toy of chaos." He turned in anger and beat the philosopher on the head with the handle of the device, knocking his pointed hat onto the floor.

The philosopher would have lost more than his hat that afternoon had the king's anger not been interrupted. Just as Pious was about to order a beheading, the captain of the guard strode into the garden, carrying something wrapped in a piece of cloth.

"Excuse me, your highness," he said, "but I come with urgent news."

"For your sake, it had better be good," said the king, still working to catch his breath. He slumped back into his chair.

"The company that I led into the forest last week has just

now returned. The remaining forest people have been captured and are in the stockade under guard. There are sixty of them, mostly women and children and elders."

Pious straightened up in his seat. "You have done very well," he told the soldier. "What of the witch?"

"We came upon her in the forest, standing in a clearing amidst a grove of willows with her arms crossed as if waiting for us to find her. I quietly called for my best archer and instructed him in whispers to use an arrow with a poison tip. He drew his bow and just before he released the shaft, I saw her look directly at where we were hiding beneath the long tendrils of a willow thirty feet from her. She smiled just before the arrow pierced her heart. Without uttering a sound, she fell forward, dead on the spot."

"Do you have her body? I want it burned," said Pious.

"There is no body, your highness."

"Explain," said the king, beginning to lose his patience.

"Once the bowman hit his mark, we advanced from the trees to seize her, but before we could lay hands on her, her very flesh, every part of her, became a swirling storm of dandelion seed. I swear to you, before my very eyes, she spiraled like a dust devil three times and then the delicate fuzz that she had become was carried up and dispersed by the wind."

Pious nodded, thought for a second and then said, "Very well. What is that you carry?"

The soldier unwrapped the bundle and held up a book for the king to see. "We found this in her cave," he said.

The king cleared his eyes with the backs of his hands. "How can this be? he asked. "That is the copy of the Good Book I keep in my bedchamber. What kind of trickery is this?"

"Perhaps she stole it, your highness."

Pious tried to think back to the last time he had picked the book up and studied it. Finally he remembered it was the night of Kairn's execution. "I keep it near the open window. My God, those horrid birds of my dream." The king looked quickly over each shoulder at the thought of it. "A bag of gold to the bowman who felled her," he added.

The captain nodded. "What of the prisoners, your highness?" he asked.

"Execute the ones who refuse to convert to the faith, and the others I want taught a hymn that they will perform on the day of the tournament this spring. We'll show our visitors how to turn heathens into believers."

"Very good, your highness," said the captain and then handed the book to the king. He turned and left the garden.

By this time, the philosopher had crept away to hide and Pious was left alone in the pleasure garden. "Silence!" he yelled in order to quell the birdsong, which now sounded to him like the whispers of conspirators. He rested back in his throne, exhausted from the day's activities. Paging through the Good Book, he came to his favorite passage—one that spoke elegantly of vengeance. He tried to read, but the idea of the witch's death so relaxed him that he became drowsy. He closed his eyes and slept with the book open on his lap while that day's butterflies perished and the universe lay in shards scattered across the floor.

The tournament was held on the huge field that separated the palace from the edge of the forest. Spring had come, as it always did, and that expanse was green with new-grown grass. The days were warm and the sky was clear. Had it not been for the tumult of the event, these would have been perfect days to lie down beneath the sun and daydream up into the bottomless blue. As it was, the air was filled with the cheers of the crowd and the groans of agony from those who fell before the sword of the Red Knight.

Pious sat in his throne on a dais beneath a canvas awning, flanked on the right and left by the visiting dignitaries of the southern kingdoms. He could not recall a time when he had been more pleased or excited, for everything was proceeding exactly as he had imagined it. His visitors were obviously impressed with the beauty of his palace and the authority he exhibited over his subjects. He gave orders a dozen an hour in an imperious tone that might have made a rock hop to with a "Very good, your highness."

Not the least of his pleasures was the spectacle of seeing the Red Knight thrash the foreign contenders on the field of battle. That vicious broadsword dislocated shoulders, cracked shins, and hacked appendages even through the protective metal of opponents' armor. When one poor fellow, the pride of Belthaena, clad in pure white metal, had his heart skewered and crashed to the ground dead, the king leaned forward and, with a sympathetic smile, promised the ambassador of that kingdom that he would send a flock of goats to the deceased's family. So far it had been the only fatality of the four day long event, and it did little to quell the festivities.

On the final day, when the last opponent was finished off and lay writhing on the ground with a broken leg, Pious sat up straight in his chair and applauded roundly. As the loser was carried from the field, the king called out, "Are there any other knights present who would like to test our champion?" Since he knew very well that every represented kingdom had been defeated, he made a motion to one of his councilors to have the converted begin singing. The choir of forest people, chained at the ankles and to each other shuffled forward and loosed the first notes of the hymn that had been beaten into their memories over the preceding weeks.

No sooner did the music start, though, than the voice of the crowd overpowered its sound, for now there was a new contender on the tournament field. He stood, tall and gangly, not in armor, but wrapped in a black, hooded cloak. Instead of a broadsword or mace or lance, he held only a long stick fashioned from the branch of a tree. When the Red Knight saw the surprised face of the king, he turned to view this new opponent. At this moment, the crowd, the choir and the dignitaries went perfectly quiet.

"What kind of mockery is this?" yelled Pious to the figure on the field.

"No mockery, your highness. I challenge the Red Knight," said the stranger in a voice that sounded like a limb splintering free from an oak.

The king was agitated at this circumstance that had been no part of his thoughts when he had imagined the tournament. "Very well," he called, and to his knight, said, "Cut him in half."

As the Red Knight advanced, the stranger undid the clasp at the neck of his cloak and dropped it to the ground. The crowd's response was a uniform cry torn between a gasp and a shriek of terror, for standing before them now was a man made entirely of wood. Like a tree come to life, his branch-like limbs, though fleshed in bark, somehow bent pliantly. His legs had the spring of saplings, and the fingers with which he gripped his paltry weapon were five-part pointed roots, trailing thin root hairs from the tips of the digits. The gray bark of his body held bumps and knots like a log, and in certain places small twigs grew from him, covered at their ends with green leaves. There was more foliage simulating hair upon his pointed head and a fine stubble of grass across his chin. Directly in the center of his chest, beneath where one's heart might hide, there grew from a protruding twig a large blue fruit.

The impassive expression that seemed crudely chiseled into the face of the wooden man did not change until the Red Knight stepped forward and with a brutal swing lopped off the tree root hand clutching the stick. Then that dark hole of a mouth stretched into a toothless smile, forming wrinkles of joy beneath the eyes. The Red Knight stepped back to savor the pain of his opponent, but the stranger exhibited no signs of distress. He held the arm stump up for all to see and, in a blur, a new hand grew to replace the one on the ground.

The Red Knight was obviously stunned, for he made no move as the tree man came close to him and placed that new hand up in front of his enemy's head. When the king's champion finally meant to react, it was too late. For as all the crowd witnessed, the five sharp tips of the root appendage grew outward as swiftly as snakes striking and found their way into the eye slits of the knight's helmet. Ghastly screams echoed from within the armor as blood seeped out of the metal joints and onto the grass. The knight's form twitched and the metal arms clanked rapidly against the metal sides of the suit. The broadsword fell point first and stuck into the soft spring earth. When the stranger retracted his hand, the fingers growing back into themselves, now wet with blood, the Red Knight tipped over backward and landed with a loud crash on the ground.

Pious immediately called for his archers. Three of them stepped forward and fired at the new champion. Each of the arrows hit its mark, thunking into the wooden body. The tree man, nonchalantly swept them off him with his arm. Then he advanced toward the dais, and the crowd, the soldiers, the visiting dignitaries fled. The king was left alone. He sat, paralyzed, staring at the advancing creature. So wrapped in a rictus of fear was Pious that all he could manage was to close his eyes. He waited for the feel of a sharp root to pierce his chest and puncture his heart. Those moments seemed an eternity to him, but eventually he realized nothing had happened. When he could no longer stand it, he opened his eyes to an amazing scene. The tree man was kneeling before him.

"My liege," said the stranger in that breaking voice. Then he stood to his full height, and said, "I believe as winner of the tournament, I am due a feast."

"Quite right," said Pious, trembling with relief that he would not die. "You are an exceptional warrior. What is your name?"

"Vertuminus," said the tree man.

A table had been hastily brought into the pleasure garden and laid with the finest place settings in the palace. The feast was prepared for only Pious and the wooden knight. The visiting ambassadors and dignitaries were asked if they would like to attend, but they all suddenly had pressing business back in their home kingdoms and had to leave immediately after the tournament.

The king dined on roasted goose, whereas Vertuminus had requested only fresh water and a large bucket of soil to temporarily root his tired feet in. Soldiers were in attendance, lining the four walls of the garden, and were under orders to have their swords sharp and to keep them drawn in case the stranger's amicable mood changed. Pious feared the tree man, but was also curious as to the source of his animation and bizarre powers.

"And so my friend, you were born in the forest, I take it?" asked the king. He tried to stare into the eyes of the guest, which blinked and dilated in size though they were merely gouges in the bark that was his face.

"I was drawn up from the earth by the witch," he said.

"The witch," said Pious, pausing with a leg of the goose in his hand.

"Yes, she made me with one of her spells, but she has abandoned me. I do not know where she has gone. I have been lonely and needed other people to be with. I have been watching the palace from a distance, and I wanted to join you here."

"We are very glad you did," said the king.

"The witch told me that you lived by the book. She showed me the book and taught me to read it so that I would know better how to wage war on you."

"And do you wish me harm?" asked Pious.

"No, for when I read the book it started to take hold of me and drew me to its thinking away from the forest. I joined the tournament so that I could win a place at the palace."

"And you have," said Pious. "I will make you my first knight."

Here Vertuminus recited the king's favorite passage from the good book. "Does it not make sense?" he asked.

Pious slowly chewed and shook his head. "Amazing," he said, and for the first time spoke genuinely.

"You are close to the Almighty?" asked Vertuminus.

"Very close," said the king.

There was a long silence, in which Pious simply sat and stared as his guest drank deeply from a huge cup.

"And if you don't mind my asking," said the king, pointing "what is that large blue growth on your chest?"

"That is my heart," said Vertuminus. "It contains the word."

"What word?" asked Pious.

"Do you know in the book, when the Almighty creates the world?"

"Yes."

"Well, how does he accomplish this?" asked the tree man.

"How?" asked the king.

"He speaks these things into creation. He says, 'Let there be light,' and there is. For everything he creates, he uses a different word. This fruit contains the green word. It is what gives me life."

"Is there a word in everything?" asked Pious.

"Yes," said Vertuminus, whose index finger grew out and speared a pea off the king's platter. As the digit retracted, and he brought the morsel to his mouth, he said, "There is a word in each animal, a word in each person, a word in each rock, and these words of the Almighty make them what they are."

Suddenly losing his appetite, the king pushed his meal away. He asked, "But if that fruit of yours contains the green word, why is it blue?"

"Only its skin is blue, the way the sky is blue and wraps around the earth."

"May I touch it?" asked Pious.

"Certainly," said Vertuminus, "but please be careful."

"You have my word," said Pious, as he stood and slowly reached a trembling hand across the table. His fingers encompassed the blue fruit and gently squeezed it.

The wooden face formed an expression of pain. "That is enough," said the tree man.

"Not quite," said the king, and with a simple yank, pulled the fruit free from its stem.

Instantly, the face of Vertuminus went blank, his branch arms dropped to his sides, lifeless, and his head nodded.

Pious sat back in his throne, unable to believe that defeating the weird creature could have been so easy. He held the fruit up before his eyes, turning it with his fingers, and pondered the idea of the word of God trapped beneath a thin blue skin.

The ruler sat in silent contemplation, and in his mind formulated a metaphor in which the acquisition of all he desired could be as easy as his plucking this blue prize. It was a complex thought for Pious, one in which the blue globe of the world from the philosopher's contraption became confused with the fruit.

He nearly dropped the precious object when suddenly his lifeless guest gave a protracted groan. The king looked up in time to see another blue orb rapidly growing on the chest of the tree man. It quickly achieved fullness, like a balloon being inflated. He gave a gasp of surprise when his recently dead guest smiled and brought his branch arms up.

"Now it is my turn," said Vertuminus, and his root fingers began to grow toward the king.

"Guards," called Pious, but they were already there. Swords came down on either side, and hacked off the wooden limbs. As they fell to the floor, Pious wasted no time. He dove across the table and plucked the new blue growth. Again, Vertuminus fell back into his seat, lifeless.

"Quickly, men, hack him to pieces and burn every twig!" In each of his hands he held half of his harvest. He rose from his throne and left the pleasure garden, the sound of chopping following him out into the corridor. Here was a consolation for having lost his Red Knight, he thought—something that could perhaps prove far more powerful then a man encased in metal.

When Pious ordered that one of the forest people be brought to him, he had no idea that the young woman chosen was the daughter of Moren Kairn. She was a tall, willowy specimen of fifteen with long blonde hair that caught the light at certain angles and appeared to harbor the slightest hues of green. Life in the stockade, where the remaining rebels were still kept was very difficult. For those who did not willingly choose the executioner over conversion to the faith, food was used as an incentive to keep them on the path to righteousness. If they prayed they ate, but never enough to completely satisfy their hunger. And so this girl, like the others, was exceedingly thin.

She stood before the king in his study, a low table separating her from where he sat. On that table was a plate holding the two blue orbs that had been plucked from Vertuminus.

"Are you hungry, my dear?" asked the king.

The girl, frightened for her life, knowing what had become of her father and having witnessed executions in the stockade, nodded nervously.

"That is a shame," said Pious. "In order to make it up to you, I have a special treat. Here is a piece of fruit." He waved his hand at the plate before him. "Take one."

She looked to either side where soldiers stood guarding her every move.

"It's quite all right," said Pious in as sweet a tone as he was capable.

The girl reached out her hand and carefully lifted a piece of fruit. She brushed her hair away from her face with her free hand as she brought the blue food to her mouth.

The king leaned forward with a look of expectation on his face as she took the first bite. He did not know what to expect and feared for the worst. But the girl, after tasting a mouthful, smiled, and began greedily devouring the rest of it. She ate it so quickly he barely had time to see that its insides, though green, were succulent like the pulp of an orange.

When it was finished and she held nothing but the pit in her hand, Pious asked her, "And how was that?"

"The most wonderful thing I have ever tasted," she whispered.

"Do you feel well?" he asked.

"I feel strong again," she said and smiled.

"Good," said Pious. He motioned to one of the soldiers to escort her back to the stockade. "You may go now," he said.

"Thank you," said the girl.

"Once she and the soldier had left the room, the king said to the remaining guard, "If she is still alive by nightfall, bring me word of it.""

It tasted, to him, something like a cool, wet ball of sugar, and yet hidden deeply within its dripping sweetness there lay the slightest trace of bitterness. With each bite, he tried to fix more clearly his understanding of its taste, but just as he felt on the verge of a revelation, he found he had devoured the entire thing. All that was left in his hand was the black pit, shaped like a tiny egg. Since the blue-skinned treat had no immediate effect on him, he thought perhaps the secret word lay within its dark center and he swallowed that also. Then he waited. Sitting at the window in his bedchamber, he stared out into the cool spring night, listening, above the din of his wife's snoring, to the sound of an unseen bird, calling plaintively off in the forest. He wondered what, if anything, the fruit would do for him. At worst he might become sick unto death, but the fact that the girl from the forest was still alive but an hour earlier was good insurance that he would also live. At best, the risk was worth the knowledge and power he might attain. To know the secret language of the Almighty, even one green word, could bring him limitless power and safety from age and death.

Every twinge of indigestion, every itch or creak of a joint, made him think the change was upon him. He ardently searched his mind, trying to coax into consciousness the syllables of that sacred word. As it is said of a drowning man, his life passed before the inner eye of his memory, not in haste but as a slow stately procession. He saw himself as a child, his parents, his young wife, the friends he had had when he was no older than the girl he had used to test the fruit. Each of them beckoned to him for attention, but he ignored their pleas, so intent was he upon owning a supreme secret.

The hours passed and instead of revelation, he found nothing but weariness born of disappointment. Eventually, he crawled into bed beside his wife and fell fast asleep. In his dreams, he renewed his quest, and in that strange country made better progress. He found himself walking through the forest, passing beneath the boughs of gigantic pines. In those places where the sunlight slipped through and lit the forest floor, he discovered that the concept of the green word became clearer to him.

He went to one of these pools of light and as he stood in it, the thought swirled in his head like a ghost as round as the fruit itself. It came to him that the word was a single syllable comprised of two entities, one meaning life and one death, that intermingled and intertwined and bled into each other. This knowledge took weight and dropped to his tongue. He tried to speak the green word, but when he opened his mouth, all that came out was the sound of his own name. Then he was awake and aware that someone was calling him.

"King Pious," said the captain of the guard.

The man was standing next to his bed. He roused himself and sat up.

"What is it?" he asked.

"The forest people have escaped from the stockade."

"What?" he yelled. "I'll have your head for this!"

"Your highness, we found the soldiers who guard them enmeshed in vines that rooted them to the ground and, impossible as it sounds, a tree has grown up in the stockade overnight and the branches bend down over the high wall to touch the ground. The prisoners must have climbed out in the night. One of the horseman tried to pursue them but was attacked by a monstrous black dog and thrown from his mount."

Pious threw back the covers and got out of bed. He meant to give orders to have the soldiers hunt them down and slay them all, but suddenly a great confusion clouded his mind. That ghost of the green word floated and turned again in his mind, and when he finally opened his mouth to voice his command, no sound came forth. Instead, a leafed vine snaked up out of his throat, growing with the speed of an arrow's flight. He clutched his chest, and the plant from within him wound itself around the soldier's neck and arms, trapping him. Another vine appeared and another, until the king's mouth was stretched wide with virulent strands of green life, growing rapidly out and around everything in the room. At just this moment, the queen awoke, took one look at her husband and fled, screaming.

By twilight, the palace had become a forest. Those who did not flee the onslaught of vegetation but stayed and tried to battle it were trapped alive in its green web. All of the rooms and chambers, the kitchen, the tower cell, the huge dining hall, the pleasure garden, and even the philosopher's hiding place were choked with a riot of leafy vine. The queen and those others who had escaped the king's virulent command, traveled toward the south, back to their homes and roots.

Pious, still planted where he had stood that morning, a belching fountain of leaf and tendril, was now the color of lime. Patches of moss grew upon his face and arms, and his already arthritic hands had spindled and twisted into branches. In his beard of grass, dandelions sprouted. On the pools that were his staring eyes, minuscule water lilies floated. When the sun slipped out of sight behind the trees of the forest, the last of that part of the green word he knew to be *life*, left him and all that remained was *death*. A stillness descended on the palace that was now interrupted only by the warblings of nightingales and the motion of butterflies escaped from the pleasure garden into the wider world.

It was obvious to all of the forest people that Moren Kairn's daughter, Alyessa, who had effected their escape with a startling display of earth magic, was meant to take the place of the witch. When they saw her moving amidst the trees with the crow perched upon her shoulder, followed by Mahood, they were certain. Along with her mother, she took up residence in the cave beneath the stand of willows and set to learning all that she could from what was left behind by her predecessor.

One day near the end of spring, she planted in the earth the seed from the blue fruit, the origin of her magic, that Pious had given her. What grew from it was a tree that in every way emulated the form of Vertuminus. It did not move or talk, but just its presence was a comfort to her, reminding her of the quiet strength of her father. With her new powers came new responsibilities as the forest people looked to her to help them in their bid to rebuild their village and their lives. At the end of each day, she would come to the wooden knight and tell him of her hopes and fears, and in his silence she found excellent council and encouragement.

She was saddened in the autumn when the tree man's leaves seared and fell and the bark began to lift away from the trunk, revealing cracks in the wood beneath. On a cold evening, she trudged through orange leaves to his side, intending to offer thanks before winter devoured him. As she stood before the wooden form, snow began to lightly fall. She reached out her hand to touch the rough bark of his face, and just as her fingers made contact, she realized something she had been wondering about all summer.

It had never been clear to her why the fruit had been her salvation and gift and at the same time had destroyed King Pious. Now she knew that although the king had the green word, he had no way to understand it. "Love," she thought, "so easy for some and for others so impossible." In the coming years, through the cycle of the seasons, she planted the simple seed of this word in the hearts of all who knew her, and although, after a long life, she eventually passed on, she never died.

JEFFREY FORD is the author of *The Physiognomy*, winner of the 1998 World Fantasy Award and a 1997 *New York Times* Notable Book of the Year, *Memoranda*, and *The Beyond*. Ford's short fiction has appeared in *Event Horizon*, *The Magazine of Fantasy & Science Fiction*, *Space & Time*, *The Northwest Review*, and *MSS*. His story, "At Reparata," has been selected for publication in the anthology *The Year's Best Fantasy & Horror* (Vol. 13). For the past twelve years, he has taught Research Writing, Composition, and Early American Literature at Brookdale Community College in Monmouth County, New Jersey. He lives in Medford Lakes, New Jersey, with his wife and two sons.

Author's Note:

On summer afternoons when there is a strong breeze, I leave my house and walk, with my dog, Woody, two miles to the local school. Once there, we sit on the edge of the soccer field in the shade of pines and watch, at a distance, the giant elms that define the boundary of the woods. Their broad leaves stir in the wind, and if I watch closely enough, I begin to see images in the shifting patterns of green—rabbits running, the continent of Africa, a bearded old man nodding in agreement, a witch on her broomstick, a minotaur smoking a big-bellied pipe. This is how I communicate with the Green Man.

I am often surprised to find that we have similar things on our minds. Sometimes in these figures he shows me pieces of stories to write, and sometimes reminds me of promises I have forgotten that I wanted to keep. Perhaps this summer I will see you there, in the leaves of the elms at the edge of the field.

About the Editors

ELLEN DATLOW is currently editor of SCI FICTION, the fiction area of SCIFI.COM, the Sci Fi Channel's Web site. She was fiction editor of OMNI for over seventeen years, during which time she published everyone from William Gibson, Bruce Sterling, Lucius Shepard, and Pat Cadigan to Joyce Carol Oates, Jonathan Carroll, and Patricia Highsmith. She has also edited a number of anthologies, including the annual *Year's Best Fantasy and Horror, Sirens and Other Daemon Lovers, A Wolf at the Door* (for middle grades), and the six-volume adult fairy tale anthology series beginning with *Snow White, Blood Red,* all with Terri Windling. Solo, she has edited *Little Deaths, Alien Sex, Lethal Kisses,* and a science fiction anthology on the theme of endangered species, *Vanishing Acts,* among other books. She has won the World Fantasy Award six times and the Bram Stoker Award once. She lives in Manhattan.

The Sci Fiction Web site is located at www.scifi.com/scifiction.

TERRI WINDLING is an editor, writer, painter, and passionate advocate of myth and mythic arts. She has won the World Fantasy Award six times and the Mythopoeic Award once.

As an editor, she has created numerous anthologies, including those edited in partnership with Ellen Datlow, and solo, *The Armless Maiden* (on the subject of child abuse), the Borderland series, and others.

Previously the Fantasy Editor for Ace Books, she has been a Consulting Fantasy Editor for Tor Books' fantasy line for sixteen years. As an author, she has published *The Wood Wife, A Midsummer Night's Faery Tale, The Winter Child,* and other books, as well as columns on folklore and myth in *Realms of Fantasy* magazine. As an artist, she has exhibited paintings on folklore and feminist themes at museums and galleries in America and England. She divides her time between homes in rural England and the Arizona desert.

Please visit her Web site, The Endicott Studio for Mythic Arts: www.endicott-studio.com.

About the Artist

CHARLES VESS's award–winning work has graced the pages of numerous comic book publishers, and has been featured in several gallery and museum exhibitions across the nation, including the first major exhibition of Science Fiction and Fantasy Art (New Britain Museum of American Art, 1980). In 1991, Charles shared the prestigious World Fantasy Award for Best Short Story with Neil Gaiman for their collaboration on *Sandman* #19 (DC Comics)—the first and only time a comic book has held this honor.

In the summer of 1997, Charles won the The Will Eisner Comic Industry Award for best penciler/inker for his work on *The Book of Ballads and Sagas* (which he self-publishes through his own Green Man Press) as well as *Sandman* #75. In 1999, he received the World Fantasy Award for Best Artist for his work on Neil Gaiman's *Stardust*. He is currently working with Jeff Smith on *Rose*, the prequel to Smith's *Bone*, as well as two collaborations with his friend, Charles de Lint.

His Web site address is www.greenmanpress.com.